Paranormal Nonsense

Blue Moon Investigations
Book 1

Steve Higgs

Table of Contents

She didn't see the man until she was quite close to him, her focus instead on the phone under her nose as she typed a scalding text message to her friend, Sarah. She had regretfully agreed to a double date so Sarah's boyfriend's pal, Darren would have someone to talk to. Sarah claimed that Darren was really good-looking and athletic, which turned out to be true, but he was also an utter bore who talked only about himself. Walking home in the dark and angry about her crappy evening, she was texting Sarah to tick her off for abandoning her so she could sneak off to suck face with Chris. Darren hadn't even offered to buy her a drink, so with her purse now deflated, she was walking home because she couldn't afford a taxi.

It was only when she pressed send on the message and looked up, that she saw the man on the dark path ahead of her. Instantly feeling anxious, she wished now that she had taken the longer route home along the main road and not the shorter route by the canal. The canal path was far faster, but it was also dark because half the lamps to illuminate it had long since stopped working.

The man wasn't moving, and her feet had come to an involuntary stop, so they were now facing each other on the path about ten yards apart. He looked to be wearing a dark suit, the little bit of light coming between the trees was catching on the shine of his shoes and the white vee of the shirt between his lapels and either side of his dark tie. He still hadn't moved but there was nothing threatening about his stance and she could see both his hands; they hung empty and loose at his sides. His face was hidden in shadow, but what she could see, from his shoulder to waist proportion, told her that he was seriously muscular.

1

Feeling silly, now that she was just standing still and becoming ever more aware of the cool September air on her exposed skin, she called out to him. 'Hello?'

In response, he raised his head. Slowly and deliberately, he brought his eyes up to meet hers. In the darkness of the shadows, she hadn't realised that he had been looking down but now he leaned forward just a little, so his face became illuminated by a thin shaft of light coming through the trees.

Then he smiled at her.

There was nothing pleasant or engaging about the smile. The man's smile inferred bad things were about to happen and when he opened his lips, the smile suddenly contained far too many teeth and canines which were distinctly longer than they ought to be.

A heartbeat passed as they stared at each other, but then he moved, exploding into action toward her. Too shocked to scream, she spun away, her feet slipping on the debris and mud of the path causing her to pitch forward. Almost falling, she corrected her motion with a hand on the path and took off at a sprint back in the direction of the pub.

Naturally athletic, she had been a sprinter through her school years and was able to hit full speed after a few yards. With the passage of air whipping her hair around, she felt a growing confidence that she could outpace the man. The pub would soon be in sight; a faint glow from the outside lights already visible through the trees. There would be safety there, so as her breath started to tug in her chest, she pushed harder, determined to get away from whatever menace the man intended.

The blow to her head came as a surprise. She had no sense that he was even close to her, but it landed hard behind her right ear, instantly knocking her off balance and stunning her at the same time. She stumbled, legs tangling as the sideways shunt ruined her forward motion.

As the concrete of the path became a painful eventuality she could barely see, she put her hands out to arrest the impact. Out of control though, she hit first with her right hip, and, still spinning, crashed over onto her back here her left shoulder bit painfully into the rough path to tear her skin. Finally, the back of her head smacked into the ground to bring a taste of blood. As she came to rest in the nettles and litter at the side of the path, she rolled onto her back so she could fend off his attack.

He wasn't attacking though. Instead, he was standing calmly next to her feet. Involuntarily, she made a little choking sound of fright and glanced around for help, already knowing that none was coming.

His suit looked unruffled and his expression was calm, serene almost as if nothing untoward was occurring and he perhaps wanted to ask her the time.

Confused, though still terrified, she propped herself up on her elbows and squirmed back a few feet to get some distance between them. The move rewarded her with fresh stings on the exposed skin of her shoulders as she backed into yet more nettles. She barely registered the pain though.

'What do you want?' she demanded, getting angry that he had chased and hit her and now seemed to have no purpose.

She regretted the question though for it prompted the man to crouch. He didn't touch her but came as close as he could without doing so. Then, he leaned forward, so his face was mere inches from hers.

'I want to drink your blood, little lamb,' he said, his voice calm and almost soothing with a faint European accent.

3

Then he hit her.

As she reeled from the blow, a massive hand grabbed her hair and twisted her head cruelly to one side. She grabbed at his hands, but it made no difference; the hand continued to twist around until it pushed her face into the dirt. She scrambled with her legs, trying to find purchase so she could fight him off, but she was no match for his strength or superior body weight. His knee went into the small of her back and she could no more move a building than shake him off then.

She felt him move closer yet, bending right over her to nuzzle her neck like a lover might and then he bit down into her soft flesh. Hot liquid ran over her skin and she knew it was her blood. It began to pool under her chin and was getting in her hair. She wanted to fight back but all too soon she found that doing so felt like a lot of effort.

The man held her in place as her frantic struggles lessened. Blearily, she could see something silvery. He had moved again, fiddling in a pocket to produce a small jug and he was doing something with it now, touching it to her skin where he had bitten her. She tried to focus on it, but she was getting a headache from her hammering pulse and the jug didn't seem all that important. Her heart felt like it was banging in her chest and her eyes were getting heavy. Wondering why her eyes were so heavy was her final thought as unconsciousness thankfully took her.

In the moonlight, the man stood back to watch her final breaths, the silver chalice held carefully in his left hand. Its contents threatened to spill over, so as he set off back down the path, he cradled it with both hands and was soon swallowed by the dark.

PC Amanda Harper checked her watch: 0513hrs. It was neither light nor dark, that time of the morning when the first rays of sun have begun to pierce the gloom yet hadn't really done anything to lighten the surroundings. She was standing on a narrow path that bordered the river Medway near to Maidstone. The path was tranquil, picturesque and thoroughly safe during daylight hours. She had walked along it many times, but in the dark, it was far less pleasant. Starkly, she found it was foreboding and anxiety-inducing and was telling herself to man-up and stop imagining that the things rustling in the undergrowth were coming to get her. Her shift had started at 1800hrs last night, a Wednesday, and she should be finishing her shift in less than an hour. Experience had taught her that it was not going to go like that though. After seven years on the beat, this was not her first murder scene and there was no way they were going to replace her this side of breakfast. If anything, they needed more people on the scene to manage human traffic, keep crowds back and assist SOCO to conduct their investigation. She would be swept up into the day of important tasks that needed doing fast.

She checked her watch again and shifted her feet a little. Trying not to look like she was dancing, she moved her arms about a bit to keep the stiffness out and the cold away. The warmth of August was long forgotten, replaced by the coolness of autumn. Amanda was thankful that this September morning was dry. However, the early morning mist forming on the river was still damp and the cool air had penetrated her layers of uniform a good half hour ago.

Sgt Dave Barnet appeared out of the gloom a few yards away from where he had undoubtedly been involved in something far more interesting than perimeter security. Dave fancied her, she knew it, although he had never said anything and was quite polite and avoided

5

flirting in general. She could tell though when she caught him glancing away when she turned, when he smiled at her and gave one too many work-related compliments. She was attractive. She accepted that as one accepts that your hair is brown, or your eyes are blue. She understood that genetics had given her an athletic figure, high cheekbones, flowing hair and a strong jawline that could have led to modelling. It was not a career choice that had interested her, although right now the thought of a bikini shoot in the Bahamas for some new swimwear firm sounded like a vast improvement. Come to think of it, topless glamour modelling sounded good about now when compared to freezing her nipples off next to a river in the middle of the night, guarding a murder scene in Maidstone.

Dave looked over, caught her eye and began walking towards her. Emerging from the gloom, his face was grim.

'What have we got?' she asked.

'Nasty and weird murder, that's what,' he answered, 'Another bitten throat. Poor girl would have bled to death and it was clearly quite violent.' Neither said anything for a moment while the river mist swirled about them.

'Is it like the others? Same MO?'

'I wouldn't go on record with that, but yes essentially it appears to be the same.' Even up close it was difficult to see his features in the dark, but he sounded weary and stressed. Amanda had seen a few bodies. Murder in Kent was relatively rare but she had been around long enough to have attended a fair number of murder scenes. The recent series, if they could call it that, were something else though. Each of the three victims, assuming this was number three, had been alone when attacked at night and were found with a wound to their throat. The press had gotten hold of it almost two weeks ago, two days after the second murder and were already calling it the vampire attacks, or other such crude but catchy names. The term *The Vampire* had been coined immediately by The Weald Word, a local paper more used to reporting jumble sale successes and prize-winning turnips. Their lead reporter led with the legend, "Vampire killer loose in Maidstone." It was published the morning following the second murder. This had been seized upon by the National press in what was a slow news week and now it was hard to think of the perpetrator by another term.

Amanda squinted at her Sergeant's face, trying to get a read of his expression in the gloom. 'So, what is the scene like? Likelihood of usable evidence? she asked.

'Just like the last two, I think. Not much of anything to help us,' he replied, his tone carrying little inflection, 'There will be saliva around the wound, but that has already been checked and lead us nowhere. Other than that, this guy does not leave anything we can use. The SOCO chaps will be thorough, but whether they are able to find anything helpful...' he trailed off just as his radio squawked, the sound cutting through the quiet stillness of the dawn in a shocking burst of noise. The call was for him, so he left her there with a brief nod as he went.

Another forty-five minutes passed as the sun struggled lazily upwards. It lit the sky, making it feel like morning by the time PC Brad Hardacre emerged from the trees surrounding the tented crime scene. She spotted him because she was looking the wrong way again, thoroughly bored with watching the ducks sleep on the bank next to her. Just before 0600hrs, she had actually performed her function and turned away two joggers as they ran down the path towards her, presumably on their usual route. Other than that, she had done nothing for the last two hours.

She checked her watch: 0602hrs. 'Good morning, Amanda, how has your day been so far?' hallooed Brad as he approached. Brad was an okay guy, most of them were with the odd exception, but she quite liked him and might have been interested if they did not work together.

'It has been sucky mostly, Brad, but nowhere near as bad as the girl lying over there had it,' she gestured with her head to the tents.

'Another Vampire victim?' Brad asked while making his canines stick out below his top lip.

'Didn't you check in with control when you arrived?' she asked with exasperation, 'You know the protocols, Brad. How can you know what is happening if you avoid getting a brief?'

He smiled and waggled his eyebrows conspiratorially, 'I quite like the idea of a vampire in Maidstone. It adds a bit of badly needed cool and hipness to the dreary landscape. Vampires are cool, right? Besides, the Chief can eat my pants.'

'If you are a teenage girl and a virgin and have watched too much Twilight then maybe vampires are cool. Otherwise, they are for geeks with Buffy the Vampire Slayer fantasies.' She looked him dead in the face, 'I doubt the victim will agree that vampires are cool.' This was a little hard on him, a little banter around horrible events is completely normal, a coping mechanism, but he needed to reel it in for his own good.

'Well, now that you are here, you can stand watch on this lonely, boring path while I get warm, get some blood back into my limbs and get a cup of tea. I'm off to see what is going on.' With that, she headed over to the tents covering the body.

I was oblivious to the latest murder at this point and was sitting in a coffee shop opposite my office in Rochester High Street sipping a fresh, strong coffee while reading the papers. I should probably introduce myself though since this story is largely about me. My name is Tempest Danger Michaels. You are probably thinking that I have a ridiculous name. Most people do.

It was not of my choosing, of course, you understand how it works. As a child, I thought nothing of it until I started school and the reactions began. Of course, I introduce myself as Tempest, which raises an eyebrow occasionally but little more than that. It is not until my middle name is discovered that real comments begin.

My Father explained that he had wanted me to have a memorable name that would assist me in life. Personally, I think he watched too many adventure films and got carried away with romantic notions of heroes saving the day. I admit that I have used the line "Danger really is my middle name" and proceeded to prove it a few times as an adult by producing my driving license, and that once or twice it has resulted, part way at least, in getting me laid. So, I guess there are advantages and disadvantages to my name as much as there are to any other. The problem generally, is that people assume I have changed my name, that I chose it myself because I wanted to say, "Danger is my middle name" before diving out of a window or something equally moronic.

Now that I have explained the name, I am still faced with the unfortunate task of telling you what I do for a living. I have my own business and that of course always sounds good, but when you are on the second date and the lady wants to hear more about you, there is simply no good way of telling her that you are a paranormal investigator. The reactions have been entertaining I suppose. Some freeze and ask me to

9

repeat myself, some laugh and ask me what I really do. One called me a total loser and walked straight out of the restaurant. However, not one lady has ever been impressed with my current job. Doubtless, you are on their side but let me explain how it came about and let me first reassure you that I in no way believe that the paranormal exists.

My two-room office sits above a cheap, and by all accounts crap, travel agent in Rochester High Street. The location is fantastic though, sitting in the shadow of the Cathedral and surrounded by amazing architecture. Outside my door are myriad public houses, restaurants, and shops selling baked wares, the smells from which combine to assail the nostrils and imbue hunger. The pavements are cobbled, the mere fact that it is a tourist location means it is always clean and litter free, and at different times of the year, such as Christmas, it is delightfully decorated and cheer-inducing.

The office is rented from the owner of the travel agent, a chap that appeared to have been boil washed. Tony Jarvis Travel was a sorry little place which might have been a booming business twenty years ago but had the appearance of a shop lost in time and purpose. The décor and displays were at least a decade old and poor Tony had the haunted look of a man that had already given up. Mousy, thinning ginger hair and a very pale complexion on a tiny frame led to my boil washed analogy. I had heard his wife, had to be a wife because no one else would speak so harshly to a person, berate him for not trying hard enough to bring in customers. Despite her feelings on the matter, a slow, but steady stream of pensionable age citizens shuffled in and out.

Anyway, I lost the point there. I joined the British Army as a young man and made a good career of it. However, they very generously offered me a substantial sum of money to leave during one of their drawdown periods and I took it. I was mid-thirties by then and was due to end my contracted twenty-two-year career at forty anyway. The pay-out from the voluntary redundancy combined with my gratuity and immediate pension benefits made my bank account look quite healthy, so I felt no desperate rush to move into my next career. I had no idea what I wanted to do after the army anyway, so for a period I bummed around walking my dogs, visiting places I had only seen on TV and doing a bit of DIY to the house I had bought as an investment a few years ago. This went on for a few months until my mother asked if I was ever planning to work again.

My mother generally didn't leave much wriggle room, so I set about finding a job. Disinterested in virtually everything that was on offer to me, it was only when a friend enquired whether I had considered setting up my own business that I hit upon the idea of being a private investigator. I didn't come up with the idea all by myself. I happened to be leafing through a magazine designed for forces personnel leaving the services and looking for new careers. There, I found a half-page advert for starting your own investigation business. Curious, I grabbed the yellow pages and discovered that in my local area, which had several million people in it, there was not one private investigator advertised. This, I considered meant there was a niche market, a gap, an opportunity and thus I applied to take the course and buy the equipment.

I contacted the Yellow Pages and they were jolly expensive, so I went with a local newspaper that advertised local businesses. Best to start out small and keep the overheads down was my thinking. Life likes to laugh at my plans though, so what happened was the paper ran my advert under the title Paranormal Investigation instead of Private Investigation. In a loud and somewhat apoplectic voice, I asked them how this happened the day the paper came out. They explained that the girl writing the ad saw the Blue Moon name I had chosen for my business and wrote paranormal without even noticing she had got it wrong. They apologised and made some placating noises, offered to run my advert correctly for a month for

11

free, that sort of thing. The paper was published and in circulation though, so whether I liked it or not, for the next two weeks I would be a paranormal investigator at the Blue Moon Investigation Agency.

I remember being distinctly irked about the advert and sitting in my office convinced that I could just shut up shop until the advert ran correctly again in two weeks' time. Well, I was wrong. The morning the advert ran I received my first phone call at 0912hrs and had a further three enquiries the same day. I have enjoyed a steady stream of business clients ever since.

That was six months ago. I kept the business name, kept the advert running and keep wondering if maybe I need to take on additional staff. Mostly, I investigate strange events which turn out to be one too many vodkas but mixed in with the stupid ones are cases that take some effort to solve. Included in this list have been a man that was attacked by a werewolf, which turned out to be a drugged-up, hairy, homeless person with no shirt, a couple that had suffered a series of bad luck incidents and believed they had been cursed by their great Aunt Ida (who is definitely a witch, she has a black cat), but were just plain unlucky and an old lady who was being kept awake by ghostly noises but turned out to have a flatulent dog.

Knowing with utter conviction, like any sane person, that the whole paranormal world is a load of fantastic nonsense, meant that I could ignore exploring the possibility that a werewolf was genuinely running around Chatham or Aunt Ida really was a witch throwing curses at her lesser relatives, and thus find a solution to each case that generally presented itself as obvious once the paranormal had been discounted. The best bit was that people paid me to politely point out how daft they were.

Today was a day like any other day. It was a Thursday, so my internal calendar was programmed for me to be doing some form of work, however on this Thursday, I had no live cases. Despite that, I had risen early, lifted some weights and walked the dogs. I was now sat in a coffee house opposite my office reading the news and relaxing with a cup of tea. The front page of the Times was mostly dedicated to further trouble in Syria with a large picture of the new Princess baby being held for the camera at her first outing. It was nothing that I found noteworthy

I switched to a local paper, the one that ran my business advert actually. On page four, just after a report of a stolen riverboat, I found an interesting headline which declared, *"Bluebell Hill Big Foot?"* below which was a grainy picture of a blob on a landscape. The first few lines gave the usual overview of the entire story, which was about reports of a large beast that had been seen several times in the last few weeks. Kent has a lot of countryside, but not so much that a Sasquatch could be living in it with no one noticing. The paper was not given to tabloid nonsense though, so I read on. The first sighting had been three weeks ago, on a Sunday afternoon. Mr. and Mrs. McCarthy of Aylesford had been walking their Labrador when they saw a large, hairy bipedal creature walking upright no more than thirty metres away. It disappeared into the treeline before Mrs. McCarthy, fifty-seven, could get her phone out to take a picture. The Labrador gave chase but returned when they called it back. Clearly shaken, they stated that the creature was not a bear, which was their first thought but moved like a man and by judging the apparent height of the beast against the trees they estimated its height at over seven feet. There were no footprints they said because of the recent dry period and hard ground. The creature was muscular around the thighs and shoulders and thick at the waist. They did not report the sighting until a local radio station ran a story a week ago following several other sightings. The radio had brought in local Doctor of Zoology and second person to have made a sighting, Dr. Barry Bryson. Their *expert witness* had

13

apparently supported the notion that there could indeed be a large bipedal mammal living in Kent but was quoted as having said, "The United Kingdom has over seven hundred thousand hectares of forest, most of it linked to support wildlife migration patterns. That there are creatures we have not yet discovered, living right next to us, is highly likely. Sightings of a creature matching what I saw have been reported several times before in the same area over the last few decades. It is entirely tenable that a large nocturnal bipedal mammal exists and that we have not seen it because it lives underground and only ventures out at night to forage." Was there a Big Foot living in the Kent Weald? Where had it come from? The article went on to recount in less detail the reports of three other persons that had claimed to have seen the Big Foot. Each one reported more or less the same description. Dr. Bryson had gone on to tout a novel that he had written loosely based on the subject. When asked if he felt the creature posed a threat his response was, "Absolutely. It is most probable that this creature is either carnivore or omnivore, it is doubtful that it would see a human as a viable meal but if startled it may attack as a defensive measure."

I looked up as the door chimed. Two young ladies dressed for office work came in chatting. Both were pretty, but a little young for further attention.

I cast my gaze back to the article. Dr. Barry Bryson, Manager at Kent Predator and Prey Park, a failing local wildlife park just outside Maidstone had seen the creature from his car, he claimed. Driving to work early on a Tuesday morning he had suffered a puncture and pulled over onto the hard shoulder of the A229 to deal with it. It was early morning, so traffic was very light, and he spotted the creature moving away from him. He pursued it and found a giant footprint perfectly preserved in thick mud where the Big Foot had disappeared into the wood line. The print measured over eighteen inches in length and showed five toes with no claws. The writer proceeded to discuss what creatures in the natural kingdom could leave such a print, concluding with none other than the North American Big Foot. The footprint was shown in a picture which was better quality than the grainy photograph shown earlier and was considered to be fairly concrete evidence that *something was out there.*

The story had not attracted the interest of the National press yet. It was the first I had heard of it, which made me feel like I was failing in some way since I am the only paranormal investigator in the book. It was probably a homeless man, or a chap out shooting ducks illegally and wearing a camouflage suit, so I was not going to let it trouble me too much.

Sat there pondering whether I should pop to the gents now or wait until I had walked the fifteen metres to my office, I was interrupted by my phone receiving a text:

Third vampire victim found by the river 200m south of River Angel Pub. Fresh scene, go check it out.

It had been sent by Sharon Maycroft, a former several nights stand and current local newspaper journalist for the very paper I held in my hands. Sharon was one of the few that accepted my profession without the slightest interest, it had no impact on what she wanted me for, which was mostly sex but on occasion, we had managed some conversation. It had been several months since I last saw her, but we moved in the same social circles and had an amicable relationship. She clearly believed I would be interested and was very kindly supplying me with information.

Would the information from Sharon require reciprocation? If so, would that mean a nocturnal activity session? Buoyed by the thought of that, I folded the paper and returned it to the little rack on the wall. I had discovered some time ago that an old school-friend, a chap I met on my very first day in school, in fact, was a PC in the Maidstone police force and had utilised the connection a few times to get vital nuggets of information. I flicked to his number and pressed the green button to dial his mobile.

Calling Darren Shrivers was displayed on the phone, but it did not connect. When it switched to voicemail I hung up and tried the number I had for his work desk. It rang briefly and was answered by a female voice.

'PC Callwell,' was all I got.

'This is Tempest Michaels calling for PC Shrivers.'

'May I ask what it is pertaining to?'

'I'm an old school-friend, I am just calling to arrange meeting for a few beers,' I lied rather than compromise him in any way, 'Please don't drag him away from anything he might be doing, I can catch him later. Or could I leave a message for him?' I suspected she would not disturb him if he was busy anyway.

'I'm afraid he is away on a course and won't be back for several weeks.'

Well, that ended that line of enquiry. Even if I could get him via his mobile later, he would have no idea what was going on with cases back at the station.

'Oh,' I said simply, 'Well, thank you anyway. I'll catch up with him later,' I added just to wrap up the conversation.

I popped the phone in my bag, slung the bag over my shoulder and stepped out into the street.

16

It was cool out, one of those early autumn days that people call fresh rather than cold. It would be cold if you stayed out in it but, of course, most don't, they merely travel through the cool air on a brief transition between house and car, car and office. There was no need to button my coat though as it was only a handful of strides from the coffee shop to my office door.

I bounded up the stairs to my office, unlocked the door and left it open while I pulled together the gear I would need. While I had not been engaged by anyone to investigate *The Vampire* murders (might as well call it that since everyone else was) I had nothing better to do and perhaps solving this would get me a truckload of publicity.

When I set the business up, I had invested in decent cameras, recording equipment, hidden microphones and professional looking stationery and notebooks that I could take to client meetings and wherever else my work took me. Since then I had bought ancient looking texts and grimoires to complete the image of the serious paranormal investigator and carried ridiculous extras such as salt, stakes, and silver. So far, I had seen a lot of weird stuff but nothing that could convince me that the supernatural existed.

I carry a shoulder bag with me just about everywhere I go. I started doing so not long after I left the army and no longer had a backpack for daily use. I have phones, business cards, notebooks, cameras and recording equipment in it generally and trivia like a pack of tissues because you never know when a lady might need one and a condom because the lady might be impressed by the tissue. I'm a man, okay? It's how we think.

Bag packed, I locked the office and jogged down the stairs, out the front and around the back to the car park where my car was waiting for me. I love my car. My twin sister says I am compensating, but I think that is a load of clichéd nonsense. If I swapped it for a 1970s battered Austin Allegro in shiny, turd-brown, it would not suddenly transform Mr. Wriggly into Penisaurus Rex, so having a car that I enjoy driving does not mean I am hung like a baby carrot. It was a beautiful red, 2009 Porsche Boxster S with a full Porsche body kit and fat nineteen-inch Porsche cup alloys.

I plipped it open and got in, swinging my bag of goodies onto the passenger seat. The journey was perhaps five miles or so and would take anything between twenty and forty minutes depending on traffic. I used to run a lot of the route I was about to take whenever I was spending time at my parent's house in Rochester, so I knew the roads could often be jogged faster than driven. Nevertheless, driving was the right option and I got there in twenty-four minutes.

I parked at the River Angel pub that Sharon had said was near the scene. The pub was an attractive two-story building set on the riverfront. I had no idea how old it was although it had old oak beams set into the walls and a several centuries old look to it. It was shut, no lights on but at 0937hrs this was no surprise. I wondered if anyone lived there. It looked like a nice place to live so perhaps the landlord and his family were in residence.

I walked around the side passing the wooden trestle tables laid out for al fresco dining and spotted a police officer on the river path. From where I stood, the river looked lovely. The setting was beautiful and must draw scores of people all year round, making it a great site for a pub. Mooring points allowed boats to pull up right outside and they were fitted along the river bank as far as I could see in either direction.

Beyond the police officer were the familiar white tents they erect to preserve a scene and prevent gawking passers-by from having anything good to look at. There were several persons moving about in full-body forensic suits and several more police officers in uniform along with one

18

or two others in suits and coats that were probably also police. All were near to the tents and not visibly doing much. The established perimeter was set at a distance that meant conversation at the site could not be heard and the detail of what people were doing was impossible to make out.

The tents were tucked in under a few straggly trees just off the path that follows the river. It was cooler here than elsewhere, the local temperature kept low by the river. I approached the uniformed police officer blocking access to the site.

'Good morning. I understand there has been another murder. I am a private investigator looking into the deaths for a third party.' Okay, so I was the third party, but the lie was far better than saying, *'Hi I investigate weird stuff like vampires and werewolves for a living.'* I have found doing so never gets me very far.

I didn't really expect help or an invite to see the victim for myself. However, much to my surprise the Officer said, 'I know who you are, sir.' I noted his number in my notebook just in case I needed to refer to whom I had spoken with. 'I saw you in the local papers after that Werewolf thing,' he was grinning now, 'Watch too many episodes of X-Files by any chance?' clearly entertaining himself.

It occurred to me that I could simply be an equal arse to him and leave him feeling small and pathetic, but that would not get me any information. I grinned back in what I hoped was a congenial way, 'Too much Buffy the Vampire Slayer actually, but what I proved in the incident to which you refer was that the supernatural does not exist. I get paid to prove it does not exist by people that fervently believe that it does,' this was mostly true, 'The very fact that this is being called a vampire slaying means a payday for me, so I am hoping you can help me out with a few very basic facts.'

At this point over his left shoulder, I spotted a second uniformed officer heading over towards us. Very different in appearance to the chap I was currently conversing with though - this one was gorgeous. I have never been impressed by ladies that dress for a night out like they are auditioning for the Pussycat Dolls, nor am I inspired by flawless makeup, so the fact that the lady walking towards me now in copper's boots, a heavy, unflattering uniform and bereft of makeup and hair-styling could grab my attention so instantly meant she must be a knock out in her usual clothes. Get a grip, Tempest, I chastised myself. There are plenty of attractive ladies around, no need to start dribbling. Opting to look focused and professional I hoisted the camera out of my shoulder bag and took a few shots of the area in general.

'My turn again. There are bacon sandwiches if you are quick,' the new officer informed her colleague on arrival.

He turned to go but looked back and offered, 'Good luck with the investigation, Mulder,' as he went. I had considered that he might just be bored and thus the initial thrust and parry of our few shared words were merely to brighten his day, but no, I concluded, he is in fact, just a dick.

'What did he mean?' asked the vision in uniform. Her face betrayed boredom and little else.

'I'm the guy in the papers investigating supernatural events. Not that I expect you to have heard of me, but he clearly had.'

'That thing with the werewolf?'

'Yup. That was me. I'm Tempest Michaels. I think this attack is linked to the previous two, which is no great leap given the proximity of the crimes to each other. Solving it will assist my business.' I was looking beyond her rather than at her but focused now on meeting her eyes.

20

Wow! They were fantastic. I realised I had stopped speaking and was just staring at her. 'What can you tell me about the circumstances?'

'Nothing, sir. Official statements will be issued once the details of the crime have been verified and the victim has been identified.' It was the answer I expected although it never hurts to ask.

'I'd like to give you my card,' I said while fishing in my bag, 'I would be very interested in following up on this with you when you are off duty.'

'To what purpose?' she asked. Okay, brain, get it right and you have a shot, get it wrong and the lovely lady will identify that you are a complete knob and that will be that. How can I get across that I am a cool guy just looking to solve a crime and be professional but that I am also available and interested? I opened my mouth to express that I find senior police officers have no time for me and that her colleague was clearly not interested in helping and thus I hoped that she could provide some perspective so that, through spit-balling our ideas together we might both do well. But before I got the first word out, a voice came from behind me.

'Wotcha, Dangerman. I knew you would get here before me. Still convinced that there are no vampires?'

'Nuts,' I muttered to myself

'Chatting up another fine woman I see. I don't know how you keep up with them all.'

Perfect.

The voice, I knew without turning belonged to Frank Decaux. Frank was the owner of an occult bookshop and believed with a foaming-at-the-mouth fervour that everything supernatural existed. He stood about five feet five inches tall, had a forgettable face, a scrawny body and light

21

brown hair which was not complemented by a sallow complexion. The overall effect was as if a witch had transformed a weasel into a man and not done a very good job. Frank arrived at my office about ten minutes after the advert for paranormal investigations went out and I had not been able to shake him since. Largely this was because he was determined to be there when I came up against something that proved to be genuinely supernatural and partly because he turned up anywhere that might have a supernatural link. Such as the site I was now stood at. I think he is harmless and generally well-meaning and I have called upon him on occasion for expert advice. He can be an annoying tit though.

'Good morning, Frank,' I replied, ignoring my desire to throw him into the river, 'How unsurprising to find you here. The officer and I were just discussing the case. Or rather, I was asking questions and the officer was deciding how to answer them.'

PC Hotstuff, as the chunk of my brain controlling my penis had now labelled her, had a question, 'I have been stood here for two minutes and so far, you have been called Mulder and Dangerman. Do you get called a lot of names?'

Halfway through turning to look at Frank I turned back to her, smiled and said, 'What I get called depends on whether I have been naughty or not.'

She just rolled her eyes. I had been aiming for cheeky scamp but had clearly missed in her opinion.

'So, what's the plan Tempest? What are we up against? Lone vampire or nest? Personally, I think a lone vampire is more likely and a very young one. Very unusual for them to make this much mess and leave bodies around the place. Only a young, inexperienced vampire, a new-born, would be so amateur,' I swivelled to look at Frank's face, but he was of course completely serious, 'Traditionally, vampires prey on those that won't be missed or on rural communities, which has, of course, become far harder this century with the internet, CCTV, mobile phones etcetera. The TV wants to show them as flamboyant creatures that live among us and impress us with their charm and looks, but they are shadow creatures in reality, keeping to the dark and trying to remain unnoticed.'

'In reality?' PC Hotstuff had an incredulous look on her face and was staring at Frank as if trying to decide whether he was dangerous or just stupid, 'A young woman had her throat ripped out twenty yards from her door by a crazed murderer. If it turns out that the perpetrator is some pathetic moron acting out a vampire fantasy...' she trailed off as if unsure how to end the sentence.

'What she said,' I chimed, agreeing completely but also noting that the victim was a young woman and very local, which given the geography must have meant that she was on her way back from the pub and only had a two hundred metre walk. That alone explains what she was doing out by herself in the dark on a dodgy looking path at night. Not a good place to walk, but if it is only a few hundred metres and the alternative well-lit route is over a mile then I'm sure most would have taken the same option as she had. Doubtless, she had taken the same route home hundreds of times before.

'Frank, you are completely mad, yet thoroughly entertaining at the same time,' I said turning back to face PC Hotstuff, 'You have my card. See you around.' I popped the camera back into my bag and left to head back to the car.

Behind me, I could hear Frank explaining to PC Hot stuff that the world Joss Whedon created for Buffy the Vampire Slayer had been quite accurate on some of the details.

Walking back to the car, I considered my sum total of facts pertaining to the case. Three victims over two weeks, all within a mile or so of each other and all brutally murdered by having their jugular punctured. Details regarding the first two murders had been sketchy and I had not paid much attention to the case until now. I needed to know where they had been killed, what they had been doing before-hand and try to find some kind of link. From memory, the first victim had been a middle-aged man and the second a little old lady. No obvious connection with either of them to the third victim, but perhaps some delving would reveal something.

I pointed the car back to the office and continued to mull over the vampire case. It would be easy enough to search for all the reports written in the papers and more specialised paranormal press. It might not reveal much but would allow me to create a timeline and map and sieve through some data to get a handle on what was known.

The phone began to ring in my bag and a second or so later the hands-free kit in the car picked it up so that I could answer it while driving.

'Blue Moon Investigations, Tempest Michaels speaking.'

The call was from a Mr. Winston Cranfield of 37 Buckley lane, Rochester.

He reported that he had a poltergeist in his house and both he and his wife had fled to the Travelodge on the Rochester/Maidstone Road. A quick mental calculation told me that the address was not far from my office, so I sold him the concept that it was clearly *a high priority task* for me and he seemed somewhat relieved that someone was taking him seriously. I told him I could be there in under thirty minutes and got off the phone.

25

I pulled into the Travelodge car park twenty-two minutes later and went into reception to wait for Mr. Cranfield. The lady manning the reception desk by herself called through to their room to check they were expecting a visitor and buzzed me through the entry door anyway. I met Mr. Cranfield coming out of his room.

Mr. and Mrs. Cranfield, or Winston and Barbara as they insisted I call them, were a lovely couple in their late sixties or early seventies which I had already guessed from Winston's voice and mannerisms on the phone. Winston had a firm handshake and commented on the veterans badge I had pinned to my collar just before I left the car. I suspected he would at least have completed National Service and I was right. Like so many of his generation, he could remember the war, sort of, but most certainly the sense of pride the Nation felt towards the services at the time. His father had served, and we spoke briefly about the army following the usual question about which branch I had been in.

Winston was neither short nor tall at about five feet nine inches and had probably been taller in his twenties. He wore a pair of hopsack trousers with a collared shirt and pullover, all in new condition. His wife Barbara, "Call me Barbara," she had instructed, was wearing what I believe was called a housecoat dress. I may have that completely wrong, but it was the sort of patterned dress that little old ladies wore and still managed to look smart in. I remembered my grandmother wearing them along with a scarf around her head when she went outside.

The clothes told me that the Cranfield's were not poor, and I knew their house to be in a good area of Rochester. This was important because I don't want to rip people off but must still charge them a sensible rate for the work that I do. I can't work for free but had done so a few times in the past when presented with a case I wanted to take on involving persons without the funds to pay me. Anyway, it seemed likely that I need not be concerned this time.

Mrs. Cranfield busied herself making tea. I noted that she only had two cups due to the nature of their lodgings but bit down my initial need to tell her to *keep it for yourself* as it seemed likely her dignity would prefer to be able to offer me something. She had apologised several times already for the lack of biscuits and the fact that it was not her usual brand of tea nor her good china.

While Barbara made the tea, I took over. There were two chairs and a table in one corner of the room by the window, so I sat on the edge of the bed, which was still perfectly made, leaving space for the two of them to sit close to each other at the table. To me, they seemed calm but perhaps a little upset or confused.

'It all started about two weeks ago,' stated Winston when I encouraged him to tell me in slow and patient detail what had led them to make contact, 'Barbara and I,' he motioned to his wife who had now delivered the teas and had sat beside him at the table, 'went up to bed after Midsomer Murders on Saturday night.'

'So, that would have been just after ten o'clock,' Barbara interjected.

'That's right, love,' he said, patting her hand across the table, 'We usually go up around that time.'

'And then we read for half an hour before we turn out the lights,' Barbara chipped in again.

'That's right, love.'

'So, this is Saturday night?' I clarified, making a note on my pad and jotting down the date.

'Yes, Dear,' confirmed Barbara.

'And then what happened?'

'Well, we woke up when there was a bang from downstairs and then...'

'One moment, please. What sort of bang?'

They looked at me without responding.

'I mean, was it like a firecracker exploding or like a book falling off a shelf or something completely different?'

'Oh,' they said more or less together. They looked at each other for a second or so and I wondered if they just needed to think about it or if the question had thrown them because this was all made up and rehearsed poorly. It would not be my first wasted call.

My concern evaporated when they said simultaneously, 'Like a book.'

'Okay. Please continue.'

'Then we heard an awful wailing from downstairs and yelling and more noises like things being thrown around and a noise like you get when you drag furniture across the floor,' Winston paused to have a slurp of tea. His hand was shaking a little and he used the other to steady his mug.

I watched while he took a drink. Someone had done a number on this lovely older couple. They were genuinely scared. Barbara was also watching her husband. Her hands were clasped in her lap and her feet were crossed one over the other and tucked to one side under her chair. I wondered if this was a pose she had been taught as a girl - this is how a lady sits.

Winston put his mug down. His wire-rimmed spectacles were a little steamed as he looked back up at me and I took a sip of my tea as he removed them.

I was about to prompt more story when he restarted anyway.

'So, I went downstairs to see what it was.'

'Well, we both went, Dear,' reminded Barbara.

'Yes, Dear you did come with me. But the noise stopped as soon as we got out of bed and when we got downstairs, we found that our living room was wrecked. The furniture had been moved and the pictures were crooked.'

'Two of my ornaments were broken,' chipped in Barbara again, 'One of them was the little crystal mouse my mother gave me. I can't replace that. How am I supposed to replace that?'

I assumed it was a rhetorical question and pressed on, 'Was there anything new in the room?'

They looked at me quizzically 'Something new? Like what?' asked Winston

I was wondering if the culprit has gone to the trouble of leaving ectoplasmic slime or something of that nature. I had encountered it on a previous case a couple of months ago, collected it and had paid a chemistry teacher at a nearby college to tell me what it was made from. The answer was:

- 1 teaspoon soluble fibre (e.g., Metamucil psyllium fibre)

- 8 ounces water

- food colouring

29

- glow paint or pigment

Not remotely paranormal and could be made in a few minutes from ingredients found on eBay.

'I was just curious,' I offered rather than giving them the full explanation, 'Was there anything missing?'

'That was what Winston said,' replied Barbara, 'Winston said we had to put the room straight and work out if anything was missing. I was going to call the police, but Winston checked the doors and windows and they were all still locked, so Winston said it could not be a burglar.'

'Was there anything missing?' I asked after no one spoke for a few seconds.

'Oh. Err, no,' finished Barbara, 'Not that we could see, and we even checked the level of the brandy in our decanter in case it was tearaway kids breaking in.'

'So, we went back to bed,' this from Winston, 'But we didn't really sleep, and we got up around six o'clock.'

'I checked the living room again in the morning in case we had imagined the whole thing, but my ornaments were still broken.'

'We pretended like nothing had happened and we didn't tell anyone because we didn't know what to tell them.'

'I almost called our son, but he would have sent for the men in the white coats. I think we both knew it was a ghost even then, but we didn't talk about it.'

'Then it happened again a few nights later and again the night after that and we moved out after the third time and went to stay with our son in Brighton. When we told him we had a ghost he said we were being silly and that we must have imagined it all.'

'We called the police, but they said they had no time to look into hauntings,' Barbara said this with a tut, 'We came home after a day and then it happened again the next night. Winston slept in the living room the night after that and the night after that but the only thing that happened was his back gave out from sleeping awkwardly,' Barbara gave her husband a look that may have been annoyance that he did not catch their ghost or may have been sympathy. I found it hard to tell.

Winston fidgeted slightly before restarting his story, 'So, then I went back to our room to sleep, that would have been on Saturday night and we had the worst attack yet that night.'

'We couldn't stay there after that, so we packed a few things and came here,' added Barbara, 'It's my Auntie Margaret you know,' she stated, looking directly at me and speaking with a hushed voice like it was a big plot reveal.

'It's not auntie Margaret, love,' said Winston

'She always resented me getting the clock. It must be her. It's ten years since she died.'

'But it's not ten years to the day is it, love? Margaret died in the July.'

'What clock?' I interrupted.

It turned out the clock in question was a family heirloom antique looking thing that sat on their mantel. A glass face hinged open at one side so the movement could be wound by use of a key. It did not look like it was worth much to me, but I acknowledged that I didn't know much about clocks. It had been passed down through several generations but had gone to Barbara's mother Ophelia rather than to her older sister Aunt Margaret due to some long-running dispute between Margaret and her mother. When the clock was passed down again to Barbara the Aunt had turned up demanding that the clock be turned over to her as it was rightfully her heirloom as the eldest child. Barbara had said no, and the rift continued. Quite why someone would think this might cause a haunting was beyond my comprehension. Clearly, it made sense to Barbara though.

I convinced them to return to the house with me right there and then after promising them that I would stay at the house with them. They changed out of their house slippers and into shoes, sort of bumping into each other politely in the confined space of the room and I excused myself to make some extra room.

Waiting for them in the car park, I checked my emails and ate an apple from my bag. They shuffled out of the door before I had finished it, both getting into a new plate white Vauxhall Astra. I signalled that I would follow them even though I knew where I was going, and it was almost one straight road from the Travelodge to their house. Four minutes later we were in their road. They pulled onto their drive and I parked in the street in front of their house. It was a 1930s-semi-detached place with several period features around the door, windows, and roofline. The front garden was well tended with mostly maintenance-free plants and overall it looked like a house that was loved. I noticed though that by contrast the house to which theirs was attached was overgrown with weeds, the windows were dirty, and the paint was flaking off.

Inside, the house was pleasant in an older couple sort of way. The décor was dated but very neat and tidy. We went into the lounge straight away without exploring the rest of house. There were lace thingies on the corners of the felt covered sofa and armchairs and more lace under pot plants and the like. The real point to note though was that the room was trashed. If I was making a room up so that it looked burgled this is the look I would have gone for. Pot plants were dumped on the floor, the contents spilling out. Pictures were either skewwhiff on the walls or now sat on the floor with the frame cracked in several cases. Nothing was straight. On the mantelpiece, very prominently as if all the other ornaments were set up to draw one's eye towards it, was the clock. The face was open, and the hands were both bent outwards at a stark angle.

'When did this happen?'

'On the third night,' replied Barbara, 'On the first two nights, the clock was just moved about or turned a bit.'

'Have either of you touched the hands of the clock since you found it like this?'

They looked at each other again. Winston had his left arm around Barbara in a protective stance, perhaps as much for his comfort as hers. 'I didn't. Did you?' he asked.

'No, Dear. I didn't even notice it at first. You had to point it out to me while I was cleaning up the dirt from the clematis.'

'You are both sure?'

They looked at each other again and briefly discussed it but decided that they were indeed sure that neither one had touched the hands of the clock. The clock hands were delicate and made of brass, if a person were to adjust the time, they would do so by moving the hands manually. However, to do so one would press lightly on the edge of the clock hand, not grab hold, so the fingerprint I could clearly see on the reverse side of the big hand was left there by the culprit.

I said, 'Good. My dear Winston and Barbara, there are fingerprints on the hands and ghosts don't leave fingerprints, so whoever is doing this it is not a ghost, phantasm or spirit from the netherworld,' while I explained this to them, I had my hands fishing around in my shoulder bag from which I produced a basic fingerprinting kit.

'Oh,' said Barbara sounding distinctly deflated, 'So, who is it then?'

I fixed them with an intense stare, 'I intend to find out.' I dusted the clock hands and then had them point out a few other items that had been moved so I could take more prints and then took their fingerprints to eliminate them. I had bought a basic fingerprinting kit online when I opened the business and it came with software that would take the scanned images and allow me to match fingerprints to them. It did not connect with a criminal database or anything like that, but it had proved useful several times in the past.

I definitely had a third set of fingerprints. Thus, I formed a plan but needed to discuss costs with the couple before we went any further. I sat them down on the sofa to explain how I planned to solve their mystery and what I would need to charge them.

Winston and Barbara were staying at their house for the rest of the day now that they were back there. I was to return in a few hours with equipment and would be staying the night at their house. Barbara still seemed quite convinced that it was her Aunt Margaret despite any evidence I had shown her. I just hoped the poltergeist would make an appearance tonight so that I could wrap this up quickly. I did not wish to charge them for multiple nights of me sat on their sofa waiting for the poltergeist to turn up.

Outside their house, I plipped the car open and got inside. Then it struck me then that I was hungry. I had planned to be healthy today and eat raw vegetables for lunch with fresh hummus and perhaps a piece of fruit and a pint of water, but those supplies were sat in my office and that was not where I wanted to go right now. I headed for home instead, letting my stomach and my vanity wrestle over what to eat.

My home was barely two miles away, so I was still debating what was in my fridge and whether I could justify a cheeseburger as part of a nutritious diet if I put enough salad in it, when I pulled up.

My house is tucked away in the corner of a village just outside Maidstone. The village is quiet and surrounded on all sides by green fields and open pasture. There is a pub and a village shop which sells groceries and all manner of other daily necessities. The village is quite typical of small villages anywhere in England.

My house is a three-bedroom detached with a wrap-around garden. I parked on my drive next to the flower beds and nicely manicured lawn I had added. On the other side of my door, my two dogs Bull and Dozer barked a warning then fussed around my feet as I went into the house.

35

Bull came to live with me a few years ago while I was still in the Army. He is both my companion and my sounding board. His brother (same parentage, different litter) came along a year later when I decided Bull needed a companion. They are both fierce and protective, make a lot of noise to deter intruders and are solid muscle from the tip of their noses to the end of their tails. They are also miniature black and tan Dachshunds and weigh about as much as a roast chicken. Arguably, they were not the manliest dogs, but I did not care what anyone else thought.

I am not a big man, but I carry a reasonable amount of muscle and have at times been ridiculed for having such small dogs. The chaps weigh less than fifteen pounds each but have character and attitude far beyond their size. I have had to point out to people that I don't need a big dog and that stereotyping would say that small dogs are ladies' dogs and thus that ladies like small dogs. If this case proves correct then ladies will be attracted to the small dogs and since I am attracted to ladies I fail to see where the downside is.

Anyway, I patted their heads and gave each a small treat from a jar in the kitchen. Their bottoms disappeared around the kitchen doorframe as they trotted off to the garden content with their efforts and left me to sort the mail. It contained nothing of interest. No bills, no postcards, just a few pointless pizza flyers and some opportunities to transfer my credit.

I settled on a fresh tuna salad for lunch, which killed my hunger but did little to satisfy my meat cravings. Dirty plate and mixing bowl went into the dishwasher and as the dogs reappeared, I settled in front of my computer to research the recent vampire murders.

I used general search engines to find almost all the information I wanted but found excellent information on the paranormal web pages that would not appear anywhere else. The paranormal press services online were run by various oddballs who reported anything that might have a vaguely supernatural connection. A lot of it was conspiracy theory and crazy ideas, yet I found truth amongst the outlandish as well and I was learning to sift the content.

Forty-five minutes on Google and other sites had revealed all that I felt was going to be available online. The first murder had occurred fourteen days ago on the outskirts of Aylesford. The victim's name was Brian Grazly, a single fifty-seven-year-old groundsman at Chilwell Castle. His body was found at night and still bleeding. The body had been found by Mrs. Stephanie Dunne on her way home after closing the staff kitchen at the castle. The report said that she generally took a shortcut in front of the onsite cottage where Mr. Grazly lived as the groundsman and had found him lying on the path. I wondered if she had screamed and drawn attention or screamed and drawn no attention at all and had then had to calm down and go looking for help. I would need to get a look at the police report to gain any better information. The second victim was Rita Hancock, sixty-eight. A retired school secretary at Aylesford primary school. Found by a Liam Goldhind while walking his dog, Simon, at just before 0600hrs in the morning. Leaves behind two children and seven grandchildren. She lived in Allington and was last seen at a friend's house following a night playing canasta with a small group of other old ladies. Her body had been left in bushes at the side of the road. The cause of death was massive loss of blood from trauma to the throat i.e. jugular punctured. Her murder came two days after the first, so more than a week had elapsed between second and third victims. The third Victim was killed last night making it three linked deaths in a short period. A serial killer in Maidstone.

The vampire case presented a chance to make headline news. If I could get in and solve it first of course. The case was right on my doorstep. The serendipity of its geography too fortuitous to ignore. I was not used to tackling murderers though, the worst my line of work had thrown at me so far were some unsavoury thieves and a few persons happy to commit grievous bodily harm on either random persons or their own supposed loved ones. Each case somehow fell under the banner of mysterious or supernatural goings-on and had either never been reported to the police or had been dismissed by them upon initial investigation because it was, "Very clear Mr. Harding that the Loch Ness Monster is not living in your pond".

I was also curious about the Bluebell Hill Big Foot but not curious enough to do anything about it until someone offered me money or some other reason why I should. However, adding up what I knew about the vampire case didn't really give me anything. Scratching my ear and pondering what to do next, I decided it was time for a cup of tea. Tea always helps, so I left the computer to put the kettle on. Bull followed me just in case it was treat-time again. I picked him up for a fuss and was rewarded with a lick to the nose. The lick was probably designed to elicit a treat rather than deliver a specific message, so I hugged him and popped him back on the floor since it was no good making him fat with titbits. He could wait until 1700hrs when his evening meal would be due. The problem with Bull was that he was above average intelligence. I don't mean above average for a dog, but above average for a human. Now you may scoff but I have watched this little dog working things out before. Not blessed with opposable thumbs, he still does his best to defeat me when I try to keep him out of a room that he wants to be in or put food where he can't conceivably reach. Also, I know some pretty thick people and he seems quite a bit brighter than them. Dozer, however, was thicker than a whale omelette and had an appearance to match. Where his brother has defined features and a quizzical brow that seemed to be considering everything and possibly plotting world domination, Dozer had slightly fat chops and oversize front paws that made him look dopey. If I drew a cartoon of him, the thought bubble would be empty.

With steam rising from my freshly made tea, I drifted back to the iMac and started again. The key to solving most crimes was finding some kind of link or motivation. For the vampire case, this theory worked unless the killer was a total nut bag and was killing at random, which unfortunately seemed entirely plausible. I researched *vampires and Maidstone* in the same search bar and got hits for groups that met up for role-playing and such like and a couple of groups that met up specifically to discuss vampire TV shows. I expanded it to *vampires+kent* but the results here were not much different. I was not even sure what I was looking for. I tilted the computer chair backward and closed my eyes to consider the subject…

…and woke up over an hour later. I checked my watch to find it was 1530 hrs and time to get on with doing something constructive. I let the boys out into the garden and watched them water my lawn before shutting them back inside while promising to return in a couple of hours to take them out for a proper walk. I locked up and left the house with my bag of kit. I was heading for the address I had found for Liam Goldhind - the chap that had found the second victim.

His address was listed as 134 Halsted Drive, Cooper Estate, Chatham. This was miles from where he had found the body, but the body had been found near a park in Aylesford, so my assumption was that he was walking the dog there instead of around the streets at home. I wasn't happy about visiting his address though because the Cooper Estate is a hole, even by Medway town's standards. Lawn ornaments were white goods and cars on bricks. I wouldn't live there for free. In my army days, they used to send soldiers in there on a Saturday night to toughen them up before operations in Iraq or Afghanistan. Nevertheless, that is where the man lived, so that was where I had to go.

Best brave pants on.

I parked right in front of Liam's address. It was 1552hrs on a Monday and any decent person would be at work. Of course, any decent person would not be living here. It was benefits country, so I expected to find him at home with Simon the dog, drinking Supertennents lager and smoking rollies. Okay, I am stereotyping to an extreme, but I am probably still right. The house was a mid-terrace that had been painted what had probably once been white or cream, but the paint was now mostly on the concrete yard at the front of the house having peeled off. I was familiar with this design of house, there were many thousands of them in the Medway area. Probably two bedrooms with a box room and small toilet upstairs with the stairway right behind the front door when it opened.

Up the short driveway, I passed discarded pizza boxes, a few pieces of motorcycle and a refrigerator. There was also a shiny, heavily modified Mitsubishi Evo VIII. I guess that is where he put his money because he certainly didn't spend it on the house. The door was shut but looked like it had given up on life a long time ago. The doorbell was smashed, so I knocked.

The door erupted in a cacophony of barking as Simon the dog did his best to eat it. My dogs did the same of course but in a far less convincing manner. They also went away when I instructed them to do so. This was not happening for Mr. Goldhind. From behind the door the dog was still barking and growling, but the effect was now joined by the swearing of Liam as he chastised the dog for its exuberance. With a final expletive, Liam slammed a door somewhere deep in the house and a few seconds later he opened the front door.

I smiled and extended my hand for the obligatory shake saying, 'Good afternoon. My name is Tempest Michaels. I'm a private investigator looking into the Vampire murders,' I fetched a card from the tin in my bag to give him. He had not spoken directly to me yet and was now looking down at the card which he held with both hands.

Liam Goldhind wasn't exactly a catch. Less than five feet six inches tall with unkempt hair, maybe fifty pounds overweight and wearing a stained t-shirt and dirty jeans. He wore no shoes and his socks had holes in them.

'Who is it?' came a voice from within the house.

'I don't know yet, do I?' his response.

'What?' the voice again.

'Mind your own business. You old bag,' he muttered so that she could not hear.

'I hoped I might be able to ask you just a few questions about the second victim,' I said pressing on, 'I believe you were the one that found her.'

'That's right. Well, actually, Simon found her. Simon is my dog,' he explained, 'I caught him lifting his leg on her,' Liam looked up for the first time since he had opened the door. I decided I preferred looking at the top of his head.

'Well, I don't wish to take up too much of your time, I am sure you have better things to do,' I said while fishing out my notebook and pen, 'If I can just start by asking what position she was in when you found her?'

'I have photos if you like,' he said, interrupting me. He produced a phone from a back pocket, pressed a few buttons and there it was, the crime scene shot from several angles, distant and close-ups including shots of the wound. The poor lady was lying on her back but not peacefully, as if asleep, more as if she had been brutally murdered and thrown away like a rag doll. Her left leg was bent underneath her, her coat was still done up, but her tights were ripped in several places. There were bits of twig or leaf in her hair, her skin was deathly pale and her still-open eyes stared unseeing to the right.

The wound itself, I observed, was a bloody hole rather than two puncture marks. So far as I knew, no pictures of any of the victims had been published, although details of the deceased persons had been. My prevailing thought was that this was particularly nasty. I had seen death plenty of times in my life, not that I had ever killed anyone, but this was still pretty grim to look at.

'You want me to tooth them over to you?' Liam asked.

'Yes, please.'

'Well no chance, mate, but I will sell them to you at twenty quid a shot.' No great surprise there.

My head snapped up at the sound of someone behind him. His mother was my initial guess, but then I determined that she did not look quite old enough. I placed her age at forty perhaps to his twenty-six or twenty-seven. The older girlfriend then, which would probably make this the house she got in the divorce (assuming there had been one) and he was the new, younger stud muffin. She was about as butt-ugly as he was.

'I asked you who it was, Liam. You should speak more lovingly to me. You did last night,' she purred at him in a voice that I am sure was supposed to be sexy but had made my nuts shrink and try to hide behind each other. She leaned up against him, putting a basketball sized boob on his arm where it was bent to hold his phone, 'What's your name?' she asked me.

'Tempest Michaels,' I introduced myself.

43

I was just about to explain what I was doing when her eyes bugged out at me, 'Tempest! It's me, Sarah Griffiths, of course, I'm not Sarah Griffiths anymore, I'm Sarah Campbell now and before that, I was Sarah Heaton,' she looked at me expectantly as if this was a big reveal that should mean something to me, 'We went to school together,' she explained further, 'Edgewear Road Juniors in Rochester. You wore glasses then and I was a little skinnier than now. You sat next to Darren Smith in the last year with Mr. Baker.'

Okay, so she clearly knew me, but I was going to have to bluff this and what did a little skinnier mean exactly?' Sarah was a few pounds over what a chart would suggest was her ideal weight and was not doing much to look after herself. Her hair was lank, greasy-looking and lifelessly brown, her face a confusion of tiny red veins and laughter lines.

I could neither confirm nor deny her claim that we had been in school together. So, I faked it, 'Hi, Sarah, how is life treating you?'

'I'm fine, Tempest. I have this lovely house,' she gestured, 'and it is all free from the government because I have a child with a disability. Plus, I have a handsome man to look after me and I don't have to do anything all day long. I love being me. You sure grew up big and strong looking. You were skinny in school.'

'I grew up. I joined the Army. I filled out.'

'You sure did. Come in for a beer,' she suggested/demanded while making urgent gestures to get me in the house, 'It would be great to catch up.'

Not a chance.

The interior of the house looked like it had been decorated in the style of a Mogadishu slum during a particularly unpleasant fight between warring gangs. Rubbish in bags was strewn at the base of the stairs. On the stairs, various items of clothing had been discarded along with about twenty items hooked on the end of the banister rail. The carpet, what little I could see of it through the hall, was filthy.

'Thanks, Sarah. Perhaps another time. I have a lot that I need to do today. I am investigating the Vampire murders case and Liam here is assisting me with my enquiries.'

'No, I'm not. I'm selling you pictures if you want to pay for them, mate,' stated Liam, his tone beginning to annoy me.

'What? You are trying to charge an old school-friend of mine for pictures that you shouldn't have taken anyway?'

This might actually work out for me. My plan to bargain with the man would have ended with me paying something. Now maybe I would get them for free after all.

'Are you mental, woman? These are worth money.'

'Do you want to hump your hand for the next week?' A wonderful picture now in my head, 'A word Liam,' Sarah demanded, indicating with her head back into the house, 'Now,' she insisted when he failed to move.

They retreated, bickering as they went. I won't provide a detailed narrative of their discussion, but I can say that it was heated and short and contained a surprisingly unbalanced number of words starting with either an F or a C. They had gone through a door as they argued, but Sarah re-emerged now with his phone in her hand. Behind her and further into the house a door slammed. Hard.

'Here you are, Tempest,' she said handing the phone to me, 'Liam can be a proper idiot when he wants.'

45

'Thank you, Sarah.' The phone was simple to operate, so although I was not familiar with the make, the icons were the same universal ones that I had on my phone. The photographs were in a folder labelled *"Dead lady"* which made finding them easy. 'Can you send them across to me please?'

Sarah took the phone back to fiddle with it and we engaged in chit-chat about school while the files were transferred.

Once it was done, I had no desire to linger outside the house, so bid Sarah goodbye and escaped as soon as I could. She waved me goodbye with repeated requests to return when I had more time for a proper catch-up. I dodged giving any kind of commitment as there was no way I was ever going back.

My car was still in one piece, but I suspected that was only because I had never actually been more than five yards from it.

Fifteen minutes later, I was sitting in my car checking through the pictures in a supermarket car park halfway back to my house. The pictures were solid gold. Liam might be a thoroughly unpleasant chap, but these were as good as a crime scene photographer would have taken. There were over fifty in total. I gave them a cursory inspection, but they needed proper scrutiny, a task I would have to tackle later as I still had a lot to do today including getting ready to deal with the Cranfield's Poltergeist.

I checked my watch: 1653hrs. Time to feed the dogs. I fired up the engine and was home in a few minutes. Bull and Dozer were happy to see me as always and buzzed around my feet as I scooped kibble into their little bowls. Once they had eaten their dinner, which took about eight seconds, I let them out to scare the pigeons off the lawn and sat out on my decking to watch them snuffle about in the undergrowth.

Tomorrow I would track down friends and relatives of the victims and visit crimes scenes and see if I could wheedle some better information out of contacts in the police force and papers.

Tonight though, I had a Poltergeist to catch.

I had convinced the Cranfields that the most likely culprit was someone with a key, entering and leaving without needing to force entry and that the best way for me to catch the perpetrator was to set them both as bait and lie in wait. So, it was now 0213hrs and I was sitting in their living room in the dark. I had tucked myself into one corner where no light from outside would illuminate me. I was dressed in my standard rip-stop, hard-wearing, black, combat gear and boots and had blackened my face for good measure. I had not brought any weapons with me as I felt it unlikely I would need to use them and because bringing them shows intend to use in the eyes of the law. Should the perpetrator elect to fight I did not want there to be weapon-inflicted injuries to explain to the police.

As agreed with the Cranfields, I had snuck into their house by entering from the street behind and jumping over a fence. There was a slight risk that I might be spotted by a neighbour and cause alarm, but there seemed a greater chance that the house might be watched by the culprit and I wanted anyone watching to think it was just the Cranfields here.

The clock kept ticking on despite the bent hands. The annoying tick, tick, tick had been keeping me awake but it was late now and with nothing to do I was beginning to fail in my fight against sleep. My eyes were getting heavy and I really wanted to get up and move about as my back was stiffening from keeping still. I felt that I needed to remain quiet and motionless though.

A few minutes later I realised I had dozed off anyway and as I snapped my head back up, I heard a noise coming from the fireplace. No. It was to the left of that. The fireplace was ornamental and had a well-polished brass coal scuttle one side and an equally well-polished set of brass tools for tending the fire on the other. Above the aperture was a brass hood which, unsurprisingly, was well polished. To either side were built in cupboards where perhaps a younger Winston had fashioned storage and shelves in the two recesses created by the prominent chimney breast.

I did not know what I could hear but it sounded much like someone patiently moving things about inside the cupboard. I resisted the temptation to get up to investigate and was rewarded by the cupboard door opening slowly outwards a few moments later. In the shadows created by the street light a few doors down, I could now see a head emerging followed by the rest of a man's body.

'Wooooo,' he said. 'Wooooooo,' as he clambered stealthily out of the cupboard and stood up. 'Arrgggh, woooooo, arrrgggh!' was his next sentence. He was making ridiculous, cartoonish ghost noises that shouldn't have fooled a ten-year-old. However, he was both loud and confident. He continued the general Wooooo Arrrgggh theme while kicking the sofa on the opposite side of the room from where I sat and beginning to tilt the pictures which hung on the wall behind it. I had instructed the Cranfields to stay in bed regardless of what they heard. Sitting here now watching there poltergeist, I was thankful that they had obeyed me.

He was working steadily around the room and I was content to let him continue as I had two cameras placed high up on bookshelves recording the entire event. Dim light from the window revealed that the chap was mid to late thirties and five feet eight inches tall with a slight build. His hair was beginning to thin and he had a weak chin and a big nose. He was wearing a tracksuit, the grey flannel type with elasticated cuffs at the ankle and wrist. I could see tattoos on his neck.

Knowing that it was not a poltergeist had meant it was always going to be an idiot and my first thought had been that someone was trying to scare the Cranfields from their home for some kind of financial benefit. To rob them while they were out being an obvious motive. Since they had not been burgled at any point, I had struck that theory from the list. Alternatively, I could believe that they were being persecuted over some family dispute. I had seen this before and it was usually a relative, so my instant, but unspoken suspicion, was their son. He seemed likely to have a key and thus be able to achieve the unforced entry. I had seen a picture of their son and he was not only older and wider but also shorter and better looking. Quite how this chap got in through the wall was a mystery still, but not one that was going to be difficult to solve.

I felt it was time to introduce myself.

The poltergeist was moving around the room still. Having gone along the wall opposite the window tilting every picture and tipping a lamp over, he was now in the corner by the light switch. He tripped on something invisible in the dark and uttered a ghostly, 'Bollocks!' as he got up again. His next steps would take him to the dresser where Barbara kept her nice ornaments and I did not want any further breakages. I elected to use minimal force in order to avoid problems with the police later, although I will admit I wrestled momentarily with the concept of whacking him with the solid oak paper rack next to the chair I was sitting in.

As he stepped in front of the dresser with another good, 'Wooooooo!' I stood up, and in one fluid motion, planted my right foot solidly behind his back, grabbed him around both lateral muscles and using my body weight as a lever I turned him into a pendulum, swung him around and off his feet and threw him onto the sofa.

The next, 'Wooooo!' changed halfway through to an, 'Aaarrrggg!' and then into a, 'What the fuuu...?' Before his face slammed into a cushion and silenced him.

'Excuse me,' I said politely and calmly as I stepped to the wall and turned on the light. I then fixed him with the best menacing stare I could muster. Of course, menacing stares are not something one practices in front of a mirror, so I just hoped it was menacing and that I didn't just look like I needed to poo.

The man looked like he wanted to jump up and leg it. He had come to land face down against the back of the sofa, then rolled over onto his back and now had one leg over the end of the sofa and one leg on the floor. He was clutching his chest with one hand and breathing heavy. His face was white - like he had seen a ghost. I ha-harred to myself.

'You scared the crap out of me, man. Who the heck are you?' he asked from his prone position.

'I scared you? You think I scared you? What do you think the old couple upstairs have been going through with this ridiculous act of yours?' I was a little incensed. Of course, without idiots like this chap I had no work, but picking on an old couple and scaring them from their home seemed like such a cowardly and awful thing to do that it had made me somewhat irrationally angry. I was keeping it under control for my own sake rather than his. The righteous bit of me wanted to break his arms off and feed them to him.

His arms were now either side of him, palms down against the sofa as if ready to push off. 'Stay there, Sir. Or, I will make you stay.' I saw him look me up and down and then come to a conclusion. It was not the right one. He tensed, which was a lot like announcing by loudspeaker that he was going to try something daft. He then threw himself up and off the sofa. I actually thought he was just going to bolt for the cupboard he had come out of, or possibly for the door out of the room just so that he could get away, but he was braver, or crazier than that and he actually came at me.

51

Ready for him anyway, I met him as he rose towards me, stood on his right foot, placed one hand on the top of his rising head to deflect his motion then shoved him to the right and onto the floor. I grabbed his left arm as he went and pulled it around from the wrist into a classic arm-bar.

'Arrh,' he said again, but with less Scooby-doo-esque spookiness than before and then, 'ooofh,' as his chest impacted with the floor and the air left his lungs in one go. I had him in a position I felt was secure enough, so I called for the Cranfields to join me.

I could hear them moving around upstairs now. Doubtless, they had been unable to sleep wondering what might happen or had been woken by the idiot noises as their *Poltergeist* had started his routine. I had his left arm behind his back and could keep him pinned with very little effort, but I put a knee between his shoulder blades anyway for good measure.

'Stay there now. There's a good fellow.'

'Who the heck are you?' he managed between breaths.

'The chap the good folks here hired to investigate the strange goings on recently. So, my question to you is: Who are you?' He didn't answer, but I noticed a wallet shaped lump in his back pocket. Partly surprised that tracksuits came with pockets for wallets given their intended use was running and other sporting activities, I plucked it out and flicked it open. It was a cheap, black, leather-effect thing that must have been years old given that the fake leather was falling off. The first card announced that I was currently sitting on Leslie N Davy.

'Leslie? I asked him. He still didn't answer but swung his head to the side to try to look at me better.

I could hear the Cranfields coming down the stairs now. I called for them to come in, advising that I had the culprit restrained. I leaned down so that my mouth was a few inches from Leslie's right ear. 'I am going to lift you up and sit you back on the sofa whereupon you are going to answer some questions. I have taken fingerprints from broken and damaged items in this room. I also have two cameras that have recorded your performance this evening. So far you are guilty of several counts of breaking and entering and of wilful destruction of property.' I adjusted my position slightly so that I would be able to lift him off the floor without releasing his arm. 'You have some explaining to do and I had better like what I hear.'

With that thought still in his ear, I grasped his right shoulder and keeping hold of his left wrist, I pulled him off the carpet and pushed him onto the sofa. I released him then but stayed right in front of him, so that I formed a physical block between him and the Cranfields who were now entering the room.

'Meet your Poltergeist.' I invited.

'Oh goodness, oh my,' said Barbara.

'Leslie?' asked Winston, 'What are you doing here?'

'You know this man?'

'We both do. He is our next-door neighbour.' A piece of the puzzle clicked into place. The cupboard next to the fireplace must be hiding a hole through from his house. I would check shortly.

Leslie looked terrible now. His face appeared to be trying to decide whether to cry or wail or find a quick way to become invisible. He was shrinking into the sofa, physically making himself smaller and clearly embarrassed.

'Barbara, would you like to make some tea?' I enquired. It seemed like time to calm everyone down, get some answers from Leslie and wrap this case up.

Her reply came immediately, 'Stuff that, I need a brandy.'

'Here, here,' agreed Winston

'Me too,' said Leslie. I fixed him with a raised eyebrow, 'Sorry,' he offered.

'Nothing for me, thanks.' I had to drive home yet, but a stiff glass of something did sound like a cracking idea. Behind me, I heard a decanter being moved and the quiet glugging of a spirit into one glass, then another. I moved slightly to one side so that I was still standing and closer to Leslie than the Cranfields but no longer blocking their view of him.

'Start explaining.'

'No need really,' said Winston, 'I know what this is about.'

It transpired that Leslie had moved in five years ago, and the once tidy house next door with its delightful clipped privet hedge had gradually declined under his ownership. I had observed that the garden was overgrown myself when I first arrived. Further inspection later would reveal that the drain pipe was hanging loose, the paint was flaking off and in general, the property was fairly grubby. The driveway had two battered looking fast Fords parked on it. A tarpaulin was hanging from one.

About six months back, after a period of politely asking Leslie to tidy his bit of the street, Winston had become a little firmer in the tone of his requests, and then when his requests had been rebuffed with unpleasant language, he had complained to the local authorities. Eventually, someone had paid attention and the net result was that he has been awarded an Anti-Social Behaviour Order and a fine. Leslie had taken umbrage and refused still to address the appearance of his house, instead striking upon the idea that he could alleviate the complaints by driving the complainers away.

He had discovered the loose brickwork leading from the cupboard next to the chimney in his property when he was installing a television unit a few weeks ago. Removing a couple of bricks, he saw immediately that he could get into the house next door and the poltergeist idea had just come to him.

'Well, Leslie,' I said to the rather withdrawn form sat on the Cranfields' couch, 'You have something of a problem now. You have committed several crimes,' I turned to face Winston, 'Winston it is time for you to call the police.'

'Wh wh wh what? The police?' Leslie stammered, somehow surprised that he might actually be in trouble for his actions.

55

'What you have to realise, Leslie,' I began, 'Is that you are a bit of an idiot. So, of course, the police.' I wanted to pontificate but stopped myself. I would get paid for my work and there was no further need for involvement on my part. 'You broke into someone's house, destroyed their property and generally menaced them. I am an investigator, not a vigilante, my task was to determine what was going on here. Punishment is down to the authorities.'

Winston nodded his head slowly in agreement or perhaps to acknowledge that calling the police was necessary, and he shuffled out of the room. Minutes later a muffled half of a conversation could be heard from deeper in the house. It did not last long; the audible click of the house phone being put down preceded Winston returning moments later.

'They will be here in a few minutes,' he announced. I simply nodded and watched as Winston joined his wife at the cocktail cabinet and took a healthy slug of his brandy. Thankfully only a few minutes of uncomfortable silence had to be endured before flashing light began to illuminate the gaps around the edges of the now drawn curtains.

I turned to Winston and Barbara. 'What you do next is your choice. He has broken into your house and damaged your property. There is a hole through to your house from his which ought to be professionally repaired. The police will escort him from your property, probably under arrest and will process him and give you a case number for insurance purposes should you need it. I will provide you with a statement detailing my investigation and video footage which is still running and has recorded all of tonight's events. It can be used by the police and I will attend any interviews and a court case if necessary. I will send you an invoice for my services in the next couple of days. Is there anything else you need me to do?'

'We would just like to get this finished and get to bed, if that's alright, Mr. Michaels,' replied Barbara.

I checked my watch: 0257hrs. 'I don't appear to have anything further to do, mystery solved and all, so getting to bed sounds good to me as well.' We stood for a moment just staring at each other waiting for someone to speak. If it lasted any longer it was going to be weird and they were clearly waiting for me to say something. I gave a sort of *I'm off* motion with one hand, saying, 'You have my number if you need me. Good evening to you both.' I gave them a cheery smile and headed into the night, passing the police on the driveway.

The dogs greeted me at the door as always, forcing me to shoo them back so that I could get in. I was tired, so after letting them out and giving them a pat, I shrugged off my gear, shucked my clothes and got into bed. It was 0334hrs and I had no plan to get up at 0530hrs for a workout.

I awoke at 0914hrs with a dog asleep on my neck. The bed was low enough that the boys could clamber on and snuggle into the duvet if they wanted to. I wondered sometimes whether it was an entirely hygienic practice but had elected to not care too much as I liked having them there. Perhaps this satisfied some unfulfilled longing for a dog to be curled at my feet when I was a boy. I reached up to poke the warm ball of dumb, but it just wriggled a bit and snuggled in deeper to my neck. The tip of one ear was draped across my mouth with the tip tickling a nostril as I moved.

Reluctantly, I reached up with my other hand and using both arms lifted him to the side. I could now see that it was Dozer, although I had suspected it would be because this was typical behaviour for him. As I levered him off me and back onto the duvet, he opened an eye but closed it again and went directly back to sleep. Bull was somewhere under the covers having burrowed there during the night. I left them to it, slipped out from under the delightfully warm goose-down duvet and went for a shower.

A little later downstairs, I ate scrambled eggs and smoked salmon on whole-wheat toast deciding what to do with my day. The simplicity of the Cranfield's case had made it a quick boost to my cash flow, provided they paid in a timely manner of course. I had taken a deposit upon engagement so there was at least some money in my account already. Now though, I was back to having no paid work to deal with again.

That was mildly concerning, but *The Vampire* was killing people in the local area and I didn't feel that I could ignore the case. There were three victims so far and no reason to believe the death toll would stop until someone caught him. I had spoken with Liam and although I now had pictures of the poor Mrs. Hancock I did not really know any more than I had before. Liam had chanced upon the body and there appeared to be no more to it than that. The first victim seemed equally random and the name of the third had yet to be released. I needed to speak to Darren Shrivers, an old friend at the local constabulary, but he was inconveniently off getting trained for something or other. With the option of getting free information from the police seemingly closed to me, I was going to have to do things the hard way.

Since I had no live cases, I could dedicate the day to investigating the vampire, but do I focus on Mrs. Hancock or Mr. Grazly first? I flipped a mental coin and elected to continue looking into Mrs. Hancock. Her friends had been named in the newspaper article online and given the geography, I felt confident I would be able to find one or all of them in the phone book.

The three ladies were Mrs. Jean Winters, Mrs. Rebecca Masters, and Miss Rosemary Green. I got lucky on my first look with Mrs. J Winters. There was only one in the book, which with an Allington address had to be the right one. She answered a phone like my mother did by saying the phone number. It had always struck me as an odd thing to do. If you had just dialed the number, then you already knew it. Answering with a hello or maybe saying your name made more sense. But I got, "902301," as my hello. Perhaps all persons over a certain age answered the phone like that.

Mrs. Winters was very keen to meet with me and invited me over straight away. She then paused to have a brief discussion with herself about what would be best. The decision she arrived at was that the other two ladies would never forgive her if they were not involved, so I should come to her house at 1230hrs although she said it as, "Half-past twelve," like a civilian always does. With time on my hands, I turned my attention towards the first victim, Mr. Brian Grazly.

An internet search revealed numerous newspaper articles about him, or more accurately about his murder, but by piecing together the snippets of information in each report I was able to build a picture of Brian and his life. Brian was unmarried with no children and no living relatives. He worked at Chilwell Castle on the banks of the river Medway. I googled Chilwell Castle to learn that it was a privately-owned stately home that had been built in 1647 by Mr. Robert Chilwell. It had remained in the Chilwell family for centuries until poor financial decisions in the 1960s, by the then resident Mr. Antony Chilwell, forced its sale.

The current owner was a gentleman from Dubai whose family had made their fortune in steel. There was no further information about the family on the page I was reading, and it seemed unlikely I needed to know anything much about them. I read that they were not in residence at the time of Brian's death but had expressed their shock and apparently, they had pledged money for his funeral costs.

Brian was the groundsman and lived in the grounds of the castle where his body had been found at the edge of the garden of his little cottage. My guess was the cottage came as a perk of the job. I flicked to a newspaper article which showed it. The front façade was painted bright white but had exposed wood beams running across it, along with it and up it, which were undoubtedly original structural fittings. They were painted black to contrast with the bright white paint and there were flowers in well-tended beds around the outside of the cottage at the front and a path centered to the house which ran in a straight line from the short garden wall to the front door.

Between the articles relating directly to his murder and a few associated searches, there was not a lot of information and what there was did not give me much. It gave me a background picture of the man though, which might prove helpful at some point. I noted that the castle grounds bordered the river almost directly opposite the River Angel pub and that the address Mrs. Winters had given me was less than half a mile away. I wrote on my scratch pad: *Three murders are all very close to each other.* Then looked at the note for a minute, tapped my pen twice on the paper and then circled it. It didn't mean anything yet and the police would be well aware of the geography involved.

I pushed my chair back and got up. Dozer raised his head to see if I was going to do anything interesting - like bring him a sandwich. We locked eyes briefly and he concluded that it was not worth being awake, so plunked his head back onto the sofa and began snoring again in seconds.

Not long afterward, but still an hour before I was due to arrive at Mrs. Winters house I was in the car heading to her general area. Bull and Dozer were on the passenger seat, one atop the other as usual. I had decided that they needed a decent walk, that the ladies would probably welcome them and that if they did not then they could just sleep in the car while I was inside. Walking them along the river path that bordered the castle grounds also gave me a chance to have a little look at Chilwell Castle. From memory, quite a bit of the grounds could be seen from the river path and as it was now autumn, I expected the summer foliage to have died back so I could see in. I might see nothing worthwhile, but if so, I had lost nothing, and the boys would be walked.

I parked the car at the end of one of the streets that terminated at the river. Parking was easy as it was a working day and only a few cars were present in the street. I clambered out, scooped the dogs and plopped them on the grass next to the car. They immediately scampered off heading towards the river, so I let them go. I tucked some baggies into a back pocket, tapped my other pockets to make sure wallet and phone were in them, plipped the car shut and headed after them.

I had last brought the dogs to walk this route perhaps six months ago. The temperature was probably about the same then as it was now which was warm enough for me to be out in just a T-shirt, but still cool at the same time. It was warmer today than it had been the last few days. Even so, I would be too cool for my outfit if I were standing still. Leaves were turning brown and yellow, creating colourful patterns on the path as they fell. The river was flowing towards Maidstone but moved so slowly one could only tell which way it was going by watching the progress of waterfowl. There was no one else about which made the walk all the more pleasant for me.

On this side of the river, the path was more regularly used than on the other as on this side there was a small housing estate bordering it in places. On previous visits, I had seen people walking their dogs, joggers taking advantage of the picturesque, traffic-free route and persons in suits and office wear clearly on their way to a job somewhere.

The path was a mix of some kind of shale that had been laid at some point, concrete here and there and well-trodden dirt. It was a little muddy in places but easy enough to pick around. The path was several feet higher than the river and mostly bordered it, however in some places there were trees or bushes between the path and the river and in other places there was just grass and in yet other places the path edge was at the river, so a wrong foot would leave the unwary person in the drink. Along the way there were spots were the bank led down to a platform for anglers and a few bins for litter or doggy poop. In the weeds, brambles, and nettles that bordered the path there was quite a bit of litter, making me wonder whose task it was to clear it up and how much was just dropped here by the uncaring and how much blew in on the wind or got deposited by flood tides.

With the river on my right, to my left I could see houses and garden fences perhaps fifty feet away through the trees. As I continued along the path, the land to my left began to angle sharply upwards so that there was now a bank to scramble up. Between the trees, the same brambles and weeds had tiny paths winding through where children had adventures. At the top of the bank, I could see more houses, the new brickwork visible through only a few small gaps in the foliage. To my right between the path and the edge of the river, there was an old wooden fence, the type made from roughly hewn branches held together with twisted steel wire. From its condition, it was probably decades old. There were bits missing, the wire was rusted completely through in places and I could see that kids, or perhaps anglers had forced holes through to the bank here and there leaving some of the fence posts sticking out at odd angles.

I had to stop at one point because the fence had simply been levered up from the ground to permit access underneath it. The pointed end of the posts were mostly broken off or rotted away, but two were jutting out perpendicular to the ground at a height of about five feet. They were not actually obstructing the path but to me there seemed a danger that a cyclist or someone not paying attention might walk into them. It was more likely they would get dirty in the process of disentangling themselves than get injured, but it struck me that the decent thing to do was make them safe. This simple task proved not to be so simple though. Where the fence ran through the undergrowth it had been caught up in shrubs and no matter what I did I could not get the posts to face back downwards. I tried then to twist the fence, so it went upwards instead but achieved nothing doing that either. So finally, I looked at whether I could just snap the two offending posts off. After five minutes of grunting, I was starting to feel like a vandal myself and I gave up. I used my handkerchief to clean off my hands as I walked away and inspected my clothing for chunks of dirt, thankfully finding none.

I walked another half mile and as I did the land to my left dropped back down again. I soon reached the castle grounds and an ancient looking stone wall. The wall had almost boulder-sized chunks of rock held together with equally ancient mortar. It had been vandalised and graffitied in places but was still solid looking. It was five feet tall, so I could comfortably see over it into the grounds of the castle when trees and bushes the other side permitted.

I lost the dogs for a moment. They had mostly been trundling along in front of me quite happy to be going for a walk but were now nowhere to be seen. I stopped for a moment to listen. No sound from the undergrowth but before I needed to call for them both one and then the other reappeared a few yards ahead of me, both emerging from under a bush.

I continued onwards, looking through the trees as I went and soon spotted the groundsman's cottage. I had probably glanced at it dozens of times before without even registering it. Now it meant something, and I could see rose bushes at the front of the property where I was guessing he had been found.

The path dipped down a little, making the drop to the water less than a foot. The two dogs were stood at the bank staring at some ducks idly paddling a few feet out in the river. The ducks paid them no attention but while I studied the ground of Chilwell Castle, the dogs were wagging their tails and dancing from foot to foot in their desperation to give chase. I would need to turn around soon and head back to the car to ensure I

64

arrived on time for my appointment with Mrs. Winters and the other ladies. Then, just as I opened my mouth to call the dogs, I noticed a small door in the old castle wall. It had always been there, the stone around the door was shaped to form the aperture that the door filled. The door itself was oak and looked both ancient and solid. At little more than four feet tall and two feet wide, it was designed for small people and probably had a specific purpose a few hundred years ago. Around the base of the door, there were vague footprints in the dirt and it was clear that the undergrowth, which must have partially obscured it, had been torn away recently. I picked at a piece of ivy. The broken end was rough, so had been ripped rather than cut, suggesting the person doing it had not brought tools. I looked around a bit and a few feet down the path found a balled mass of ivy, bramble and other foliage that was now drying out and looking withered. It was, I judged, a week or so old.

I went back to the door. There was a keyhole about halfway up on the left-hand side. It was just a big hole in the wood, so I had to crouch to look into it where I could just about make out the inner working of a metal lock. There were no spider webs or sign of other insect activity, so it must have been used recently. Did that mean anything? Maybe. I stood up again and looked over the top of the wall. On the other side were the same species of trees and plants I had seen so far. I checked left and right, placed my palms on top of the wall and levered myself up to get a better look.

Not far from the gate was another stone building. It was not very big, perhaps ten yards by ten yards and was almost completely obscured by trees and shrubs growing around it. I could just about make out the roof, which was pitched to form a centre apex and was made from a black slate. It was largely covered in lichen and had weeds and plants growing from it, though everything looked intact from my current angle.

65

I briefly considered going over the wall for a better look, but time was getting on and there would be other opportunities should I feel the need. I did not know what I was looking for after all. I dropped lightly back to the ground, called the dogs and headed back to the car.

Mrs. Jean Winters lived at number 93 Leadbetter lane. It was in Allington which would once have been a small village a couple of miles from Maidstone but was now absorbed into the city's suburbs so that one could not really tell where one postcode ended and the next began. The house was a semi-detached property in a cul-de-sac running parallel and one street over from the main road running through Allington.

The house was of 1930s design with a recessed front entrance, chequerboard path leading from the road to the door and many period features which undoubtedly had specific names I had never learned. The front garden was resplendent with clipped topiary in various neat globes and through the open ironwork of the latched gate, I could see Buxus clipped into low-level box hedges bordering both sides of the narrow path. The front garden itself was large compared with my vision of similar properties, perhaps thirty feet or more. In all the house was quite charming.

I had parked directly in front of her house as there was a space there. The property had a drive but no garage and there was no car visible, which might mean that she had a husband that was out or that she no longer drove, or perhaps that she had never driven. I dismissed it as unimportant. As I moved to open my door, two children dressed in their school uniform walked by heading from the rear of my car towards the front. I checked around me to see if there were any more and could see a few in the distance behind me. None were close though, so I left the dogs on the passenger seat and slid out of the car. The door to the house opened before I could take a second pace and a cheery looking lady in her late sixties or early seventies appeared in the doorway.

'Mr. Michaels?' she asked, raising her voice slightly to make sure I heard her over the length of the path.

67

'Yes indeed,' I answered closing the distance and producing a business card, 'Mrs. Winters?'

'Yes dear, the other ladies are indoors fixing some tea,' she paused, which I thought odd until I followed her gaze back to my car and the two little noses pressed against the driver's side window. 'Are they Dachshunds?' Mrs. Winters took a step towards them to get a better view. Bull barked at that point and before I could answer Mrs. Winters spoke again, 'I used to have Dachshunds when my Percy was still alive. Oh, aren't they adorable? You must bring them in.'

'Very good, Mrs. Winters,' I fetched the two over excited idiots from the car, although fetched is a tenuous term. I opened the door a crack and they wedged their heads and then bodies through the hole, hit the ground running, shot along the path and didn't stop at Mrs. Winters as the sprinted into her house. Perhaps they could smell cake.

I plipped the car locked again and found myself alone in the street as Mrs. Winters had already followed the dogs inside. I let myself in and closed the door behind me. Inside, the house was surprisingly modern in its décor and furnishings. Where I had expected perhaps oil paintings on the walls or souvenirs and knick-knacks on shelves, there were none. The wallpaper was modern and very new looking. In the living room, a minimalist approach had given the room an airy and spacious feel. The carpet was new or at least unmarked by the passage of feet, its soft woollen appearance matching the tan brown leather three-piece-suite elegantly. The curtains also matched the theme and to one corner of the room stood a brushed aluminium television cabinet with a Sky TV system and a fifty-inch flat-screen. I might have decorated the same if it were my place.

I could hear the ladies bustling towards me from the kitchen and the familiar rattle of a tray laden with cups, saucers and the accompanying silverware. The other two ladies were carbon copies of Mrs. Winters, each of the three with grey hair neatly moulded to their heads and kept short, each was a little large at the hips but in a womanly, friendly-grandmother kind of way and each wore simple clothing that looked new but bought from a shop that tailored to pensionable aged ladies.

Mrs. Winters introduced them both in turn and instructed everyone to sit and make themselves comfortable. As she did so, Mrs. Rebecca Masters poured the tea while Miss Rosemary Green handed the cups out and offered cake.

Being polite I took a piece of cake but elected to leave it untouched for now rather than devour it and risk having a second slice forced upon me. I try hard to avoid cake in general, as delightful though it is, it provides very little by way of nutrition and just makes me fat.

Bull and Dozer were instructed to stay down for fear they would climb onto the ladies' laps, spill tea and steal the cake. They did look at me when I gave them their orders but promptly ignored me as the ladies cooed and welcomed them onto the couch. I kept a wary eye on them though, ready for cake thievery.

'So, how may we help you, Mr. Michaels?' asked Mrs. Winters, taking the lead before I felt the need to.

'As you know ladies, I am investigating *the vampire* murder case and it is important for me to create the most complete picture possible. This should just be a simple case of me asking a few questions and you answering where you can.'

The three ladies were looking at me expectantly, so I placed the cup and saucer on a side table adorned with a doily, reached down into my bag and produced a notebook in which I had roughed out some questions I hoped to ask them. I started at the top.

'What time did Rita leave here on the night in question?'

Jean was sitting in the middle of the three-seater sofa with Rebecca to her right and Rosemary to her left. Rebecca and Rosemary both leaned forward so the three women could each see the other two.

'I think it was about half-past eleven, wasn't it?' asked Rebecca of the other two.

'About that wouldn't you say, Jean?' asked Rosemary.

'Yes, ladies. I think that is about right,' agreed Jean.

This pattern then continued with pretty much every question thereafter as I worked through my list. I would ask a question, the three would confer briefly and Jean would provide the answer. It was a bit like watching University Challenge where only the spokesperson could give the answer.

Nevertheless, I got to the end of my sheet and by then had jotted two pages of notes. None of it seemed to mean anything though. The ladies met every week on the same day and played canasta, they had been doing so for years although they were not sure what to do now as they were missing their fourth player. They drank Sherry and wine and always met at Jean's house because she had the nice card table. They would take it in turns to do food and I had collected several other meaningless and banal facts. Rita always walked home, her husband had been dead for six years and she lived alone as did they all, although Rosemary had never married, she told me with a wink.

As I scribbled notes, the two dogs had made themselves very comfortable and had the look of two contented and very sleepy dogs nestled as they were, either side of Jean so the sofa went old lady, stupid dog, old lady, stupid dog, old lady. I was not fooled though for had a

70

crumb of cake been offered to them they would have reacted faster than your average superhero.

The walk from Jean's House to Rita's was less than half a mile and took her only a few minutes. They had been very shocked and horrified to hear the news of course, but that was about all I got from them. Tea drunk and cake eaten, I packed my notepad and pen away, ushered the dogs towards the door and stopped to shake the ladies' hands, each in turn. I thanked them one last time and went back outside to the car. A light drizzle had set in during the hour I had spent with them, so the dogs, who perpetually avoided any form of wetness, ran to the car and looked pointedly at me and then the door and then me until I arrived to scoop them inside.

As I pulled away, I ran a quick mental calculation on whether I needed any groceries, decided I did and pointed the car towards Sainsbury's. I was gathering information on the vampire case, but so far, I was not making any of it join up or lead me anywhere. It was odd to be without a paying case, but I doubted it would last very long. Oh well, it was Friday afternoon, so I could enjoy not having a regular job, maybe get a bath and watch some TV. Tonight, I was out with the chaps for a beer.

Good times.

I showered and changed selecting Caterpillar boots, jeans and a polo as suitable for going to the pub attire. It was 1846hrs, a little early to be heading out and I needed to eat first. Bull and Dozer were sat watching TV on the couch, but soon appeared in the kitchen when I rattled a few pots. Ever hopeful, like all the rest of their canine brethren, they forget each meal as soon as the last bite is swallowed and immediately revert to hungry.

I kept my cupboards stocked with healthy food because like so many people I found it all too easy to open a wrapper and start chomping something easy and less nutritious whenever my stomach demanded sustenance. I grew vegetables in my garden and made sure that I got my five-a-day whenever possible. I never, or at least rarely, ate processed food and never had white carbs in the house. It was not so much that I was dreadfully vain about my appearance, although I will admit that I want to look good but I was quite focused on being healthy and convinced that regular exercise and a nutritious diet made a person more focused, more capable and in many ways happier at a basic level. Of course, I do still drink alcohol and do still eat burgers or pies on occasion simply because they taste good.

What to eat then? An eternal conundrum. I had turkey mince in the fridge, so dinner was brown rice with a turkey and vegetable chili and lots of avocado pear diced into it at the end. Healthy, nutritious, filling and low in anything that might be considered fattening which is a good thing as I planned to put four or more pints of beer on top of it.

The dogs had wandered off when it became clear I was not fixing a second meal for them but reappeared as my spoon scraped the bottom of the bowl for the last few morsels. Looking down at them, I said, 'Sorry chaps. There is no way I am giving you chili to finish. Especially you Dozer, since you fart like a warthog with dysentery anyway.' Undeterred they continued to wag their tails until the bowl and the cooking pots went into the dishwasher. Disappointed, they retreated to the lounge and slipped under the cover on their bed, leaving two little tails hanging out.

My phone rang, the screen claiming that it was Big Ben calling. I had known Big Ben for many years, meeting him in Bosnia when he had been transferred into my section from another unit following an 'incident' (he hit someone he really shouldn't have). Big Ben was… well, he was big. He stood six feet and seven inches tall and was mostly muscle. He was classically good looking, his ability to pick up women was legendary, and I still didn't really understand how he did it despite years of studying his technique. He was also a complete cad with women, had no belief in relationships and would expound his theories on the subject given even the slightest opportunity and stated that he was constantly in danger of creating mini-versions of himself because women spontaneously ovulated when they saw him naked. A couple of years ago, his parents were killed in a road traffic incident that proved to be caused by negligence on the part of a national haulage company and he received a substantial payout. He promptly left the army to pursue *full-time shagging*; his words, not mine. By blind serendipity, we had grown up just a mile or so apart, so when I took my uniform off for the last time and moved home, we had met for a pint and a chat and had been hanging out together ever since. Today, Big Ben lived in a nice penthouse apartment overlooking the river Medway in the middle of Maidstone where he could easily predate on the ladies of the town. He didn't work, as he didn't need to, so filled his time with going to the gym and playing golf. Occasionally he helped me out as back up on my cases because it gave him the chance to do something different and a slim chance that he might get to thump someone.

'Ben. What's up?' I asked as the call connected.

'Nothing man, everything is sweet at my end. Shagged a totally hot Swedish chick last night and she was still in my house when I got in from golf, so I gave her another seeing to and then tossed her out. Let her get a shower first though.'

'So, considerate.'

'Nah mate, it was so I could get her phone and erase my number from it. She took it last night when I was chatting her up.'

'But she knows where you live, Ben. Won't she just come back when she discovers your number is not in her phone?'

'They never have done before. It is, of course, possible, I suppose.'

'You make me sick, Ben. I spent last night sat on a client's sofa waiting for a poltergeist and before that, I watched a couple of episodes of Buffy the Vampire Slayer as research. Nearest I got to sex last night was when Bull licked my nose.'

'When were you last at the gym?'

'Err, Tuesday, no Wednesday evening.'

'Were there hot girls in the gym?'

'There are always hot girls in the gym, Ben. Going to the gym makes them hot generally.'

'And did you approach any of the hot girls? Poor lonely ladies with nothing better to do on a Wednesday night than to go to the gym, hoping desperately that they can hone and tone their bodies to the point where a man, maybe any man, will take an interest. Did you try to save them from the perpetual struggle they must engage in just to make themselves attractive enough to warrant a man's attention? No, you didn't. You left them to suffer, didn't you? You utter git. Those poor girls had to drag themselves home again all alone. You could have spent the night making one of them feel special, helping her get clean again after the sweat of the gym.'

'I don't think it works like that for anyone but you, mate.'

'And that is why you fail, my little Padawan.'

'Ben what did you call for?' I asked impatiently.

'To tell you I shagged a totally hot Swedish bird,' he replied, clearly exasperated as if I was being particularly dense, 'Anyway, get to the pub, I'll be there in ten minutes.' He hung up.

Git.

'Boys! Get your collars on.' I hollered through the house. I listened for the onrush of feet across the stone floor.

Nothing.

'Boys!' I called again as the lazy little monkeys had failed to move, 'Come along chaps, it is pub o'clock,' I called as I went through to the lounge to find their two tails still poking out of their bed covers. I hustled them up and out into the garden. Better to pee in the garden than the pub. Two minutes later and with their collars on, the three of us went out the door.

The pub was a couple of streets over from my house on the main road through the village. If I went directly there it was less than five hundred metres and would take perhaps three minutes. It was a pleasant evening though, so I took a long route to the pub as it meant that the chaps could exercise themselves and would arrive at the pub ready to curl up in a corner and sleep.

Bull and Dozer knew the way to the pub, which they demonstrated by increasing their pull on the lead as we neared it. They dragged me the last few yards through the car park, not that I was exactly kicking and screaming, and I pushed open the door to pass over the threshold and into the warmth of the Dirty Habit. I had taken the time to make sure the dogs were walked, and we arrived at 1937hrs which was neither early nor late.

Natasha was behind the bar as usual. Friday night was her shift and the chaps were already sat in the right-hand corner, their pints in varying stages of emptiness.

'Alright, fellas?' asked Big Ben of the dogs, leaning down, and ruffling their fur. This was usual routine for the dogs, so I left them with the guys and headed to the bar.

'My round, chaps,' I announced as I passed them. Always good to make sure you get a round in early I find. Besides, I had been trying and failing to chat up Natasha the barmaid since I moved into the village. Natasha is above average when it comes to looks, intelligence, and probably everything else. If I met her somewhere else, I might stand a chance, but everyone knows an attractive barmaid gets hit on but drunk idiots constantly, so I'd sensible chosen to never add my interest to the list of losers and though I wanted to right now, I chose the wise route and just ordered my drinks.

While she made up my order, I glanced across at my drinking buddies sat around one of the small tables. The pub was old and beautiful, poorly lit in places, but typical of village pubs all over England. It sat on a corner of the main road running through the tiny village of Finchampstead, just outside Maidstone in Kent. After so many years in the army living away from England, there had been a yearning to return to the joys of village life and the simplicity of a good pub. This one had been in the same spot for centuries, surviving against competitors as other pubs had opened and subsequently closed over the many years. In the eighties, the small village had three pubs, but only the Dirty Habit remained despite the village population increasing when a new, small estate was built. The origin of the pub's name was a play on words due to the Friary located just about a mile away between this village and the next.

I got back to the table with three pints of Kronenberg and returned to the bar for an ale and a cider. I took a spare chair and pulled it up between Jagjit and Ben.

'So, what now mate?' asked Jagjit. Jagjit and I had gone to school together, met on our first day still aged four and had attended each other's Birthday parties until we left School. I joined the army and left the country, Jagjit had stayed where he was and was still there every time I came home on leave. When I finally came home for good, it was Jagjit that organised my homecoming. When I say homecoming I, of course, mean that we went for a curry and had a few pints. Jagjit worked in some kind of sales and judging by his car he was making out okay. His parents were still alive, and he lived with them. He had been married briefly before the lady in question ran off with his cousin and he had moved back home at that point. That was more than a decade ago and he steadfastly refused to entertain getting married again much to his mother's annoyance. He had four brothers though and each had multiple children, so I was not sure what her issue was. Much like Big Ben, Jagjit had offered to come on jobs with me and then, after I had not taken up his offer, he began pestering me. I think maybe Big Ben had made the stakeouts and occasional confrontations sound more glamorous or adventurous than they are, but he wanted to join in, so I had relented and Jagjit had helped on a couple of cases so far.

Across from me sat Hilary, whose actual name was Brian Clinton, but… well, it's obvious really. He had been Hilary for so long that even his wife called him it. Her name was Anthea and she very definitely wore the pants in their relationship. I wondered sometimes if she wore the penis also. Hilary was allowed out on a Friday night though because his wife said so. I had met him in the pub a few months ago and he was a solid member of the Friday night crowd now. Hilary was tall and thin, and his hair was starting to recede, he was wearing an outfit probably provided by his wife that was designed to make him look as unattractive as possible while still being modern and almost trendy in appearance. His top was a Ralph Lauren polo shirt but in a colour that could best be described as portaloo blue. His jeans were probably expensive also but looked too big for his skinny waist, so the cinched-in belt gave the appearance of a potato-sack tied with string in the middle. He worked in telemarketing, a job in which he was clearly capable as he was some kind of senior manager, but one which he had never had anything positive to say about. His face bore a perpetually morose expression, but he had the driest sense of humour I had ever encountered.

Finally, there is Basic. James Burnham is called Basic because God only loaded him with the basic package. He could breathe and walk and perform basic tasks, but that was pretty much it. He lived with his mum and we liked him because he made each of us feel like Stephen Hawkins' brighter brother. He had shaggy black hair that hung down past his ears at the front and sides and back, his clothes were generally dirty because he tended to spill on himself, but he was clean enough because his mum looked after him. He had found employment stacking supermarket trollies when he left school and had been doing it ever since. Like Jagjit and Big Ben, Basic had asked if he could come along when I needed muscle. Muscle was something he had as if nature had compensated for his lack of IQ with an abundance of strength. More Quasimodo than Adonis, Basic looked like he could have been the world's greatest caveman and might be able to break rocks with his head. Just like with Jagjit, I had relented and brought Basic along with Big Ben and I a few weeks back when the extra person seemed an appropriate step. I worried afterward what the person I had tracked the case in question to, and thus needed to have a word with, had thought as he opened his door to me with my two henchmen flanking me one on either side.

The conversation was paused when I returned with the beverages, but it never takes Big Ben long to turn it around to who he shagged last night. He was just getting started when Hilary held up a hand to stop him. 'I'd rather not hear it, if I'm honest, Ben.'

Big Ben raised an eyebrow. 'Hilary you need to hear more than anyone else. You've been married so long I bet the only action your mattress gets is when you turn it every month.'

'What my wife and I get up to and how often is none of your business, thank you, Ben.' Hilary picked up his pint to take a swig.

'Mate. The crux of all your woes is that you got married in the first place. Marriage crushes a man's soul.' This was not the first-time Big Ben had elected to rant on the poison of marriage.

'You have no respect for women Ben, that is your problem,' Hilary shot back.

'I do respect them though. I respect them enough to tell them up front that I intend to ruin them for all other men and never call them again. Quite often they laugh because they don't believe me, but what can I do about that? The way I see it, no relationship can last past six months and still be interesting. If I could get away with it, I would have them sign an agreement on the first date stating that we automatically break up at the six-month point if the relationship makes it that far. It would do away with daft aspirations of holidays in the sun, or gifts of jewellery just because they are a year older. Relationships go stale.'

'How would you know, Ben?' asked Jagjit, 'You have never had a girlfriend that lasted more than a few weeks.'

'That's not true. I dated a girl for three years once.'

There was a moment of silence while we tried to take in this revelation. 'How old were you at the time, Ben?' asked Hilary.

'I was ten when we broke up, but don't tell me it doesn't count. I have had my heart broken just like everyone else and now I have learned my lesson it can never happen again.'

I needed to chip in my opinion, 'I'm on the fence with this. A lot of what Ben says is true, relationships do lose their spark and the rampant sex bit does diminish.'

'Is that true, Hilary?' asked Jagjit, 'You are the only married one here and no one else managed to score more than a couple of years when they did marry.'

Hilary picked up his pint for a swift draught. 'I am not answering that question. However, I do wish to make it clear, Ben, that you are without a doubt, and being completely fair to you, a complete and utter dick.'

'You really are,' Jagjit and I agreed

'Acknowledged. But it does not appear to be affecting my chances. Hey, Natasha, how about a shag?' he asked as she passed him on her way back to the bar with empty glasses.

'I'd rather sleep with a dog, Ben. You disease-ridden man-whore,' Natasha dumped the tray of glasses on the bar and came back to pet the dogs, 'Ben is a disease-ridden man-whore, isn't he Bull?' she cooed into his ear, cradling him on her ample chest and kissing his head. 'Isn't he? Yes, he is.'

Natasha placed Bull back on the floor and patted Dozer once more before going back to the bar and the customer waiting there. The conversation turned to work and rugby as it usually did, and the beer continued to flow.

By 0730hrs on Saturday morning I had finished a good fifty-minute-long workout at the local gym and was heading home in the car with my muscles warm and twitchy. I had trained alone, which is less favourable and less enjoyable than training with a motivated partner, but very few want to join me that early on a Saturday. Most of the people I knew would be still in bed and staying there for a lie in. I had no set hours though, just tasks that I needed to complete and avenues to pursue to solve cases. I could lie in anytime I felt the need.

I got a shower and threw on a pair of jogging bottoms and a zip-through hoody. Breakfast was rolled oats in skimmed milk and a banana which was boring but healthy and the slow release carb would keep me going until mid-morning. The boys vacuumed up a bowl of kibble each and ran out into the garden, tiny legs feverishly propelling them across the lawn to chase away the pigeons. Content that they had secured their territory from aerial invaders they snuffled off across the grass and into the shrubbery to look for frogs.

There were still a lot of people on my list of people to interview, however the phone rang before I could consider whom to speak with first. 'Blue Moon Investigation Agency. Tempest Michaels speaking. How may I help you?' Professional, right?

There was a pause at the other end of the phone and the small sound of someone breathing before their voice came onto the line, 'Hello?' a woman's voice, soft, perhaps pensionable age.

'Hello. This is Tempest Michaels of the Blue Moon Investigation Agency. How may I be of assistance?

'I really don't know if you can help.' The voice was wavering and unsteady as if frightened or unsure of itself.

82

I moved to the kitchen counter and grabbed up a pen and paper in case I needed to take notes. 'Can I ask your name?' I enquired, wanting to make a connection. I kept my voice soft and even, hoping I would impart a soothing effect.

'It's just... I don't know who else to turn to.' No name given. No real information at all.

'I pride myself on being completely confidential, madam. Whatever you tell me won't go any further. If it helps, I have an office where we can meet,' I offered. The lady making the call might be a complete nutjob or a genuine client or even a witness to something that would be of interest to me. I had no way of knowing unless I pressed her for more information. There was little sound from the other end of the line, just the quiet sound of breathing and another noise which might have been a lip being chewed in deliberation. To me, it seemed as if the lady was trying to make a decision. Do I prompt her before she chickens out? Or do I stay quiet and let her get there by herself?

'I think my grandson might be a vampire,' she said all at once as if the words had been welling up and had finally forced their way out in one go. Grandson meant I was probably right about her age.

'You most certainly called the right person then, Mrs...'

'Cambridge, Vera Cambridge. My Grandson is Jim Butterworth, although he calls himself Demedicus Solomon now. Can you come? It is really quite urgent.'

'What makes you think your Grandson is a vampire, Mrs. Cambridge?'

I listened then as Mrs. Cambridge launched into a long-winded summation of her grandson's increasingly odd behaviour with several claims that he used to be such a lovely boy. He wore dark clothing, he

83

slept all day and stayed out at night, his curtains were never open and when she had insisted on drawing them open, he had bought paint and painted the window so that it was opaque. The list of typical sad fanboy wannabe vampire behaviour droned on until I was suddenly snapped back to reality.

'Say that part again please.'

'I found blood on his clothes. It doesn't show up all that well because his clothes are all black, but it turned the washing machine water red once a week ago, so I looked for it since then and when I took his clothes out of the laundry basket this morning there was blood again.'

My mind was spinning at high RPM now. This could be the guy. Just like that, I could have solved the Vampire murders case. I might not be getting paid for it, but this was a case I could not turn down. Okay Tempest, calm yourself a little. What are the chances that this is the same maniac out committing murder? Slim of course, but blood on the clothes is fairly damning evidence. Whose blood is it? If she found bloody clothes last night they could be from the latest victim. How much blood does it take to colour the water in a washing machine? Quite a bit was my guess.

'Where are you now, Mrs. Cambridge?'

'I am at home,' she replied, her voice still unsettled, but at least forming answers to my questions.

Now for the more important question, 'Mrs. Cambridge, where is your grandson?'

'Well, it's daylight so he is asleep. All vampires must sleep during the day. Even I know that.'

'Quite correct, Mrs. Cambridge, but specifically where is he asleep?'

'He took to sleeping in my basement months ago when he became a vampire, so that is where he is now.'

Bingo.

'Mrs. Cambridge, I need to point out that I am a private investigator that specialises in paranormal cases. My clients usually engage me to investigate circumstances that they believe are of supernatural or occult origin.' I wanted to see if the poor old dear did have a crazed murderer in her house, but it was far more likely that I was going to find a spotty teenager in love with Kirsten Stewart or with a Goth fixation and therefore getting paid seemed attractive. 'I think I need to establish what it is you would like me to do.' Please don't say drive a stake through his heart, please don't say drive a stake through his heart – I repeated in my head like a mantra.

'Can you do some tests to prove that he is a vampire?'

Easy, since obviously, he was not a vampire at all. 'Yes Madam, I have a number of simple methods to determine if he is a vampire or not.'

'Oh, good,' she said, seeming quite relieved, 'Then you can drive a stake through his heart, yes?'

Nuts.

'We shall have to see, Mrs. Cambridge. We do need to discuss my fee, I'm afraid.' I explained my daily rate and that I was willing to waive it given that I had no actual investigation to conduct. We agreed on a fixed call-out charge much like one might pay to a plumber. I got her address, assured her that I would be there within the hour and got off the phone.

Time to calmly consider what to do? Let's suppose that the grandson in question is, in fact, *The Vampire*. Would that make him dangerous?

Probably.

In which case, do I want to alert the authorities? Not a good option I surmised because of two very good reasons: If I am wrong and it is just some fool in a costume and the myopic grandmother is finding ketchup, I will look like a royal idiot. If I am right, and it is him, I will get no credit for the capture as the police make the arrest and pose for the national news claiming their detective work led them to the quick apprehension etcetera.

So, what is my next move?

Make a cup of tea.

Mrs. Cambridge lived in a small cottage in nearby Aylesford, so the journey took no more than a few minutes and I pulled up well inside the hour I had allotted for thinking, preparing and collecting Big Ben. Her address placed her in the old part of town, the original village where the buildings were probably all several centuries old.

It was necessary to park around the corner as the houses had not been built with cars in mind and parking was at an absolute premium. Her house was a small cottage, perhaps two bedrooms and a bath upstairs, galley kitchen, small lounge and dining room downstairs, small basement underneath. It was certainly pretty, and the postage stamp front yard was well kept, giving the cottage the appearance of the quintessential English village dwelling.

'Is there a plan?' asked Big Ben as we got out of the car. I had explained what we were doing on the drive over once I had roused him from sleep, forced him to get dressed and bundled him into the car.

'These are old buildings with only an internal access point to the cellar. If he is in there, he will have to come through us to escape. Once inside, we can quiz the old lady and get her out of the way. With her gone, we head into the basement looking mean and drag Mr. vampire-wannabe out of his crypt. If he looks likely to be the killer, we subdue him and call the fuzz.'

'What am I getting paid again?'

'Nothing. You are doing this because you love me and because you still owe me a hot blonde from about six years ago.' Big Ben and I were both dressed in hard wearing gear: Cargo trousers, the sort made from a rip-stop material with plenty of utility pockets, ass-kicking, black combat boots, t-shirts and Kevlar vests. Big Ben was happy to come along on my busts because it gave him cool lines to use on the ladies, but he wasn't buying into the whole paranormal thing any more than I did. He wore the clothes because they look kinda cool and it meant he wouldn't ruin anything of his.

Before we went in, I briefed him, 'Right mate, this guy might actually have killed three people, so we need to cover each other and take this seriously.' We were paused outside the house next door to Mrs. Cambridge dealing with equipment and formulating a brief series of planned responses to certain scenarios.

'The chances this is actually the guy are slim, right?' asked Big Ben.

'Instinct says that I am not that lucky and that this is going to turn out to be a spotty teenage scrotum that has watched too many Twilight movies. However, the lady was convinced that she had found blood on his clothes, so we proceed with caution.'

'How about plan number one is that we ask where he is, drag him out and thump him?' Big Ben was totally serious. 'Or, better yet, a swift knee to the 'taters. Vampire or not he will drop just like anyone else.' Big Ben had a firm grasp of biology.

'Not the best plan,' I explained in the most neutral tone I could manage. Big Ben's exuberance could be a problem at times. 'If he is innocent that would be considered as ABH or worse. With luck, he will be willing to talk, and I can get the clothes from the old lady and test for blood simply enough as I have a kit in the car.' I felt that we had been standing in the street for long enough and would begin to attract attention if we stayed out here much longer. The outfits did not exactly blend in.

Big Ben followed me through the gate and down the short path. Near out-of-control wisteria covered one side of the house and looped over the frame of the door, hanging down low enough in places that we both had to duck. Mrs. Cambridge opened the door before I could knock. She was stooped and probably closer to eighty than seventy. She had tightly curled silver hair and wore a granny dress. I have no idea what the correct term for the outfit is, but I see old ladies wearing them all the time. Anyway, she was a run of the mill old lady with a face like leather and a troubled expression.

'Come in boys,' she beckoned, turning back into the house herself.

Normally I would have introduced myself on the doorstep and shown a business card, but she seemed happy that we were the vampire hunters she had called. Following behind her, I felt a need to speak anyway, 'Mrs. Cambridge, good morning. My name is Tempest Michaels, this is my associate, Ben Winters. Thank you for calling us.'

Mrs. Cambridge took very little time in getting to the task. In her hands, she held a plastic carrier bag from a National supermarket in which she had placed the blood-stained clothes she had found this morning. I pulled them out to inspect them using a tool rather than my hands to avoid putting my DNA on them.

There was a black shirt and a pair of dress trousers like one might find with a Dinner Jacket. It was hard to make out, but the fabric of the shirt was definitely stained with something. I licked my latex glove covered finger and rubbed at the fabric just a little. It came away with a distinctive pink tinge. It was sufficient to convince me it was blood. I placed the bag on the floor by the front door to collect on our way back out and asked Mrs. Cambridge to show us to her Grandson. She showed us the stairs down to the cellar and invited us to proceed.

I crept down the cellar stairs, not because I was concerned about going into the dark of course, but because I wanted to find Jim asleep or at least catch him by surprise. If he was down there, he was being very quiet, and all the lights were off. Big Ben waited at the top of the stairs to turn on the lights on my signal. I reached the last step. There was enough light coming from the stairwell to see the basic layout of the room, but little more than that. Mrs. Cambridge said his coffin, because of course he slept in a coffin, was against the far wall adjacent to the small window that should be letting natural light into the basement.

I clicked my fingers and Big Ben hit the switch to bathe the room in light. The room was a gothic temple to all things vampire. Jim clearly had little imagination and an account with Vampires R Us because there were candles, black and red velvet and occult looking silver artifacts adorning every surface. The floor was covered in rugs and furs, there was a large

90

mahogany sideboard / altar-looking thing with dusty tomes arranged on top. There were also Buffy the Vampire Slayer comics though, so perhaps he wasn't completely committed to the crypt look after all.

The coffin was exactly where Mrs. Cambridge had said it would be and there was a figure in it. I took all this in during the first second or so, by which time I was moving across the room and Jim was coming awake.

'Bwwwah?' said Jim, his hands gripping the sides of the coffin and his feet beginning to flail. The coffin was set a couple of feet off the floor on top of a structure sheathed in black velvet. The coffin looked high end to me, not that I had much experience when it came to coffins, but it was made from a shiny black material and looked expensive.

Jim was getting up, which is not what I wanted. I wanted him incapacitated or immobile while I asked him a few questions. I crossed the room in two paces, raising my hands to my sides to show they were empty. 'Take it easy, big fella. I am a private investigator here at your Grandmother's request. I just want to ask you a few questions.'

'You dare to disturb me from my slumber?' He certainly got into character pretty quick. His voice was pitched somewhere between angry and disbelieving, 'You will perish, foolish mortal. Be gone while you still can.' He was half sat in the coffin now with his hands gripping the sides. What I noticed though was that he didn't seem to want to get out and deal with me.

I crossed my arms and gave him my stoniest look, 'Jim tell me, do you really think you are a vampire? Or are you just being a moron?' Above me, I heard Big Ben snigger.

Jim was not tall, perhaps five feet eight inches or a little more. It was hard to tell with him in a coffin. He was also skinny as if the diet of blood was not very filling. I reminded myself that he was potentially guilty of

91

several murders, but it was hard to imagine the brutal murders being carried out by the gimp in front of me. He was wearing black drainpipe jeans, no socks, a black silk shirt open to the waist nearly, heavy eyeliner and black nail varnish on his fingers and toes. He also wore an abundance of silver jewellery.

'Not exactly Robert Pattinson, are you?' I was goading him unnecessarily.

'I will suck your soul out!' he screamed, rising from the coffin. I placed a firm hand on his chest and pushed him back down.

He swatted at me and then ducked his head to bite my forearm. I pulled my arm away, no telling what he might do, and bites are painful. 'Behave now, Jim.'

'My name is Demedicus Solomon,' he interrupted me, his voice an angry growl, 'Jim Butterworth was my useless, pathetic human form before I was transformed into a vampire.' He looked quite pissed off, but he didn't attempt to get up.

My time in the army provided plenty of opportunities to learn when a person was going to fight and when they were not. A lot of chaps wanted to sound tough and would threaten and make a lot of noise, their nervous energy would manifest as general agitation causing the would-be protagonist to stay in motion, hands clenching, body vibrating. One soon learned that they posed very little threat though. The ones to watch were the calm ones, the ones that said very little, choosing to observe instead. My analogy was that of a sword being drawn. Drawing a sword makes very little noise, but means it is going to be used, the noisy man was just rattling the sword in its scabbard and thus had no intention of drawing it at all. Jim / Demedicus was just rattling his sword. Looking at his seventy-kilogram frame I was not sure he even had a sword.

I'm not much of a fighter myself, I tried a lot of boxing and martial arts but found I did not have the temperament required to have people hitting me. Constant effort at the gym, plus years of fight training, meant that I looked the part though and I use this to my advantage when I need to.

'You are a vampire hunter? Come to destroy me in my crypt? I see the stake sticking out of your belt. You won't find me easy to kill mortal.'

'Jim, I have no intention of causing you any harm and will be gone as soon as I can confirm that you are a true vampire,' his eyebrows lifted, 'and get a couple of answers regarding your supply of blood.' Jim seemed caught between anger at my intrusion, excitement that I believed he may be a vampire and indecision about what to do next.

'Do you want to get out of the coffin and do this over a cup of tea?' Tea makes for a relaxing atmosphere, probably because it is such a normal activity, but my hope was that I could prove he was neither a vampire nor the crazed murderer and get out of there.

'Vampires don't drink tea,' he stated snippily.

'How about a Bloody Mary?' Big Ben called down from the next floor. Clearly Big Ben was enjoying himself.

'Jim.'

'Demedicus,' he snapped again.

'Okay. Demedicus,' I relented, 'My name is Tempest Michaels, my colleague upstairs with your Grandmother is Ben Winters. I am going to invite him down now.' I made it a statement rather than a question - no need to invite his opinion.

'Ben, come on down. Demedicus is willing to let us test him to prove that he is a vampire.' Again, it was a statement - it is happening.

93

'What do these tests involve?' Demedicus asked, eyeing the stake in my belt once again. His eyes were bugging out a bit and he was starting to sweat. To my mind, the sweat had already proved that was not a vampire, but I proceeded to explain the tests anyway.

'Nothing that will harm you in any way, Demedicus. Your Grandmother wants me to prove to her whether you are a vampire or not because she is concerned about you. As everyone knows vampires are part of the undead and therefore have no heartbeat, their body temperature is far below the human normal range and they have no breath or reflection.' My years of studying Buffy, Charmed and True Blood was clearly put to good use. 'My tests will merely confirm your status as positive or negative.'

His eyes were bugging out even further now and he was beginning to look quite unsettled. The prospect of having one's ridiculous illusion exposed I assumed.

'I'm not happy about this,' he muttered.

Behind me, I could hear Big Ben coming down the stairs, but he clearly had someone else with him from the pattern of footfalls. I turned to see Big Ben arrive in the basement accompanied by Mrs. Cambridge. Mrs. Cambridge had a bible clutched to her breast and a crucifix in her left hand.

'I can't allow you to do these tests,' stated Demedicus in what was a fairly authoritarian tone, 'I am a vampire and won't be subjected to ridicule by lesser mortals.' He was still sat in the coffin but appeared to have finally found some gumption.

'You do as you are told, foul hell beast,' spat Mrs. Cambridge.

Caught between Demedicus and Mrs. Cambridge, I found myself moving my head like I was watching tennis, 'I thought Mrs. Cambridge had gone to her neighbour, Ben,' I pointed out with a degree of exasperation.

Mrs. Cambridge then clearly decided that progress was not being made fast enough and despite her advancing years, she grabbed the stake sticking out of Big Ben's belt and launched herself across the room at her grandson.

Big Ben and I both lunged at her, catching a shoulder each. She twisted and kicked, wailing that the hellspawn had to be destroyed.

Where do these people come from?

Big Ben and I had to hold on for dear life, despite each of us weighing twice as much as her. Demedicus meanwhile had pulled a mobile phone from somewhere and had already connected to someone.

'Obsidian? Obsidian, you must help me. There are people in my crypt trying to kill me,' he was yelling into the phone. I assumed that Obsidian was another vampire-wannabe. Do vampires have friends? I could remember Buffy and Faith taking out nests of vampires, so I suppose they cohabit or something. 'It's my grandmother and friggin' Van Helsing man. Get over here,' a pause while whoever was on the other end spoke, 'Don't give me the daylight rubbish, man. Get over here. Get everyone and help me out before they put a stake through my chest,' his voice was a desperate squeak.

Big Ben and I had finally subdued Mrs. Cambridge and had settled her onto a chair next to the stairs without popping her hip completely. 'You must kill the beast while the sun shines,' she ranted, 'They are weakest then. If you won't do it, then I will. Just hold him for me.' She was full on bonkers at this point, eyes fixed firmly on her Grandson. This was getting

95

way out of hand. I needed to calm her down, grab the blood-stained clothes and leave before it got any crazier.

Big Ben was the next to move though. 'Vampires burn in sunlight, right? So, let's prove dummy here is not a vampire and then maybe we can move on.' With that, he crossed the room, flipped the handle on the small window to the outside world and flung it open. The window had been painted black on the inside, but now natural sunlight flooded into the room.

'AArrrrgghh!' screamed Demedicus, 'Arrrrggh! I'm burning.' He was sort of dancing around a bit flapping at his face, but then he grabbed at the velvet sheet under the coffin, gripped it in both hands and yanked it out from under the coffin which flipped over and crashed onto the floor sending up a fog of dust. He then threw the sheet over his head to keep the sun off, not that I was buying into the charade.

Mrs. Cambridge jumped back up. Actually jumped! 'See! I told you he was a vampire. Kill him now!' She came at Demedicus again. Big Ben and I both moved to intercept her, which left Demedicus with a direct path up the stairs and out of the room. And that's exactly where he went. Still screaming and cursing, he ran, flailing the velvet behind him like a cape. It was wrapped around his head though and I guess it affected his ability to see because there was an almighty thump as he ran into something.

Now what? Neither my time in the army nor private investigation training had prepared me for situations such as this. It was all getting quite ridiculous.

'I'll go see to vampire boy, you take care of Mrs. Cambridge,' I yelled at Big Ben as I headed for the stairs, 'Mrs. Cambridge?' I called to get her attention, 'Mrs. Cambridge, I want no more crazy vampire talk and attempts to kill your grandson.' I thought it necessary to put this point across in unambiguous terms before she went ahead and stabbed him with something.

'Jim is no more vampire than I, which should be perfectly obvious to anyone. You must calm down so that Ben and I can ask him a few questions.' I headed up the stairs to the living room where I could hear Jim / Demedicus groaning and moving about. Sure enough, Jim was on the floor in the living room. He appeared to have run head first into one of the oak joists supporting the upper story of the house. There was a cut to his head and blood leaking out of his hairline and down across his forehead. The oak joist would have been an odd feature in a modern house but seemed perfectly at home in the middle of the room in this quaint little cottage. Jim had forgotten its location in his haste.

I knelt and gently removed the velvet sheet from his semi-inert form. His skin, now exposed to daylight, was not crisping or bursting into flame, which seemed conclusive enough proof to me of his mortality.

'Let's get you up and into a chair, shall we?'

Please let me get this over with and get out of here with no further madness.

Jim was conscious, perhaps a little dazed, but he accepted my hand and let me help him up and into one of the chintz-covered armchairs. As he was settling back into the chair, Big Ben appeared at the top of the stairs leading up from the basement.

'Mrs. Cambridge promises to behave now. Wow, what did you do to him?' Big Ben asked as he saw the blood now dripping down Jim's face.

'I didn't do anything. The thump we heard was Jim running blindly into the oak joist over there,' I replied, motioning with my head. I had slipped on a pair of latex gloves, I always keep some in my pocket, and was

97

checking the convincing wound on Jim's head. The skin over the scalp is thin and has a great supply of blood, so even a small cut will bleed profusely. This was not a small cut.

'Mrs. Cambridge promised to behave if I let her come back upstairs,' Big Ben repeated his previous sentence, 'She looks a little exhausted from all the excitement actually, I doubt she will give us any more bother.'

'I sure hope so.'

'First-aid kit?' Big Ben asked.

'There is one in the car,' I advised then turned my attention to the old lady, 'Mrs. Cambridge?'

'Yes, Dear?' She had taken a seat by her small dining table and although she was still eyeing Jim suspiciously, she appeared to have calmed down and did indeed look quite exhausted.

'Mrs. Cambridge, my associate is going to pop out to my car to fetch a first-aid kit. Jim has a nasty cut to his head and may need treatment at A&E. First, though I need to do what I can to stem the bleeding. Can I expect any more trouble from you? You will observe I hope, that Jim is now in daylight and has not burst into flame. Furthermore, the presence of blood should convince you that he is not a vampire since vampires have no heartbeat and therefore don't bleed.' I had stepped slightly to the side so that she could see Jim bleeding and not burning.

'Yes, Dear. Sorry about before. I'm not sure what came over me. Are you alright, Jim?

'Demedicus,' he slurred quietly, still not quite ready to let his fantasy go.

Big Ben had been bent over next to me examining the inch long cut to Jim's head. He stood up now though and moved to the door to get the first aid kit. My back was to the door, but I sensed it opening as light flooded into the room. Big Ben gasped quite audibly, a noise of inrushing breath followed by the sound of the door being slammed shut.

'Tempest, we have a problem,' he squeaked. I looked up to see him bracing the door with his body. Back to the door, feet planted firmly on the wooden floor. 'There is, like fifty morons dressed as vampires outside, man.' His eyes were showing way too much white for my liking.

Before I could get off my knees and ask him any further questions, faces started appearing at the windows. The faces each wore too much eye makeup, one had a bleached flat top hair-cut, another wore his hair in black spikes, yet another was a girl with black lips and a dozen facial piercings. I scanned the room, it had four windows positioned on two different sides. At each window, I could see more faces appearing so that now they were several deep in places. They were cupping their hands to the side of their faces like people do when they are looking into somewhere dark and need to shut out as much peripheral light as possible.

'They've got Demedicus!' I heard one of them say, 'He's friggin' bleeding man!'

Oh, nuts!

The call to Obsidian that Jim made downstairs. I had totally forgotten the call for help.

Big Ben had bolted the door and was looking out the small window above it now. 'There's more arriving, Tempest. A whole bunch of them just got out of a van. This is not cool. I can't be murdered by a bunch of vampire-wannabe losers. I'm supposed to die underneath a pile of dirty

99

women while celebrating my ninetieth birthday. I promised myself I would.' Big Ben was looking genuinely nervous, which in turn was beginning to affect my efforts to stay calm.

I reminded myself that this was not my first time in an uncomfortable situation. Not my first time trapped in a building with hostiles outside for that matter. Panicking gets you nowhere. The only thing you can do is breath and focus. I did a mental checklist: Have we secured the premises? And that was as far as my mental checklist got because I heard the back-door open.

Big Ben and I reacted together, or rather we failed to react, but we did that together. For a heartbeat, we just stood looking at each other, but then the spell was broken as vampire-wannabes began to stream in through the door from the kitchen to the rest of the house. Leading the bunch was a hefty, hairy man with black hair and a beard, wearing a full-length, black, leather coat he could have stolen from Morpheus in the matrix. He had kept with convention and was wearing a ton of black eyeliner, probably mascara and a plethora of silver rings and chains. Obsidian perhaps? Let's call him vampire-wannabe number one for now.

Vampire-wannabe number one was running. It took nanoseconds from the time he rounded the door to the time he was into the room and moving towards me. He was a lot bigger than me and had a face that meant business.

My adrenalin spiked instantly and since flight was not an option, I adjusted my stance for fighting. I had fought big guys before, although I don't make a habit of it and try to avoid fighting altogether if I can. When they rush you, it is easy to convert their momentum and throw them. This was my intention, but I never got the chance because Mrs. Cambridge punched him in the nuts.

Just like that.

She didn't even get out of her chair, she just flung out a fist at his crotch as he drew level with her. He folded up mid-run and crashed to the wooden floor at my feet. Behind him, a small sea of advancing vampire-wannabes screeched to a confused halt. In front of them, Mrs. Cambridge got to a wobbly, standing position from where she had been sitting in silence during the few seconds that all this had been playing out.

'Now just you stop all this,' she commanded, her voice that of a grandmother admonishing some unruly children, 'I have had quite enough nonsense for one day already.'

In the doorway that came from the back of the house into the living room, were rows of vampire-wannabes. Those at the front looked like they wanted to be elsewhere and were being shoved forward by those behind that could not see. From somewhere in the crowd came a voice that still felt they had a purpose here. 'We came to rescue Demedicus from those vampire hunters,' he said aiming for forthrightness and not quite making it.

The faces I could see had all been focused on Mrs. Cambridge, but, as if remembering why they were invading someone else's property, they now looked across at me as one. What they saw was Big Ben and I still poised for fighting, wearing Kevlar and combat boots while behind and to our side were their fellow vampire-wannabes still pressing their faces to the window and probably trampling Mrs. Cambridge's geraniums. Just to the side of me was Demedicus still covered in blood and looking dazed.

Not good.

Crowds are stupid. It was something I had learned long ago in Bosnia, but back then a short warning burst from the gun mounted on my

101

armoured vehicle would get their attention and split them up pretty quick. I did not have that option here.

'Ben?' I enquired.

'Yeah?' he answered.

'Just checking.' Time to try talking my way out of this. I dropped my ready-to-fight stance, straightened myself and attempted to combine a look of relaxed and non-threatening with absolute authority, 'Assembled vampires,' might as well play along with them and try not to upset them any further, 'My name is Tempest Michaels and I am investigating the recent spate of murders associated with vampirism. It was reported that this man,' I pointed to Demedicus, 'may be able to assist with my enquiries. His injuries are self-inflicted and not of our doing. We intend him no harm, but now that he is injured, my priority is to tend to him before continuing any line of questioning. I ask you to go about your business, but to elect one member of your party to remain here to aid Demedicus and to report back to the collective.' I didn't actually want any of them staying here, but this was my best shot at calming the situation and getting them dispersed.

The sea of faces was all fixed on me and no one was saying anything.

'It's a hive,' came a voice from somewhere near the kitchen door.

'What?' I found myself forced to ask.

'A group of vampires. It's not a collective, it's a hive,' the voice advised.

'No, it's not, you plonker,' argued another voice, 'It's a nest.'

'What? Whoever heard of a nest of vampires,' asked the first voice again. In the gloomy room, I could not make out which of them were speaking, but the heads were turning away from me and towards each other as the subject came under greater scrutiny.

'In Buffy the Vampire Slayer, episode seven of series four, Faith tells Buffy that she has found a nest and they proceed to clean it out. It's a nest,' returned the second voice, who I could now pinpoint as a scrawny ginger vampire-wannabe with glasses and what looked like a Count from Sesame Street doll sticking out of a coat pocket.

'Joss Whedon's ridiculous view of vampires as aggrandising master villains with plans for world domination was an insult to us all. How can you respect yourself in this company if you look to him for reference?' The new voice was from a large woman, well probably a woman, but kind of hard to tell really. She/he had purple lips and eyes, crazy black and purple hair and stood a foot taller than most of the other vampires around her/him. 'All the greats say it is a hive of vampires and I shall give a lecture on this subject at next week's meeting.'

The discussion was quickly turning to a fight between the vampires and I wanted to leave. It was not that I was scared necessarily, although I recognised the potential danger in my current situation, it was more that the only fight you really win is the one you don't have. The army teaches you a lot of things when you join up and there is an inevitable change to your personal characteristics, but it took me a while to realise some of the changes the experience had made to my personality. How can I explain this adequately? If you cast your mind back to school, there was probably one kid in your class whose first reaction to any situation was to just thump someone. Generally, people have a natural resistance to harming other people; they need to be wound up or motivated to break social boundaries and strike out. The army removes that natural resistance, so that like a sociopath, the need to factor in the other person's emotions and concerns is not present. At some point many years ago I saw the truth of this and recognised that I was quite able to switch from well-mannered and polite to aggressively deadly with little thought involved. Nevertheless, I would rather avoid thumping anyone today.

I looked down at Demedicus, who just shrugged up at me. He was still sat in the chair holding a rag to his head. He still looked deathly pale and was still leaking blood. I was not going to get any answers here.

'Mrs. Cambridge, I think it best if we take Jim to hospital. The cut to his head is quite deep and will need stitches. Would you like to come with us?' I wanted to get the hell out of there before any more trouble started and I wanted to isolate Jim as the ever more unlikely murderer.

Big Ben was hovering near the door. 'Time to go?' he asked.

'Yup. I think it best, but watch for the idiots outside.' I turned to Demedicus and gave him a hand up. He got shakily to his feet and with my arm around him for support, we moved to the door.

'Coming, Mrs. Cambridge?' I asked back over my shoulder. We were at the front door and ready to leave. I needed her because the blood-soaked clothes had been moved and I wanted to take them with me. I suspected it would lead to nothing, but I knew I would forever regret not checking if I failed to follow up what might stop a killer. 'We really need to go, Mrs. Cambridge,' I called again.

'You go ahead, love. I need to get this lot out of my house and tidy up the mess.' Mrs. Cambridge looked royally upset about the house invasion and ready to grab a broom and start whacking people. I elected to get Demedicus out of the house and off to hospital with Big Ben. Then I would come back for the blood-stained clothes and help Mrs. Cambridge disperse the crowd. This was partly out of a sense of duty to little old ladies everywhere, even those that could put a big man down with one punch, and partly because I was now getting concerned about negative publicity. How long before the cops turned up? Or the press got hold of the story?

'Ben get the door. We get Demedicus to the car and you get him to A&E while I clear up this mess, mate. Sound good?'

'Any plan that gets me out of here will be good enough.' Big Ben opened the door and went out but following close behind with Demedicus propped against me, it all went to hell again.

The vampire-wannabes waiting outside had not been waiting patiently it seemed. As I stepped over the front doorstep, Big Ben disappeared under a pile of them as they all rugby tackled him as one. I hardly had time to register this and react before Demedicus was ripped from my grasp and I too felt hands grabbing me.

Anyone who has ever been in a fight knows that it is probably going to end up on the ground within a few seconds if the first flurry of blows does not end it. It is not a comfortable place to be, but there are advantages to it. The weight of my attackers bore me to the concrete, but I turned as I fell to get my back against the ground and thus my limbs available for striking out. It was a sea of black all around me and any number of ineffective blows were landing on my skull, arms, and legs while I protected my face and waited a few seconds for an opening. It was hard to see where one person ended and the next began, but then I spotted a nose and whipped out my right leg. It connected just under the target and I drove my leg hard off the solid surface beneath me. Suddenly daylight streamed in where the now departed vampire-wannabe had left a hole and I caught a foot that was trying to kick my ribs. The blow hurt but I was now able to angle my body and punch the attacker in his stationary groin.

Then the sweet sound of police sirens filled the air and as heads went up, I sent a stiff hand into the throat of the now doubled over, sore-groined vampire-wannabe whose foot I still held.

I glanced over to see Big Ben's feet poking out from between someone else's legs. As the police neared, the hands clutching me let go and I was able to stand up and take in the scene. Demedicus was sitting on the garden wall accompanied by two female vampires, one of them cut quite an attractive figure in her tight leather trousers, but he seemed to be okay if a little pale still. His head was covered in blood from the head wound and it had run down over his face and onto his clothes. Big Ben was also getting up, so he was okay. I doubted his attackers were feeling too clever though. All around him were injured people, people holding themselves, people bleeding, people tending to someone else who was probably bleeding, and they were all dressed as vampires. I had a fleeting premonition that I was not going to get a great deal done today.

A police car screeched to a halt in front of the property and I could hear more coming. First out of the car was PC thinkshesfunny from yesterday morning at the river. Out of the driver's side emerged PC Hotstuff. Both PCs looked nervous as if expecting trouble and prepared to deal with it. They had their hands on their batons and were ready for action. The fight was over though, the danger gone. I stepped forward to speak with them but was immediately jostled by vampire-wannabe number one, as he tried to get to the police first. I guess his nuts had recovered. Perhaps this was a shrewd move on his part - point out the perpetrators and lay the blame early. I wondered if he would turn out to be Obsidian - the man Demedicus had called.

We were in a tiny front yard laid to lawn with a few rose bushes now bereft of flowers in the mid-Autumn. To beat Obsidian to it, I would have to trample the flowers which seemed unfair and I had faith that the truth would be revealed by Mrs. Cambridge soon enough. I let him crack on.

PC thinkshesfunny spoke first though, giving possibly Obsidian no chance to voice his side of the story. 'Nobody move. Especially you, Mulder,' still funny then. He took a few steps to his right, never taking his eyes off the people in front of him. 'You lot, move around to the front of the house.' I guess he had seen more of the vampire-wannabes lurking at the side of the property which was confirmed when they began trudging around to the front as instructed. Not all of them clearly though as he yelled after someone that had elected to hop the fence and head for freedom. PC thinkshesfunny leaned his head down into the radio pinned to his lapel, spoke with someone else and the lead police car coming down the hill towards us swept straight past the property to head off anyone fleeing the scene. I doubted it would be too difficult to spot them given the outfits being worn.

Two more police cars pulled up, the rearmost containing a Chief Inspector going by my limited knowledge of insignia. He stood up and turned to face us, putting his hat on as he did so.

The rest of the morning turned out to be distinctly boring. An ambulance arrived to take Jim away. Before leaving with him, the medic on board treated several minor injuries, mostly cuts, and bruises from the scuffle. Big Ben and I were handcuffed and left sitting on the garden wall for more than an hour while the Chief Inspector spoke with Mrs. Cambridge and several of the vampire wannabes.

PC Hotstuff had taken preliminary statements from us as we were handcuffed, which had at least given me a chance to explain that we had reacted to a request for our presence and that none of the property damage if there was any, nor any of the injuries sustained, were our fault. My statement was received with little emotion until I got the part where

Mrs. Cambridge believed she had blood-soaked clothes that could tangibly make Jim the serial killer. At that point, she had hustled off to find the Chief Inspector, leaving us with PC thinkshesfunny. Then there was much radio squawking and in less than fifteen minutes two more police cars arrived on the scene followed by vans with SOCO looking chaps and cases full of equipment for gathering evidence.

It was not an easy task to check my watch with my hands cuffed behind my back, but I always felt more balanced if I knew the time. I stretched my arms as far to the left as possible, hooked my right hand upwards to snag my sleeve and wriggled to get a look at my watch: 1143hrs. Nearly three hours had passed since we arrived, so my thoughts were turning to lunch and to what my dogs might be doing. They would have happily spent the morning asleep but would need to go out soon.

'What do you think will happen next?' Big Ben asked me.

'You will be taken downtown and spend a night in the cells while we try to work out why you started a riot in a peaceful village on a Saturday morning,' PC thinkshesfunny offered. I really didn't like him. 'You need to learn to leave investigative work to the professionals and take up something you are better suited to.'

'What are you doing, PC Hardacre?' Ah, the voice of tranquillity and reason. At least I hoped it was. PC Hotstuff was speaking from behind us as she left the house and walked down the garden path, 'A word, if you please.' She came into view as she left the garden, motioned to PC thinkshesfunny and continued to the other side of the road.

I wanted to say, 'Run along now,' but it seemed too juvenile and unnecessary. I let him go without a look in his direction.

'Is it me or is he quite difficult to like?' I asked Big Ben

108

'Tempest my friend, he is a practicing dick bag and should be ass-banged to death in public by donkeys.' Goodness. Not much grey area there. Big Ben had little tolerance for people he didn't like.

Across the road there appeared to be an exchange which looked less than friendly. I could not hear it, but it looked like PC Hotstuff was berating PC thinkshesfunny. I liked her even more, although I doubted she was doing it for me. She finished speaking and left him across the street as she came back to us. As she approached, I tried hard to focus on ignoring the voice in my pants and his ideas about handcuffs and police uniforms.

'It seems your story checks out. The Chief Inspector wants a word, but I expect you will be released soon.'

'Any chance we can have our handcuffs removed?' she turned to look at Big Ben who flashed her his most winning smile. Usually, the smile is enough to get him into a girl's pants, but he must have suffered a misfire or something because it had no effect at all. Her face registered no emotion, but she shifted her focus to look behind him just as we heard male voices exiting the building.

'PC Harper you can release them.' PC Harper then, not Hotstuff, but perhaps my name was more apt. My guess was that the voice came from the Chief Inspector which was confirmed when I turned my head to look. Big Ben and I stood and turned so that our handcuffs could be removed. 'Gentlemen, you have had a busy morning,' the Chief Inspector said.

'Not really,' said Big Ben, 'We have been sat on this wall for most of it.' Probably not the time for annoying the nice Chief Inspector but too late now.

He seemed not to notice the comment though as he introduced himself, 'I am Chief Inspector Quinn.' Chief Inspector Quinn was a shade

109

over six feet tall and modestly built, like a triathlete perhaps. I judged that he had been born locally given his accent. I guessed his age as early forties, but perhaps older given that he appeared to look after himself. There was a small scar on his nose that probably had an interesting story but could have been from a childhood accident and he had the air of patient authority that senior public officials must develop in order to survive. 'You are being released, but you may be called for questioning later so don't leave the area. You have not committed a crime, but what you should have done is called the police,' Inspector Quinn was displeased clearly, and his voice had an angry tremble at the back of it that I felt he was doing well to suppress, 'The suspect has a head wound that may complicate the investigation and you have contaminated the building, which may have contained key evidence. Thanks to you there are dozens of additional fingerprints that we now need to catalogue and eliminate. Mrs. Cambridge appears none the worse for her eventful morning; a tough old bird that one, but I want to make this completely clear - I don't like what you do. You strike me as charlatans with all your paranormal nonsense. Stay away from this case, or I may find the time to investigate your business. I believe I will enjoy that more than you will.'

He was stood directly in front of me, speaking directly at me and giving additional emphasis with his eyes to show me that he meant it. This was a bust. I would not get paid for responding to Mrs. Cambridge's request, nor would I get near Jim again. If he was guilty, which to be fair seemed unlikely, I would not be involved or credited.

'Very well, Chief Inspector. Are we free to go?'

'Yes, Mr. Michaels.' There was no point in trying to get in the last word. He was wrong about me, about my motives and about my business, but I would only be able to prove that with actions.

'Let's grab our gear and get out of here, Ben.' I hated being on the losing end. Who does? I was going to be in a crappy mood for a while, but just as I turned to go, PC Hotstuff winked at me and gave me just a little smile. It was fleeting, but I didn't imagine it. I paused to see if there was more, but she turned her head away to speak with a colleague and was already walking away.

We travelled home in silence, each thinking our own thoughts. I should be angry about what had happened, not that being angry was constructive, but I felt it was a natural reaction. Instead, I was thinking about PC Harper. She was very attractive that was for sure. Mr. Wriggly had all kinds of activities planned, but ignoring that I had to wonder now if she had smiled at me, or at Big Ben. He had been laying the charm on thick and it rarely failed. I was interested in her from a basic attraction level, nothing more. Acknowledging that allowed my thoughts to move on to more pressing subjects like what to do next with the case. Before I could frame my next thought, Big Ben broke the silence.

'It's not my fault they picked a fight with me. I was merely defending myself.' It was the same explanation he had given to the police. Their questioning had largely corroborated this. He had thumped several bonkers vampire-wannabes, and this constituted a good morning for him. 'I like hitting people. Is that wrong?' he asked from the passenger seat as we had driven home. He looked across at me to gauge my opinion.

'I think there is a certain balance brought to the universe when the righteous hand out a well-deserved slap, but I worry that this morning was not quite a case of that. People should have the right to dress as vampires and be as weird as they choose to. That kind of freedom was one of the things the army had us fight for. This morning I think they were genuinely convinced we were the bad guys and they were fighting on the righteous side.' Big Ben thought about that for a moment.

'Rubbish, mate,' he decided, 'If just one of them takes off their make-up and never puts it back on then I will call it a success. The drive back to Big Ben's apartment took no time at all but we went the rest of the way in silence, each mentally licking our wounds. I dropped him off and pointed the car back to my place.

Bull and Dozer met me at the door propelled by their perpetually moving tails. 'Hey, boys. Are you well rested?' I asked as I let them into the back garden and ran up the stairs two at a time undoing my clothes as I went. I flicked the shower on and stripped off the rest of my clothes, dumping them into the laundry hamper. I had not expected to end up in an all-out fight and be rolling around on the floor this morning, but I had and now I was sweaty and felt grimy.

As the warm water started to steam up the shower door, I examined myself in the large mirror I had installed on one wall. I had several abrasions, a few bruises and the first traces of unpleasant body odour. Sweat is an inevitable side effect of rushing adrenalin, no way to fight and avoid it. A couple of ribs on my right side were tender to the touch, I had a vague memory of taking a kick to my side when I was on the ground, and I had bruised knuckles which were making my hands stiff. Otherwise, I was fine. I berated myself briefly for being weak and stepped into the shower.

Shortly afterward, I was dressed in more normal gear and relaxing on my couch. On the small table next to me was a now empty mug that once contained tea and a plate that held a few crumbs from a ham sandwich and an apple core. Both dogs were sat next to me eyeing up the core. I made them wait, but when I got up, I broke the apple core in two and dropped the pieces in different directions so that one dog could not grab both bits and run.

I had a prior engagement to have dinner with my parents, so shortly Dozer, Bull and I would be taking a chilled bottle from the fridge and heading to their place. I felt lucky or privileged that my parents were still together - so many people got divorced it seemed. They were getting old now though and I liked to visit at least once a week to make sure they were not trying to tackle any tasks that were too strenuous, or trying to lift anything that was too heavy.

113

Dad had been a serviceman in the Royal Navy, working throughout the world and largely dragging my twin sister and me around with him. We knew no different of course and I personally had no complaints. Dad had enjoyed a successful career that had ended early due to injury. Now at sixty-eight he was essentially retired but worked an occasional shift at the nearby Royal Dockyard tourist attraction as a guide. He didn't need the money, but I think he went because he got to tell tales of seafaring and enjoy banter with likeminded chaps.

Mum and dad still lived in the house they bought when he retired from the Navy. It was a semi-detached in a street of semi-detached houses and was neither big nor small and they were neither rich nor poor, but they were happy together as far as I could tell, and I liked that my parents were still together. As I turned into their street, I could see my dad in the small front garden. He was bent over, facing towards me and had a garden fork in one hand that he was leaning on. It looked like he was weeding.

He looked up as I pulled into the space in front of their house and chucked a brief wave in my direction. The dogs had been asleep and quiet on the passenger seat for most of the journey, but I could never get to my parent's house without them knowing where they were and leaping about with excitement. How they knew and could tell where they were while asleep, I would never know. They always sprang to attention two corners before I reached mum and dad's place and were now standing on their back legs looking out the passenger window at my dad, wagging their tails like mad.

Their noses left little prints on the glass, something I was always fighting to remove because I doubted passengers would appreciate dog snot marks next to their face. I checked the path was clear then leaned across and opened the door. They exploded outwards and shot up the short drive to join dad as he bent down to fuss them.

'Wotcha, kid,' Dad said as I stepped out of the car and locked it. He had an easy smile that was rarely missing, and he really loved my dogs although he had never had one of his own. His smile was broad now as he scratched their heads, down on one knee. They took a few moments of fuss then buzzed away around to the back of the house to see if there was a cat to chase.

'How are you doing, dad?' I asked as we shook hands.

'Better than ever, my boy,' his response typical as we were not ones for moaning.

I turned to follow the dogs around to the rear garden where I would find mum bustling about making dinner through the kitchen window. Dad hooked the fork under one arm and with a calloused hand on my right shoulder, he came with me. A cacophony of barks lit the air to suggest that the dogs had indeed found one of mum's cats. Not that the dogs posed any real threat. If cornered, I thought it more likely the cat would take a Dachshund's nose off. Arriving in the back garden, I couldn't see mum anywhere, so dad and I stood chatting in the yard like we often did.

'What are you working on now then, Tempest?'

'You hear about *The Vampire* case?'

'Mm-hmm.'

'Well, that. And I am thinking about looking into that Bluebell Bigfoot thing. I have a rare quiet period with no paid casework, but I did solve a Poltergeist haunting this week.'

Dad considered my report for a second as if summing up how I made such an odd statement sound so normal. 'What do you make of that Bigfoot thing then? Do we have a bear loose from some rich fool's private collection?'

'Could be I suppose, the reports are not exactly reliable.'

'Not buying the Bigfoot theory then?' Dad was smirking at me because he felt the same as me about all things paranormal.

'It will be some guy in a suit.' The cistern flushed in the house, the sound travelling through the open patio doors to explain where mum had got to. 'I have a couple of ideas about it, but I need to pursue paid work, so even if I do look into it, I will have to drop it if the phone rings with a real case.'

'I'm sure that's the right thing to do.' Dad was very agreeable about pretty much everything, which made a nice balance to mum, who err, wasn't.

'Hello, Tempest,' said my mother as she came out of the house and into the back garden.

'Hello, mother.'

'We have roast pork for dinner. It's your dad's favourite.'

'Jolly good, sounds great.' Mum wasn't much of a cook really although she was convinced that she could be on Master Chef provided they didn't want her to do, "All that fancy nonsense". Growing up she had ensured there was always home-cooked food on the table for us and was not afraid to open a book and cook something she had never tackled before. The results were a little mixed at times, but that is probably true for everyone. She had mastered the art of producing a roast dinner though,

117

so I habitually made sure that was what she was cooking before I arranged to visit.

We were all still stood outside in the yard a few seconds later when the dogs reappeared. They had probably scoped out the garden for cats, found none or chased them all off and were now coming to see if mum or dad wanted to pick them up and fuss them. It was generally third on their list after eating stuff and chasing stuff.

'Let's go in, shall we?' I asked. Mum turned around to do just that but stooped to pat first Bull and then Dozer as they flitted between my parents until the fussing began to dry up. I stepped towards the house then remembered the wine I had left in the car.

When I walked in with the bottle in my right hand, my father gave me a nod of appreciation, 'Let's get that open before it ruins, son.'

The house was filled with the glorious smell of roasting dinner. The sounds were of spuds sizzling and pans bubbling, and I breathed in deeply and held it for a few seconds before exhaling. The house had changed over the years of course. When I was very young there had been far less money around as mum and dad wrestled with the mortgage and the cost of raising my sister and me. Cheap furnishings and fittings had gradually been replaced with nicer objects and conveniences such as central heating and double glazing had been installed. The décor was neither modern nor old, it followed no particular style and was nothing more nor less than a reflection of the lives of two people that had been married for decades and did everything together.

Standing in the dining room, around me there were family photos on the wall and on the display cabinet which also served as a dinner-service receptacle and drinks cabinet. Knick-knacks from various holidays adorned each available surface and must make dusting a nightmarish task, but the house still looked and felt like home and always would, I guess.

Dad had taken the wine to open, so I was in the dining room alone while mum and dad were both in the kitchen and I was feeling warm and happy until I saw the incongruity.

'Mother.'

No answer.

'Mother,' I called a little louder, 'Mother why are there four place settings?'

'We have another guest coming, dear,' she replied, now standing in the kitchen doorway looking just a little guilty.

119

I sighed deeply and slumped my shoulders in an exaggerated display of defeat.

'Who is it this time, mother?'

'It is Deborah Tailor. You remember her, don't you? We still see her at church every week.' She hit the *every* a little harder than was necessary as if I was suddenly going to start attending.

'Yes, mother. I remember Deborah Tailor, but why is she coming to dinner with us? Have you been playing matchmaker again, mother? You know how I hate when you do that.'

'Tempest, you need to meet women. You can't stay single forever.'

I groaned, and even to me I sounded like a sullen teenager. Dad was staying silent and hiding in the kitchen. I would deal with his treachery later.

This was not the first time my mother had pulled this stunt. The ladies in question were always from the church or the daughter of one of the ladies in her circle of friends. To date, she had yet to produce a lady that I could even be attracted to. I may come across as shallow but surely it must start with attraction. The last woman she introduced me to looked like an Ewok after it had lost a fight with a strimmer. Weighing up my options, I considered just bolting for the door. I was hungry, and the food would be both good and plentiful but just as my foot was starting to twitch, the damned doorbell rang, the sound piercing my thoughts like a peel of doom. Mother stripped off her pinny quickly, bundled it and handed it to my dad who had now appeared in the kitchen doorway.

I scowled at him and mouthed, 'You're dead meat.' He waggled his eyebrows and smirked at me.

The dogs were doing their usual routine of barking insanely at the door, so I snagged them both from under mother's skirt and took them back into the dining room, one under each arm. They were both wagging their tails madly and straining to see who was now coming through the door.

Whoever it was spoke and the dogs launched into a fresh series of barking until I gave them both a squeeze and a shush. I could hear mother bustling around at the door and the two women exchanging pleasantries. Mother was probably taking her coat and inviting her in. I had not seen Deborah Tailor in perhaps twenty years or more. We went to the local infants and junior schools together, although she was a year below me. I knew her only because our mothers both went to the same church and as children, we had been taken with them and ended up in the same place every Sunday. As teenagers, there had been a passing attraction because she had boobs, and at fifteen that was about all the motivation I needed. Nothing had ever come of it though and I had probably seen her once or twice as an adult but could not recall when or where.

Mother came back into the dining room followed by Debbie. I couldn't guess whether she was a willing participant in this caper, or an equally ambushed victim. I hadn't seen her in some time, but I recognised her instantly. I felt my Dad's hand underneath my chin as he pushed my mouth shut. Apparently, it was open.

Deborah had filled out a bit since I had last seen her. No doubt she is a lovely person, and I honestly don't believe that I am particularly shallow. I admire ladies who look after their bodies of course but I would like to think that I would take a lady as she comes rather than worrying too much about their gym habits. A womanly shape can be just as attractive as an athletic one and once a relationship is embedded, does it really matter if the lady is a size 8 or a size 16, if what you enjoy doing is spending time

121

with one another? I was telling myself that the answer was no but could not avoid observing that Debbie also had some facial hair on her top lip. Some ladies develop a little of it and some of those that do are not as diligent as others in dealing with it. It is their personal choice of course and I pass no comment, but Debbie had a mustache like Lando Calrissian and I suspected that would be a bit too much for me to ignore.

'Hi, Tempest,' beamed Deborah.

'Hello, Deborah,' I managed weakly, feeling a little intimidated and wondering if she was here willingly or had been pressed into it by her mother.

'Debbie please,' she replied.

'Well, I'll leave you two to catch up then,' mum said and headed to the kitchen dragging my dad with her.

I turned to look at Debbie, suspecting that she was equally misled by my mother and was probably here only because she had been pestered for months and had finally given in. Debbie was not unattractive. Her hair was brunette and there was a healthy-looking cascade of it hanging over her left shoulder. Her makeup was simple but well done, her nails were freshly manicured, and she was wearing a knee-length dress with a wide belt and a pair of knee-length, leather boots. Overall, Debbie looked like she had given thought to her appearance.

'Nice dogs.'

I was still holding the Dachshunds.

'Ur, yes. Yes, they are,' I replied.

'Are they yours?' she asked.

'They most certainly are. I doubt many others would be dumb enough to have them. Are you okay with dogs because I am going to have to put them down and the first thing they will do is run over to investigate you?' I didn't wait for an answer, but Debbie said that yes, she loved dogs before I could get them both safely onto the floor.

As predicted, both scurried across to investigate her boots and climb her legs. I was glad that she had boots on and not tights of some kind which they would most likely snag and hole while searching for attention. I took a couple of steps and reached into the kitchen, snagged the bottle of wine before dad's hand could close around it and offered it to Deborah who was now kneeling on the floor to pat the dogs. She was making cooing noises and had both dogs rolling on their backs for belly scratches. Perhaps this meal would be pleasant enough after all and mother would not spend the whole time trying to mate me off.

'Ooh, yes thanks, Tempest,' Debbie said on seeing me offer the wine bottle. 'Your mum says you catch ghosts now?' It was a question rather than a statement.

I plucked a glass from the place setting that would be hers and poured her a large glass. I took another large glass for myself and handed the dregs to dad who was standing in the kitchen doorway waiting for it. He frowned at the amount I had left him but took it on the chin without comment.

'Not quite, Debbie. Mother gets a little confused sometimes.' *Because she is a senile, interfering old bat*. 'What I actually do is investigate cases where people think they are being haunted or think their brother is a werewolf or believe there is a demon cat living in their garden. I advertise as a Paranormal Investigator,' I paused as Debbie crossed herself, 'but of course, there is no paranormal. Vampires don't exist and neither do ghosts, so my task is to find the truth behind each case and in doing so, solve the mystery I have been presented with.'

'What about the Holy Ghost?' Asked Debbie, crossing herself again.

'Hmm?'

'The Holy Ghost? The Holy Ghost existed because it is in the Bible.'

'That's true,' came mother's voice from the kitchen.

Super. A religious debate. Just what I was hoping for. I gave myself a mental head slap. 'Well, of course,' I replied, 'but that is very different from suggesting that people are being haunted by their Great Aunt Mavis or that a malevolent spirit is trying to drive a family from their home because they have built it on an ancient Indian burial ground.'

Debbie seemed to consider that for a moment but nodded. I prayed (no pun intended) that discussions about God, church, and religion in general could be avoided for the rest of the afternoon.

'So, what do you do now, Debbie?' I asked, hurrying the conversation along.

Debbie explained that mostly she looked after her four children and that the child support payments etcetera provided enough money for her to be a full-time mum. At the mention of children, my mother had beamed a big smile at me, somehow missing the point that Debbie already had four children. Both mum and dad had come through from the kitchen and we were all now standing around the dining table sipping wine. I say sipping but that was what I was doing. My mother and Debbie were putting it away like there was an unannounced competition. As I watched, Debbie upended her glass and reached for the half-empty bottle dad had brought through with him.

'Tempest can you get another bottle from the fridge, dear?' asked mother. 'I am about to serve.'

Wine was kept outside in a fridge in the shed. I think mother got through too much volume for it to be stored in the house, so a dedicated fridge was needed. By the time I returned, there was food steaming on various platters and in oven-to-tableware receptacles and everyone was waiting for me before sitting down. Mother had moved dad from his usual place so that Debbie and I could sit next to each other.

I did what I was supposed to do and pulled out Debbie's chair, so she could sit. I took my seat next to her and clicked my fingers under my chair until the dogs came to me and settled. The wine was screw top, so I popped it in the now empty wine cooler on the table and forked a couple of roast spuds onto my plate.

Mother got the conversation moving again, 'Tempest, why don't you tell Debbie what you are working on at the moment.'

'Mmm, yes, please. Tell me all about it,' agreed Debbie.

I spent the next few minutes regaling Debbie and my parents with tales of the recent past: The Cranfield's Poltergeist, my interest in the Maidstone Vampire murders and the possibility that there was someone dressing up as a Sasquatch and roaming around Bluebell Hill. Debbie replied with oohs and aahs in a few places to indicate she was listening but kept on chowing her food without looking up. By the time dinner was done, mother's cheeks had a healthy glow from the wine and the plates of food were all but empty.

Debbie was picking the last few morsels from her plate. 'That was excellent, Mary. The best meal I have eaten in ages.'

'Well, thank you, dear. You are very welcome. Tempest is an excellent cook, you should have him prepare a meal for you sometime.'

'Mother,' I warned.

'That sounds nice,' Debbie said, smiling at me.

'Doesn't it?' I agreed, not meaning a word of it. Debbie was pleasant enough, but I wasn't attracted to her. So far, she hadn't shown anything more than a passing interest in me though, so perhaps I was concerned for no reason.

'Michael give me a hand to clear these things away,' my mother insisted as she stood and grabbed the plates and dishes nearest to her. I began to get up, but mother flapped her arms at me and told me to stay and entertain our guest.

As they left the room, Debbie leaned forward as if she intended to whisper something to me, but as I leaned my ear toward her unthinkingly, she stuck her tongue in it and grabbed my head while simultaneously grabbing my upper thigh with her other hand.

Quite actually shocked, I leapt from my chair, hit my testicles on the edge of the table, twitched at the sudden jolt of pain in my lower abdomen and knocked over my glass of wine. Trying to stand straight and to not cup my bruised nuts while ignoring the cramping pain in my gut, I watched with horror as Debbie swivelled towards me. She licked her top lip meaningfully, place a hand either side of her chest, pushed her giant boobs together and slowly parted her legs. If performed by a more attractive woman, the act might have me dribbling and hoping my penis was not straining the front of my trousers. Performed by Debbie, my entire genitalia was hurriedly throwing belongings into a suitcase and grabbing its passport.

Mother stepped into the room from the kitchen, took a sharp breath and vanished again backward, audibly bumping into dad as she went. I could hear a brief and hurried under-the-breath discussion before mother loudly announced, 'I have pudding. I hope you are both hungry.' I groaned internally with the prospect of dealing with this later. Mother had caught the briefest glimpse and would have seen Debbie shoving her boobs at me with her legs open and me holding my crotch. Chances were, she was already counting how much wool she had in the cupboard to knit the clothes for our first-born child.

Debbie took her hands away from her boobs and swivelled back towards the table just as mother appeared with a steaming sponge-pudding concoction and dad followed with a tub of ice-cream, on which was balanced a scoop, and in his other hand a jug of steaming custard; all bases covered.

The dogs were doing their utmost to trip them both, so I grabbed first one collar and then the other to haul them out of the way. They could have an empty bowl to lick between them, but I wanted their waistlines to stay where they were. Snagging the dogs reminded me that my nuts still hurt. Mostly, I wanted to curl into a foetal position and nurse them, but decorum dictated that I take a helping of pudding and enjoy it, so I did. It was really good, but I swear I could feel my waist expanding as the calories hit my bloodstream.

Spoons scraped against bowls and dogs danced beneath chairs until I nodded to mother and she took both her bowl and Dad's and placed them on the floor. The boys, rather than take one bowl each, plunged together into the first before switching to the second and then back to the first to make sure they were completely clean.

Mum straightened up and appeared to have had a thought, 'Will you be in tomorrow, Tempest?'

'In and out I guess, mother. Why?'

'Your Father and I were planning to pick chestnuts and there's such an abundance of sweet chestnuts trees on the green in Finchampstead that we decided to go there for them. I thought we might pop in to warm up with a cup of tea. Or if you are out, we could take the dogs out to collect nuts with us.'

It seemed reasonable to me. Sunday ought to be a day where I relax, read a paper, roast a chicken and watch TV, but it was likely that I would be continuing my investigation into *The Vampire* case instead. Making sure the dogs went out for a good walk without me being involved sounded helpful.

'Do you like chestnuts, Debbie?' Mum asked. 'Maybe you and your children should come with us, we can all go to Tempest's house afterward.'

Oh, for heaven's sake!

'Mother, I am sure Debbie has plans already and has no need to see my house.' Please be busy, please be busy, please be busy.

Debbie seemed to think about it for a while before speaking, 'Charlie has a party at a friend's house tomorrow, the other kids are with their father and I have lunch with friends organised after church. I could cancel though.'

'No, don't do that, Debbie,' I implored.

For once I got lucky and Debbie decided that she was otherwise engaged for the suggested event. The conversation ranged for a while, but it was not long before I felt it was acceptable for me to make my bid for freedom. I bid them all goodbye, kissed mother lightly on the cheek, shook dad's hand and waved to Debbie. I was unsure about Debbie's intentions, although her display at the table suggested they involved sweaty sex and little else.

An hour later, I was back at home on my sofa with my feet curled under me and a dog on my lap. The six o'clock news came on followed by the local news that I wanted to see. The first report was the incident in Aylesford. I had suspected it might be and wanted to prepare myself for the inevitable phone call. The report showed the outside of the house and footage of police standing next to the crime scene barrier tape. All the vampire-wannabes were gone but there was an excellent shot of Big Ben and me sitting handcuffed on the wall outside the house. My phone rang as I knew it would. I pressed pause on the TV remote and answered the call without needing to look at the screen to see who it was.

'Good evening, mother.'

'Tempest!' she shrieked. 'I just saw you and that big friend of yours, what his name?'

'Big Ben.'

'Yes, Big Ben, on TV and handcuffed. What on Earth were you doing this time?' I opened my mouth to speak but was cut off, 'No, never mind. I don't want to hear anything about it. This is what I get for letting you join the Army. None of the other ladies at the church have their boys on TV in handcuffs. Must you ruin my reputation?'

'Mother,' I replied in as patient a tone as I could muster, 'I responded to a little, old lady who asked for assistance. There were a few complications and the police showed up. The cuffs were taken off as soon as the lady told the police her story.'

'Well, that's not what it looked like.'

129

'Mother. If the ladies in the church ask you about this, you can tell them I was mistakenly arrested while aiding a pensioner. I am sure you can put some spin on this to make you look even more beneficent than usual.'

'Hmm. We shall see,' she replied grumpily.

I could tell she had run out of steam, so I bid her goodnight and disconnected. Then pressed play and watched the rest of the news. The coverage was not extensive but referred to a vampire gang and suspected ties to the recent murders. The report was delivered by an on-the-scene team with a suitably serious tone.

The report ended with a short clip of Chief Inspector Quinn making a statement in which he said that human blood had been found on articles of clothing in the house and that a suspect had been taken into custody. He finished by speculating that he expected a swift conclusion to the case now.

I wondered about that.

Harold McBeak had worked as a taxi driver for thirty-seven years, clocking up the most recent anniversary just a few days ago. During that time, he had changed cars eighteen times, worked for five different companies and been offered sex, or a quick fiddle, as payment by drunk girls unable to pay their way home more times than he cared to remember. Only on one occasion had he succumbed to the girl's advances and had never done so again because he felt so dirty afterward.

He thought on that now as he waited in line across the road from Tequila Sunshine nightclub. The late crowd leaving town were the worst, you never knew what you were going to get, but he rarely had a fare that proved uneventful. Sometimes they vomited in the back of the car, he had learned long ago to have wipe clean seats fitted. Sometimes he would pick up a horny couple and they would practically have sex in the back of the car. Sometimes a group of young men would decide they didn't need to pay for their ride, so he kept an equalising stick under his seat. He couldn't make them pay, especially once he had made one or two of them bleed, but he could drive away believing that they would think twice before pulling the same stunt again. The equalising stick was a shortened pick axe handle which tucked neatly alongside his seat and was invisible from the outside. It was always clean because following any use he would discard it as damning evidence. So, bring them on, he thought to himself. Let them try to not pay. Me and my old friend the equaliser will keep the score even.

Harold sat waiting his turn in the taxi rank outside Tequila Sunshine nightclub hoping that he would get a fare that was none of the above and perhaps just fell asleep instead.

He watched as a young man of perhaps twenty-five approached the cab in front, leaned down, exchanged a few words and got into the rear of the vehicle. The car pulled away, making Harold's cab the one at the front of the queue. Glancing down at the clock on his dashboard, Harold idly observed that it was 0234hrs as his back door opened. He glanced over his left shoulder to see a couple get in. The girl was inappropriately dressed for the time of year and outside temperature, wearing a thin top with a spaghetti halterneck strap and a micro denim skirt. Harold couldn't see her shoes but expected them to be stupidly tall. As she scooted along to let her boyfriend/ male companion/ tonight's shag in, she flashed a brief exposure of white cotton between her legs. Harold looked away self-consciously, but the girl was oblivious.

'Shut the door, its freezing,' she demanded of the man settling next to her.

In the rear-view mirror, the man was hard to see. He tucked into the corner of the car behind the driver, but Harold could tell he was big. Really quite big. Certainly, twice the size of the girl. He was well dressed in a suit made from a dark material, possibly blue, but it was too dark to make out much detail and the man's face was hidden behind Harold's headrest.

'Chart Sutton please,' the girl requested from the back seat. She was looking at her companion and leaning into him. The door clicked shut as she spoke again, 'I'll give directions as we get closer.'

There seemed to be little need for conversation, so Harold swung his attention to the road, checked his mirror and pulled out. As he accelerated down the hill towards the A229 he glanced into his rear-view mirror, the couple were locked at the lips, the man had a hand inside her top and hers were in his hair.

Better than vomit Harold thought as he turned left and joined the frugal late-night traffic heading out of the city.

132

Bull and Dozer exploded into a cacophony of barking which brought me from peaceful slumber to instant disorientated alertness. The clock told me it was 0817hrs. Too early for anything mundane to be happening and then the next series of thumps and doorbell chimes told me what it was that had woken the dogs and got them so excited.

I sat up more fully in bed. The dogs were still barking, both facing the bedroom door, tails wagging like crazy.

'Okay, Okay. Enough now chaps, I'm up. Let's go see who it is.' Obedient as ever, they paid no attention to my request to cease their noise and kept right on barking.

I fumbled for sweatpants and a t-shirt and had to lean over the dogs to open the bedroom door while they were head-butting it in their haste to get out. Tiny legs propelling them along the hallway, they got about four yards before they had to stop at the top of the stairs because Dachshunds don't go down stairs. The length of their legs and depth of the steps means that they bash the first step down with their chin before their feet can find it. They learn this very young, usually by falling down the stairs.

Scooping them up, one under each arm, I headed down the stairs just as the doorbell went once more. The dogs barked their reply but stopped as I gave them a gentle squeeze and a shush.

'Just a minute.' I said to the shadowy visitor at my door. The frosted glass gave no indication of gender, age or race. It had to be someone I didn't know, or they would have called out to me or phoned me. I shooed the dogs out the back door so that I could answer the front without the visitor getting two daft dogs clawing at their legs. The boys would run around the side of the house and strain their heads against the gate to

134

bark once more at whoever might be there, but that was still a better solution. I left the back door open a crack so that they could get back in.

Heading back to the front door I ran through different scenarios in my head. This is my personal address, not my business address, so only friends and family have it. Although of course addresses are not that hard to come by, so I supposed that it could, in fact, be anyone. Why though would anyone be so insistent on getting my attention this early in the day? Had I forgotten to do something? Was I supposed to be somewhere?

Oh, my God. Someone has died!

It was going to be a relative on the door that knew my address, but not my phone number and they were here to tell me mum or dad was in the hospital or the morgue. Having now filled myself with dread, I opened the door.

PC Hotstuff was stood illuminated in the early morning light outside. I silently acknowledged that my most recent fantasy woman was waiting to be invited in and prayed that any remaining morning glory wasn't visible.

'There has been another murder. In fact, there has been a double murder with the same M.O. as the previous Vampire killings,' PC Hotstuff said. She was still outside, the cool air spilling in around my feet. While my sleep addled brain fought for something intelligent to say, the voice from below reminded me that he didn't like the cold and now was not a great time to appear to be the size of a baby sweetcorn.

'Come in, please,' I beckoned and stood back to allow her passage. She crossed over the threshold and I shut the cold back out where it belonged while failing, but really trying, to not check out her bum. PC Hotstuff was not in uniform and the transformation from a clearly attractive woman in a dowdy and unflattering uniform into a sex goddess in jeans and a jacket was startling. With no effort at all, she was stunning. Her hair was loose and curled a little at the edges as it hit her collar. Her clothes appeared new: blue jeans, tan, calf-length boots with a chunky heel and matching short, tan leather jacket. The jacket was by Karen Millen, I could tell from the buttons, which meant it was neither cheap nor stupidly expensive, suggesting that she gave thought to her appearance, but didn't spend without consideration. She carried no handbag and wore very little makeup - just a swipe of mascara and she looked fantastic.

Worried that I might start to drool, I pushed by her into the kitchen as she hesitated in the entrance lobby. 'Please, come through,' I invited as I switched on the light.

'Can I offer you tea?' I had no coffee in the house, which I was suddenly regretting.

Her answer of, 'Yes, please. If you have sweetener,' gave me cause to shake that pointless concern from my mind.

'Milk?'

'Just a splash. Thank you.'

'It's skimmed milk, is that ok? It's all I have.' Skimmed was the only form of milk I had drunk for years, the result of a period in Bosnia many years ago where all we had for months was UHT (Ultra Horrible Tasting) milk because it would last. We were in the mountains overlooking Sarajevo in the winter, so a hot brew was very welcome, but the war-torn country had no supplies to offer. When we finally got back to somewhere with real milk it had been skimmed or nothing and to me, it had tasted like nectar from the gods. Since then, any other milk was unpalatable.

Anyway, Amanda said she was fine with it and given the choice of it or nothing I might never know if she was just being polite while secretly wishing she had opted for water. The kettle began to bubble behind me as

136

I leaned on the counter. The dogs were sniffing about her feet and she bent down to see them.

'Be careful they don't jump up at your face,' I advised. She looked up smiling. 'They can be a little excitable around new people and might nip your nose if they can get close enough. You are certainly in danger of being licked,' I explained.

'They are wonderful. What are their names?' I told her which was which as she continued to coo and pet them, their tails whizzing like metronomes on acid. The kettle boiled, and I made two cups of tea. I was up now, so the caffeine would do no harm and I could hit the gym early. Of course, I had coolly still not asked why she was at my house. The voice from my pants was certain it was just for sex and was begging me to get on with it.

'So, a double murder?'

'Yes. Out near Chart Sutton.' Bull was on his back letting her rub his belly.

Distracted by my dumb dogs she had fallen silent again. 'Chart Sutton, you say?'

'Sorry,' she said standing up. 'I'm a sucker for small dogs.' She took the tea as I offered it to her and took a small sip before wrapping her hands around it as if to warm them up. 'Like I said, there was a double homicide. Maybe I can help you catch the killer.' She locked eyes with me as she finished that sentence, holding my gaze for a few seconds before looking down to her cup as she took another sip.

'Help me how, exactly?'

'I looked you up last night when I finished my shift. You have a colourful past, but you are solving cases and this one seems right up your alley. Chief Inspector Quinn thought he had solved it yesterday when SOCO found human blood at Jim Butterworth's place. The fool even went on TV last night announcing that he had a man in custody and he believed the case to be nearly closed. I don't think my lot are going to get to this guy before he does it again, so maybe you can. I can assist with information I guess.'

I let a few seconds of silence pass to see if she would feel the need to fill the lack of void and tell me more. She did.

'Plus, I have applied for promotion to detective four times and Chief Inspector Quinn knocks me back, or gives me the wrong date for the exam, or somehow always manages to scupper my plans. He is the lead investigator and I want him to fail. If I can help you to find the killer maybe you can let me have the arrest and I can get out of uniform and finally make this into a career.'

I considered what she had said for a moment and then thought about what she had not said. There was a definite undertone. I looked squarely at her eyes and gave her a second to decide if she wanted to hold the gaze or not. When she looked away, I spoke again.

'Is there some history there with Chief Inspector Quinn?' I asked the obvious question.

'You are quite astute, but that is not something I wish to discuss at this time.' No eye contact. She was looking into her cup, reflecting on something. Was he a filth bag that made her skin crawl? Not important at this point.

I put my teacup down, then pushed myself back and up, to sit on the kitchen counter. Electing to leave whatever issue she had with Inspector

Quinn to one side, for now, I asked instead for more detail on how I could help her, 'So, just to be certain I have this right: you want me to help you catch *The Vampire* because it will further your career and you think I have the necessary skills to achieve that. I feel quite flattered but tell me why I should help you.'

Her eyes snapped up at the question, her face seemingly unsure which emotion to go for and caught between disappointment, anger, and surprise.

'Please don't misunderstand me,' I continued, 'I am not saying no, I just want to hear more detail on what my part in this is and why I should feel motivated to help you. I just realised that I don't even know your name.'

PC Hotstuff smiled across at me, lighting up my world again as she stepped forward with her hand extended. 'Amanda Harper,' she said.

'Tempest Michaels,' I replied, letting my hand fall away. Her hand was soft and very warm where it had been gripping the mug of tea. Leaning in to shake her hand was the first time I had touched her. The move brought me close enough that my nose picked up the gentle feminine twang of her perfume, not that I was able to determine what it was, but it smelled exquisite and expensive.

'Middle name Danger, Isn't it?'

Oh, that's right, she had looked me up last night. Super.

'That's a story for another time.' It was my best deflection and one which had occasionally worked so that *another time* turned out to be in bed. 'So then, Amanda. Why me and why now?'

'Because I think you will solve this anyway and I want to ride on your shirt tails. I can assist, I have holiday I can take and use for the next two weeks. I have four days off now anyway due to my shift pattern.' She was buttering me up for her own gain and I was fine with that. I had no idea why I was resisting because I knew I was going to say yes.

'Let's go through to my office and discuss this in there.' I hopped off the counter and led her through to what would have been a dining room but served as my home office. I still had a dining table and chairs in the room pushed up against one wall where they were largely forgotten. The walls were dominated by newspaper articles, whiteboards with scrawled theories and post-it notes of varying sizes, colours and ages. At the far end of the room was a patio door at which the dogs were now sat. I let them out. 'Please feel free to nose about, I am going to put some more substantial clothes on, but won't be long at all.'

I drained the last of my tea, set the cup on the dining table and headed upstairs. My need to get dressed was driven by the danger of Mr. Wriggly deciding to get up a head of steam and show through my jogging bottoms since I had no restraining underwear on. In the bedroom, I grabbed slacks and a shirt/jumper combination that looked business casual and popped on some shoes. Glancing in the mirror I discovered that my hair was sticking out at every angle.

Perfect.

Momentarily angry at myself for not checking my appearance before opening the door, I thought instead that it spoke volumes about Amanda that she felt no need to say anything, nor stare at it. Then I thought that perhaps she didn't say anything or stare because she had no interest in me other than as a means for forwarding her career. Chastising myself for thinking at all, I tidied it with a little product and went back down to find her.

140

'So, what do you think?' she asked as I walked back through the door. 'Are we forming a partnership to get him? I have the inside line on the investigation and can provide details for all the witnesses and families of the victims and will hear about any new developments long before you might otherwise. I can help you with questioning people and stitching together the evidence to lead us to the perp.' She said perp like she was Judge Dredd and I loved her for it.

Giving myself a mental slap, I pretended to take a few moments to think before replying. 'Let's give it a few days and see how we go. How does that sound?' I didn't want to appear too keen. 'I have never had a partner before, a few assistants when I needed extra muscle, but never a partner. This is not a paid investigation. You do understand that, yes? I have not been commissioned and won't be paid for expenses or anything else while this goes on so there is no reward money, but there are bills to pay.' I let that hang for a moment but started speaking again before she had a chance to, 'I don't expect you to pay, other than fuel in your car and perhaps snacks if we stakeout. Do you have a site for the murder last night? Can we get access to it?'

'I was expecting to pay you actually, not that I can afford it, so thank you for not giving me a bill.' Her shoulders seemed to slump a little as if she had been holding her breath and now felt able to finally exhale. 'The victims were found by a passing motorist at 0400hrs this morning on the B2163 going to Chart Sutton. I don't know much currently other than that there are two victims, a man and a woman and that the M.O. is the same as the other murders. I came pretty much as soon as I found out. One of the other girls gave me a call to say she was heading to the scene. We were meeting later today as she was going to be off shift at breakfast and now won't.'

That seemed like explanation enough to me. What would I need to do before going out? Did I have enough gear in my car and the house? 'I need to change my footwear and grab a few bits, but we should get going as soon as we can. Five minutes sound good?'

In less than six minutes we were in my car, having elected to take that and not hers because all my gear was already in it. The cab of the Porsche is small, comfy and plush, but definitely small and I brushed her arm every time I changed gear. Her perfume filled the small space. It was a fantastic scent on her, and I had to try not to glance at her despite my brain demanding that I study her face, her hands, the exposed flesh of her neck, the swell of her breasts.

For goodness sake! Concentrate, man.

Thankfully Amanda started speaking which distracted me and probably prevented me from dribbling. 'With the murders last night, this officially became a serial killer case. Chief Inspector Quinn will be getting pressure from the Superintendent to wrap this up before the National Crime Agency swoop in and cut him out.'

'Why is it only a serial killer case now? Is that to do with body count thresholds combined with a period that defines it as different to a spree killing?' I asked.

'Essentially, yes. A serial Killer is only defined as such after the third murder, but it is a specific category with an abundance of writing on the subject. Honestly, once it was defined, it was romanticised almost to the point that it became something to aspire to,' she paused, perhaps noticing that she was beginning to rant, 'Sorry, I wrote my dissertation on the growth of the serial killer from 1970 – 2000 when reading Criminal Psychology at Uni. Would you believe the number of identified serial killer cases globally increases by one hundred percent every year? There are so many now that they don't even make the news unless they are truly wacko.'

'Like our vampire?'

143

'Pretty much.' Amanda lapsed into silence again and before I could think of anything to say we passed a sign announcing our arrival in Chart Sutton.

Chart Sutton is a pleasant enough village, not too far from the lovely village of Leeds with its fabulous castle and grounds. It is a bit too remote for me to want to live there but I imagined the demand for property was high enough to keep the house prices up. The roads mostly empty due to the early hour although there were a few people heading out for weekend pursuits. With little traffic with which to contend, the thirteen-mile journey had taken just over fifteen minutes, the crime scene easy to spot from a long way off even in the poor light of early morning. As we slowed to pull off the road just before all the tents and barrier tape, a police officer jogged across to wave us off. Amanda powered down her window, exchanged a few words and directed me to park along the road, after the screened-off area.

We exited the car with me having to step into the road to get out. Traffic was still light so swinging my door into the lane of oncoming cars was easy enough. I popped the boot open and grabbed my shoulder bag, then hustled after Amanda as she had not waited for me. I caught up to her just before she got under the cordon tape.

'Will I be allowed free movement here? Or will I need to stay with you?' I asked.

'Probably best if you stay outside for now. I will be able to go where I please and should be able to take you with me, but if Chief Inspector Quinn is here, he may cause a problem. Especially after your arrest yesterday.' She turned to me then, perhaps wanting to see what my face was saying about having to wait outside for her to check the coast is clear. 'Okay?' she asked.

'Yup. I'll hang around outside until you have had time to see if our friend is already here.' It was no problem for me, I was used to not being let into crime scenes. Getting into the tent to see what the killer had done was a new experience. Amanda ducked under the tape and into the tent passing one of her colleagues who gave her a brief nod. He looked across at me with an unreadable expression, then looked away dismissing me.

I took out my notepad and jotted down what I knew.

1. Five murders over the course of just over two weeks.
2. Each death (assuming these were the same MO) was the result of a vicious and frenzied attack during which the attacker had bitten a large hole in each victim's neck. The resulting trauma caused catastrophic blood loss and almost immediate death.
3. The dead so far had no apparent connection. They were of different races, ages, genders, social groups and lived in different villages.
4. They were all killed at night or in the early morning.

It occurred to me as I wrote the list that there really was no paranormal connection other than the press had dubbed the killer as *The Vampire* because of the neck wound. Was that important? No, I decided, it was not because there is no paranormal, just a lot of people willing to believe in it. My primary (and self-appointed) role as a paranormal investigator was to find the ordinary truth behind the mysteries I faced.

So far, I had never had a case that I had not been able to solve by producing a perfectly ordinary criminal acting out as a werewolf or ghoul or whatever for their own gain, or a set of circumstances that explained why the client had convinced themselves they were being haunted or visited by an apparition. In one case, I had a lady that had convinced herself that her late father, a fisherman, had returned and was haunting her house because she could smell him. It turned out her cat had been catching fish from the pond of a neighbour and was eating them under the stairs where a fishy mound of half-eaten bodies was now producing the scent, she thought she recognised. Even after removing the fish carcasses myself and cleaning the area with bleach, she continued to question whether I was sure her father hadn't returned. Paranormal investigation can be quite lucrative, but I often feel that I am robbing people when I prove their case was all in their head.

Amanda reappeared to break my train of thought. 'Tempest you can come through,' she said, holding the cordon tape up for me to pass easily underneath. 'It is pretty gruesome though. I hope you have a strong stomach.'

I followed her through the screen flap to the scene beyond. I was not worried about losing the contents of my stomach, it had been hardened against such things a long time ago. Always best to be warned though as I had no desire to vomit in front of the lovely Amanda.

Beyond the screen was the back end of a 2006 Maroon Ford Mondeo. A further screen obscured all but the boot lid and tail lights, but as I drew closer, I gained a view of the driver's side back door. It was open and a person in a full forensic suit with mask and gloves was taking pictures of the interior. From where I stood, I couldn't see much of anything; no blood, no pale foot sticking out of the car door, no sense of anything to indicate it was a murder scene really.

I had my notebook out already and my phone which I used to snap the vehicle registration. Unsure what information I would be able to gather here without getting in the way I stayed where I was, out of everyone's way and jotted down a few questions:

1. Name of victims?
2. Ages?

146

3.   Any connection between the victims?

4.   Taxi firm?

5.   Where did the driver collect the fare?

6.   Was the taxi despatched from a base or waiting outside a bar or club?

I was struck by how quiet the scene was. Road noise came from the occasional passing car, but in between, I could hear birdsong. I had seen perhaps twenty people on site, but each was going about their business with minimal conversation. There was no radio chatter, just an occasional quietly spoken instruction from one colleague to another. This was my first time this close to a fresh murder scene. I had never been able to get beyond the barrier tape before, so I could not gauge whether this was normal or not. I guess I expected more banter, more action, more something.

As I stood considering what my next move should be Amanda reappeared, moving at a fast walk. She grabbed my right elbow without slowing down. Quietly she said, 'We need to go, Chief Inspector Quinn just pulled up. I doubt he will be pleased to see you here and that will embarrass Michael, the chap I sweet-talked into letting you in with me.' Clearly, we were leaving.

'I know you didn't get to see anything, but I should have all the information you need.'

'Super,' I replied as she wove me through the screening and back out on to the road. We exited the opposite side to where I had parked about fifty metres down the road and would need to go back past the cordoned area to get to my car. I paused outside the screening to put my notebook and phone back in my shoulder bag, not sensing the urgency that Amanda clearly felt. She displayed this by grabbing my hand and pulling me after

147

her. She wanted to get going, but hey, I was now holding her hand. Actual flesh to flesh contact.

We skirted the edge of the road between the cars and the barriers still holding hands. Her arm stiffened to make me stop as we got to the end of the barrier screens. I watched her peer around the corner and I guess she decided it was clear as her grip on my hand loosened. I let her hand go as she turned to look at me. "All clear," she mouthed silently.

'Jolly good,' I replied with far more volume than was required. As I passed her going to my car, my stride was confident. I am not in the habit of showing fear and all the sneaking around was making me feel ridiculous. Perhaps I was compensating because I had no power in this environment. Not bothering to analyse why I felt the need to strut, I arrived at the car still fishing in my bag for my keys with my left hand and holding the bag open with my right. Amanda had fallen behind briefly as I set off, but caught me now as my scrabbling hand finally located the keys and plipped the car open.

Amanda caught my eye across the roof before we got in. 'I think it best if we get out of here before he spots us,' she said. 'Not that we can't be here, but he is an annoying arsehole and I would rather avoid the questions. Do we go back to your office?'

'My house. I have more space there to spread the information out. What can you tell me about the latest victims?'

Amanda was quiet for a moment as I focused on finding a gap in the increasing traffic. Seeing my opportunity, I spun the car off the grass verge, trying not to churn it up and fill my tyre treads with mud, crossed both lanes and headed back towards Maidstone and my house. Once into traffic, she started speaking again.

'The two victims are a man, probably the taxi driver, and a young woman. The male victim was Harold McBeak, age fifty-eight, looks like he tried to defend himself. He had a bat of some kind,' she explained. 'The cause of death appears to be massive blood loss from a neck wound. He was found several metres from the car. It looks like he was dragging himself away from the car towards the road when he bled out. The bat was abandoned behind him in the blood trail. The girl we have yet to ID, but she was petite, blond and attractive. From her clothes and complexion, I would place her at maybe nineteen or twenty and most likely on her way home from a club in town. She was left on the back seat of the car, same cause of death. No other obvious injuries to either victim.' She had delivered the details as a report, keeping emotion and cadence from her voice.

'What makes you think the man tried to defend himself?' I asked pressing for more information.

'The presence of the bat and its proximity to his body coupled with traces of wood that match it alongside the driver's seat. My guess would be he kept it for dealing with problem customers. It could be that the killer brought it with him, but so far, he has left no trace of himself and never used a weapon. Leaving a bat with his fingerprints on would seem clumsy. Also, there is no blood on it, so it was not used by the attacker.'

Reasonable enough, I thought. 'What do the throat wounds look like?'

Amanda paused before answering, possibly to order her thoughts so that she could answer the question accurately and without opinion, or possibly because it was gruesome stuff and she didn't really want to remember at all. I gave her a few moments, but she started speaking before I felt the need to prompt more from her. 'They seem to fit the pattern of the first three victims. Forensics will need time to confirm

149

whether it is the same mouth that inflicted the bite to the earlier victims, but I would say it is the same person. Same murderer.'

'Did the attack seem frenzied?' The murderer was killing people in quick succession, five now in seventeen days, three in the last four days and with no apparent connection between the victims. Was the killer acting out a sex fantasy? Meeting a pathological need of some kind? Were the five victims we knew of the only ones he had killed or were there more elsewhere? The questions were piling up and answers were proving elusive.

Amanda had taken time to consider her answer again. 'I don't think so. The girl's clothing was a bit skewwhiff as if she had been having sex in the taxi. Bra undone, but not ripped, skirt pulled right up, but there were no obvious bruises on her arms and legs, so it is unlikely she fought much, if at all. If I had to guess I would say there was a second passenger that was known to the girl. They were travelling together, and he bit her throat in the back of the taxi while it was being driven. The taxi driver careened off the road as the blood started squirting, coming to rest where we saw the car this morning. He then either took the bat and attempted to stop the attack or panicked and fled only to be caught and overpowered. Does that sound plausible?'

'I think I need to give that some thought, but I don't see any immediate holes. It is probably close enough for now.'

The conversation had taken us back into Maidstone town centre. I was on the one-way system and it was 1145hrs. I needed breakfast and a cup of tea. Amanda took that moment to yawn and stretch and in doing so pushed her shoulders back and her chest out. The fullness of her shirt filled my vision, involuntarily I stared at her fantastic twin mounds of swollen flesh and my thoughts turned from crazed vampire murders to the potential future nakedness of my companion. Mr. Wriggly instantly

150

stirred, which when stuffed into trousers and jammed into a bucket seat was not comfortable. He was endeavouring to stretch out and in doing so was tugging on some pubic hairs that were probably tucked underneath him. Now distracted by a pinching sensation coming from my groin I remembered why I was having trouble in the first place and flashed to another image of PC Hotstuff, this time reclined in lingerie on my bed.

'Nice car,' she said breaking the spell like a pin to a bubble. I twitched the wheel as my focus returned and I realised I had not paid the slightest attention to the road for the last few minutes.

'Thank you. It is a little impractical, but I love it.'

'Do you put the dogs in it?'

'Yes. They sit on the passenger seat quite happily, although I never take them very far. To the park and back or the vets when their jabs are due. Mostly they curl up and go to sleep.'

Amanda lapsed into silence, her line of conversation seemingly exhausted and we finished the short journey back to my house without speaking again.

The dogs performed their usual routine of barking excitedly as we entered the house, followed by tearing off towards the back door. I let them out and shut the door, the sound of their feet on the decking ceasing as they hit the grass.

Back inside, Amanda was leaning on my desk looking at pictures pinned to the wall. I had printed off several I got from Liam Goldhind.

'Tempest, where did you get these pictures?'

'Liam Goldhind, the man that found the second victim. Whoever the police had conduct the investigation and deal with the crime scene, failed to confiscate his phone, or whatever it is the police do, because he had over a hundred pictures of Mrs. Hancock on it.'

'These should be in police hands, they may be important.'

'You can have copies of everything. I assumed the police would have their own pictures.'

'We will have. Every bit of evidence though...'

'Well, just let me know what you want or if you want to get someone in to make copies. Whatever.'

Bull, then Dozer appeared at the back door looking to come back in. It was nearing lunchtime, so they would try to convince me that they needed something to eat. My own stomach rumbled lightly at the thought.

'I'm going to put the kettle on and make a sandwich, can I interest you in anything?' I asked Amanda over my shoulder as the dogs whizzed between my legs.

'Both sound great,' she replied. She was still looking at the pictures of Mrs. Hancock, her hands tucked into her back pockets as she leaned forward to scrutinise something in one of the photographs.

I passed her on my way to the kitchen where the dogs were excitedly dancing in front of the fridge looking hopeful. As I strode past them to the kettle, they swivelled to maintain eye contact and began dancing again once I had filled the kettle, switched it on and turned back to face them.

'Carrot?' I enquired.

No answer came, but I assumed, based on experience, that they would eat anything that came out of the fridge, so fished out a decent sized carrot, snapped it in half and chucked the two pieces into the lounge. Their paws slipped a few times as they propelled themselves from stationary to full speed on the stone floor. As I snagged the milk from the fridge door, I could hear crunching from the next room.

Amanda wandered through from the dining room/office just as I was pouring hot water into two mugs.

'Two sweeteners, right?'

'Yes, please.'

Tea on the breakfast bar, I gathered bread and butter, ham and cheese, lettuce and pickles and the general accoutrements and tracklements that made sandwiches so very interesting.

'Help yourself, please,' I invited, as I cut several slices from a farmhouse style loaf and furnished her with a plate.

As Amanda began to butter some bread, I fetched an A4 pad and pen and began to make notes of what she had already told me about the latest murder victims. Where they had been picked up, where they had been found, the probability of a third person in the Taxi who was most likely the perpetrator.

I had lots of questions which I now started to jot down.

- Names of victims?
- Any connection between them? – seems unlikely
- Witnesses to the taxi driver making his pick-up? – interview other taxi drivers from last night to see if anyone saw them
- Is there CCTV outside the club? – probably
- Did it catch a view of the killer?

I could have kept going for quite a while.

'Do you need to be anywhere this afternoon, Amanda?

'There is nothing I can't cancel,' she answered without answering the question.

I had several simultaneous lines of thought. The first thought was that I could get Amanda to supply me with information from the investigation since Darren Shrivers was out of town and thus not available, then it occurred to me that it was Sunday and I might be able to get Amanda to stay for dinner, which was a pleasing prospect as I could not deny my attraction to her.

However, before any of my thoughts could coalesce into a sentence, I heard the front door handle turn. The dogs heard it too and were up and off and running through the house to see off the intruders... who turned out to be my parents.

'Ah,' I said to no one, rather brainlessly.

Mother was in the house now and pulling off her coat and bending down to undo the laces on her walking boots. 'Yes, yes. Hello, Bull. Hello, Dozer. No, I don't need a wash, thank you,' she advised the dogs.

'Move your bum please, Mary. So, I can get in, would you?' This from my dad.

'Give me a moment Michael. I'm taking off my boots,' she answered with a little impatience and irritation.

'Well then, shut the door, Mary. You are letting all the cold air in. It's not like I can get around your bum, is it? It fills the door.'

'Shut yer face,' she replied instantly, accompanied by a punch to his ribs.

Dad made a suitable ouch noise to placate his wife but shoved her over the threshold and into the house anyway. The door slammed shut behind him.

'Amanda,' I whispered. 'Their eyesight is largely based on movement. If we stay still, they might not see us.'

'Hmm?' Was all I got in reply accompanied by a single raised eyebrow. She had no idea what I had just referenced. I felt a little disappointed.

'Hello, mother,' I called through from the kitchen.

'Hello, Tempest,' her reply drifted back through. She had still not looked across to see that I had company. 'We thought we would stop in on our way to pick sweet chestnuts, see if you wanted to join us. You did say you might not be in, so we were just going to get the... oh.' Having finally finished faffing with coat and boots and looked in my direction, mother had spotted Amanda. That she had been silenced mid-flow was something to make a note of.

155

'Michael.' Mother was staring at Amanda and I and motioning desperately behind her for her husband. Dad was taking his boots off and paying no attention.

'Michael!' this time with a bit more insistence behind it.

I was clearing the chunk of sandwich from my mouth so that I could speak when Amanda beat me to it.

'Hi. I'm Amanda,' she said advancing across the room to shake my mother's hand.

I saw dad jerk his head forward to look past my mother's legs having heard Amanda speak. Mother had taken Amanda's hand and was now examining her like one might a prize sheep before buying it.

'How you doing, kid?' asked dad from the floor.

'Fine, dad,' I called through, not taking my eyes from my mother and Amanda.

'Mother, Amanda is a police Officer, she is assisting with a case I am working on, nothing else.'

'So, you didn't stay the night?' my mother asked Amanda like it was a perfectly normal thing to enquire.

'Mary!' cried dad from the floor. 'You can't ask such questions.'

'Why ever not, Michael? It is a simple yes or no answer. How am I ever going to get grandchildren if he never has a woman stay over? Besides,' she said, turning her attention to me. 'I thought you and Deborah hit it off last night.'

Amanda had retrieved her hand and had taken a step back to get some room between her and the crazy woman. 'Well, I have to say that I did not

156

spend the night last night or any other night I'm afraid. Of course, Tempest hasn't gotten around to asking me yet.' On saying this Amanda turned around to grab her tea from the breakfast bar behind her and winked at me with an amused smile. I could not read the wink. My brain told me she was winking to say that she was playing along, and the wink was conspiratorial, the voice in my pants was utterly convinced the wink meant that she was instructing me to get on and invite her for sex because she was only here for that and growing impatient. Amanda was clearly quite entertained by my plight and mouthed in mock anger, 'Who is Deborah?' Well, at least I had discovered that Amanda had a sense of humour, even if it was at my expense.

I had to bury my face in miserable exasperation at this point though. I was going to try very hard to explain to my mother that Deborah was a whale and that there was no way on Earth I would entertain a liaison with her. I knew, however, that it was a futile endeavour.

'Mother I will make this as clear as I can and hope with an absolute desperation that you listen to the words I am saying: I have no interest in Deborah. I did my best to be pleasant to her while she was a guest at your house, but we did not exchange numbers.'

'I already gave her your number,' she replied.

'I won't be making any plans to see her, and I implore you to stop ambushing me with blind dates at your house when I come over for dinner.' I turned to Amanda wearing a weary expression. 'Sorry about this.'

'Whatever is wrong with Deborah?' demanded my mother.

'Leave the boy alone, Mary,' demanded my Dad, knowing of course that my mother would completely ignore him.

157

'Mother,' I started. I had my hand on my forehead wondering how to explain this in terms that she would understand. 'Mother Debbie and I are incompatible.'

'You mean you don't like her because she is fat?' Mother had pursed her lips now and was looking annoyed.

'Mother, Debbie is overweight.' I didn't want to fall into the bait of labelling people as fat. 'Ignoring that element though, we have nothing in common, she already has a handful of children and she is not the type of woman I am looking for.'

Mother stood still in the middle of the kitchen and seemed to be considering my last statement. Amanda was sipping her tea, I was trying to work out how to get mother away from the subject but thankfully dad came to the rescue. 'I need a cup of tea,' he announced loudly.

'Good idea, dad,' I said, turning to refill the kettle. 'Amanda if you had not already gathered these are my parents. They are both a little odd.'

'Pleased to meet you,' Amanda said.

'Are you single then?' asked my mother, sticking with the same singular line of thought. I rolled my eyes, thinking I was probably lucky that she had not yet asked if she is ovulating.

'Erm, yes, actually.' Amanda then did her best to deflect my mother by speaking to my dad, 'Did I hear your first name is Michael?' she asked. 'Which makes your name Michael Michaels. I've never heard that combination before.'

'Well, Tempest's middle name is...'

'Danger,' she completed his sentence. 'Dare I ask what your middle name is?'

'You can my dear, but I'll never tell. At least not while the lights are on.' Dad's cheeky smile was short lived as mum flicked her hand at his spuds and struck home.

Dad instantly sagged against a kitchen cupboard, one hand on the counter, one hand on his nuts. Mother had turned her back on him and was moving to the cupboard where I keep the tea and cups.

'Sorry about this, Amanda,' I managed. 'I would like to claim that this is unusual behaviour, but I can't.'

The kettle flicked on behind me as my mum busied herself making tea. Dad was recovering and managed to straighten himself to get to one of the breakfast bar chairs. Amanda had to take a sidestep so he could sit.

'Amanda, shall we take our sandwiches and retreat back to the study?' I asked already gathering my plate and mug.

On the way to the study, which is just about ten paces, my phone rang. I juggled my tea and plate, trying to free a hand to fish for my phone, but had to accept defeat and dump the tea mug on the first available surface I found, which was a stair. I had long ago given up putting anything edible on the floor as I always found a Dachshund on it or in it a few seconds later. Tea was an absolute favourite of theirs and I had been mugged while watching TV on the sofa before; eyes on the box, the Dachshund would take advantage of my distraction and dive headfirst into the mug resting on my leg. I would only discover my tea was beyond saving when the sound of frantic lapping reached my ears.

Hand finally available, I retrieved the phone from my back pocket, saw the name Jagjit on the screen and pressed the answer icon.

'Hey, man.'

'Dude! What are you up to later? I got a cool movie to watch and a pack of beer.'

'It is Cobra?'

'Suck it, douchebag. Just because I am Indian, it does not mean I have to drink Indian beer.'

'It's Cobra, isn't it?' I said laughing.

'You are such a dickhead, Tempest.' His voice now whining.

I said nothing, forcing him to answer the question.

'Okay yes, it is Cobra, but that is just because it's what my dad bought.'

'You want food? I have some T-bones in the freezer I can take out.'

'You know it, man. Six o'clock work for you?'

'You mean 1800hrs? Sure.'

'1800hrs? You are such a robot.' He disconnected.

'So, where were we?' I asked Amanda, who had now finished both her sandwich and her mug of tea and was looking over some of the printed pages I had on my desk.

'The Brotherhood of the Dead? This is an actual thing?' she asked, holding up the club flier I had.

'Apparently so. I did some research and found that there is a whole vampire-wannabe network of clubs. Each has a founding member that is supposed to be an actual vampire and they meet and dress up and pretend to be vampires, do LARP and that sort of thing. It is probably not connection to the recent murders, it was just something I stumbled across when I was poking around.'

160

It was time for me to press Amanda for some help. I was a little uncomfortable asking her as I had no favour to offer in return at this time, but I needed better information than I was getting.

'You remember that you offered to help fill in the blanks in my investigation?'

'Yes. I think I can do that.'

'Well, I guess it is time to earn your keep.'

I explained as best I could that I was used to getting information from a friend at the Maidstone station without giving away any details about the person. Amanda said that in principle sharing information, if it was not sensitive or personal to the victim was permissible and she would see what she could do.

I asked her specifically for as much detail as she could give me regarding the Brian Grazly murder and outlined what I already knew, which was what the papers had reported only.

'I will go to the station this afternoon and will get back to you once I have something. Now though, I think I will make good my escape before your mother asks if I am ovulating today.' She said with a laugh.

Her laughter was like music, but the best music I had ever heard. Everything about her was just fantastic.

'I'll see you out.'

Amanda still had her boots on and all the things she came with were still in her pockets. As we neared the door, she pulled her keys from her jacket pocket, paused, leaned in through the kitchen door frame and then back out again.

'Want to give your mum something to talk about?'

'Hummh?' I grunted, wondering what she was asking me.

'Nice to meet you both,' Amanda called through to the kitchen.

My mother appeared suddenly from behind the kitchen counter. 'Oh, are you leaving, dear,' she enquired, advancing towards us.

'Yes, I have work to do.'

'On a Sunday?' She asked, her tone now horrified.

'Police work is never done I'm afraid. Got to be going then,' she said. Then waved to my parents, leaned in and kissed me on the lips. I was so taken by surprise that I dropped my teacup. It thunked on the carpet, somehow not breaking. She winked again as she broke the kiss and with a little laugh, she opened the door, waved once more and was gone.

I closed the door behind her and slowly turned back towards my kitchen deep in thought. What the hell had the kiss been about? It was only a peck on the lips, but did that mean she was interested? Surely, she must be? Not because I am fantastic but because why else would she kiss me? Surely, she must know how she looks and what effect she has on men in general? Or did it mean nothing and that was just for show? Again, with the wink.

Still thinking, I looked up to find both parents staring at me from inside the kitchen and both dogs staring at me from the floor. The dogs wagged their tails as I made eye contact with them.

'Um,' I said, showing off my huge intellect.

'She has great hips, Tempest,' Oobserved my mother. 'And good breasts.'

162

'Definitely good breasts,' chipped in my dad.

'Shut up, Michael,' Instructed my mother without looking away from me.

'Good breasts,' I echoed, deep in thought. 'I shall make sure I congratulate her on them next time I see her.'

'You will do no such thing, Tempest. I am just saying that she is a young woman with all the bits she needs for raising children.' Mother had moved to join me in the entrance hall now and was picking her boots up to go again. 'Is it too much to ask that there are Grandchildren before I am in my grave?' Mother liked to lay in on thick if she could.

The conversation was an old one and I wondered sometimes when it had started. There was a long period in my late teens and early twenties when she was convinced I was going to produce children out of wedlock and expected me to stay a virgin until my wedding night. My dad never really offered an opinion on the subject either way but had warned me to *be sensible* on a couple of occasions. At some point, she had changed tack and suddenly needed me to procreate lest I miss the window of opportunity. It seemed likely that others suffered the same as I, although I could not recall being lamented with all that many stories.

I wanted to reiterate that Amanda was just a colleague of sorts, but the kiss had made any denial of a relationship seem lame.

'Off to collect chestnuts then? Would you like to take the dogs with you?' This was my attempt to navigate past further discussion of babies and Amanda's breasts. Amazingly it worked.

'Yes. Have you noticed if they are many?'

163

'They are abundant, and you know how few people actually stop and pick them up so there should be plenty for you.' I turned to call for the dogs but found them at my feet. 'Time for a walk, chaps.'

A minute or so later, both my parents, accompanied by my two faithful dogs, were out the door and heading down the path. As I closed the door, I could hear her complaining about grandchildren again. They would be back soon enough. I checked my watch. It was 1322hrs. I pulled my phone from its usual hiding place in my back pocket and wrote PC Hotstuff a text. 'Confused. The kiss was very pleasant, but not sure what it meant.' I hovered my finger over the send button then elected to delete it while berating myself for being indecisive.

I had time to kill, so I prepared some vegetables to accompany the steaks, performed some basic housework tasks and set the washing machine to clean some laundry. Then I got changed and went out for a run.

There were great running routes around the village located on the North Downs as it is. Plenty of contour, different surfaces and so much better than running on the pavements where the impact jarred my knees and made them ache. Just shy of an hour later I arrived back at my door sweaty, devoid of stress and feeling mentally positive about my day.

I headed to the shower.

Jagjit arrived at 1806hrs with a ten-pack of Cobra beer in glass bottles and two movies that both starred Jason Statham. It took us about eighteen seconds to get the first pair of bottles opened and less than fifteen minutes to drink them. It had been a while since we had done this, so we chatted about work and stuff and enjoyed the cold beer.

I served the steaks at 1930hrs on the dot. We sat and ate them in near silence at the breakfast bar in the kitchen rather than on trays in the living room or at the table in the dining room. Plates clean and in the dishwasher, we went back to the movie.

Sat on the sofa talking about nothing much at all, I told him about having Amanda turn up at my house that morning and how she had then kissed me in front of my parents.

Helpfully, Jagjit just laughed at me and called me a hopeless knob.

'I need the loo,' announced Jagjit getting up. 'You want another beer while I'm up?'

'Go for it.' I reached for the remote and paused the film as he left the room.

It was just cool enough now for me to have the fancy ornamental electric fire on in my lounge. With the lounge door shut, it stayed nice and warm and there was no need for me to turn the main central heating on. Jagjit left the door open so I hopped up and pushed it closed again to keep the warmth in.

I fiddled with my phone a bit while I waited for him to return. I was checking out local news stories when I heard him scream loudly. I was out of my chair and moving fast and for once not having to trip over a dog as

165

they had not bothered to react at all. Some guard dogs they were - bark like buggery if there was a knock on the door, but if someone broke in and started killing me, they would sit and wait for a biscuit.

I went through the kitchen and into the entrance hall to find Jagjit leaning against the wall holding his chest. I saw no blood, he was alone, and his face looked like he couldn't decide whether to laugh or scream again.

'What the hell, man?' Seemed to be the obvious question.

'Outside,' he said indicating with his arm. 'Outside,' he paused again, stood himself up and gave an exaggerated full body shake.

I gave him a few moments to sort himself out, curious about what he was going to say. I noted that the outside security light was not on and I could see no one the other side of the door. I folded my arms and gave him a quizzical eyebrow.

Jagjit finally pulled himself together. 'Tempest, there is a something terrible and scary outside your house.'

'Terrible and scary?' I repeated his words mockingly.

'Dude. Outside your house is a woman wearing lingerie and a trench coat. I heard a knock on the door when I came out of the toilet, so I opened the door and she flashed me.'

'And that made you scream?' I enquired.

'You didn't see it, man! The woman has a mustache like Lando Calrissian.'

Oh, my God. It was Debbie! I hesitated, but then opened the door because hiding inside just felt a bit too weak. It was the wrong thing to do

166

though because Debbie had been vanishing back up the path, beating a retreat to her car, I guess. She caught sight of the shaft of light from my front door and turned to come back when she saw me framed in the doorway.

Behind me, Jagjit moved from where he was slumped against the wall. 'What are you doing man? Shut the door before she sees you.'

'Too late,' I whispered.

'Oh. Oh, hold on. Tempest, are you shagging her? She looks like Mrs. Potato Head auditioning for a porn movie!' Jagjit's voice was incredulous, which it damned well should have been. He was also being a bit cruel about her figure.

'What?'

'I know it been a slow year for you on the lady front, but seriously man?' I wanted to protest my innocence, the evidence was damning though, and she was back through my gate already, so I shut myself outside with her and left Jagjit inside.

'Debbie, what are you doing here?' I asked as she came to a halt in front of me. She did indeed have on a rain mac, some stilettos, sheer stockings, the type with the seam at the back, and no evidence of anything underneath.

'I came to surprise you, Tempest. Would you like to get rid of your friend and invite me in?'

No, I bloody wouldn't.

'Sorry, Debbie. This is not something that is going to happen between us. I'm just not ready for anything right now despite what my mother believes.'

167

'Are you sure?' Debbie opened the mac and showed me what she had for me. It was not the most appealing packaging I had ever been presented with. Unwillingly, I noticed that her pubes were escaping either side of her gusset like a hundred spiders making a bid for freedom.

My sole thought was that I could never unsee the sight in front of me. Debbie took a step forward and my penis took control of my base motor function, slammed into reverse, and had my back pressed against my door before I knew I had moved.

'I don't give up easy, Tempest. You should know that.' I think I gulped at that point. 'Your resistance is sweet. I look forward to breaking it down.'

I was trying to find the door handle with my right hand so that I could open the door and spill inside. As I edged closer to it, Debbie leaned forward, placed a hand on the door by my head then breathed into my ear, 'I'll be back soon, lover.' Then she licked the edge of my ear sensuously, tapped my groin playfully and spun around to head off into the night again, pulling her coat around her as she went. The click click of her heels on the path like a staccato beat to match my heart rate. While Mr. Wriggly was considering suicide options, I found the door handle and stumbled back inside.

'You dog,' laughed Jagjit, clearly entertained by my horror-stricken face.

'Dude, that is easily the scariest experience of my life thus far.' I sat on the floor and leaned back against the door, my limbs just hanging loosely like I had fallen from a great height. Bull and Dozer wandered out to see what we were up to, their wet noses on my hands causing me to get moving again.

'So, who was that?' Jagjit wanted to know.

168

'Someone I won't be sleeping with.' My phone pinged to announce the arrival of an email. Leaning to one side I found the phone it is usual place in my back pocket under my right bum cheek. The email was from Amanda and had attached files.

'Want to see some crime scene pictures?' I asked without looking up.

'Will there be horribly mutilated dead people? Because the answer is no if there is, but probably yes if there are not.'

'Then grab a couple of beers, buddy, while I get these on a bigger screen.' I levered myself off the floor, plopping Dozer back on the tile as he had curled on my lap and gone to sleep already.

The contents of the email would be impossible to make out on the tiny phone screen, so I opened the same email on my iMac in the home office/dining room. By the time Jagjit reappeared with two fresh, cold beers, I was scrolling through pictures of Brian Grazly's cottage.

'So, what are we looking at?' Jagjit wanted to know as he placed a bottle on a Spiderman coaster next to the keyboard.

'I clicked back a couple of pictures which brought up the outside of the cottage at night illuminated by portable lamps. 'This is the scene of the first vampire murder victim. Or, at least the first one reported.' I corrected myself.

'Are you working this case?'

'Sort of.'

'Sort of?'

'Well, I have not been engaged to investigate it by anyone, but I don't have a current case, and this is National press stuff. I thought it worth looking into. If I get a case that pays, I can always drop this again, but if I can get anywhere with this, I reckon there is some serious exposure for the business. Plus, a hot girl asked me to.'

'Hot girl?'

'I'll tell you about it later.'

'Gotcha.'

I clicked back to the email from Amanda.

Tempest,

The attached files show the pictures and case notes that you need. Obviously, physical evidence is not something I can get you access to easily. The only way to achieve that, is to have you taken on as an official consultant which is unlikely with Chief Inspector Quinn involved.

You do realise that this is me unofficially leaking you this information and that should you allow it to go to anyone else I won't only be fired but in all kinds of trouble.

I am trusting you.

Amanda

It had been sent from a private email address. I opened the case notes, which ran to quite a few pages and pressed print. As the machine began to whirr and chew through paper, I clicked back to the pictures.

Jagjit put his beer down to grab a chair from the dining table behind me. He pulled it up back to front and to the side of me so he could see the screen and sat down leaning on the back of it.

'What are we looking for?'

'A good question mate, but the simple answer is that I don't know. My experience thus far has taught me that what I see rarely makes sense until later. I am trying to build up a picture of the victims. Through that perhaps I will establish a trend or pattern or find some connection that will enable me to look at something else, which will then focus me in on something that helps me find the culprit. It is very much not an exact science.'

'Okay, so we just look at pictures, make notes and hope something proves to be useful later?'

'Pretty much,' I conceded.

'Okay. Feels a bit voyeuristic, like we are stalkers or something looking inside the lives of other people.'

'Yup,' was all I could say to that.

We were scrolling through shot after shot of the cottage exterior. There were a lot of pictures and none of them seemed to show me anything useful. I clicked forward until the pictures changed from the building exterior to that of the victim. Mr. Grazly had come to rest face down across his path facing away from the house. His face was turned to the right with his neck exposed and horribly torn. His arms were by his sides and his legs straight and together as if he had been standing to attention and simply fallen forward. His head was between two rose bushes, each pruned well down at the end of the season, so they were little more than thorny lumps. There were a few scratches on his face where he may have fallen into one of them.

I made a few notes on my pad. As I did, Jagjit took up the mouse and scrolled through a few more pictures.

I took the mouse back, backed up and clicked to print a couple of shots I thought pertinent and pressed on. There were over a hundred different shots of Mr. Grazly from different angles where the photographer had recorded his hands, his feet, a scrap of mud where his hand had grabbed for purchase in a bid to get away. In all the shots, there was no obvious wound anywhere other than his neck, his clothing was not dishevelled but he was dressed for being indoors with house slippers and a light jumper on rather than shoes and a coat which he would have wanted if he had been intending to be outside for more than a few moments.

I noted this, then drew a short line and wrote: *"lured outside?"*

The photographs moved inside the house next. I expected that every room had been catalogued, in which case, there was no sign of a struggle anywhere that I could see. There was no spray of arterial blood on a wall or ceiling, no overturned lamps or smashed photograph frames. The cottage was neat, tidy and well organised.

Most of the walls were painted in a basic white, matt finish. The wooden window fittings all contrasting in deep glossy black. The furniture was solid oak looking items that might have been in the house since it was built. The few modern touches, such as a chrome toaster and a flat-screen TV with satellite system, stood out in bold contrast to everything else in the house.

In each room, the photographer had taken wide shots of the room and then a close up of various items such as a key press, drawer contents, items spread out on a desk.

'Go back to the keys,' Jagjit demanded suddenly.

I scrolled back a couple of frames until the single shot of the key press came into view. I went back to the previous shot, which was taken from across the room as a wider shot and showed the small glass-fronted cabinet mounted on the wall about five feet up next to a door to the outside. Probably the back door.

It was a cheap store-bought cabinet made specifically for putting keys into. The back panel was perforated so that keys could be hung at any height in neat little rows using plastic hooks that went into the holes. There were three rows of keys and about ten keys per row. Each had been labelled with a plastic label from an old style dynatape machine, the type where the operator is turning a dial and pressing a hard letter into a plastic strip to create the label, which probably meant they had been there for twenty years or more.

Jagjit leaned forward and pointed to the screen. Under his finger was a label that read, *"Family Mausoleum"*.

'What?' I asked unsure what point he was making.

'Nothing, I guess. It just struck me that they have a mausoleum in the castle grounds,' he shrugged. 'Press on mate. I was just surprised and wanted to check what I had actually seen.'

We continued going through the photographs for another ten minutes, but they revealed nothing new. I felt I had taken up enough of Jagjit's evening looking at crime scene evidence when we were supposed to be watching Jason Statham kick people in the teeth.

'Let get back to the movie, shall we?' I asked getting up.

Jagjit nodded his approval to my suggestion and pushed his chair back under the dining table as I reached down to the printer. The wad of paper got a staple through the top left corner to keep it in order, then left on the desk for another time.

As Jagjit headed out of the room, I paused and went back to the computer, calling that I would be through in just a second. I wanted to reply to Amanda and had a question that would keep me awake.

I wrote:

Amanda,

Many thanks for the case file and the trust. I shall not let you down.

I do have an unrelated question though, which is entirely because I am a man and we are confused easily: Why did you kiss me?

Tempest

I hovered my finger over the send button wondering if I should reword it or not but chastised myself once again for being indecisive and clicked on the send icon.

Now, back to Statham.

As he settled into the seat of his BMW i8, Simon Munroe considered that it was cooler today than he had expected. Cool enough, in fact, to make him wish he had started the car ten minutes ago while he was still having breakfast. He rubbed his hands and blew on them while he waited for Michelle. Simon Monroe felt that he had done well in life. He lived in a large house at the top of Bluebell Hill which overlooked the Kent Weald. He owned and ran a successful Public Relations business and had a very pretty girlfriend who was spending most nights at his place now. He liked having her stayover as her presence meant sex every night and most mornings. This morning she had joined him in the shower, which was an absolute favourite. It was only six weeks into the relationship though, he mused to himself as the passenger door opened. Too early to get excited.

'Ready, fair lady?' he smiled across at her as she settled into her seat.

She turned to him, slid a hand across to cradle his stubbled chin and pulled him into a light kiss. 'Take me home so I can get ready for work.'

'Yes, ma'am.'

He pulled the car off his drive, turned left and headed towards town. Michelle fiddled with the radio, bringing up a channel that she favoured and when he next glanced at her she was scrolling through her phone. He checked the clock to see that it now read 0714hrs. He had plenty of time to drop Michelle off and get to his office. He liked to be first in so that he could see his staff arriving and know that he was putting in more hours than anyone else. As he shifted his eyes back to the road, Michelle started screaming. Properly screaming. On the road ahead of them was the most enormous creature. It appeared to be crossing the road from left to right just a few metres away and he was closing on it fast. He yanked the wheel to the left and squeezed around behind the creature, clipping the

175

hedgerow with his mirror as he went. It must be at least seven feet tall, he thought. The observation causing him to stare into his rear-view mirror as it disappeared into the treeline behind him.

'What the hell was that?' He asked, more to himself than Michelle who was out of breath from screaming and now hyperventilating in the seat next to him.

His next thought was to question whether the dashcam was on or not, but as he brought his eyes back from the rear-view mirror to the road, he saw that he had allowed the car to drift. It clipped a bush on the left just as he twitched the wheel to avoid doing so. He overcompensated and in the narrow confines of the country lane, immediately found himself pointed towards trees with too little time to avoid them.

Aiming for a gap, he hit a small silver birch with the left front corner of his car just inboard of the left-hand headlight. A branch smashed through the passenger's window, showering Michelle in glass. She screamed again while he pumped the brake and fought the wheel, but the car was no longer his to control. The area was called Bluebell Hill for topological reasons as much for the local flora. He was heading down a steep decline and gathering speed.

Bouncing off another silver birch, the light sports car spun, then slid sideways until a few feet later the wheels on his side dug into the soft soil. The car flipped, then barrel rolled enough times that he lost count before it slammed mercilessly into the unyielding trunk of an oak tree.

At the top of the slope, the creature looked down at the wrecked car, hesitated, then hurried away.

The morning had started off normally enough. Perhaps if I had turned on the local news, I would have seen what was to come, but I sipped my tea and ate my rolled oats blithely oblivious to the craziness ensuing just a few miles away.

My plan for the day was to swing past the office to check physical mail and to go over email messages. I get emails to my phone like everyone else, but a quiet hour in my office would allow me to sift them properly and to respond to any client enquiries I had received yesterday and had so far given only a cursory response to. I wondered again if I needed an assistant. It was not the first time I had acknowledged the potential need. I even started writing an ad to put in the local paper once. However, I had stopped when I could not work out how I would advertise a job at a paranormal investigation agency without getting morons dressed as the Ghostbusters, or whatever, turning up to be interviewed.

The roads were quiet, so I parked the car in its usual spot, opened the door leading up to my office and then decided to pop into the coffee shop across the road so that I could flirt with Hayley. My mental clock told me she would be there.

Flirting aimlessly with Hayley started several months ago when I saw her nudging her colleague and discussing me as I looked at their sandwiches. From the expression the pair of them had at the time, they were either laughing at me because I had something stuck to my head or were making salacious comments to each other the way people do when they spot someone they fancy. Putting my paranoia aside, I chose at the time to assume they were being naughty, so I had cranked the charm up to eleven and left a big tip. Hayley was short, maybe a shade over five feet and a good few pounds over what the world would consider ideal. I didn't care about that one bit and she was very cute, perhaps mid-

177

twenties, large breasted with straight brown hair that fell to her waist and she smiled all the time.

'Good morning ladies,' I hailed to them both from halfway across the room.

'Hi, Tempest,' I got back from Hayley while her colleague continued serving.

'One of your delightful sticky-toffee Mochaccinos please, Hayley.'

'Skinny, sugar-free syrup, no cream, in a cup to go?'

'Yes, please.'

'Anything else you feel tempted by?' she asked, clearly not meaning the cakes.

'I do have unsatisfied appetites,' I replied, locking her eyes with mine. She had a paper cup in one hand and a pen in the other to write my name and order but had frozen in place, staring at me while the heat amped up. Her tongue darted out to wet her lips as if she were about to speak.

The door chimed behind me as more people entered. Hayley glanced across at them, which broke the spell and we both looked away. Hayley smiled at me once more, her cheeks tinged with pink as she hustled off to make my drink.

I moved to the end of the counter to wait the few moments required and pulled out my phone. No messages this morning, I doubted that would last. Slipping my phone away, I looked up to see three gentlemen dressed as Dog the Bounty Hunter, by which I mean they were clad head to toe in black, wearing big boots and full-length, black leather coats. At the counter, the tallest of them, he must have been six feet and five inches tall, was ordering. Straight blond hair fell to his shoulders, and as

178

he moved, I could see a silver earring dangling from his left ear. Next to him was a shorter man dressed much the same, although his coat nearly touched the floor as if they could not get one short enough for his body frame and he could not consider a different style. His hair was black and spiked, and he had on sunglasses. The rearmost of the three locked eyes with me as I moved my gaze to take him in, he appeared to be trying to look mean. I had no need of pointless distractions, so I broke eye contact.

Hayley brought me my beverage, we exchanged smiles again and I left the shop.

Across the road, Tony Jarvis was waving off an elderly couple from the front step of his Travel Agency. He shook the old fella's hand and he was smiling so my guess was that he had made a sale.

'Hi, Tony. Business doing okay?'

'Not too bad. Just sold a round-the-world trip to that lovely couple for a little over ten thousand pounds. They have been coming to me for over thirty years to book their holidays. I could do with a few more customers like them.'

'I'm sure we all could,' I agreed.

'How about you then, Tempest? Can I interest you in a city break? A week skiing? You look the sort for some winter sun. There must be a young lady you need to take away somewhere.' Tony tried the salesman's approach of sale-by-bombardment every time I ever spoken to him and it was a recognised long-running joke now.

I had never once spent so much as a pound in his shop but the thought of a week skiing in a fabulous resort sounded pretty darned good. Maybe if I got my act together, I could shoehorn something in after Christmas. The trouble was, I always had a case, or cases, ongoing and was too invested in the business to not be available when the phone rang. It was something to consider though.

'Tempting Tony, tempting, but not this time. I need to catch a few more ghosts before I can afford your rates.' I joked.

Up in my office, I set my coffee down and popped the top off so that it would cool to drinking temperature more quickly. I had a few pieces of mail on the mat but they all looked like rubbish. I opened Outlook Express, scrolled to the start of yesterday and began reading and responding to my mail. I had not received a text or email from Amanda regarding my message to her the night before, which was disappointing me a little. There was nothing I could do about it though and while I was itching somewhat to send her another message, checking that she got the first one, there was no way I would permit myself to make so desperate a move.

I had sixty-three emails in total, although many were offering cruises to the Caribbean or drugs to enlarge my penis, so I probably only had ten-real ones. Near the top was one from an odd address that my eye was pulled to: ghidorahsmite@hotmail.com. Ghidorah was a mythical three-headed dragon. Yes, only a geek would know that. Okay. I clicked on it ahead of the other mail.

Mr. Michaels,

Stay away from my quarry little man. You are messing with creatures you cannot hope to survive. Back off and let the professionals tackle this beast.

Vermont Wensdale

Okay, that was fairly weird.

Before I could give it any more thought, I spotted another email two above this one from an equally odd address: ambrogiosilvano@bloodnet.org. Bloodnet? Really? So, what did this one say? I clicked.

Mortal,

You have attacked my followers. I have been killing your kind for over one thousand years and will do so for thousands more. You will die this week, as will all your kin. I will end your bloodline and bathe in your soul.

Ambrogio

The wierdometer was cranked all the way up today. I pushed back in my chair and swivelled to look out the window while I contemplated the two emails. I had one guy telling me to stop pursuing his quarry, although I had no idea which quarry he was referring to, and another that was threatening to kill me and all my family for involving myself in the first place. Involve me in what though?

I knew nothing about Vermont Wensdale nor Ambrogio Silvano, so I performed a most basic google search. Ambrogio Silvano was simply not in there, although it did reveal that Ambrogio was an Italian word meaning immortal. Vermont Wensdale, however, produced loads of hits. He was a famous American that killed vampires and werewolves and other supernatural creatures for a living. He had several books one could buy which I assumed would chronical his activities. I wondered if he was a genuine nutbag or just an author who had found a great way to promote his books. The picture of him looked like the chap in the coffee shop, the tallest of the three Dog the Bounty Hunters.

I further searched for Ghidorasmite to see if that was a company name but turned up nothing except Wikipedia references to the three-headed dragon. Bloodnet, however, did produce a result. It was a cyberpunk game from the nineties and a forum for Angel and Buffy fans. Not a lot of help there then.

I bet myself that Frank would know more about the subject so got up out of my chair and went to see him.

Frank Decaux turned up at my office on the morning the first advert for Blue Moon Paranormal Investigations ran. He was nearly foaming at the mouth with excitement that there was another true believer with which he could converse. He had expected to find Buffy the Vampire Slayer or the Winchesters from Supernatural, so was thoroughly deflated to discover I had no belief in the paranormal and simply sought to exploit the foolish nonsense my numerous clients clung to. He had bounced back quickly though, determining that he would be my inside source, my font of knowledge and that through my investigations I would prove to myself that there were occurrences that could not be explained. That werewolves, ghouls and other creatures were, in fact, living amongst us and not just fictional. Frank was mental. Safe mental though and weighed less than fifty kilograms so could not easily be dangerous without getting hold of some decent weaponry.

He owned and ran an occult bookshop called Mystery Men just around the corner from my office, so I was at his door in under a minute. It was an odd little place which he had opened straight out of school in the mid-eighties. Upstairs from a florist, in what would once have been a back bedroom of a terraced house, he had dark fantasy and horror novels stacked floor to ceiling. On the walls leading up the stairs to the shop were posters from old horror movies or sci-fi movies and grainy pictures of beasts and creatures taken years ago, such as the Loch Ness monster and Bigfoot. In the shop, the piles of books arranged on numerous shelves at first appeared to be completely haphazard, but soon one discovered that rather than alphabetically by author or title, they were arranged by creature and then by fiction and non-fiction. The more serious the book, the closer it was to the counter. Inside the glass counter at the front were old leather-bound books that one should probably call grimoires.

183

There were a few limited-edition models around that had unbelievable price tags on them, such as a model of Buffy the Vampire Slayer dispatching a pair of Vampires. One was caught mid-dust as the stake hung in the now exploded body and the other was reeling from a freshly delivered spin kick to the head. It was perhaps fifteen inches tall and the price tag was twelve thousand pounds. I wanted to scoff, but had once checked out Mystery Men on Companies House and found that it was doing very well. I had to acknowledge that he knew what he was doing.

As I went up the stairs past the posters, I wondered if Frank's assistant Poison would be working today. Although I doubt Poison is her actual name, it is the one on her name badge and what she appears to be called by everyone. She wears goth make-up, or should that be Emo now? Regardless, that is the style she goes for, she has black nails and several piercings, hair which changes colour quite often. She is nineteen, athletic and is super, super hot. She also flirts openly every time I see her. I say flirts, but a not uncommon opening sentence from her would be: "So when are you going to let me bed you?" I can't for the life of me work out why I am resisting, but there seems something wrong with bedding girls that are easily young enough to be my children. Plus, I am not sure if her flirting is serious, given that she could have virtually any man she chose and might very well flirt with every customer as a sales tactic.

With that thought dying on my brow, I pushed open the door, which Frank has rigged with a chime that does not chime but creaks like a crypt door being opened. Inside the shop, with their backs to me, I found the three Dog the Bounty Hunter looking chaps from the coffee shop. The tallest of the three was at the counter flanked by the other two on either side like guards. The pair of them both turned to lock eyes with me. A beat passed with me stood in the doorway. I was looking at them, they were looking at me. I glanced to the till to see Poison, but not Frank, then the spell broke as Frank emerged from a back room behind the till.

184

He was carrying a large grimoire and spoke before looking up. 'Rasfell's Undead Guide should provide all the information you require gentlemen.' He set the book on the counter carefully then looked up. 'Oh.'

'Good morning, Frank.' I closed the door and moved into the shop which had barely enough room now that there are six of us in it. I was damned certain I was not going to hang around by the door looking intimidated and had no reason to be. These chaps dressed uniquely but they had given no indication of animosity thus far.

'Be with you in a moment, Tempest. I'll just help these gentlemen out and...'

'Tempest?' interrupted the one with the long blond hair, turning around. 'Tempest Michaels?'

'Yes. Pleased to meet you.' I recognised him immediately as I had been looking at his face online just a few minutes ago. It was Vermont Wensdale. I reached into my pocket for a card, but his friends moved forward to block me and I could hear their leather gloves creaking as they curled their fists. I took a step back to give myself moving room, already feeling my pulse quicken. 'Not a great place to fight, chaps,' I said through gritted teeth.

'Now, gentlemen,' interjected Frank, but I cut him off

'Let's take this outside before we destroy the shop, shall we?'

Vermont raised both his hands, palms towards me and blocking his companions. 'Stand down,' he instructed them, which resulted in the pair instantly relaxing and visibly losing interest in me. He was very clearly the boss. 'I apologise for my associates,' he drawled slowly in an American accent. I couldn't place the accent to any region, I was not worldly enough for that but somewhere among the Southern states was accurate enough

185

for me. 'I am Vermont Wensdale of the Vermont Wensdales. You will have received an email from me this morning but have negated my desire to seek you out by finding me instead.'

'I got your email.' I saw no reason to expand.

'I hunt supernatural creatures, Mr. Michaels. I hunt them and kill them and have travelled the world doing this for many years. I am experienced, tenacious, I know my enemy, I have a team of people supporting me and I am protected by God.' The last one made my eyebrows rise.

'Are you protected by God, Mr. Michaels?'

This was not a question I had been asked before. I found myself jostling between making fun of this guy because he was clearly bonkers and wanting to disarm him with a sensible answer that would satisfy him and get him out of the shop and out of my way. In the end, I settled for, 'Why were you looking for me?'

'Because you are in my way and likely to get yourself killed, Mr. Michaels. You are looking for a vampire, a particularly aggressive one and I doubt you possess the ability or the nerve to defeat and destroy him. I, however, do have the nerve, Mr. Michaels. I know this because I have killed over one hundred vampires already on four continents. I am not here to brag, Mr. Michaels. I am here to destroy a monster and to save lives. Yours amongst them.' This was all delivered in a voice that could have made commercials. It was silky and smooth, and each word was carefully and exactly delivered. 'I want to compliment you on your recent investigation of the werewolf. The story had just come to my attention when I learned that you had revealed the beast to be nothing more than a man. It is fortunate for you that it was not a true lycanthrope for you would not have survived such an encounter.'

186

I didn't see much point in arguing with this guy. He clearly believed he is out there killing vampires which made me wonder what he was killing, which made me wonder if I stood toe to toe with a crazy serial killer who offs anyone with slightly long canines. Time to wrap this up. 'I shall consider myself well advised, Mr. Wensdale. I wish you good luck in your quest,' I attempted to deliver it with sincerity so that he would take the hook and leave me in peace. I could investigate him more fully later.

We stared at each other for a few seconds, which I didn't like because I had to look up at him, but he slapped me hard on the shoulder and turned away. 'Well done, Mr. Michaels,' he said over his shoulder. 'I did not expect you to see reason. Stefan, please pay the lady, we must make preparations while our quarry sleeps.'

The shortest of the three with the spiky hair and sunglasses must be Stefan since he reached for his wallet and handed a card to Poison. The grimoire went into a bag and I saw four hundred pounds rung up on the till. Nice one Frank, I thought to myself.

'Thank you, come again,' Poison called after them as they filed out the door and down the stairs. Then I heard her say, 'Hi, Tempest.'

I turned from watching Vermont leave to see Poison smiling at me still behind the counter. She had on a royal blue crop top that matched her eye makeup and lipstick and a black sports bra thing underneath. Her toned belly was visible above the counter with something black and sparkly adorning her excellent midriff.

'Good morning, Poison.' I replied while forcing my attention away from her perfect body. I focused on Frank. 'Rasfell's Undead Guide, Frank? Do you make these yourself?'

187

'That book was first published over three hundred years ago Tempest, it is incredibly rare and obviously no longer in print. I have another copy though if you wish to know what they know,' Frank said smiling.

'Another time perhaps, Frank. But tell me, what did they want.'

'You don't know Vermont Wensdale do you, Tempest?'

'No, should I?'

'Tempest, Vermont Wensdale is a legend. His books are on the shelf behind you.' I looked where he was pointing and sure enough, there were several books just a few feet from me. I selected one at random and turned it, so that the cover was facing me. The title read, "Supernatural Beasts of Lower Saxony." There is a picture of Vermont Wensdale holding a sword, cape fluttering in a breeze. 'I have some signed copies if you are quick. I didn't mess around when I saw the chance to improve the value of my stock. Signed copies are worth five times as much. I did nearly mess my pants when he just walked into my shop. Imagine it, Vermont Wensdale, living legend just popped into my shop. I will be blogging about this. Poison did you get pictures?'

'Of course, Frank. It was kind of hard not to get the hint that you wanted them. I even got a shot of you and he bent over looking at his latest book.'

'Great,' said Frank, beaming ear to ear. 'Get tweeting and Facebooking on all the usual groups please.' Poison pulled her phone from a back pocket where my groin instantly assured me it must have been deliciously warm from its proximity to her pert, tight, athletic little bum.

Frank's attention swung from her to me, diverting my attention thankfully from her derriere. 'What was it you came in for, Tempest? Is it the *Vampire* case?'

188

'Sort of. I guess. I wanted to ask you who Vermont Wensdale is, but I seem to have covered that one. I also got an email from Ambrogio Silvano last night. Ever heard of him?'

'Ambrogio Silvano? Not a name I recognise. What is it in connection with?'

'He emailed to tell me I had meddled in his business and he was going to end my bloodline. My assumption is that he is another kook that thinks he is a vampire and feels offended by the minor debacle in Aylesford yesterday.'

'Well, if he is a vampire,' Frank would usually pick up on my dismissal of the possibility that it could be a supernatural creature, 'then the name would be in Rasfell's Undead Guide. I'll get my copy, shall I?' Frank tutted and shook his head while he turned to retreat into the same back room I saw him emerge from earlier. A few seconds later he came back out carrying another copy of the leather-bound tome.

He placed the book on the counter and thumbed it open close to the last few pages. 'Vampires are at the back next to werewolves. You might think that alphabetically obvious, but this is the only guide that works that way and that is because most of them are translated directly from whichever language they were originally written in. Anyway, I digress.' He thumbed a few more pages. 'Ambrogio Silvano. Here he is. Italian vampire from the 9th century. Thought to have been killed in 1576AD during the great vampire purge set by Pope Pius V. You say you had an email from him?'

'Yes, I got it last night. He seems quite upset about something I have done but was not specific about what it was. He was however specific about killing me and everyone in my family. I wondered if there could be some connection with the Maidstone vampire-wannabes I met yesterday.'

Frank looked like King Arthur had just offered him a seat at the roundtable. He had a stunned yet euphoric look on his face as if something wonderful has just happened. 'Are you asking me to join you on a quest?'

'Well, not exactly,' I began.

'You need my help to solve a mystery, Tempest. You won't find me wanting.' He seemed utterly gleeful. 'I'll get right on it. Leave it to me to track down the source of the email. Can you forward it to me?'

I pulled my phone and clicked a few buttons. 'On its way to you now, Frank. Now if you will excuse me, I am going to leave that with you and get back to work.' I put my phone away, but before I could move, Frank came around the counter and grabbed my arm. I turned back to face him.

'Tempest, I am worried for you. You continue to deny the existence of the very creature you pursue. A creature that is most probably ancient, immortal and incredibly powerful. Vampires preying so openly are rare, so this one is either so powerful that he believes he can't be stopped, or he has gone crazy which makes him an immortal, indestructible death machine. Let me help you if you must pursue him. I can help to protect you, I have weapons, I have knowledge. I'm not saying I can fight a vampire, but I can help to keep you safe because you can't fight one either and I worry that you might just try to do so.'

'Frank, I am touched. Deeply. But the recent murders have been committed by a person with a fetish. A vampire-wannabe, not an actual vampire. I don't know who he is, or where he is, or why he is doing it, but I plan to find him and hurt him.'

'Why?' Frank was stood there waiting for some revelation from me. What was driving me to pursue a criminal that was already being pursued by the police and now by a professional vampire hunter? 'Frank, I may

190

discuss my motivation one day,' I paused, smiled and turned to Poison to deliver the killer line, 'but not with the lights on.' Okay, I stole the line from my dad, but it was a good one and I managed to deliver it without someone whacking my nuts.

Poison smirked and dipped her head to look at me cheekily through her fringe. Frank tutted and shook his head.

'You are my font of knowledge, Frank. Let me know what you find on crazy Italian vampire dude.' I grabbed the door handle behind me, pirouetted flamboyantly and exited the store. As I went down the stairs a text pinged in my pocket. I checked the screen and saw PC Hotstuff as the sender. Damning myself for being hesitant, even as I was hesitating, I opened the message.

It read: "Hi, Tempest. Sorry about the kiss, I couldn't resist it. Your mum is just like mine - always trying to marry me off or find me a husband."

That was all she wrote.

I was walking back past the coffee shop towards my office rereading the message and trying to work out what it meant, when my phone rang. I didn't recognise the number, so answered with my professional voice. 'Blue Moon Investigations, Tempest Michaels speaking. How may I help you?'

'Mr. Michaels?' A woman's voice, middle-aged, fifties or early sixties maybe, educated and confident. 'You investigate unusual events? The paranormal and all that?'

'That is correct. I specialise in cases that have a supernatural or unexplained element.'

'Then we need to meet, Mr. Michaels. My name is Rita Sweeting-Brand. My daughter is currently in hospital swearing she was attacked by a seven-foot creature that was neither bear, nor man, nor anything else of this earth - the so-called Bluebell Bigfoot. Her boyfriend crashed his car when they came across it early this morning. He died at the scene.' her voice failed to waver at all in breaking that news I noticed. 'The police are not taking her account seriously. The two of them were doing drugs last night and he was still under the influence, whatever you call it, this morning.'

I had fumbled for my keys and opened the office door as I listened to Mrs. Sweeting-Brand. While scribbling names and brief details I asked, 'Where are you now, Mrs. Sweeting-Brand? How soon can we meet?'

'I am still at Maidstone hospital A&E as that is where the ambulance took my daughter. Her injuries are minor but,' she paused. 'Perhaps you should come here.' I noted again how calm and unflustered her voice seemed, but also detected an angry and possibly impatient undertone as if this were all simply unacceptable.

192

I checked my watch: 1150hrs. Mental calculation ran for a second or so before I answered, 'I can be with you within the hour, Mrs. Sweeting-Brand. I have your number but should be able to find both you and your daughter easily enough. I will meet you in A&E.'

'Within the hour, Mr. Michaels.' She hung up.

I checked my watch again, more from habit than needing to see what the time was. I packed a few bits, closed the office again and went home to grab a quick lunch and let the dogs out on my way to the hospital.

Those few small tasks took less than forty minutes and the drive to the hospital a further six. Parking at Maidstone Hospital is a pain though, so despite the ticking clock, I could not predict how long it would take me to find a space. They had expanded the car park a few years ago but finding a space was a fight unless it was particularly early or late. Luck was on my side though, as just then I saw reverse lights come on a few cars in front of me and an aging Austin Allegro began to inch out of a convenient space.

There was an older gentleman at the wheel, with a well-dressed, but equally aged lady sitting in the passenger seat. She appeared to be chatting amiably while he drove, so they had not been in to receive grave news. Allowing myself a few happy thoughts about long-married couples, I pulled into the now empty space and killed the engine.

I passed an out of order car park ticket payment machine on my way in, making a mental note that I would have to look around for another one on my way out. The reception door swished open as I got to it, the automatic sensor working overtime to keep up with the continuous flow of people. I squirted a blob of sanitary wash stuff on my left hand from a dispenser on the wall. Above it was a poster of a stern woman in hospital scrubs looking down at me and warning of infection. I paused to check the hospital colour coordinated map as I rubbed the alcohol into my hands, and set off to the left where I already knew A&E was located.

Entering A&E, I checked my watch to make sure I had arrived within the hour. Mrs. Sweeting-Brand did not seem the type to tolerate tardiness. Only fifty-three minutes had elapsed, so I was safe.

I stopped at the A&E reception desk where a short dumpy lady in her mid-fifties with greying hair and a bored expression, was already dealing with someone. However, I could identify Mrs. Sweeting-Brand as the lady ten metres away talking to a younger version of herself in the bed next to her. She was easy to pick from the crowd, as ruling out the very young and very old adults in the room left a diminished subset of options. Listening earlier to the voice of Mrs. Sweeting-Brand it had sounded to me like she wore clothing by Hobbs and coats by Laura Ashley. It was exactly what the lady in front of me had on.

'Mrs. Sweeting-Brand?' I called at a volume she would hear.

The lady I believed to be Mrs. Sweeting-Brand turned towards me at the sound of her name and motioned her head ever so slightly to beckon me over.

I extended my hand. 'Mrs. Sweeting-Brand, good day to you. This is your daughter?' I enquired, quite certain that it was. Her daughter looked to be in her mid-twenties and was a very attractive brunette who would have captured my attention under any circumstances. The bedclothes were pulled up to just below her breasts and above them, she wore a hospital gown of the backless type as if ready for surgery. She had on no bra and the cool breeze flowing through A&E from the Ambulance/ Paramedic entry doors had made her nipples stand out beneath the cloth. I focused away from them and onto her face which was a mass of bruises

194

and small cuts. Her hair was a mess where she had cut her head and bled profusely into it.

'I am Michelle Sweeting-Brand,' stated the woman in the bed, raising her own hand to shake mine. Her voice was even and calm. Whatever excitement had led her here it had passed, and she seemed over it for now.

I pulled a card from my pocket and handed it to Mrs. Sweeting-Brand. She had shaken my hand but did not consider that I needed to know her first name or even that she should return my salutation. I ignored it, hospitals and loved ones in accidents were stressful, trying times and could make anyone's manners slip.

'Mrs. Sweeting-Brand. How may I help you?' I asked.

'Mr. Michaels my daughter has been injured and claims...'

'I don't claim, mother,' interrupted Michelle. 'It was a seven-foot beast creature. I'm sorry I didn't stop to take pictures for you while Simon was crashing the car and dying.' A tear escape the corner of her right eye as she looked away.

'Well, there you have it, Mr. Michaels.' Mrs. Sweeting-Brand locked eyes with me for a second and walked away, clearly expecting me to follow. 'My daughter is a high fashion model and her looks are her career. The injuries to her face are ruinous, she may never work again. She has so little other talent, I can't imagine what else she might do. I don't for one minute believe that what Michelle saw was a genuine creature, it will be some fool dressing up. I want this person found Mr. Michaels, found so that I can sue them. Sue them into the ground.'

Mrs. Sweeting-Brand was a little scary.

A nurse had come over to calm Michelle who was now sobbing quietly and being ignored by her mother. 'My daughter is also given to taking drugs, although she thinks I am too blind to see it. Cocaine, that sort of thing. Whatever she saw could be dismissed as a bad trip if it had not been seen by several others, so I am prepared to accept that she saw something. Can you focus your attention on this matter, Mr. Michaels?'

I wondered if she was ever anything but direct. 'I can Mrs. Sweeting-Brand and I can start my investigation today.' She nodded as if acknowledging that this was satisfactory, and I thought for a moment she was going to ask why I was not busier.

'Good. I can't abide waiting.' I believed her. 'How soon will you be able to reveal this miscreant?'

'I can give you daily reports by email if you wish, but I can't make any predictions about what I will find or how quickly I can resolve this if at all. You understand that at this point I have very little to go on and would be very foolish to guarantee a result.

'But I expect a result, Mr. Michaels. Otherwise, why engage you? I will give you three days. If I see no compelling reason to retain you after that I will look for a more qualified investigator.' Good luck finding one I thought to myself.

Our business seemed concluded, so we briefly discussed costs and she assured me she would transfer funds in full for three days by the end of the day. She shook my hand once more and I left, glancing over my shoulder only once to find she had not bothered to return to her distressed and injured daughter but was at the counter berating the woman there for something.

I pulled up at my house to find Frank's car parked on the road and him sitting in it. It was not the first time he had ever come to my house, but it was a rare occurrence nevertheless. From my car, I could see he had spotted my arrival and was now wrestling with something heavy on his passenger seat. As I got out and locked up, he was still wrestling so I opened his passenger door and crouched down to see what he was doing.

'Need a hand, Frank?'

Beaming, smiley face as usual. 'I think I know what the Bluebell Bigfoot is. I brought some reference material over.'

I looked at the pile of books and A4 pages on the passenger seat. 'Shall I take these inside?'

'I could use a hand,' he agreed and together we scooped it all up and headed down the path to my place.

'I thought you were looking for information on vampires, Frank. In particular, the one that is threatening to kill me and all my kin.'

'Ah well, that was easy research, so I had Poison do it while I busied myself looking into the Bluebell Bigfoot. Don't worry though I have lots of information about Ambrogio and his followers.'

'He has followers?'

'Oh, yes. He is one of the oldest vampires in Europe, at least of those that are known to still be hunting and therefore he has many children'

'Wait. Children?'

'You know, turned vampires,' Frank explained in a tone that suggested I was being particularly dense.

198

I juggled the books I was carrying so I could get my keys up to the door and used them to push it open, shooing the dogs with my foot as I went to prevent tripping on them.

'So,' Frank continued, 'Ambrogio will have turned many former lovers' etcetera into vampires across the many centuries he has lived. Of course, I can't say exactly how old he is, but I was able to trace him back to 12th Century Rome as I showed you earlier, so let's call it an even thousand years at least. Each of these children will have turned some more, so he has quite a family. Then there are those that want to be turned.'

'Vampires-wannabes,' I interjected. I suppose it made as much sense as putting a poster of a footballer on the wall.

'Essentially yes, Tempest. Vampire groupies might be a better term of reference though. They form groups and communicate with the real vampires in the hope that they can perform tasks for them. Then, through their display of loyalty earn their trust, and in so doing, the right to be turned.'

Both Frank and I had arrived in the kitchen just a few paces from the front door. We dumped the piles of books onto the kitchen counter where it formed a breakfast bar. I grabbed the kettle and held it up to Frank by way of a question.

'Always, Tempest. Milk, two sugars please.'

NATO standard brew I reflected, remembering my army days. Funny that I could not hear milk and two sugars without connecting the military term for it. White no sugar was Julie Andrews… white none (nun) or Whoopie Goldberg for black no sugar (black nun): army humour.

I flicked the kettle on. 'I just need to let the dogs out,' I explained as I headed out of the room to find the boys in their usual feverish excitement by the back door. Seconds later I could hear them outside chasing unseen birds or cats as I came back into the kitchen. The kettle clicked off, so I made the tea while Frank sifted the pages and books into some kind of order. I glanced across as I stirred the milk in, I could see perhaps one hundred little, coloured flags stuck to pages in the various books he had assembled.

'You were telling me about vampire groupies,' I prompted.

'Yes, vampire groupies. You met some the other day actually, Obsidian Dark and his bunch - local Kent vampire group.'

'You mean they were not real vampires?'

Frank stopped moving and stared at me, his face incredulous. 'They were out in daylight, Tempest. Of course, they weren't real vampires.' I had momentarily forgotten that Frank took everything very seriously and that my flippancy was wasted on him.

'No, Frank. Of course not. However, Ambrogio is a real vampire?'

'Yes, Tempest. How is it that you came to be a paranormal investigator again? You don't seem to know anything about the paranormal.'

I was looking at the paperwork in front of me, wondering, not for the first time whether he might have a point. Did I need to engage in some serious study of the subject? Sighing, I replied, 'I appear to know enough for now.'

'Well, there seem to be some considerable gaps in your knowledge, Mr. Michaels. So many in fact that I am not sure where to begin.'

'Let's start with you telling me about the Kent vampire groupies and how they fit in with Ambrogio and then tell me about Ambrogio and don't forget to include lots of detail about why he wants to kill me. How about that? Then you can tell me what you think the Bluebell Bigfoot is if it is not some nut in a suit.' I picked up my tea for a sip and wished I had a chocolate digestive to go with it.

'Alllrighty-then,' said Frank, as he sat on one of the breakfast-counter stools. He sifted through a ream of paper - some loose single leaves and some a stack of pages stapled together. 'Here we are,' he said producing what looked like a colour flyer.

The flyer was for the Brotherhood of the Dead LARP vampire club. LARP I knew stood for Live Action Role Play, I found the concept ridiculous, but it was not my role to judge and I had no right to any opinion on other person's hobbies and pursuits. The Brother Hood of the Dead met twice a week on Mondays and Thursdays. The font was in red type and appeared to be leaking blood. The flyer advertised real vampire encounters, true believers welcome, come along and join the undead.

'Where did you get the flyer?'

'Off the wall in my shop.'

'Lovely. Will they be kidnapping virgins and draining each other's blood?'

'No, but they will be fantasising about both those things I expect. We get them in the shop sometimes. The clubs all follow real vampires, they contact them, perform tasks for them, beg them to visit and turn them. That sort of thing. I believe they all partake in drinking blood which they claim to be human. I can't tell you where they get it from or if it is chicken blood or something else, but they can be quite intense and a little scary when they want to be. And they are all believers.' Frank went quiet for a moment thinking. 'You saw on the News that the Demedicus kid had human blood from one of the murder victims on his clothes?'

'Yes, it was blood from the second victim - the little old lady. I got information from a friend on the force this morning. He has confessed to the murders, so I guess they keep him I until they can prove it wasn't him.'

'You think he is innocent?'

'Innocent might be a stretch, but the kid I met did not give off a violent vibe. I doubt he could have overpowered the first victim either, so I don't think he killed anyone, but I think he knows who did. He got the blood from somewhere. You said they perform tasks. Like what?

'I don't know actually. I am just patching bits together from conversations in the shop but typically I should think it would be arranging collection of their coffins and delivering them places when they visit certain countries, providing volunteers for them to feed on. Ooh, I bet Ambrogio will turn to them to deliver on his threats to you!' Frank appeared excited at the prospect of vampire nutters attacking me.

'Okay,' was the only answer I could come up with. 'So, what is the deal with Ambrogio? Why does he want to bathe in my soul?'

'My guess would be that he is in direct contact with the Brotherhood of the Dead vampires, given how soon after the incident with Demedicus and Obsidian he emailed you, and that he has taken personal insult in your meddling. It could be that he is the founder of their group or that they do his bidding. He is an old vampire and therefore very powerful.'

'Alright, Frank. I get the picture,' I cut him off. 'I need to go talk to the Brotherhood of the Dead and get this settled now before someone does something stupid. You really think they would attack me just because some nutter tells them to?'

Frank kind of shrugged. Helpful.

'So, Ambrogio is a master vampire from Italy who may be controlling a bunch of local vampire groupies that may or may not have orders to kill me. Got it. Now tell me about the Bluebell Bigfoot.'

Frank's eyes lit up and his grin broadened.

Frank had filled me in on the recent sightings but had then produced older reports of a beast with a similar description from the sixties, seventies, eighties, and nineties. There were credible and, in some cases, detailed reports of a large bipedal creature that had been spotted at various sites in the area. No attacks were reported though, so the excitement, if one wished to call it that, was simply because they could not identify what they had seen. It was little more than background information and would have no bearing on what had been seen recently unless it proved to be the same chap doing the same daft thing for fifty years.

Frank had also produced a picture that had been drawn in pencil by one of the persons that had encountered the beast in 1983. Mr. Carl Morris had drawn a creature that anyone could recognise as the known image of the North American Big Foot or Himalayan Abominable Snowman. Also known as Sasquatch, it was drawn in a fearsome manner as if caught frozen in mid-attack. The creature had a row of pointed teeth and huge canines such as one might find on a lion or other big cat. Both hands were raised to show clawed digits. The appearance of these features could have been taken from a werewolf drawing and I had to wonder how much Carl had embellished the drawing. Had he been attacked by this creature, surely, he would not have survived.

Frank's theory was that the creature currently being spotted in the Bluebell Hill area was, in fact, a Cowlco, an ancient creature that hibernated for much of its life, was mostly nocturnal and fed only every several years. Frank showed me a drawing of one, similar in many ways to the drawing by Mr. Morris in an old book on mystical creatures. But he dismissed the drawing by Mr. Morris as, according to the text he was showing me, the Cowlco was not known to be carnivorous. I dismissed it all as utter nonsense.

I had a list of sites where the Bluebell Bigfoot had been seen. There were only four of them and they were all within a couple of miles radius of each other. I noted where each of them was and fetched my walking boots. It was threatening to drizzle but it was still dry for the time being, so I called for the dogs. Not more than two minutes later we were out the door and piling into the car.

The nearest site was less than a mile from my house. I parked as close to it as I could get, clipped the dogs to their leads and set off to see what I could find. I entered a field in which the McCarthys had claimed to have seen the Bigfoot several weeks ago. I estimated from the picture the paper had shown, that I was now stood in the general area they had been and that the creature would have been in the tree-line now opposite me and up the hill.

Bluebell Hill is jolly steep in places, so it was a slog to go the short route that I took directly across the field. The field was firm underfoot but damp from recent rainfall. It appeared to be a crop field, possibly some kind of corn, which at this time of the year was nothing but tiny nubs of stalk poking from the dirt.

I got into the tree-line and worked my way along it. I was looking for signs of movement. A large creature will break twigs, leave footprints in the soil or scraps of fur on the branches of trees and bushes as it passes close by. I found nothing. The dogs were happy to look for rabbits and I had to keep calling them back lest they saw one and were too far away for me to retrieve. Dachshunds are small enough to get down a rabbit hole and difficult to get out.

I got on my hand and knees to look at suspect scrapes in the leaf litter and soil a few times but soon decided that there was simply nothing to find.

'Oi!' said a voice from behind me.

I turned to face it and found the owner of the voice to be an older gentleman with a shotgun in the crook of his right arm.

'This is my spot,' he said.

'Your spot for what?' I wanted to know.

'Don't play silly buggers, young-un.' I was such a fan of being talked down to. Ire already rising, I took a definite step forward into his personal space and then looked down at him. He was wearing a green tweed-mix with his socks rolled over the bottom half of his trousers and a heavy roll neck jumper to keep the cold out. His hair was a thick wave of grey and white with just a few bits of black left to show the original colour. The style of it looked like he had set it in 1974 when this look might have last been fashionable and then never changed it since.

I gave him credit for not taking a step back, but it left me almost pressing chests with him. I was not going to step back either, so instead, I grabbed his shotgun. In one swift move I snatched the weapon with my left hand and pushed him back a pace with my right. With neither hand on it, the shotgun was mine before he could get his hands out of his pockets. I broke the breech and ejected the cartridge. It plopped onto the soil and was snatched up by Dozer who then ran off with his prize.

'Hey, what the devil are you playing at?'

'I am walking my dogs and I don't like your tone.' He reached for the shotgun, so I slapped his hand away. 'Now, my question again. Your spot for what?'

He looked distinctly less confident now. 'For catching the Bigfoot.'

You must be joking was what I wanted to say, but in my line of work, I would spend all day saying that. Instead, I went with a straightforward, 'What?'

'The Bigfoot was seen here. If it comes back, I am going to kill it and be famous.'

I sighed. 'If you shoot the Bigfoot you will find a man inside a suit and will be guilty of manslaughter, but you will definitely not be famous. Are there any more of you out here?'

'I, I don't know,' he said looking around. 'What do you mean about a man in a suit? Do you mean the Bigfoot isn't a real Bigfoot?' He looked stunned at the possibility that he might be wasting his time.

'Of course, it is a man in a suit. Dear God, man. While you are out here getting cold and damp, the fool that has been dressing up is at work, or at the gym or doing anything other than wandering around in a Bigfoot suit waiting for you to shoot him. After the death yesterday, I doubt he will be seen again.' I offered him his gun and called to Dozer who still had the ejected case. 'Go home. Stay there.' Dozer had seen that I was after the casing so had run off so I would chase him.

'Are you sure it's not a real Bigfoot?' he called after me, but I had already walked away. I didn't bother to answer and when I caught sight of him as I left the field, he was trudging slowly down the hill and back towards the road.

The second site, where Dr. Bryson claimed to have seen the Bigfoot, was just as devoid of any trace of hair or fur or marks that might indicate a large creature had been through. I tried to find where he had discovered the footprint, but any trace of it was long gone. Leaves were falling to cover the ground so even if it was still here it would be well covered.

I didn't bother going to the other sites. Instead, I went home, made tea and looked up the people that had reported seeing the creature.

It took a couple of attempts to find a number for the McCarthys, but I managed to catch Mrs. McCarthy at home. She recited her tale to me quite willingly and it matched what I had read in the reports online and in the papers. I believed that she and her husband had seen something. I asked her what she thought it was, but she did not want to be tied to an answer. She expressed that she doubted very much that there was a Bigfoot roaming around Bluebell Hill but that she also had no idea what she had seen if it was not a Bigfoot. She also said that she would not be going anywhere other than the park to walk her dog for a long time.

I thanked her for her time and called the next person. The next person believed they had definitely seen a Bigfoot, no doubt about it. Once again, I felt sure they believed what they were saying. The next name was the last on my list and the one I considered to be the most interesting - Dr. Barry Bryson. Dr. Bryson was a chap who ought to know his stuff given his knowledge of Zoology and such.

Online searches revealed basic information such as a relationship with an estranged wife, pictures of a couple of children and information such as his education, career, and current employment. Dr. Bryson was the manager of a wildlife park less than a mile from my house. I switched my search and found the postcode, grabbed my keys and jacket and headed out to see if he was there.

I could have walked there with the dogs given the distance involved, but then I doubted a wildlife park would welcome domesticated dogs and leaving them outside in the cooling air for an indeterminate period seemed folly. Instead, I left them at home sleeping and whizzed two minutes around the corner to a place I had passed thousands of times, but never once thought to stop at.

Kent Predators and Prey Wildlife Park was not a large place and looked like it badly needed a new investor. The car park could easily hold one hundred cars and I could see a sign for an overflow carpark leading to a field but there were only two cars present at 1504hrs on a Tuesday. Perhaps they did better in the holidays. The cars both had foreign plates, one I recognised as French and one had an E on it. Is that Spain or Estonia? I could not remember.

The wooden fence at the leading edge of the property was old, worn and broken. The path leading into the main building was full of weeds and no longer even. A post where a litter bin would once have been mounted held just a fraction of the broken lid mechanism, the bin and the rest of the lid may have been missing for some time.

I could see through the windows and into what looked like a reception/shop area, but there was no sign of life. I pushed the door open and went inside. There was no noise other than that from the motor of an old drinks dispenser whirring away to my left.

'Hello?' I called with a measured amount of volume and authority. There was an almost immediate sound of movement from somewhere behind the reception counter and a lady appeared. She was perhaps in her early fifties, just over five feet tall and plump with a pleasant face. Like a stereotyped farmer's wife perhaps with red cheeks from seasons spent outside.

She met me with a smile. 'Good afternoon and welcome to Predators and Prey,' her greeting delivered with practiced polish.

'Good afternoon, Margaret,' I responded, reading the name badge on her chest. 'How is today treating you?' I held that people were in general much more likely to provide answers if you established a brief rapport before quizzing them on subjects they might well otherwise resist interrogation over.

'Very well, thank you,' came her reply. 'But we close at four o'clock. If you were hoping to come in, I'm afraid you will be very short on visiting time.'

'Actually, I am here to see Dr. Bryson. Is he in today?'

'One moment please while I check that he is available.' She bustled off into the back office. I could hear a brief exchange, although I could not make out what was being said. I heard the scrape of a chair as someone stood to get up and it was a man that came out into the reception area first.

'Dr. Bryson?' I enquired with a hopeful and cheerful tone, wanting to set him at ease. I left any further words until he had confirmed or denied I had the right man.

'Yes, I am Barry Bryson,' the man looked unhappy. I need to embellish that to get the picture across though. The man in front of me, whether it was Barry Bryson or not, looked hopelessly lost, as if the entire weight of the world was on his shoulders and there was no escape from the horror that was his life. He was a tall and broad-shouldered man, perhaps six feet eight inches tall, but he was hunched over as if deflated, so it was hard to gauge an accurate height. His shoulders were drooping, and his head quite bowed as if it were hard to hold up. Even his face appeared to be sagging.

I knew his age to be forty-five or forty-six just from his school year which I found on Facebook, but he looked ten years older than that. I logged this information for later consideration.

Margaret had followed Barry back in and had taken up position a few feet away straightening the little handouts at the side of the counter, clearly doing something vaguely work-related while conveniently eavesdropping.

'Dr. Bryson,' I started.

'Barry, please,' he interrupted.

'Barry, I'm Tempest Michaels. I am investigating recent reports of a Bigfoot seen in this area for the mother of Michele Sweeting-Brand, the woman who was injured yesterday and hoped we might talk about what you saw.' I focused on his face to see what reaction would surface. If possible, he sagged a little further. Was it guilt I was looking at? Had he made it up? He would not be the first person to report a paranormal sighting that turned out to be a big fat lie. Sounding and looking utterly defeated, he invited me back to his office where we could chat in private.

Barry's office looked like the rest of the Park, and like Barry himself for that matter in that, it was tired and worn out and sagging at the seams. Shelves dominating one wall contained mostly box files, arranged by year on some shelves and by alphabet on others. Most would not stand straight and were battered to breaking point.

Barry went around the desk and sat back in his tired looking chair. It was an office swivel chair that groaned a little under his weight. There was an additional chair opposite me against the far wall. Barry waved his hand in the general direction of the chair and leaned back.

'What is it that you wish to know? I told the reporters everything more than once.'

'Barry, so far you have retold your tale to people that did not believe you, I am here to listen to what you actually have to say. I get paid to investigate the paranormal, so I want to hear your story first hand.' I expected Barry to brighten at this. My experience was that people with an unbelievable story to tell, wanted desperately to tell it, but found no one believed them. Presenting them with an interested and willing listener always seemed to generate a retelling with gusto and often exaggeration. If Barry was not so inclined, then was it because he had in fact not witnessed anything and now felt exposed by my potential probing?

'Ok, Mr. Michaels,' Barry said. 'I'll tell you what I saw.'

Less than half an hour later I was home. Barry had not had much to tell, leaving me utterly convinced that he was lying and had seen nothing at all. I was now stood in my kitchen looking at the dogs snuffling in the garden while I stirred a tea bag idly around my favourite R2D2 mug.

I wanted to dismiss Dr. Barry Bryson, but somehow, I could not shake the feeling that there was more to his story, fake or otherwise. Barry had retold his story almost verbatim from the article published in The Weald Word. I had prodded him for more information. 'What was the light like? Did the creature turn towards you at any point? Did you notice any other wildlife about and how was it acting? How far away were you from the creature? How could you be sure it was not a man in an outfit?'

He has answered all the questions with practiced and bored ease as if the answers were rehearsed. I suspected that they were. Barry had apparently been on his way to work at the Kent Predators and Prey Wildlife Park on the morning of Tuesday 21st. He usually arrived at 0700hrs to open up and prepare for the day, but on the day in question,

212

he had left home early because he wanted to spend some time using the computer in work to conduct research for a new book he was writing. He was a published author he assured me. His home computer didn't work, and he did not currently have the money to replace it or get it fixed. Anyway, his usual route brought him down Bluebell Hill. His car took a puncture causing him to have to fight the wheel to keep control. He admitted that his car was also in need of attention but that he had no money to attend to that either.

With a tyre to change, he had pulled to the side of the road where there was a hard shoulder area. As he was putting the jack back into the boot along with the wrecked tyre, he spotted what he described as a large bear-like creature emerge from the wood line thirty metres away. It walked upright and was moving away from him. He was able to get his phone out and catch a series of pictures of the creature, but the lighting was poor and the quality insufficient to attract the national press who he admitted to contacting. I asked him who he had spoken to and at which papers or websites and listened as he recited names of persons at The Sun, The Mail and The Mirror which I noted for checking later.

He went on to describe the creature in great detail, estimating the hair length, weight, height etcetera and then explained that he held a Ph.D. in Zoology where his dissertation was on the Modern Evolution of the Predatory Mammals of England. He pointed behind my head to a framed certificate on the wall which I politely glanced at to play along.

Thinking back now, I should have asked him if there was, in fact, a wrecked tyre still in his boot. I had missed a chance to catch him out and prove he was lying. There was probably no need though since I was already convinced he was.

There was one point in the conversation that I was troubled by, another bit that didn't fit. He had reacted oddly when I referred to the creature as a Sasquatch. Placid throughout the interview he became animated at the mention of the word Sasquatch, stating, 'It is not a Sasquatch.' He then explained that the Sasquatch was a North American creature and should in no way be confused with what he had seen.

Bull barked at the door to be let back inside which broke my focus. I realised that the tea had gone cool and that I was now stirring the bag around a well-stewed cup. I was missing something vital, I could sense it or feel it like a non-superhero version of Spidey-sense.

I poured the tea away and went to let the dogs in.

After Frank's warnings, I decided that I needed to address the potential Kent vampire issue head-on. If they were planning to attack me then getting to them first might defuse the issue, but if not, it might force them to move early which would interrupt what might be a well-conceived plan on their part. I might be giving them too much credit, or they might not be involved at all, in which case Frank's theories were all wrong. I knew where they would be tonight though, so I could end the speculation and perhaps ask them about Ambrogio.

I let Frank know what I was planning out of courtesy and to my surprise, he insisted on coming along with me. He said he could act as an interpreter (?), and that he knew some of them because they relied on him to provide their demand for rare books (and probably vampire comics I suspected). Whatever the case, he felt the chance of violence was greatly reduced if he was there. I told him I was bringing Jagjit and Big Ben anyway and would be in Jagjit's car so could collect him. He wanted to take his own vehicle though and would meet me at the M2 motorway services at Junction 8.

With all the recent weirdness, I wanted to drop in at my office and make sure it was still there, or at least unmolested. I needed to walk the dogs anyway and Rochester High Street and nearby castle grounds are a delightful place for it.

It was 1835hrs when I pulled into my parking space behind the travel agent. Bull jumped from the passenger seat and onto my lap to look out of the window, clearly excited and ready to get out and sniff things.

I clipped both he and his brother to the same lead and opened my door to plop them on the floor. They broke into a run instantly, held in check only by my thumb on the ratchet of their extendable lead. They hauled me across the car park and pawed impatiently at the door while I fumbled for my keys in the twilight. I unlocked the entry door from the street and watched the dogs bound, now untethered, up the stairs ahead of me, keen to get to wherever they were going and unconcerned that their tiny legs would not permit them to come back down.

My office was, in fact, unmolested despite my concern, so I flicked the light on and checked my emails again.

I had a further forty-four new emails since I had last checked. I scanned quickly to dismiss the junk but found what I was looking for and hoping not to see three from the top: Ambrogio has sent me another message.

Mortal,

You and your kin will die tonight.

I had been threatened before of course. By big men. With big guns. But I had to admit that I was finding this a little unsettling and I felt exposed because I had no idea who this guy was or who he might be sending after me. Feeling unsettled made me angry though, so the fire in my belly was telling me to find this idiot and slap him around until he apologised. I shut the machine down and scooped up both dogs, went out the door and then put them down again so I could lock up.

Back on the street, I elected to get a hot drink from the coffee shop across the road. This was mostly so that I could flirt with Hayley if she was there. They shut soon, so perhaps there would be talk of what she had planned when she finished and perhaps a natural course for the conversation to flow into us meeting at some point after work one day.

As I was thinking this, she came out of the shop. They closed at 1900hrs so with fifteen minutes to go she was starting the routine of bringing the fold-out tables and chairs inside.

'Hello, Tempest,' she smiled broadly. 'Who are the little guys?'

'This is Bull and Dozer,' I said pointing to each in turn. 'They are my trusted lieutenants. I am surprised you have never seen them before.'

'I would have remembered you two,' she said as she bent down to pet them. They recognised a willing masseuse and were both struggling to beat the other to the best spot at her hands.

She straightened up and wiped her now well-licked fingers on her pinny. 'Are you coming in?'

'Yes, but purely on the chance of seeing you of course,' I ventured. This drew a sly smile as she opened the door to let me in.

'What can I get you?'

'Just a tall, skinny hot chocolate to go please.' I wondered if the dogs were allowed in, I could not remember taking them in before and could not recall seeing dogs in there. It was close to closing though and we were the only people in the place apart from whichever of her colleagues I could hear banging about in the kitchen out of sight. I took them in anyway, expecting she would object if she felt the need to.

'So, are you after the reward?' Hayley asked conversationally as she poured milk into a jug for heating.

My eyebrows went up. 'What reward?'

'Oh. It's all over the local news, some American vampire hunter has posted a ten-thousand pounds reward for information leading to the capture of the Maidstone Vampire. His name is... hold on.' She whipped her head around to face the kitchen. 'Martha?' No response. 'Martha?'

'What?' came a voice back from the kitchen.

217

'What was the name of that American guy? The Vampire Hunter.'

'Vermont Wensdale,' I said for both to hear.

'Yeah, that's it. Do you know him?'

'We have met,' I said through tight lips. A reward. That was going to bring the crazies out in droves. I had visions though of Vermont being inundated with calls and emails from people who live next door to an Emo.

'One skinny, tall hot chocolate to go.' Hayley was holding my beverage out for me to take. The cup had a number on it with, "Call me" written in her girly, rounded script.

I paused to fish out a business card. 'I will call you, but please tell me I am an idiot if I don't.' She smiled once more as I took my drink off the counter and headed out to make sure the boys were well walked before I went out to meet the vampires.

I had my rip-stop kit on again when Jagjit came for me at 2030hrs. I had too little time for a proper dinner, so had quickly made a tuna sandwich and eaten it while dressing.

Jagjit had a large, black, nearly new Japanese Utility vehicle with a double cab, so there was plenty of room for me and a bag of gear just in case. I got in the back next to Basic. Big Ben was already in the front. I paid the guys fifty pounds per hour for this kind of work and they were still doing it at mate's rates. It was rarely exciting but often entertaining and I think they did it because they wanted to rather than because I was paying. We tended to go for a beer afterward unless it was too late or Big Ben was off to get laid somewhere.

I had already explained to Jagjit that we were meeting Frank on the way there, so a few minutes later we were pulling off the motorway and into the services to join up with him.

I spotted Frank's car in an obvious spot under a lamppost as we came into the car park. It was where he said he would be, but he had failed to mention that Poison would be with him. She was leaning against the tail end of the car fiddling with her phone, thumbs going like mad as she typed on the tiny keypad.

'Who the hell is that, Tempest?' asked Big Ben who was now staring at Poison like a dog in heat.

'That, Ben is Poison. Real name no idea, but she is Frank's assistant in the shop. I did tell you to go in there.'

'But you didn't tell me there was a honey in there. It looks like a crap shop full of weird stuff. I would have gone in for her.' Big Ben was practically salivating.

219

Poison looked good. It was still warm out and she was wearing stretchy pants like you might wear to the gym and a pair of high-top trainers, both black. Her midriff was showing again, and we could all see her nipples through the stretchy fabric of her top. As if feeling our eyes on her she pulled her jacket closed and zipped it up.

'Just try not to get her naked until after we finish tonight, Ben. Okay?'

'Yeah. Yeah. Work now. Shag later. Got it.'

As we pulled up next to Frank's car, his window powered down. 'Whatcha chaps!' He said with great enthusiasm. 'Ready to go?'

'Let's just take two minutes to discuss the plan, Frank,' I replied as I got out.

'Hello, Tempest,' Poison purred in my direction, still slouched against the rear of Frank's car. 'Who is your big friend?'

Jagjit rolled his eyebrows, ignored again while Big Ben leapt at the chance to introduce himself. I could hear Poison laughing at whatever Big Ben was telling her as I moved to stand between Jagjit and Frank. They were both leaning out of their cars with the two driver's doors parallel to each other and the cars facing opposite directions.

Big Ben saw us waiting and came around to join us with Poison following him.

'Our intention tonight is to visit the Kent vampire group at their clubhouse. There I will ask them what their intentions are and whether they actually have any knowledge of or involvement with a person called Ambrogio who appears to want me dead. There is a danger that they are planning to attack me or do harm to me so we may meet hostility.'

'How many people are we talking about?' asked Big Ben.

'Frank?' I prompted.

'Maybe as many as fifty. I could not find a membership list or roster to know how many members they have, and although the flyer did not say bring a friend, I would not be surprised if there were additional non-members there as well.'

'Okay, so it is an unknown force with unknown intentions. When we get there, Big Ben and I will approach the group, but everyone else stays in the cars until we know whether they are hostile or not. Keep the engines running, please. If we need to make a fast escape Big Ben and I will have the option of getting into the back of Jagjit's truck until we are clear. Frank and Poison, likewise stay close to Jagjit, and if Big Ben and I come running you get out of there quick.'

I let that sink in for a few moments. 'Of course, this might be a completely harmless group getting together to watch vampire movies in their clubhouse. We are only guessing that they may be involved in which case we will apologise for interrupting them and for the incident at Aylesford two days ago and be on our way.'

Basic raised his hand slowly. 'You don't have to raise your hand if you have a question, Basic.' Big Ben said.

'Will it just be vampires?'

'I believe so, Basic.' Getting an actual question from Basic was pretty much unheard of, so I didn't want to discourage him, but I wanted to know why he asked. 'Why do you ask?'

'I don't like werewolves,' he said flatly. 'Werewolves are big and hairy and nasty. Vampires are sexy.'

Everyone seemed to consider this for a moment before nodding their agreement. To allay any lingering concerns, I asked Frank what he thought.

'Werewolves and vampires don't mix James,' Frank stated using Basics actual name, which I had no idea how he knew. 'Well known fact that one.'

'But on Twilight they do,' Basic pointed out, clinging to the idea like a life raft in a stormy sea.

'Twilight is a load of twaddle for teenage girls,' answered Big Ben knowingly.

'Oh, really?' Poison looked less than impressed by his generalisation.

Time was ticking on, so I wanted this show to get on the actual road. 'Okay, chaps' I said breaking the moment. 'We can continue the discussion afterward if you like but we need to go. Basic don't worry about Werewolves. I give you my personal guarantee that there won't be any.' I felt safe in my promise as there is no such thing.

Thirty seconds later we were back in the cars and heading out of the car park.

The Kent Vampires were meeting at their clubhouse, which was in a small village called Boxley, just outside Maidstone. I had driven through Boxley a few times without really noticing it. It was just another suburb of Maidstone which I had gone through plenty of times but never once stopped in.

The lane the vampire clubhouse sat on was not a place I had ever heard of and had been forced to google it just to track down its location.

The flyer had a postcode and we found the place easily enough just by following the verbal instruction from the satnav.

And then all hell broke loose.

The lane leading to what the satnav claimed was the destination was narrow with a flat grass verge about five feet wide that was probably littered with bluebells in the summer. Tall thin trees had grown on both sides to form a canopy. The trees cut out all the light from the moon and stars which made it unnaturally dark. There were cars lining both sides of the lane, half-on, half-off the road where they had pulled onto the grassy verge to leave sufficient space for cars to still pass.

As we passed the cars the road curved slightly, and we began to see dancing light between the trees. The dancing light was flames and I think we all realised this at the same time as I felt the others stiffen when I did as if the action were synchronised.

'I've got a bad feeling about this.' Big Ben murmured as we came around the trees and into the clearing that contained the clubhouse.

The clubhouse was a wooden building that was double height, but probably single story inside and might once have been a church hall. There were brick footings to perhaps three feet off the ground then the rest was timber and looked to be in a well-kept condition. Windows could be seen on the front and one side from light reflecting off them, but there was no light coming from within that I could see.

What was happening was not immediately clear, but the building was on fire all along one side and as we watched, two guys doused the other side with fuel from a jerry can. As Jagjit hit the brakes and we started to pile out I saw one of them throw a match and felt the pull of air as the fuel caught. The fire leapt into life. Now the building was burning on two sides.

As the fire went up, it illuminated the far side of the clearing and I saw, clear as anything, Vermont Wensdale, and his two flunkies silhouetted

224

against the trees. There was no way I was wrong. That the crazy idiot has caused this with his stupid reward offer did not surprise me, that he was here in person though was a shock. I had taken him for deluded rather than dangerous or irresponsible.

'Come out, vampires,' yelled someone now silhouetted in the flames not twenty feet from me. My attention swung back to the burning building. I could see maybe twenty guys all holding bats or... Christ, could I see people holding stakes?

All this took half a second, as what we were seeing became obvious very quickly. These guys were burning the vampires out of their barn and the people inside were going to burn to death if no one did anything.

I could not tell if there was anyone in the barn, however, before I could decide what to do the door opened and two vampire-wannabes made a run for it. They were met by at least half a dozen men with bats and we saw the spray of blood from a mouth as they were both tackled. The door had snapped shut again but I heard a window smash, possibly from the side that I could not see. Was it someone breaking out, or one of the attackers trying to get in?

'Let's go!' yelled Big Ben and he was gone, already running towards the men outside the barn. I waved for the others to stay where they were and took off after him. He was several paces ahead of me and I saw him pile into two guys with a hard shoulder. As they went sprawling, he swung a haymaker at a third guy who seemed stunned to be on the receiving end suddenly. He went down like his on-switch had just been turned to off. As Big Ben moved to the fourth guy, I could see he was going to get him, but lose to the fifth who was already beginning to swing what looked like a sharpened crowbar.

The two that Big Ben had already taken out were on the floor, but both were starting to get up. I leapt the nearest one gaining some height as I did and drove a knee into the face of guy number five before he could complete his backswing. As we went down, I ripped the crowbar from his hand and threw it away.

It had become a melee though in the space of a few seconds. I took a glancing kick to the jaw from one of the chaps on the ground as he struggled to get away. Doubtless, he had no idea nor any care about who was who in the dark.

As I rolled over Frank appeared above me and held out his hand to help me up.

'Get back to the car and get out of here, Frank.' Frank looked panicked, but he shook his head and helped me up.

It was of little use though as I was bundled back onto the dirt with a tackle that knocked the wind out of me. I tasted dirt and leaf litter as my mouth dug into the ground. I think Big Ben kicked the guy tackling me at that point though as he jerked violently and rolled away. As I fought for breath and to work out which way was up, I saw a whole platoon converging on where I lay. The fight had come to us.

There must be twenty of them I calculated, all dressed in various dark clothes. Some in decent looking combat or tactical gear, but most were wearing jeans and hoodies. It didn't matter what they were wearing, I thought to myself as I calculated the chances of survival. We were five in total, including Frank, who weighed seventy kilos if he ate a good breakfast and Poison who weighed less than that.

The barn was now fully ablaze on both sides with flames licking at the roof and spreading around to the front of the building. There the door, and possibly the only exit in such an old building, was positioned. The door burst open at that moment, allowing a hoard of angry, frightened vampire-wannabes to escape. With the attackers' attention on us, they had seized their chance to get out and were now heading straight for the mob and therefore right for us.

As I watched, I could see that leading the charge was none other than Obsidian Dark. He was wearing the same rig he had been in three days ago at the cottage in Aylesford. I thought I recognised one or two others. They were running but also stumbling and coughing from the smoke that must have filled the space they had just escaped from. Their eyes were streaming and making their overuse of makeup comical as it ran down their faces - the effect on some of them somewhat like a tearful teenage girl.

The mob attacking the vampire-wannabe clubhouse reached our position just as Frank hauled me off the ground for the second time. They were slowing though, their attention drawn by the yells from the vampire-wannabes. Obsidian bellowed a feral battle scream as he ran at the mob. His hair and long black leather duster were flapping behind him as he ran towards us, leaving a trail of diminishing smoke. He was unarmed, so far as I could see, but seemingly unconcerned about such trivial detail.

The yell from Obsidian drew the attention of any that had not yet noticed the latest peril.

In the clearing, the noise of the fire now engulfing the barn was deafening but his voice rose above the surrounding din and was joined by his fellow vampire-wannabes as they met with the nearest members of the mob. Big Ben seized his chance to rip a bat from the hands of a much shorter man whose attention was now focused away from us. A fast kick to the back of his knee and a chopping downwards thrust with the end of the bat put the man on the floor. Suddenly the mob was being attacked on two fronts and was outnumbered.

227

In the darkness, with staccato punctuations of dancing light from the fire, utter confusion reigned. The effect was much akin to a strobe light at a club as flashes illuminating nanoseconds of movement. I grabbed a man in front of me from behind and threw him to the floor, but it was too dangerous to follow him down with further blows.

I looked around for my team, wanting to get them out of the melee and to safety. Though only a minute or so had passed since we arrived, I had seen no one on fire and heard no one screaming in the agony that being burned provides. I clung to the hope that there was no one still inside. Anyone who had not yet escaped the clubhouse was surely lost.

I glimpsed Poison then, easy to see with her diminutive, athletic form. She was being helped off the soil by two vampires. It looked like she had rolled in a puddle.

Someone grabbed my shoulder and I spun to react and found Jagjit heaving for breath behind me. He bent over at that point and threw up. 'We need to get out of here,' he insisted between gulps of air.

He was right, but that had already been my consideration. We just needed to find everyone first.

'Get the car, mate. I'll find the others.' Just then I heard the sweet, blissful noise of sirens coming our way. Who had placed the call did not matter. It might have been one of the vampires from within the burning barn. If so, then the sirens would be both police and fire brigade and probably ambulance as well.

Jagjit turned towards the lane that led into the clearing and stumbled off at a lope clearly in some discomfort. We could lick our wounds later.

I looked for Big Ben, Basic, Frank, and Poison again and saw that the number of people visible in the clearing had reduced greatly. My guess was that some of them had fled and as I thought that I heard car engines start back out on the lane.

A girl screamed. I turned towards the sound to see three guys in combat gear dragging Poison off. They were ten metres distant and moving away from me. She was being held off the ground but was putting up quite a fight, thrashing her little arms and legs. As I started to run towards her, I had to jump one guy who was lying inert on the ground and then around two more who were tussling over a bat. I saw her break one of her legs free and proceed to kick the guy who had been holding it in the face. With that, he lost his grip on her other leg and she fell to the floor.

The loss of forward motion meant I caught up to them instantly. I threw myself over Poison and into the two guys who were still holding her arms.

'Tempest, they are after the reward money,' I heard Poison shout. 'These idiots think I am a vampire and can tell them something they can use.'

I was on the floor, rolling to my side and off the one man I had landed on. I felt dazed and beaten and my lungs were beginning to really struggle from the exertion.

'The reward is ours, bitch. Tell us what you know,' shouted the one she had kicked in the face. Having not learned a lesson he was trying to grab her feet again.

Then I was thrown to the ground for what must have been the sixth or seventh time as I was tackled hard from behind. Yet again I tasted dirt and breathed in insects, leaf litter and goodness know what. There was a weight on my back, I registered a knee pushing into my spine, pinning me to the floor. My arms were free though, allowing me to scramble for purchase, so I could flip the latest assailant off. My left arm was wrenched

229

behind me as I tried to move though, and I felt the cool hardness of steel as a cuff slammed into place over my left wrist.

Then I could hear voices shouting commands and as I looked up there were police in uniform rounding up mob crazies and vampire-wannabes alike. Somewhere in there was my team too.

I glanced to my left to see Poison lying on the dirt just a couple of feet from me. The guy that had been holding her was now face down on the ground and handcuffed like me. She had a little blood in the corner of her mouth but was sitting up onto her elbows to look around.

'Stay there, don't move.' A cop told her as he hauled the guy next to her onto his feet and led him away into the clearing proper where the police were beginning to gather.

The weight on my back shifted and a voice close to my right ear said, 'I'm going to get you up now, but I can put you down again so behave yourself. There is nowhere to go.' It was Amanda. I could tell instantly from the faint scent of her perfume which had found its way to my nose. Even in these circumstances, it went straight to my groin without involving my brain.

'Hello, Amanda,' I said. She froze and spun me around, so she could see my face. I guess she had seen someone to tackle and had tackled them. Having taken me from behind and knocked me into the dirt she had not had the chance to notice that she knew the guy she was sitting on.

'Tempest what are you doing here and why were you attacking that girl?'

'He wasn't. He was helping me. He was trying to fight three guys by himself to save me.' Poison interjected helpfully. It sounded much better coming from her.

Amanda seemed satisfied with Poison's explanation and helped me to stand. The cuffs stayed on though.

We joined the group now forming in the centre of the clearing. The fire brigade was already putting out the fire, the scent of wet wood now replacing that of burning wood. The smoke had dissipated and with the fire out the roar it had provided was noticeably absent. However, the fire engine had a compressor running to pump the water and there were several nearby vehicles with their engines running and a background mumble of conversation between the assembled police and their captives punctuated irregularly by the squawk of a radio, so it was far from silent.

Jagjit, Frank, Basic and Big Ben were already there as were perhaps twenty-five others which meant that a lot of the vampires and many of the mob had escaped, either before the cops arrived, or into the woods where they might be hiding still. I looked around hopefully for Vermont and his two goons but there was no sign of them.

Paramedics from two ambulances were treating several people, the slowly revolving blue lights on their ambulance illuminating the clearing and everyone in it as they turned. The injuries looked mostly superficial, which is to say that I could not see any blankets draped over bodies and no one appeared to have a stake sticking out of their chest.

Obsidian was being led over to the group from the ambulances now. He had a bandage around his head and blood covering most of one side of his face. He was instructed to kneel, and when he resisted the gentle pressure being applied to his shoulder, he was nudged hard in the back of his knees and pushed roughly to the ground. He gave the cop his best

231

angry face, but then noticed he was next to one of the mob that had set fire to his clubhouse and threw himself bodily at the man. Obsidians hands were cuffed behind his back like everyone else, so he was trying to head-butt or bite the guy.

Two cops grabbed his shoulders and hauled him back.

'Don't mix the groups, you moron,' instructed a sergeant. 'The ones dressed like vampires go over there.'

Obsidian caught sight of me as they hauled him back to his feet. His eyes bugged out of his head. 'You! I'm gonna kill you! You, maniac!' with that he lunged towards me and the two police officers holding him lost their grip. He pitched forward and stumbled. Unable to move his feet fast enough to stay upright, his trajectory, however out of control, was sufficient to get him the few metres he needed to land on top of me. I was on my knees already and could just not move fast enough to get out of the way.

Had I been able to react quicker, I might have been able to roll onto my back and get my feet out to parry him. Now though I was pinned under him as he was trying to get to my face.

'You dirty murdering git. You are going to die, you and all your kin! I will bathe in your soul,' he was screaming, and he was mad, like apoplectic mad, but he just told me something I wanted to know. There was no way it was a coincidence that he had used the same phrase as Ambrogio, so he must be involved with him somehow.

The police had caught hold of him again and were lifting him off me. With his hands tied he could do little but swing wild kicks at me until they forced him back to the ground using the cuffs to overstress his shoulder joints.

Once back under control, Obsidian was dragged away still swearing and threatening death to all. I could see there were two distinct groups and we were in with the mob.

'We are not with these guys,' I shouted to the sergeant.

'He doesn't care, Tempest,' replied Big Ben. 'I told him that already.'

'Hey, Sarge,' I tried again but he continued to ignore me.

'Everyone is going to the station, Tempest,' said Amanda. 'It's the only way we can sort this out.'

I could see it from their point of view. A building on fire, multiple attempted murders, probable arson, people assaulted and no idea what the hell was going on. I would have arrested everyone too. A short while passed and we were loaded into vans under guard and taken to Maidstone police station.

It was after 2000hrs and we were at the station. It had not taken long for the police to sort us into different groups. I was ushered into a room where I found Big Ben and Frank. A few minutes later we were joined by Jagjit, Basic and finally Poison. There were chairs and a table and a jug of water with plastic cups in the room but little else. We could hear conversation drifting through the walls. However, it was not loud enough to make out what anyone was saying.

I was not particularly worried about our situation. I could not come up with anything we could be charged with and therefore it should only be a matter of time before we were released. I wanted to leave now of course. Hunger, boredom and the desire to get my friends out of this awful predicament all fighting for dominance in order of priority.

I settled into a chair much as the others already had. Our phones had been taken along with all other personal effects. It was a good thing we didn't carry illegal weapons as a matter of policy as our incarceration might have stretched far longer.

The chair was uncomfortable, one of the mass-produced polypropylene ones in a dull shade of blue. 'Anyone got any injuries worth sharing?' asked Jagjit who was inspecting the knuckles of his right hand. They were a little swollen and the skin was split in several places. The blood had dried some time ago and was flaking off as he poked and rubbed.

'Is that broken?' I asked him.

'Nah, probably not. Don't even remember doing it.'

'Just the usual bruises, Tempest,' answered Big Ben. 'How about you, Poison?'

234

Poison was sitting next to Frank, against the wall opposite the door idly poking at a hole in her leggings. 'A few bruises, I think. Nothing much. I have a fat lip where some turd punched me. What were they doing there anyway? Trying to kill a whole bunch of people just for dressing up as vampires?'

The question appeared to be addressed to me although I knew as much as anyone else at this point. 'Vermont Wensdale was there. He wants to catch the Vampire, so my guess is this was all to do with that. Vermont bloody Wensdale.' I huffed.

'The dick,' added Big Ben helpfully.

'The famous Vampire Hunter,' countered Frank still in full belief mode.

'Well, I reckon they did some research and found out about The Brotherhood of the Dead and where they would be. Much the same as I did really with Frank's help. They then went there en masse and tried to get them to talk. My guess would be the vampires locked themselves inside their clubhouse and some moron decided it would be a good idea to burn them out, thinking they could force some answers from them. Something like that.'

Just then the door unlocked, and Chief Inspector Quinn stepped in followed by PC Amanda Harper. She closed the door and he looked around the room briefly as if checking out each of us.

Big Ben elected to start things off in his usual style, 'Ah, Chief Inspector Quinn, good evening to you. How's your wife and my kids?'

Chief Inspectors Quinn's eyes popped out a bit at the insult. I found Big Ben funny generally, he was just so brash and ready to be abusive to people that probably deserved it. This was not the right time though.

Chief Inspector Quinn just ignored him. 'You are free to go once we take statements from each of you.' He paused and turned his attention to Big Ben and me. 'This is the second time this week that you have been arrested. If there is a third time, I will find something to charge you with regardless of how innocent you might think you are.'

'That's a load of rubbish,' said Poison. Clearly, Poison had thoughts on the matter which differed to the Chief Inspector's. 'Were it not Tempest and the rest of us you would be dealing with a barn full of people burnt to death and not a few cuts and bruises. Do the vampire-wannabes even know that we saved them?'

'Your intervention has been reported to their leader. He was convinced you were leading the mob and wanted you dead.' Amanda piped up but was cut off from saying anything further by Chief Inspector Quinn holding his hand up in front of her face.

'Saved them?' repeated the Chief Inspector with a mocking tone. 'Surely you don't believe that? The police saved them, you merely added to the confusion and panic. You are only being released because I don't have the room to hold you and because thus far none of the injured persons has claimed their injuries were caused by any of you.'

'Who were they?' Frank asked

'It is of no concern to you. I suggest all of you ensure I don't see you again any time soon.' and with that, he left, but not before shooting Amanda a hateful gaze.

'That was pleasant,' I said getting up. 'Can we go now?

'Once I have your statements.'

'Okay.' Then I had a thought. 'Have they released Jim Butterworth yet?

'No. I'm not on this case, but I do know he is still being held and charged with the death of Mrs. Hancock.'

I gave her an incredulous look just as Big Ben spoke, 'Are they nuts? Two more people have been killed since then.'

Amanda looked across at Big Ben and then back at me. 'I think they know he is not guilty of the latest murders, but as he has confessed to the first two, he is not getting out any time soon.'

I suppose that made sense. I wondered why he had confessed if he was not guilty.

'Shall we start with you?' Amanda asked Poison.

Just about when I was being arrested at the vampire clubhouse my parents were pulling up outside my house to walk the dogs. They didn't know I was being arrested of course, only that I was out working for the evening and could not guarantee a return time.

Mum was driving. She bumped the driver side wheels just onto the pavement to leave a little more passing space in the road and killed the engine. She waited as always for my dad to get out and around the car to open her door for her.

'Thank you, Michael,' she took his offered hand.

'You are very welcome, Mary.' He helped her up and then transferred her hand to the crook of his arm, so they could walk arm in arm to my door. They were a very cute couple.

'We are coming, little dogs,' mum called out as they reached the gate. It was a redundant statement, but I often did the same myself. She fished in her handbag for the keys and pulled them from whichever corner they had hidden in after a few seconds of rooting.

My dad stood inspecting a shrub momentarily while his wife opened the door and the two dogs whizzed out between her legs before it was even half open.

Their tails wagging furiously, the pair nuzzled one then the other friendly human and then reverted to the one they were not currently with and constantly changed human for almost a minute, until a smell under a bush attracted them and they shot off to investigate that. The gate was shut so they were safe in the front yard area and were left exploring as mum then dad went inside.

'Come on in fellas. Come on. Bull, Dozer. Come on,' called my dad while mum filled the kettle.

Probably curious about the chance for a biscuit, first one then the other popped back out from under the bushes and hopped into the house allowing my dad to shut the door.

Thirty minutes later the teas were drunk, and the cups were in the sink. The dogs had excitedly crunched a gravy bone, run around the garden, performed various garden duties such as bark at birds and were now back in their bed. The only sign of their existence, a single tail tip poking out from one edge of the blanket. My mother was putting her knitting back into her bag when the doorbell chimed.

Mum hooked her knitting bag onto her right arm while fishing for her keys with the left. 'It'll be someone selling something I expect. What a time to be out bothering people. Are you ready, Michael?' she asked on her way to answer the door.

My dad slid off his stool in a theatrical move of getting up. It was either unnoticed or ignored by his loving wife. He patted his pockets to make sure everything was in place and began moving to leave.

She opened the door intending to step straight out of it so that whoever was outside would have to step away. This would give her space, so she could lock up and the caller could be politely shooed away. Instead, though she stopped dead on the doorstep still inside the house.

'You are the kin of Tempest Michaels?'

'Ur?' replied mum. In front of her stood the tallest, broadest man she had ever seen. It was dark out now, the automatic light at the front of the house throwing his features into sharp relief, but the word she would use to describe his face later was emotionless. He wore a suit of midnight blue with a tie to match and a white shirt. The suit looked expensive. He had an accent, something European that she was not able to place immediately.

My dad joined his wife at the door. Slightly concerned, he elected to lead with, 'Good evening. How may we help you?'

'You are the kin of Tempest Michaels,' a statement this time. 'I can smell the truth of it. I am Ambrogio Silvano, you must die.' Then he stood there, not attacking, not attempting to get into the house.

My mum was just staring at him, head slightly to one side as if waiting for the punchline at the end of a joke she had not understood from the start. 'I'm not sure what you mean. Can you explain yourself a little better?' she asked, ignoring the bit where she was supposed to die now.

'The farmer does not explain himself to the sheep. Step outside so that I may devour you,' instructed Ambrogio while still not moving.

Then my dad got the farmer and sheep comment. 'I say chap. I don't know what your game is, but you will apologise to the lady right now.'

'Tempest Michaels had wantonly challenged me. I don't accept insults from mortals. I have promised him that he would see his bloodline die before I killed him, would you make a liar of me? Step outside this dwelling so that I may feast on your life force. Don't fear. It will be quite the sweetest death you could imagine.'

At this he moved for the first time, slowly bringing up his right arm that until now had been held loosely at this side. He beckoned to Mary, it was an unthreatening gesture that suggested compliance was expected. He took a half step forward and reached out to her.

She began to move forward, and as her hand went beyond the door frame and outside the house, the man moved to take it. The expression on his face was peaceful as if all of this was routine and pleasing.

'Mary?' queried my dad, wondering what she was doing. He was stood right next to her, his clothing brushing hers, but she was moving away from him as she moved to leave the house.

The man outside reached to take her hand so he could draw her gently from the house. As he did so, my dad began to react, wanting to grab his wife and draw her back inside where the illusion of safety promised a better position than being outside. Before he could get to her though, she swung her bag and smacked Ambrogio upside his head accompanied by a roar of, 'Take that. You smarmy twat!' His head jerked slightly to the side as the bag connected, but he reacted fast and the arm that had been reaching for her hand now snapped out and grabbed her around the wrist.

A handbag swung by an old lady was never going to have any real effect. However, as the bag fell away it revealed a knitting needle poking from the side of his skull with a ball of yarn hanging from it. Mum liked to knit clothes for orphaned children and donated her products to the local church, she took the knitting kit everywhere and now it was impaled in Ambrogio's head.

My dad grabbed his wife around the waist and tried to get to her wrist as Ambrogio pulled them both outside with no visible effort at all. At the same instant though, the two dogs burst from between their feet and attacked his legs, each biting an ankle.

In the momentary distraction, his grip on Mary's arm loosened and both my parents tumbled back into the house under their own weight, propelled backward by their efforts to escape his grasp.

241

'Dogs. In!' commanded my dad from the floor. The pair disengaged simultaneously and bounced excitedly back over the door frame.

Ambrogio had been bent to swipe at the dogs but straightened back to his full height now. He brushed a few creases from his suit once more completely calm and in control.

'Invite me in, woman,' he commanded in his soothing, even voice.

'You can get stuffed.' she countered, still lying on the floor, propped up on her elbows. Ambrogio then noticed that her eyes were not making contact with his, instead, they were focused a few inches higher and to the right. He looked up with his eyes like someone searching for an answer then reached to feel his head with one hand. He found the knitting needle, plucked it from his skull and tossed it to the floor.

'Thank you,' she said as the ball of wool and needles came to rest on the yard paving.

At this, my dad shoved her roughly to one side, slammed the door shut with his feet and reached over to lock it. The bolt clicked home, but he snagged a dining chair and wedged it under the handle for good measure. As he did so, she slumped against the floor, the adrenalin fading and leaving her spent.

'Oh my, that was strange and unpleasant. Would you put the kettle on please, Michael? I rather fancy a cup of tea?' Mum asked from her prone position. Bull, who had been standing in the kitchen doorway wagging his tail next to his brother in anticipation of another treat, now crossed the short distance to her head and began licking her nose.

The shadow outside the door was still there. As they watched it turned, paused as if making a decision and then moved away towards the gate. My dad jumped up and dashed to the dining room window where he

242

could see the shadowed form, lit only by a distant lamppost exit the property and head towards the road.

He came back to the lobby and slumped against a wall smiling gleefully down at his wife.

'What?' she asked noticing his ridiculous smile.

'You can get stuffed. Rosemary Elizabeth Michaels,' he chuckled. 'You do like to surprise me.'

She swiped at him, but he was out of reach, so he knelt and kissed her head. 'I'll make that cup of tea.'

Finally, we were released from the police station without charge and as we collected our belongings, I noted that I had a dozen missed calls from my mother. Probably something to do with one of the dogs. The last call was over an hour ago, so I elected to call from the car, then remembered that I didn't have it with me and that the car I had travelled in was not with me either. I would deal with my friends and see them on their way and then call her. It was nearly 2200hrs, so she would not yet be in bed and was probably at home watching Midsomer Murders while downing her third brandy.

It was full dark outside, light coming only from the lights inside the police station which had a large glazed lobby. Beyond the glass were a few seats and what might be called a counter where I supposed persons went to make complaints, report lost items etcetera, anything that was not urgent enough to warrant dialling 999 perhaps.

Jagjit was still inside arguing about his car which had been left at the vampire clubhouse. He was demanding a lift back there by the police and they were smirking at him.

Big Ben had decided that it was the perfect time to stroll into Maidstone town centre and pick up girls. Of course, he meant girls plural. He had invited everyone but contentedly headed off by himself when we all made excuses.

'I'm going to get a taxi back to the cars with Jagjit.' Frank said as he came out of the station. 'When he gives up arguing with them that is. I think they might arrest him again just to shut him up if he doesn't give up soon.' Frank turned to see if Jagjit was still at the counter arguing but at that moment he slammed his hand down onto the counter, said something that was probably not very polite and stormed toward the doors and us.

'I am aggravated,' he stated, stomping down the steps to the pavement.

'I will cover the taxi fare mate. It will go under expenses.' I didn't have anyone to bill this case to so it was coming out of my pocket, but it seemed likely that the taxi would cost a few quid and I didn't want my friends out of pocket because they helped me.

'It's getting late, we should go,' said Frank. 'Tempest, can you see Poison home?'

'I hardly need an escort,' Poison pointed out. 'But, since it's you...' she smiled at me and gave a wink that went straight to my groin, then she grabbed my hand and tugged to lead me away.

'See you later, chaps,' was all I could manage weakly as I departed, largely not under my own steam and wondering what was happening.

Around the corner and out of sight of the others Poison's hand was still in mine. It felt tiny. She slowed the pace, glanced over both shoulders as if checking her surroundings and then without warning stopped and pushed me against the wall of the building we were passing.

Before I could question what she was doing, or resist, or anything else she leaned forward and stuck her tongue in my mouth. It was not unpleasant.

I felt her tongue stud brush against my upper incisors and immediately wondered what that might feel like grazing against more sensitive skin elsewhere. Her body was very pleasing against mine. Her legs were either side of my right thigh and I felt warmth there as she pressed her groin against me. My trousers began to react.

I broke the kiss off as my phone rang again. I had taken the time a while ago to assign different tones to different people, so the Jaws theme coming from my back pocket announced a call from my mother. The sudden thoughts of naked entwinement with Poison had made me forget the missed calls.

'Mother?' I had whipped the phone out with a somewhat apologetic expression at Poison. She gave me a lopsided and utterly cute, but demure look back then pulled out her own phone taking a step away from me.

'Tempest, where have you been? I have been calling for hours,' asked my mother in a demanding tone.

I felt instantly embarrassed as if I was a teenager admitting he had been caught shoplifting. I chastised myself for such foolishness and went with, 'At the police station without my phone for most of the evening. I just left there.'

There was a pause at the other end. 'You got arrested again, didn't you?' It was a statement not a question, although I could acknowledge that getting arrested was not all that unusual for me.

'Well, yes,' I started then heard my own defensive and slightly whiny tone. 'Yes, mother. But released without charge because once again I had not actually committed a crime and had been rescuing people when a few things went a bit wrong.' A better explanation could be given later. Mum was mostly worried about the ladies at the church hearing about my activities. She was already horrified that they believed I hunted monsters.

'Never mind all that now, Tempest. Your Father and I met someone at your house tonight while we were letting the dogs out and... well... he sort of tried to kill us.'

I processed that at speed. I had only two questions 'Are either of you hurt? Where are you now?'

'You Father and I are both fine, a little shaken, but I believe the man left hours ago. We were going to go home, but your father insisted on giving me a stiff Brandy, then helped himself to your rum.' I could hear the disdain in her voice and that she had raised her voice slightly to ensure my dad heard her too. He would just smile to himself at that though and smack his lips at the excellent flavour. 'It was all very strange,' she continued. 'He said we had to die but then just stood there. He was outside, and we were inside, and he just stood there expecting us to come out so he could kill us or something.'

'Stay there. I will be home in a few minutes. Just keep the doors and windows shut and stay inside. Promise?'

'Yes, dear. Stay inside, we can do that. Midsomer Murders is about to finish anyway so I am not going anywhere.'

'Okay. A few minutes. I'll be there as soon as I can.' I ended the call.

'You need to go, Tempest, don't hang around. I'll text you later.' Poison had clearly heard enough of the conversation to piece together the rest of it.

Unsure whether I should kiss her again quickly or what the right protocol was I instead said, 'Sorry.' Then turned to run off to the nearby train station where I felt sure I would find a taxi. I paused and looked back at her again.

247

'Go,' she instructed, so I went.

Sat in the taxi fidgeting with my phone, I saw that I had also missed several text messages. I opened the text icon expecting to see that they were all missed voice mail message notifications from my mother. I was right in that all but one of them were. The one that was not was from Hayley, who I had not got around to messaging yet with all that was happening around me.

She probably thought I was playing it super cool like a complete idiot.

"Hi, Tempest. I can't decide if you are just playing it cool or being a jerk. After months of flirting I kind of expected a message this evening. (smiling face). I choose to assume that you have just got tied up with other things and I shall hear from you soon (smiley face with a wink and kiss lips)."

We were still a few minutes from my house, so I composed a reply quickly wondering if my arrest would excite her because I was such a bad boy or scare her off because I must be a complete jerk.

In the end, I settled for, *"Not cool enough to play it cool, dear lady. I'm afraid I had a busy evening interacting with the police on a case. Perhaps we can get together this coming weekend."* Satisfied that I had not lied and that 'get together' could mean anything, I pressed send and put the phone away.

As the taxi driver pulled onto my road, I had him drive past my house pretending I lived further on. I wanted to check out the parked cars. Seeing no cars that looked unfamiliar and no one sat obviously in their car, I got him to stop, slipped him a twenty to cover fare and tip and stepped out cautiously into the road.

I stayed where I was in the road as he pulled away again, scanning the area for any sign of movement. I wanted to get to the house, but I was wary that an ambush might be waiting for me. It was what I would have done.

There was plenty of illumination from the streetlights but therefore also lots of shadows. The street was very still though, no movement anywhere, not even light spilling through curtains from the televisions inside to give the illusion of movement. I could hear the hum of the motorway some two miles away, so there were no local sounds to hear.

Satisfied that there was no one lying in wait for me, I covered the distance to my house and called out to my parents as I let myself in.

'In the lounge,' my dad called out

The dogs appeared at my feet in greeting but having sniffed me decided that the sofa and sleep sounded superior and trotted back to where they had come from with me following them.

My parents were clearly not traumatised by the events of this evening, as I was waved into silence by mum's arm, lest I speak over the big *whodunit* reveal on Midsomer Murders. Dad turned and winked from an armchair across the room, but they were both clearly glued to the show after investing nearly two hours on grisly death. Realising they were fine, I observed the nearly drained glasses on the coffee table and went to fix myself a drink. An industrial strength rum and coke would fix a few problems and probably help me sleep.

With my drink made, I opened the cupboard in which I kept the dog treats and two small dogs skidded to a halt by my feet. The cupboard door never made a sound, so far as my ears could determine, but they could hear it over the sound of the television or even from out in the garden. I fed them each a gravy bone and took my drink to sit with my parents in the living room.

The title music kicked in a few seconds later to indicate the show had ended and finally my mother felt she could give me her attention.

'Is it alright if we stay here tonight?' she asked.

'Of course,' I replied, thinking that perhaps she was shaken by the evening's fun and games and wanted to stay inside until it was light outside again.

'Good. I have had three large brandies and really shouldn't drive, and your dad has had just as much rum.'

Right. So not staying for fear of death then, merely from inebriation.

'Would you like to fill me in on tonight events?' I asked

'I could ask the same of you.'

'You first, mum.'

I took a long slurp of my drink. Mmmm, just the right amount of rum.

Mum regaled me with the story about the man on the doorstep. I grabbed my notepad and wrote down what he had said as she outlined the exchange. Writing, circling and underlining that he would not come in the house and kept trying to get them to come out.

I hopped up then and went through to the kitchen where the books Frank had brought over were stacked neatly to one side. I grabbed the one I wanted and took it back into the lounge. On the sofa, I leafed through trying to find the bit I wanted.

251

'What are you looking for, boy?' asked my dad. My phone pinged in my pocket sending a jolt of interest as it could be Poison or Hayley or Amanda and each of those options was enticing. I left it in my pocket though rather than cut my dad off.

'One moment. Here it is. By any chance does this fellow look familiar?' I asked, showing mum a page in the book.

'Oh, that's him. Isn't it, Michael?'

'Let me have a better look, please.' I passed my dad the book rather than make him crane his neck.

'Ambrogio Silvano,' he read, peering through the bottom of his bifocal glasses. 'Yes, I would say that was probably the chap we met this evening. Good likeness anyway.'

He scanned the page for a little while longer. Mother and I were silent. 'Says here he was running around in the 12th Century. He certainly looks good if he is that old. Italian. Well, that explains the accent.

What do you think, son?

'I think the man you met tonight is someone that looks like this Ambrogio chap and has turned the resemblance to his advantage. I enlisted some expert help on this case,' meaning Frank, 'and he believes that there are vampire clubs around the world that pay fees to people they believe to be vampires in the hope that they will be turned into vampires by their Master. Something like that. Potentially, the man you met tonight is acting out the role of master vampire to drain money out of gullible fools.'

'Well, he was very big and very strong and pretty damned scary,' said my mother.

I considered this for a moment, read my notes again and came to a decision. 'I need to call someone, but then I am going to take the boys in the garden and lock up. I am tired, so will be off to bed shortly. If you want to stay up, you are more than welcome to. I need a shower, so I'll be in the bathroom for a few minutes if you want to get in there first.'

'You haven't told us why you were arrested yet?' complained mum.

'All connected to the same vampire case, mum. I will tell you about it over breakfast. It is really not that exciting though.'

I stood up and stretched. I had several bits of me that were getting sore from being slammed into the ground, punched, kicked, and hit with things over the last few days. The bruises were beginning to join to form one whole-body uncomfortable mass. I had a lot of pieces of this case, but nothing that was going to help me solve it. Maybe tomorrow I could talk to some of the vampire-wannabes and get some information from them on Ambrogio.

As far as I was concerned, he had crossed a line now. The case was personal. Threatening me was one thing but turning up at my house and grabbing my mother was not something I could ignore. Whether he was in anyway linked to the murders or not, I was going to find him and expose him and very possibly get into a fight with him at the same time.

I wanted to ask Frank a few questions but checked my watch and hesitated. It was late already, but would Ambrogio be back tonight? Had he left, or had he gone off to get friends? I decided, given the circumstances, that it was best to see what Frank thought.

As I left the room to begin the bedtime routine with the dogs, I fished out my phone again. The message that landed a couple of minutes ago was from Hayley.

"Your life sounds so exciting compared with mine working in a coffee shop. I would like to hear all about it sometime, but it is not what I am really after you for. xx"

The dogs were in the garden doing their usual routine, so I sent an immediate reply while I waited for them. *"You seem to know what you want, so please tell me what it is. x."*

Bull was trotting back towards me when the reply came just a few seconds later. *"Being honest here, I don't really need a boyfriend, I don't have time for one and have always found men to be a bit needy once they are in a relationship. I do miss sex though, so I suppose what I do want is some cock xx"*

I picked my phone up from the carpet where I had dropped it in my surprise, then tried to find a suitable response.

"How refreshing to meet a lady that knows what she wants and can ask for it directly. I shall see what I can do." I left it at that and got a single, *"X"* back as a final response. The ball was now in my court. I had never really worked out if I was looking for Miss Right or not. Was I bothered if I met a few Miss Right-Nows along the way? No, not really, was the simple, immediate and honest answer. If attractive women wanted to use me for sex, I was not inclined to argue or resist.

I flipped to Frank and pressed call. He answered almost immediately.

'Tempest?'

'Hi, Frank. Frank, while we were having fun tonight Ambrogio came to my house and tried to hurt my parents. They stayed inside, and he pretended like he couldn't get in. Do you think my family is actually in danger?'

254

'Oh, my lord. Yes, Tempest. A danger of the gravest kind. Ambrogio will be more or less unstoppable.'

'Why do you think that? No, silly question. Forget I asked.' Frank would just explain how vampires were so much stronger and faster than humans and that they lived for centuries because they were so hard to kill. I changed tack instead. 'Frank if my parents stay inside their house when it is dark will they be safe?' This idiot Ambrogio clearly would not enter the house because a vampire can't cross a threshold they have not been invited across. If I played by his rules, then I should be able to keep my family and friends safe.

Frank agreed that they could probably avoid harm if they stayed inside but that did not allow for Thralls which the vampire might employ. I wrote Thrall on the back of my left hand with a sharpie so I could look it up later. Frank explained anyway that a Thrall was a human servant that would do a vampire's bidding and could move freely in daylight and across thresholds thus defeating many of the protective precautions one might employ.

I thanked Frank for his time and disconnected. I was not sure whether I needed to be worried or not, but I was certainly not relaxed.

I awoke at a fairly normal 0530hrs, scratched myself sleepily, yawned and briefly considered getting back under the welcoming covers. I had long ago learned though that an early morning workout came with a number of benefits. Not only did I find that no matter what the day held I would already have ticked "go to the gym" off the list and thus not be able to miss it, I also felt better physically and found myself more mentally aware. Furthermore, I could eat a hearty breakfast without too much concern because I had already achieved a calorie deficit. I left the dogs asleep in my bedroom as it was far too early for them to consider getting up.

I made as little noise as possible getting out of the house so that my parents would not be disturbed, although as I had crept passed the guest bedroom door, I observed that either someone was using a chainsaw to cut through oak or my mother was sleeping on her back again. Creeping was probably redundant.

With so many gyms to choose from I had moved around a few of them until I had settled on one that offered very few frills but had a cheap monthly rate and all the equipment worked. It also opened at 0500hrs which no others did. It was a time that worked well for me. I did not need much equipment. An old army physical training instructor had once shown me he could train a person hard enough to make their eyes bleed with no equipment at all.

I got my cardio by running or cycling so the gym was just for picking up big weights repeatedly until the muscles being engaged refused to pick them up any more. Doing this routinely meant that I was stronger than I would otherwise be and kept the fat at bay as each session blasted about half of what they say a man's daily calorie intake should be.

At just after 0715hrs I was walking back through my front door to the pleasant smell of bread baking.

'Wotcha, kid!' called my Father from the kitchen where he was peering through the oven door. 'Should be out in a minute.' he said, referring clearly to whatever goodies he had inside it.

My dad was a dab hand at anything he decided he wanted to be a dab hand at. I had inherited this ability but with less skill. Or perhaps a little less determination, but he elected to start baking bread one day and then went on to master it. Within a few months of starting, he was turning out baps, bloomers, bagels, and brioche without needing to open a book.

'I need a shower,' I announced as I dropped my car keys back onto their hook.

Mother was most likely enjoying a cup of tea and watching the breakfast news in the living room, so I stripped off on my way up the stairs, threw my thoroughly damp clothes into the hamper in the bathroom then leaned into the shower to set it running.

I posed vainly a few times in front of the big mirror I had on one wall. It was ok for my age I felt. I was never going to win a contest or get a modelling career, but I was in acceptable shape and could see a clear definition between the muscle groups. Too much fat on my abs still but the only way I would shift that would be to stop drinking alcohol forever and life was just too short to never have a pub lunch or night out.

Dressed and back downstairs, the dogs came to find me with their little tails wagging behind them. They had been in the garden when I got home making sure the neighbour's cat was evicted from its favoured spot under the plum tree. Greeting complete, they trotted back to the lounge to take up their standard daytime position on the sofa. There they would sleep until the chance of food or a more interesting activity came along.

Interesting activities included things like bark at the postman, bark at birds in the tree outside of the window in the living room, bark at the neighbour's cat visibly taunting them from the fence outside, that sort of thing.

On the side in the kitchen sat a beautiful and fresh white sandwich loaf on a cooling rack. The smell was divine and conjured up images of melting butter sliding off a warm slice and onto my wrist as I ate it.

'It's ready to eat, son,' offered my dad, opening a draw to select a bread knife.

'You first,' I countered and watched as he helped himself to two generous slices including the crust.

'Mary, would you like some toast, dear?' he called through the living room where we could hear her tutting at the news headlines.

'Coming,' she replied, her voice preceded her appearing through the door a few seconds later holding a now empty mug. 'I need a refill and a fresh mug. Bull licked this one clean.'

It had probably been left unattended I thought to myself as I selected a fresh mug for her and one for myself.

Breakfast was a very pleasant affair with my parents talking animatedly about their forthcoming cruise holiday which they had been planning for months and was almost upon them. We chatted back and forth about my garden and what I had planned for it, about the weather, as one always does and generally avoided any talk of the events of the previous night. We are great at avoiding issues by pretending they don't exist.

I'm not sure that it is healthy, but it is what we do. By 0900hrs, mum and dad had gone home, and the house was quiet again. After my shower, I had selected tan cargo pants and Caterpillar boots with a t-shirt and hoody. It was my plan to give the dogs a good walk as I might be out quite a bit during the day.

'Boys,' I called through to the living room. No reaction.

'Time for a walk,' I called again as I grabbed their leads off the peg in my utility cupboard. Still no reaction.

Sighing in defeat, I went back through the lounge where two disinterested Dachshund faces were peering at me, side by side on the sofa. I had to walk up to them and place their collars on their necks and gently tug at them while also instructing them to move their fat arses. Accepting defeat with very little grace they lazily got off their cushions.

They stretched and finally began trotting resignedly to the door. A few minutes later I was letting them off the lead to run free in the vineyards and they finally seemed to be excited about being outside. Now, with both hands free, I pulled my phone out to check emails and other messages. I scanned my emails, of which there were a few, but noticed immediately a new email from Ambrogio.

Mortal,

How dare you attack my servants! I grow impatient with your continued existence. Your kin barely escaped last night but have merely prolonged their pointless lives. Soon you will understand the futility of your resistance. Until then, since you have taken followers from me, I will take one from you.

Ambrogio

Okay, so he was upset about the fire at the clubhouse and blamed me for it. The guy wanted to kill me, scratch that - he wanted to bathe in my soul, which sounded more than a little homoerotic. I wondered exactly what bathing in my soul entailed? Anyway, since he already wanted me dead, I doubted I could make him much more upset.

I paused briefly to wait for the dogs who were now sniffing at something underneath a hedge. My guess was there would be a rabbit hole beneath the brambles they had caught a whiff of.

Before I could consider what Ambrogio meant by threatening to take one of mine the phone rang in my hand causing me to drop it.

The number was a mobile, so it was very possibly a client calling.

'Blue Moon investigations, Tempest Michaels speaking. How may I help you?' Polished.

A moment of silence on the other end and just when I was going to repeat myself the person spoke. 'Hello, Mr. Michaels. I think I need to meet with you. I need your help.' A woman's voice. Young. Local accent.

'Of course,' I replied agreeing. 'Can you tell me what this is pertaining to?'

'Um. I was at the fire last night.' she said, leaving her answer hanging in the air for a bit. 'I escaped okay, but my boyfriend was taken by the police.'

'It would be inappropriate for me to discuss the case over the phone. If you want to meet, I can make myself free today. Perhaps you should tell me your name.'

'Sorry,' she mumbled. She sounded scared and confused more than anything else, so I softened my voice and tried to coax some information out of her.

'I was at the fire last night too and I got arrested trying to help your friends get away from the fire. Were you hurt at all?' a simple question to get her talking.

'No. No, I wasn't. I think I was just lucky though. My boyfriend Nigel went out ahead of me and tackled a man with a crowbar so that I could get away to our car. He said he would meet me at home, but he never turned up and then my friend Sophie said he had been arrested with lots of the others.' She took a breath and continued. 'Then I didn't know what to do, so I went to the police station and they said he would not be released yet as he was being questioned in connection with *The Vampire* Murders. Then my other friend Becca, who is not a club member said she heard they found human blood and that was why they were all being kept by the police.' She was beginning to blurt, and I could not keep up. I didn't even have a pen to hand out walking the dogs as I was, but then she ended with a question as if she had just had a thought that dominated everything else, 'Oh my God, has Nigel actually been drinking human blood?'

Wow. That was a question. 'Why do you think he might have been drinking human blood?

Silence for a few seconds.

'At the club, we drink cocktails that are supposed to be blood. It is fake stuff of course made from corn syrup and food colouring, that sort of thing. We put vodka in it, or something else to make them alcoholic but then our Master, that's the true vampire the club was founded by, well he showed up for the first time ever. I say ever, but apparently, he started

261

the club over one hundred and fifty years ago but has not been seen since then. So anyway, he showed up a few weeks ago and everything became weird. I mean weirder than usual,' she said when I didn't respond.

I was trying to process all this at speed. I needed to meet this girl and anyone else from the club and it needed to happen soon. I put my hand over the phone and quickly called to the boys to turn them around. The walk would have to be shorter than originally intended.

'I need to meet you. Where are you now?'

The young lady was called Angela Barclay. I offered to go to her, but she wanted to meet at my office instead. I was now waiting for her to arrive.

A fresh tea was cooling on my desk in its little cardboard cup. I had a kettle and supplies in the office but had felt drawn to the chance to have Hayley smile at me this morning. Typically, she had not been in, but rather than admit I was only there to see her I had ordered a tea anyway.

My phone rang then. It was Frank's number. 'Good morning, Frank.,' I answered.

'Hi, Tempest. Is Poison with you?'

'No. Should she be?'

'Well, it is half past nine and she has not turned up for work. I can't remember her ever being late before and I last saw her heading off into the night with you.'

'Oh. Well, we only walked about one hundred yards and then I left her.'

'I thought you were seeing her home?' he said, clearly a little upset that I had not. I had not thought about it until now. Should I have seen her home last night despite my parent's predicament? Should I have taken her with me for safety?

I pondered that briefly and came to three conclusions. Firstly, Poison was a strong, independent woman who did not need a man to get her home safely. Secondly, I had a suspicion that had I escorted her to her door she would have dragged me through it and shagged me senseless and I was not sure I really wanted to pursue the undeniably attractive, but

263

most definitely half my age, sex strumpet that I would continue to bump into on a regular basis no matter how the event went. Thirdly, had I turned up at my house with Poison in tow, wearing muddy spandex and sporting face piercings, my mother's head would have rotated clean off her shoulders.

'Frank, I left her when I got the call from my parents to say they had been attacked by Ambrogio. Poison said go. So, I went. I expected her to grab a cab from around the corner and be in her house before I got to mine. I had no idea what Ambrogio might try next and expected him to still be hanging around outside. My mother said that he would not enter the house even though he intended to kill them, and they were right there. Why is that?'

'He could not go into the house, Tempest. He is a vampire, even you must know the basic lore. He is stuck outside until invited in.'

If Ambrogio believed this nonsense as fervently as Frank did, he had probably stayed outside of his own volition rather than step over the threshold and burst the bubble on his own fantasy.

'Anyway, Frank,' I moved the conversation along, 'Poison is a big girl and did not need me to escort her anywhere. Why the concern?'

'Well, she isn't here, and she isn't answering her phone and I had hoped she was with you.'

I heard the door open at the bottom of the stairs and light footsteps cautiously begin to make their way up. 'I have a client, Frank. I'll pop around when I get done, but drop me a text if she wanders in. Everyone is late for work sooner or later.'

'Ok, Tempest,' Frank replied with some resignation.

Was Poison with me? Frank clearly thought I was far more stud-like than I am. A shadow appeared outside the frosted glass and a distorted silhouette followed it as the visitor reached the top of the stairs. I jumped up to open the door, checking my watch as I went: 1016hrs.

'Angela?' I enquired of the young woman outside. Her hand was raised as if to knock on my door, but she lowered it now and nodded her head.

'Please come in and take a seat. Can I get you a cup of tea? Or something else?'

'A tea would be lovely. Thank you.' She took a seat where I had indicated, in the window where I could come to sit with visitors rather than sitting imperiously behind the desk.

Angela Barclay was dressed for office work. If she had been dressed like a vampire last night, all trace of that was now gone. I had studied her face briefly when I opened the door and had seen no sign of the facial piercings favoured by everyone else I had met from the vampire club. Her make-up was basic eyeliner and a bit of lippy. If she was wearing anything else, it was good enough that it looked natural. A grey pencil skirt and short heels and a baby pink, plaid jumper over a white collared shirt completed her look. Her outfit was such that she could be working in any one of a million different offices. She was slim, bordering on skinny, but was probably mid-twenties and quite pretty.

'This started with you calling me to help you, so let us please go back to the start and you tell me what it is that you want me to help you with.'

'This is all about The Brotherhood of the Dead, I guess. That is why I came to you. I only got involved because my boyfriend was so into it and to start with it was fun in a sexy, dark, mysterious kind of way.'

'Okay.' I said, setting a cup of tea on the table in front of her. I turned to grab a chair and notepad and sat down just across from her. 'Please continue.'

'It was just a fun club where we would meet up and have a few drinks and everyone dressed up as vampires. Some of the guys were quite geeky and played vampire-based boards games, or they would watch vampire horror flicks and every week there was a discussion about the world of vampires - who had found new evidence in the news of crimes that had not been solved and were clearly the work of a vampire, that sort of thing. The senior members though would talk about being converted into vampires and they collected club fees, which I thought just went to rent of the clubhouse or something like that. I didn't pay, Nigel paid for me, but I found out the membership fees were quite expensive, ten pounds a week and there are over one hundred members.'

I did some quick mental math and came up with over fifty thousand pounds a year.

'So, what was the money for?' I asked.

'I asked Nigel that and he said that we were paying fealty to our Master and he would soon begin turning his loyal servants into vampires. I thought he was joking, but he wasn't. We had a fight about it and he got very upset at my questions and said that if I didn't believe in vampires then I should just get out and never come back because he would be the first to be turned.'

'When was this, Angela?'

'A couple of weeks ago. I apologised in the end and we went to the clubhouse afterward.'

'So, the club is paying money to their master vampire as a display of loyalty. What else?'

'Well, like I said, it used to be all sex fantasy stuff and games and talking and drinking, like it was some kind of specialist bar, but then it got more serious and then started getting scary. About a month ago Nigel got really excited about an email he had received. He said it was from the Master. I thought the Master was just a made-up person. There is, or rather was, a big oil painting on the wall in the den which was supposed to be of the master. I figured it was just a painting someone had gotten hold of.' She stopped to take a sip of tea and then kept the mug in her lap, both hands wrapped around it. 'Ambrogio had emailed Nigel and was asking him to perform certain tasks.'

'Like what?' I interrupted.

'Hold on I need to explain something first. Ambrogio is the club's master, but no one had ever met him. Then, completely out of the blue, Nigel started getting emails from him. He was so excited. Nigel thought it was special treatment, that he had been selected and his time to be *turned* had finally come.'

I was making notes while all this went on and underlined *mass-delusion* twice. 'So, you were telling me about the tasks Nigel was given.'

'One of the tasks was to watch you.'

I snapped my head up at that point.

Ordering my thoughts quickly, I asked, 'When did that start?'

'A few days ago. After the thing with Demedicus. Nigel said he had to make sure you were watched because you might spoil Ambrogio's plans.

267

Then there was someone else he had to watch and the senior guys from the club they were all taking it in turns.'

'Who else were they watching Angela?'

'It was you and then people connected with you. I didn't hear names. I wasn't trusted to be involved, they were doing Ambrogio's bidding and that was all I needed to know Nigel said.'

My head was spinning with all the information. 'Hold on, Nigel is not a very vampire name, Angela. Does your boyfriend go by another name ever?'

'Yes. He calls himself Obsidian Dark most of the time.' Another piece slots into place.

'Ok, so what else did they do?' Angela seemed suddenly like she believed she was saying too much. Revealing facts that might get her boyfriend or others into trouble. Sensing this, I pressed her, 'Angela, I am not the police. What you tell me can't be used as evidence but if Ambrogio is murdering people and you don't tell me what you know he will just go on doing it. Worse yet for you, if Nigel is involved, he will be counted as an accomplice and you will be considered equally guilty because you knew what he was up to.' I had no idea if that would happen. However, I guessed that she would not know either and would be suitably terrified by the prospect to start spilling all the beans.

Angela seemed to think about that for a moment. She took a sip of tea and continued speaking, 'They collected his coffin when he arrived here from Italy. They were given specific instructions on where to collect it from and where it was to be taken to.'

'And they did it?' I asked incredulously. I caught myself then, I could not afford to question their motives or suggest they were wrong at this stage if I wanted to get more information from her. 'Sorry, Angela. That was rude of me. Do you know where they collected it from and where they took it to?' If she knew the destination, I would have a place to check out.

'Nigel would not tell me. He said it was better if I did not know. I do know that he collected it from a port though. At least I think that's right. They used his van to collect it and the satnav was for an address there, lockup connected to an importer.'

I thought about that for a moment. 'But you don't know where he took it?'

'To his crypt, I guess. But I don't know where that is.'

'Will Nigel tell me?'

'I don't think so. He is really invested in what he is doing. He really thinks Ambrogio is a vampire and will be able to make him into one as well. That is why he is doing all this.' She fell silent for a few seconds, then she sniffled loudly and put her hand to her face to hide that she had begun to cry. 'Will he get into trouble?'

'Yes, Angela. I think that he is already in trouble.' I was thinking to myself that if Ambrogio was *The Vampire* then Obsidian/Nigel was very probably a knowing accomplice. Who else at the club was involved?

I moved to my desk to snag a box of tissues from it. I offered the entire box to Angela as her face was now a mess. When I agreed that her boyfriend was probably in trouble, she had given in to wracking sobs that shook her whole upper body and not in a pleasing way. Mascara was now smudged, and tears had left visible tracks through the now visible foundation on her cheekbones.

'Angela, who else at the club is involved? You said there were several of them taking it in turns to do different tasks like watch me.'

'At every meeting, the senior council would disappear for a secret ceremony, at least that is what it was called. The clubhouse had a back room that they could go into and lock, but I don't know what they were doing in there and Nigel would never really talk about it.'

'How many of them, Angela?' I pressed.

'Six, including Nigel,' she answered without her needing to think about it or count them in her head. 'The Senior Council has six members and they were all involved in performing whatever tasks Ambrogio had.'

'I need names, Angela. Can you write them down for me, please? Both their vampire name and their real name if you know it.'

I handed Angela the pad in front of me but turned it to a new sheet so that she could not see what I had written. Her arms twitched a time or two as if in indecision, but she took up the pen and began to write.

The list looked like this:

Obsidian Dark	Nigel Havers
Brandeis Danto	Rick
Draven Parris	no idea
Karayan Krystol	Sarah Gaine
Thanatos Angelus	Louis Richmond
Keith Teeth	Keith something

I laughed when I got to Keith Teeth as he had the least vampiry and most ridiculous name I had ever heard. Perhaps that made him slightly less of a loser than the rest of them.

'Is there a rank structure? Which one of these is the leader?'

'I think they are all equal,' replied Angela, sniffing as she did. 'If there was a leader it was never discussed or announced, but I think Nigel pretty much took over when Ambrogio started contacted him. Mostly the others just seemed in awe of him.'

'Did they not delegate any tasks to other club members? You know, lesser errands like watching me and reporting on what I was doing, or fetching and carrying stuff for Ambrogio?'

'I'm not sure,' she said after a pause to consider it. 'I was not asked to do anything, but each of the Senior Council had at least one acolyte that performed tasks for them.'

'What sort of tasks?' I asked as I was writing acolytes in big letters.

'I'm not sure,' she said again.

'Think please, Angela. This could be important.'

Angela fidgeted in her chair for a while, her hands in her lap clenching and unclenching. She took another tissue and blew her nose once more, the sound loud in my confined office.

'I really don't know. Sorry,' she decided finally.

'Was Demedicus an Acolyte?' I had a vague theory forming.

Dreadfully, Angela nodded that he was.

271

Angela finally left my office at 1122hrs, leaving me with a far better picture of what had been going on. The police were not looking in the right place. I was not sure they were even looking really, and I was certain they did not understand what was going on.

Angela wanted me to help her boyfriend. However, I doubted there would be much that I or anyone else could do. I suspected that he was at least guilty of knowing that Ambrogio was killing people.

Before she left, I had asked her a couple of final questions, 'Demedicus was found to have human blood from one of the victims on his clothing. If Ambrogio is killing people and only the Senior Council can get hold of it, how do you suppose he got some? Could it be that he found out what it was because of his close ties as an Acolyte?' I was fleshing out ideas in my own head not expecting Angela to know either way. She surprised me though because she knew the answers exactly.

'Demedicus told me about it. He had a thing for me, I guess. It was obvious from the first time we met at the club. I got drunk and kissed him and after that, he was convinced we were meant to be together.' I was making notes hurriedly, but as she paused for breath I looked up and encouraged her to go on. 'He came to me about a week ago and said that the Senior Council were drinking human blood and that he had got some for us both to drink. He brought it to me in a silver chalice and said he had overheard Ambrogio talking to the Senior Council members and telling them that drinking the blood of his victims would start the *turn* and that it would imbue them with extra strength and faster reactions. He was completely mad for the idea that we would gain superhuman strength and power by drinking it. I said that I didn't want to. I had no idea it was really human blood. I thought it was all just make believe until the police

272

confirmed they found human blood from the murder victims on his clothes.'

'Hold on.' I had found a bit that didn't fit. 'When I went to Demedicus he felt threatened and the first person he called was Obsidian. If Demedicus was infatuated with you why would he do that?'

'Lots of the club members practice open relationships. They encourage sex between members. I was never up for it although Nigel often suggested we should. Since Demedicus was Nigel's acolyte I suppose I could have shagged them both any time I fancied,' she trailed off at that point. I suspected it was from running out of things to say rather than being distracted by thoughts of getting severely dicked. I asked a few more questions but felt there was little more to get from her and a pressing need to go over what I had learned to make sense of it. Angela left a few minutes later.

A full twenty minutes had elapsed, during which I considered the conversation with Angela and reread my notes. Then, like getting an electric shock, I leaped from my chain when I suddenly remembered Poison. I picked up my phone to text Frank. I expected to hear that Poison had turned up ten minutes after we had last talked or had called in sick but before I could use the phone, I heard the door at the bottom of the stairs open and then several sets of heavy boots coming upwards.

Seconds later, the door opened, and Vermont Wensdale invited himself in. One of his flunkies held the door open for him and then came through behind him and took up a flanking position to his right. Flunky number two was Stefan, whose name I remembered from the encounter in Frank's shop. He was last in and flanked his boss on the left side. It looked practiced. They looked aggressive. Threatening.

273

I was still in front of my desk, so I sat on it, legs loose in front of me. I wanted to appear non-threatening, but I was no fool, so I made sure I had a strong position should I need to deal with... anything. All my limbs were free to move, and I had desk objects within easy reach should I need a weapon.

They remained standing in front of me and Vermont was clearly about to start speaking when I cut him off. 'Your stunt in the woods nearly got a lot of innocent people killed last night. Your stupid reward created a swarm of idiots that set fire to a building and people got hurt. My friends got hurt and you better have a damned good reason for being here.' I felt like shouting but elected to keep my tone even as being the calm one generally gives you the upper hand.

'Your involvement and thus your exposure to danger are of your own doing, Mr. Michaels. I warned you to stay out of this affair and you said that you would. Had I known a rank amateur was going to be so foolishly brave I would have made moves to stop you. You should have been honest about your intentions.' He was equally calm, almost good humoured.

'Vermont, you are a fool on a fool errand. There is no vampire at the end of your quest. Your mob attacked a group of people that like to dress up and play make-believe. The nonsense you perpetuate creates an environment where other fools can play out their fantasies and, in this case, there is a fool killing people, draining their blood and then feeding the blood to equally deluded fools who believe they will gain from it.'

'You want me to slap him, boss?' asked flunky number one.

I held Vermont's gaze for a moment, partly because I didn't want to acknowledge the flunky's existence since, he was insignificant to these

274

proceedings, and partly because I wanted to see whether Vermont would consider the question.

'Not yet, Arthur,' Vermont replied. I noted the name.

'Mr. Michaels, you are neither sufficiently skilled nor well connected enough to have any impact on my hunt. I am only here to reinforce my warning to stay away from pursuing my quarry. You will most likely get yourself killed together with your friends and family. Should they accompany you, which I understand they did last night, will only expose themselves to the same danger.' Vermont's expression was passive. He was offering no threat and besides being a grade one nutter, he was almost likeable.

That didn't get him off the hook though. 'Vermont your reward for information is irresponsible and has already resulted in people being hurt. There seems to be little I can do to make you stop your current course of action, but I will be continuing my investigation.'

At my last comment, Arthur lunged. I had had no sense that he was about to. Usually you can see people plan to move because they tense their body, or their hands start to twitch, but he was motionless one moment and moving the next. Nevertheless, he had too much room to cross for me to not be ready by the time he arrived.

He was a shade taller than me at perhaps six feet and one inch and a little heavier, although it looked like fat rather than muscle. He came at me in a leap, thrusting off his right leg trying to land a hard punch with his left fist.

As I came off the desk, I swung my right arm around in an arc going out from my body and down which deflected his blow. Simultaneously I turned into his leap with my left elbow high and moving fast.

275

As my elbow connected with his jaw, I knew I had got it right. He went instantly limp and rubbery, but I sensed Stefan push past his boss and come at me from the other side. He was far shorter and bulkier in contrast and the bulk looked more like muscle. I had my back to him delivering the blow to Arthur's jaw and could not avoid the kick to my ribs. His heavy boot drove in on my left side which was left exposed by my high elbow. It folded me to my left and shunted me to my right. He could easily have followed that up with a blow that would have put me on the floor or could have swept my legs now that I was off balance, instead he hesitated momentarily which gave me a chance to find a balance point on my right foot. From there I spun around to face him.

His kick was being followed up belatedly with a haymaker punch that now passed harmlessly by my face. His momentum all behind the intended blow he was now off balance himself. I stepped forward onto the back of his right knee joint as his body stretched in front of me. That he would go down was inevitable but the check in motion caused his body to snap backward and his head flung itself all the way back exposing his neck which I duly punched. Hard.

Three seconds and both were down. I sprang back to face Vermont, but he was still stood where he had been, just as impassive as ever. I dropped my hands back to my sides and stood up straight once more, breathing a little harder than before.

'You do amuse me, Mr. Michaels. I shall pray that you don't get killed on my watch. Come along, chaps,' he commanded. Then he turned and walked out the door, clearly believing that proceedings had been concluded.

I sat back down on the edge of the desk. Stefan was lying on his back holding his throat and making gagging noises. Arthur looked a little dazed and was sitting a little awkwardly on the floor, leaning against a wall.

Different options were fighting for dominance. Anger at being attacked dictated that I wanted to get in a few more hits but I also knew that the fight was well over and the right thing to do was help the wounded regardless of which side they had started out on. My better side won the argument, so I extended my hand to help Arthur off the floor.

'Come on, big man. Let's get you up.' He looked up at me, frowned but took the offered hand and let me help him back into a standing position. Together we then pulled Stefan off the floor and the two of them struggled out of my office, each one holding the other up.

It was already a weird day.

With Vermont and his flunkies gone I made tea and let my pulse calm for a few minutes then elected to sift emails from prospective clients and pull together my thoughts on Ambrogio, *The Vampire* murders and everything to do with them. Hopefully, I would find some sense if I ordered my thoughts and would be able to see my next step.

First to my emails.

Fifty-six in total since this morning but most of it was crap. I had one email from a Craiglowry@hotmail.co.uk who had seen a ghost ship in the Medway and wanted me to help him get a picture of it, another from oldiron@gmail.com who had a spectral dog in his junkyard and finally one which sounded vaguely promising from shaynes@yahoo.co.uk which was well written and signed by Susan Haynes. Her message explained that her husband had died recently, and she was now being haunted by his ghost.

I printed her email off and stuck it on my to-do pile. The other two potential clients would have to wait, and I accepted that I might never get to them. I recognised once again that I needed to take on an assistant or partner. Potential customers were willing to contact me, so even if they were barmy, they did so knowing that my services would cost them money and therefore I was losing billable hours letting their emails go unanswered. Furthermore, I would suffer poor referencing from each of the people I did not get back to and risk creating the need for competition to spring up. I enjoyed being the only paranormal investigator in the book, the longer I could maintain that position the better.

I wrote *assistant* on the board behind me in big letters so that I would see it every time I walked in and vowed to do something about it as soon as I had breathing space.

Vampires. I thought to myself. Vampires, vampires, vampires. I focused on Angela Barclay and what she had revealed about the hidden movements of Obsidian and the upper tier of the Brotherhood. What did Obsidian know? He knew where he had taken the coffin and that made him the best person to speak to next. He was arrested last night. Was he still in custody?

I flipped through my phone and called Amanda. She answered on the second ring. 'Amanda it's Tempest. Do you know if the vampire-wannabes from last night have been released yet?'

'I don't, but I can find out. Why?'

'I just had a girl in here that was there last night but got away. Her boyfriend is Nigel Havers. He was arrested and is one of the club elders or whatever you want to call them. She claims he helped move their master's coffin. Anyway, I think there may be some involvement with the murders, so you and I need to talk to him.'

'Tell me why you think they are involved?'

'If she is telling me the truth then Jim Butterworth stole the blood from the elders who were going to drink it as part of some twisted ritual to turn them into vampires. There may be a central figure here calling himself

278

Ambrogio Silvano. I have no idea if that is his real name or not, but he could be the murderer and if so, he could be killing people with the full support of the upper tier of this club. I would consider it all utter tosh were it not for the dead bodies and that one of their members was found to have blood from Mrs. Hancock.'

'Give me two minutes.'

I sat back at my desk when she disconnected. What did I know? Asking myself that basic question and writing down facts, so that I could see them, was a tactic I learned to use long ago. It organised my thoughts. I grabbed an A4 pad and a pen and began to write.

- The Kent charter of The Brotherhood of the Dead believed that their Master Vampire had come to them and was going to turn them into true vampires
- The Kent vampires are paying Ambrogio a lot of money which makes this a profitable scam for him
- Ambrogio was real. I believe him to be a person that looks like a vampire from a book, but whatever he is the Brotherhood of the Dead think he is real and is doing things for him that are almost certainly illegal.
- Several people have been killed. I can't tie Ambrogio or anyone else to the crimes yet.
- Blood from the second victim was found at Jim Butterworth's house. He was not the killer of course, but if Angela was right then he had obtained the blood from the supply brought to the Brotherhood of the Dead by Ambrogio. This train of thought meant that Ambrogio had to be the serial killer the police were after.
- Ambrogio threatened my life and attacked my parents already

279

- Vermont Wensdale? Where did he fit in? He also believes Ambrogio to be a vampire.

I snatched up the phone as it rang to break my concentration. The name on the screen was PC Hotstuff.

'Amanda,' I answered.

'They were all released thirty minutes ago. Nothing to hold them for. Nothing to tie them to the murders and too many of them to hold anyway.'

'Dammit!'

'They have names and addresses for all of them, so I relayed the information about Nigel Havers without telling them where I got it and sent them to find him. With luck, they will pick him up at his house in no time.'

That's if he goes home. I had a feeling he would be going elsewhere to do his master's bidding.

'What about this Ambrogio character? What can you tell me about him?'

I gave Amanda some brief details but said that it would probably be best if she came to me when she was able. She agreed to come over directly she was finished with what she was doing.

It was nearing lunchtime when yet again I remembered Poison. Then the phone rang. Doesn't it always? I picked it up. It was Frank. 'Hello, Frank. Is Poison there yet?'

'No, Tempest, she isn't. I shut the shop and went to her place and she hasn't been home all night by the look of things.'

I was getting a bad feeling about this.

'Her flatmate let me in and went through her laundry with me to prove that her clothes from yesterday were not in the hamper or the washing machine. She had mud on her clothes from the fight at the clubhouse, Tempest. She isn't answering her phone, hasn't tweeted anything all day and no one has seen her. I am getting worried.'

'So am I. Where are you now, Frank?'

'I'm just leaving her place in Wainscott. I'll be back at the shop in less than ten minutes.'

'I'll meet you there,' I said and disconnected.

Where was Poison? With an itchy feeling at the back of my skull, I clicked back onto my emails. No, no, no, no, no, no, no reverberated around my brain as I scrolled down to find the email I needed to read again.

Mortal,

How dare you attack my servants! I grow impatient with your continued existence. Your kin barely escaped last night but have merely prolonged their pointless lives. Soon you will understand the futility of

your resistance. Until then, since you have taken followers from me, I will take one from you.

Ambrogio

The last sentence. I had just dismissed it. Now it made sense. This prick had taken Poison. I was certain of it.

I moved towards the door to intercept Frank as he arrived but checked my motion before I got to there. Something Angela Barclay had said.

Ambrogio had a crypt. If this guy was as crazy as he seemed and totally convinced that he was a vampire, then he might be at the crypt now. Could I appeal to Obsidian to reveal the location? Only one way to find out.

I dialled the number for Angela Barclay.

'Hello?'

'Angela, it's Tempest Michaels. I need you to give me Ambrogio's phone number. One of my friends has been taken, a young girl and I think he knows where she might be.'

'What?'

'Angela this is serious stuff. Give me Ambrogio's number.'

'I don't have it. I'm not sure anyone does. Nigel said that you don't contact Ambrogio, you wait for him to contact you.' This was not what I wanted to hear. Was she protecting him? Or was this information genuine?

I tried a different approach. 'Okay, then please give me Obsidian's phone number and address.'

'Oh, no. He can't be involved in anything like that,' she told me matter-of-factly.

'Angela, I need his number. If he has nothing to do with any of this then he can be eliminated as a suspect, but I need him to tell me where the crypt is.'

I could almost hear her thinking. Inside I was screaming *come on* at full volume, but I waited for her to speak again. 'I, I don't know,' she stammered. 'This doesn't feel right.'

'Angela,' I practically yelled down the phone. 'People are dying. Your boyfriend is involved somehow and if you don't give me his number, I will have the police at your place of work to drag the information out of you, dammit.' I was getting a little impatient.

Angela gave me the number and we disconnected. As I began typing in the number I had written down on my desk jotter, I heard the bottom door open and feet clomping up my stairs at speed. One set of feet though and light sounding.

I paused before I dialled, and Frank's head popped around the doorframe.

'Frank. I think Poison may have been taken.' I showed him the email still on my screen.

Frank leaned across the desk and peered through his glasses at the screen.

'My God,' was all he said.

'If she hasn't been home all night, we can assume she was taken last night sometime after I left her and before she got home. Since no body has been found and he is messaging me, I am guessing that she is still alive.' Frank grimaced at the suggestion that she might not be okay. 'Look, we don't know if Ambrogio is actually the killer yet anyway. He might just be some crazy vampire role-playing fool who Poison will beat the crap out of given half a chance. Or she might not have been taken at all. We could be jumping to conclusions. Have a seat or make a cup of tea. I have the number for Obsidian Dark, so I am going to appeal to his sense of self-preservation and get some answers.'

The phone rang for ages and just as I was going to hang up it was answered by the all too familiar voice of Obsidian Dark. 'This is Obsidian.'

'Obsidian, this is Tempest Michaels.'

'How the hell did you get this number?'

'That's not important, Obsidian. I need your help and I think you need mine. Ambrogio is using you.'

'Ambrogio is a god,' he cut in over me. 'You have no idea what you are dealing with, but you will find out soon enough.' The last remark was delivered with a half chuckle.

'I am starting to get tired of the threats, Nigel.'

'Don't use that name,' he spat. I probably shouldn't be provoking him if I wanted information, but he seemed disinclined to help anyway. 'I am Obsidian Dark, and I am a vampire.'

'So, how come you are up and talking to us in the daylight?' asked Frank calmly.

'Err?' replied Obsidian

'Basic stuff really, Nigel. You would be dust if you were a vampire. It's the middle of the day.' I added.

'I have been drinking the blood of my master's victims. I am a half vampire now you fool. I have the strength and speed and soon will join my master in immortality!' he was thundering down the phone. 'You can try to spoil things as you spoilt them last night, but you will fail you pathetic meat sack.'

285

I looked at Frank with my best is-he-making-this-up face, covered the phone and said, 'Half vampire?'

'Lore regarding turning vampire is conflicting. There is a suggestion that drinking the blood from the dead victim of a vampire can pass on supernatural vampire traits and begin the turn,' he whispered quickly.

'Okay, Nigel. Role play time will be over soon and when I catch up with you, I will enjoy slapping you around, vampire strength or not.'

'This is your fault. Ambrogio was going to turn me last night, but you and your family ruined it.'

'Ooh, what happened.' I goaded

'Your parents survived,' he responded with an audible sneer that chilled my spine. 'But don't worry, they will get theirs soon enough. Until then we have your poisonous little bitch to use for the ceremony tonight. Why don't you join us at the crypt and we can kill you too?' click. He disconnected.

'Bother,' I said. It was the only response that seemed to fit.

'Bother,' echoed Frank.

They had Poison. We knew that much at least now which was a step up from just suspecting. Did they plan to kill her? It certainly sounded like they did. If there was some daft ceremony or shite vampire hokum planned for tonight, then we had only a few hours to find her, but we had no idea where they might be.

'Frank, he said come to the crypt. I think he meant it.'

'You think he actually wants you to come along?'

286

'Well, maybe if he really intends to kill me, but what I mean is they actually have a crypt. That is where they will be doing whatever it is they are doing.'

'Well, of course, there is a crypt, Tempest. How else could Ambrogio sleep?'

Obviously.

'Traditionally...'

'Focus, Frank,' I interrupted before he could get started again on vampire lore. 'Poison is missing, probably kidnapped by these dicks and we need to find her right now.' I banged the desktop with my knuckles as I said the last word. I was agitated, nervous energy coursing through me, making me want to act.

'You're right. Of course, Tempest. So, what do we do?'

'We get everyone on this,' I said, my brain whirling as I planned. 'We call in everyone we can, including the police and we find Poison before darkness falls.'

On the west wall on my office is a map of Maidstone and the surrounding countryside. I put it up when I moved in as I had it lying around at home and thought it might be useful. I had not looked at it since but now grabbed a marker pen and went over to it.

'Frank help me out here. The first victim was found here,' I said, putting a black blob on the map next to Chilwell Castle. 'The second here and the third here.' Two more blobs. 'The fourth and fifth victims were found together out in Chart Sutton.' The blob this time was quite a distance out from the other three, which made them look more like a cluster.

'But they were picked up outside of a nightclub in the town centre,' injected Frank, getting involved.

'That's right. So, it would be about here.' Another blob not far from the first three.

I grabbed a rule from the desk to join the blobs by opposites using a fine-nabbed pen. All the points intersected just in the river not far outside Aylesford and not far from the site of the first murder.

Frank and I studied the map for a few moments. Frustrated, I said, 'I don't think that helps us much.'.

Frank, 'Hmmmd,' to himself, so I allowed him silence to focus his thoughts. 'His crypt will be underground, so in a basement or something similar I expect, but it could be in a cemetery if there are ones with enclosed crypts.' I peered at the map. There was nothing like that until you went at least half a mile towards Maidstone. It seemed like we were stretching.

Frank and I were still staring at the map when the bottom door opened again. I stepped to my left and opened the top door hoping that it was not Vermont Wensdale back again. To my happy surprise, it was Amanda. From my vantage point staring down at her, I could see the top of her head and the top bit of cleavage. I gave myself a mental slap for focusing on her flesh and was able thus to meet her eyes readily when she looked up at me in the next half second.

I got a slim smile and a, 'Hello'.

'Amanda. Glad you are here. It would appear that Poison has been kidnapped.'

Her smile froze and then dropped. 'What?'

'I just got off the phone with Obsidian. He claims that he has her and that she will be killed tonight in a ceremony to turn him into a vampire. Ambrogio is behind it all guiding his movements.'

'It is probably not just Obsidian, Tempest,' said Frank. 'I expect it is the whole top tier of the club.'

'Amanda, can you get people on this?' I knew the answer, of course, they were the police after all. 'I think Ambrogio is hiding out somewhere still pretending to be a vampire.' I heard Frank make a noise and held up an impatient hand before he could remind me that Ambrogio is actually hundreds of years old and impossible to kill. 'Given his level of psychosis, there is a very real chance he has made a crypt to sleep in. Obsidian's girlfriend fingered him for handling the coffin and taking it somewhere, so we need to find it and we need to find it right now.'

'Okay. What evidence do you have? A ransom note, an email? Anything?'

'Not a damned thing you can use,' I had to admit. 'I spoke with Obsidian on the phone. He confirmed he had snatched her last night and that they plan to kill her tonight.'

'Okay. I need everything you have on the girlfriend, so we can pick her up for questioning. I also need the two of you to complete an official report of the crime down at the station and I need whatever evidence you have that this person has been kidnapped. What is her actual name?'

I had no idea. 'Frank?'

'Err, Ivy Wong,' he stuttered.

Ivy. Poison. Obvious.

'We need to get to the station then.'

'I need to find the crypt.'

'But you have to report the kidnapping.'

'But I don't have any evidence.'

'Nevertheless,'

I cut her off, 'Amanda I can't go with you right now. I am going to work out where this crypt is and then I am going to get her back. Please do whatever you can to put people on alert. This whole vampire thing has gotten way out of hand. People are dead, and more people are going to die if no one stops them.' This was frustrating, but I was not going to spend hours at a station trying to explain why I thought Poison/Ivy was in danger when I had no evidence.

Amanda considered this but eventually nodded and assured us that she would do what she could. Then she left and Frank and I went back to staring at the map. There was a thought itching at the back of my head, but I was struggling to make it coalesce into anything tangible. Something about the grounds at Chilwell Castle.

Then my thoughts rearranged themselves slightly and I caught a glimpse of the memory I was trying to find. 'We need to go to my house, Frank. I think I know where the crypt is.'

'Hold on. A few seconds ago, we had no idea. Now you suddenly do?'

'I'll explain on the way,' I shot back as a reply. I had already grabbed my bag and pocketed my car keys.

I was almost at the car when the phone rang, so I plipped it open for Frank to get in but wandered away a bit so that my conversation would be more private. The call was half expecting, so to see Mrs. Sweeting-Brand flash up on my phone's caller ID was no great surprise.

I squinted my eyes against the expected tirade when I answered as she had come across as a person that had limited patience or need to remain polite.

'Mr. Michaels, I am gravely disappointed that I have been forced to make this call. I expected to hear some sort of report by now. I grow impatient with your lack of progress. Are you some charlatan dragging your feet to get more money from me? I paid for a professional service and I shall damned well have it.'

'Mrs. Sweeting-Brand I can assure you that I will only bill you for the hours I spend investigating your case and for the expenses, I incur in pursuit of a solution. I will provide an itemised bill when I have completed my investigation, or I can provide updates with expenses and charges daily if you prefer. All of this was outlined in my terms and conditions of contract.'

'Terms be damned, man. I want you to find the imposter and bring him to me.' I swear I could hear her vibrating with anger from being kept waiting.

'As I said at the time, this is not a simple case to investigate.' There was no one else in the phone book, so it was not as if she was going to sack me in favour of a competitor. 'The culprit has left no physical evidence that anyone has yet found, the countryside is littered with hunters trying to capture the supposed Big Foot and no further sightings have been made which means the man inside the suit has gone to ground or has abandoned his pretence. This is going to take some time. You assured me three days and it has been barely twenty-four hours.'

'You have three days,' she snapped and then hung up. Mrs. Sweeting-Brand was easy to dislike.

I had called Big Ben from the car, given him some basic information and he had asked where I needed him to be without me having to ask if he was available. As I pulled up to my house with Frank he was pulling into the street. His car stopped next to mine and we all spilled out and headed for my house. Big Ben already had his black combat gear on complete with tactical fingerless gloves with Kevlar knuckles and a webb belt of accessories.

The dogs barked as we went into the house and wagged their tails more excitedly than usual as there were visitors. I led them through to the back door and let them out for a wee.

'So, what are we looking for, Tempest?' asked Frank, as I went straight to the computer and fired it up.

'Just a couple of moments, please.' I was waiting for the computer to finish spooling and open the file I wanted. 'I have a picture I need to look at.' I drummed my fingers impatiently on the desk as the little rainbow symbol spun away on the screen. Bull barked at the door to be let in, but before I could move, Big Ben took a pace and pulled the door open. Both dogs plopped through the gap one after the other.

The computer caught up with itself, so I could get to the file I wanted.

'And.' Click.

'Here.' Click.

'It is.' One final click of the mouse and I pushed back from the screen so that Frank and Big Ben could get closer.

'I see keys, Tempest,' said Big Ben in a mockingly questioning tone.

The picture was of the key press at Brian Grazley's cottage with all the keys labelled neatly using an old style dynatape machine. On the third row, just over half way along was a space labelled *Mausoleum*. On every hook, there were two or more keys except on the hook for the mausoleum which had only one.

'Jagjit noticed the mausoleum when we first looked through these pictures. It just didn't mean anything at the time. I even know where it is.'

'Well kindly enlighten me then, Tempest,' insisted Frank.

'This is the groundkeeper's house for Chilwell Castle. He was the first victim that we know about. Maybe he was killed for the key. We don't know, but I was right there looking over the wall last week. The mausoleum is right by the river, just inside the castle wall and recently someone stripped back the undergrowth to get to a gate that leads out of the castle grounds and onto the river path.' Frank seemed sceptical, so I pressed on. 'Remember the map in my office? The point of intersection was right on the river, right by the castle. It's not conclusive, but we can be there checking this place out in ten minutes and I am going right now.'

'Do we call the police?' Frank asked.

'Not yet.' I decided. 'Let's check it out first. If there is someone there, then we can call for back up.'

'Should we not at least tell someone where we are going? What if we arrive and it is swarming with the Vampire's minions?' Frank looked quite concerned.

'Frank has a point, Tempest.' Big Ben had been quiet until now.

'Okay. So, let's tell Amanda where we are going and to send for backup if she doesn't hear from us. That good enough?' I left the question hanging for a moment to see what they thought. When they were visibly undecided, I pressed on, 'There is nothing to tell the police at this point. If I am wrong, then we waste their time sending them to the wrong place when they could be looking elsewhere for her. Plus, we have been arrested twice in the last week and we are proposing to break and enter the grounds of a stately home.'

'Okay,' they agreed, both conceding the point.

I ran upstairs to get changed into more appropriate gear. I had on office wear which is not the thing for countryside paths and leaping over walls. If I was right and we had found the crypt, then who knows what might happen.

Selecting my black combat gear, I strapped on the impact vest and the same fingerless gloves as Big Ben was wearing. My feet I clad in my old, but very serviceable army boots. Not the issue ones of course, like most full-time servicemen I had invested in a better pair that would be more comfortable for long-term use. They were less well-polished than they used to be and now had old, dried mud in the welts - a crime punishable by infinite press-ups a lifetime ago.

Back downstairs and ready to go I checked my watch: 1503hrs. Lots of time before dark still. I made to go for my car keys which were hanging in the entry lobby and there were the dogs in front of me looking expectant. If I went out now, I would miss their dinner time. It was too early to feed them, plus they needed a walk. I tussled internally for a moment and concluded that I might as well just take them with me. They would sleep happily on a blanket in my car without getting cold. I could take their dinner with me and if we did find Poison or had to go to other places, I would still be able to deal with them.

Frank was looking at Big Ben and me as if he had a question, so I encouraged him to ask it. 'Is all that gear necessary?' Big Ben and I looked at ourselves and at each other. Head to toe black with impact padding on elbow and knees, Kevlar plates on the chest and back, fingerless gloves with Kevlar knuckles, combat boots, webb belts with tools, Maglite torches - the usual paraphernalia. 'It's just that you look like you are off to start a coup,' he said when we failed to speak.

'More like storm a fortress,' said Big Ben with a huge grin.

I said, 'It's what we wear. I doubt anyone will see us unless we want them to and surely it makes us look like professional security or uniformed something?' I checked myself in the mirror by the front door. I tried a smile. 'Do you really think we look like terrorists?' Frank just shrugged. 'Too late to change now,' I concluded. 'Let's go.'

Dogs ready to go and both food and water for them in a pack by my feet I tackled the hardest subject: Big Ben and I were both combat veterans and used to being in situations where there was a tangible risk of harm, but Frank weighed about half of what I did and ran a bookshop. It was not that I felt Frank would not be any use to me or was more likely to get himself hurt. I was just used to moving around with Big Ben and our training meant we knew how to operate without speaking or discussing the next step each time. I was reluctant to tell Frank he could not come, but I would be more comfortable if he stayed behind. As Frank and Big Ben came out to the doorway, I encouraged Frank to go back to his bookshop and to wait there for news but of course, he would not entertain the idea.

What Frank said was, 'Tempest, I think you need me more than you know. What if you encounter Thralls? Do you know how to break the blood bond between them and their master?'

'Actually, I do Frank.' I replied dryly. 'I saw it on Vampire Dairies recently.' I was joking of course, but Frank seemed crestfallen that I was trying to leave him behind. 'You can come, Frank. But I don't want you to get hurt. If we find Ambrogio or Obsidian or any of the others the priority is to find and rescue Poison. With no back up the plan is for Big Ben and me to stop them or delay them so that you can get away and get help.' Frank looked distinctly nonplussed.

'So, my job is to run away?'

'This is vital, Frank. If no one gets help, then no one rescues Poison. Your task, if we encounter overwhelming numbers, is to find back up and bring them to us. Seriously though, no matter what we plan, it will all go to hell as soon as we find them, and I want to know that help will arrive.'

'No plan survives first contact with the enemy,' Big Ben recited from army doctrine.

'What he said,' I echoed. 'The best case is we find Poison with Obsidian, clobber him, rescue her and this is all over before dark.'

'Worst case?' asked Big Ben solemnly.

'Worst case is we all get killed by vampires,' was Frank's feelings on the matter.

'Worst case,' I corrected him. 'Is that there is nothing there and we still have no idea where Poison is.'

'Let's hope we guessed right on their location then,' finished Big Ben.

There being nothing left to say, we snagged bags and gear and headed out, me with two Dachshunds dancing around excitedly in front of me. Frank jumped in with Big Ben and he peeled out and past me as I was settling the dogs on my passenger seat. I had told them where to go, so

297

just a few minutes later we were pulling up back at the same spot I had
parked in earlier this week.

At the door in the castle wall, the three of us stopped. Running down the path I had outlined that this point was close to the first victim's cottage and where we thought the crypt was.

'Give Frank a boost over, Ben,' I instructed as I leapt the wall myself and dropped down on the other side into a crouch. A moment passed and when no one appeared to be coming over the wall behind to me I began to get up again to see where they were. Then the door in the wall opened and Frank walked through it, head ducked slightly, followed by Big Ben who was more or less bent double to get through.

'It was unlocked,' Frank said, somewhat redundantly.

Big Ben and I exchanged a glance just as Frank came to crouch beside me. I had no idea if there was any need for us to be surreptitious, but caution seemed the right tactic until we knew more.

The old, overgrown building I had seen over the wall in my last visit looked just the same now. There was no noise of any kind save for birds tweeting in the trees. It would be a tranquil, lovely garden to be in under other circumstances.

I motioned forward with two fingers of my right hand, a practiced move from a different life. Big Ben set off without another look, skirting between trees to cover the fifty yards to the target.

I checked behind me to see that Frank was trailing along, copying our movements and keeping both low and quiet. If we were being observed from the main building, we probably looked like complete idiots. Big Ben and I were both dressed in our standard black combat fatigues, Frank had on poorly fitting jeans and ratty old, white, hi-top Converse that had long ago decided that white was no longer fashionable and elected for a new

299

colour called cruddy instead. To finish his look, he was wearing a black Hogwarts t-shirt and a faded burgundy Black Sabbath hoody unzipped at the front.

We got to the building, or as close to it as we could get with all the overgrown plants around it and edged along it to what we assumed was the front. This part of the building faced away from the river and towards the castle so was the one bit we could not see until we rounded the side we were now edging up.

As he reached the front edge, Big Ben crouched down again. He was peering out towards the castle. I wondered if he could see someone, or if we had been spotted, but realised he was just checking if there was anyone visible as he was about to silhouette himself in front of the white stone façade at the front of the mausoleum.

He rounded the corner and disappeared from view briefly until I moved to the corner myself. The building, which appeared fairly drab from the rear was all white carved stone at the front. The entrance was framed by two large pillars either side which stood perhaps three metres high beneath the apex of the roof. The entrance itself was a massive oak door inset with black ironwork. The front was just as overgrown as the rest of the building but where we had come to the front corner, we could see that someone had recently beaten a path through it to gain access.

I remembered finding the freshly removed undergrowth at the gate in the castle wall. This looked just as fresh as if it had been cleared in the last couple of weeks. I fingered a piece of broken bramble just like I had when I was looking at the gate - snapped not cut.

I pushed on through the gap in the undergrowth with Frank on my heels.

300

'The lock has been used,' said Big Ben almost whispering. 'It's just like the gate.' Meaning that it was clear of bugs and debris. 'Do we go in?'

I nodded and watched as he twisted the ancient doorknob and pushed at the door. I expected nothing to happen as I figured the door would be locked but it swung open with almost no noise at all.

And inside staring right at us like a bunny caught in headlights was Obsidian Dark with an armful of candles. A few feet from him was another man I didn't recognise. Both were dressed in black, which seemed to be the colour of choice for this season's vampires. Both hissed simultaneously and shifted back from the shaft of sunlight now illuminating the room.

Obsidian dropped the candles and hissed again like he was an angry cat. Despite moving back into shadows, he was quite visible from where we stood, as was his colleague. The inside of the mausoleum was a single room with small alcoves in the wall that I guessed held the ancient bodies of Mr. Chilwell and his ancestors. The room was illuminated by perhaps one hundred large church candles that were adorning every surface and right in the centre was a coffin, the lid closed. The coffin appeared to be made from brushed aluminium or something similar with brasslike metallic fittings to contrast yet complement the rest of it. It lay on top of a large stone block in the centre of the room. It was draped with what might have been red velvet. Just the bottom foot or so of stone was showing.

There were two steps down into the main room from where we were, the ceiling was perhaps four metres from the floor making the room seem bigger than it was.

'Where is Poison?' I demanded through clenched teeth while staring straight at Obsidian. This paranormal nonsense had gone on long enough.

'With the master,' came the reply with a sing-song chuckle. Obsidian was smiling at me.

'You had better not hurt her,' yelled Frank, advancing past me into the room. I put my hand firmly on his shoulder and whispered that he be ready. I didn't feel I need to say what he needed to be ready for.

'She will die the sweetest of deaths tonight as we are made vampire,' cooed Obsidian from the shadows below us.

I took a step down into the room and then another to join Obsidian and his friend, let's call him vampire douchebag number two, on the floor of the crypt. 'It's over, Obsidian. The police know you have been helping Ambrogio to kill people. You are going to go to jail along with the others that are involved. They know where you live, they know where you work, and they know what you have done. Ambrogio is going to be caught and you will all go to jail. Help yourself, give us the girl before any more harm is done.' This was my one attempt to talk sense into him. The next stage was to beat him into telling me what I wanted to know.

Vampire Douchebag number two decided to pipe up, 'You pathetic mortal weakling. You fail to understand the forces you are meddling with. After tonight we won't live anywhere, we won't work anywhere, and it won't matter what we have done because we will be unstoppable, invincible and untouchable.' His voice was full of confidence like he believed every word he was saying.

'Tempest, how about if I punch him in the face? Do you think that will move things along?' asked Big Ben.

'I think it might, Ben. Let's do that.'

Big Ben was already moving, his shoulders forward and his right arm rising to land a strike when the door slammed shut behind us shutting off the light.

'And now, you die,' laughed Obsidian causing Big Ben's charge to falter as he turned to see what Obsidian was looking at. I turned also and there, just inside the door, were another four vampire wannabes - the rest of the senior circle.

I turned back in time to see Big Ben complete his intended motion and swing a haymaker fist at Obsidian. It was the first time I had ever seen him miss. The punch sailed past Obsidian who was smiling broadly as he gave Big Ben a shove. Having taken his eyes off the target to look back at the door, his strike had been timed wrong and he was off balance. The simple push from Obsidian caused him to trip over his own feet and sprawl across the floor.

'Get them,' instructed vampire douchebag number two.

My brain slammed into gear and hit the accelerator hard. The only way out was through the four vampire dicks now blocking the entrance, but if I made it through them it would leave Big Ben on the floor with a six on one situation. So, that option was out. I grabbed the shoulder of Frank's hoody and pushed us both towards the centre of the room. We needed to better the odds.

If I could just take out one of them and get Big Ben back on his feet it would be three against five, odds that could cause a standoff unless they had weapons, which they entirely might. I was dragging Frank I noticed, something I didn't have time for. He was behind me fiddling with his clothing as I powered towards Obsidian. He and Big Ben were on one side of the room, the coffin giving me separation from vampire douchebag number two. Big Ben was trying to get up as I closed the distance between us, but I could not get to him before Obsidian lined up and kicked him full in the ribs. Twice.

And then suddenly Frank tore from my grasp, pushed an arm across my body in a bid to lever himself in front of me and appeared from under my left arm brandishing a crucifix. Obsidian cried out and shielded his eyes. He backed away from Frank as he advanced. He backed away as if the crucifix was painful to see.

As I bent to pull Big Ben back to his feet, Frank spun back and away from Obsidian to vampire douchebag number two and then to the other four vampire dicks, all of which were keeping their distance from the terrible effect of the crucifix.

This is ridiculous. But since it is working why challenge it?

Big Ben was up now, a hand clutching his side where the kicks had landed. He had dirt on his face, hands, and clothes from his fall and blood on his bottom lip. Frank had positioned himself in front of us, his free hand keeping us corralled behind him. We were still very much exposed, and it was still six against three with Frank's fighting skills uncertain at best.

As usual for Big Ben in situations of dire peril he elected to throw gasoline on the fire. 'Tempest, you told me there was a woman amongst this bunch. They all look like butt-ugly blokes to me. Which one of you is the girl?'

No one answered but they began to fan out around us, one of them climbing onto the coffin so he/she could leap down onto us. Frank was struggling to keep them all at bay now and we were going to have to act. I still fancied our chances if we could take out the first two to come at us. The first two to attack were always the bravest, or most confident of their abilities, although with this bunch clearly convinced they were vampires/half vampires/whatever, I was far less certain they would act in a predictable manner.

'Ready?' I asked Big Ben. We were both in fighting stances focused on the target nearest us.

'Don't wait for me,' he responded. So, I didn't.

They were going to attack sooner or later, why give them the chance to pick their moment? I went straight at the vampire on the coffin, convinced he would throw himself at me as I came closer so watched for it, stepped underneath him in a feign move as he lunged and popped up again to lift his legs as they went over me. It didn't work as I had planned though, so instead of landing on his face or skull he rolled into Frank and knocked him over. And now that Frank was keeping no one at bay the vampires all rushed us at once. The five that remained came at us in one wave and you just can't fight them all.

I moved to meet the first of them as he leapt at me, hoping to catch his punch or kick so I could turn it into a hold or use it to force him off balance, but in the dark my grip missed, and I was punched in the side of my head by another unseen assailant. The blow sent me into the hands of the first vampire who immediately capitalised on my flailing body by getting his hands around my throat.

'Will you just die?' came a rasping voice by my left ear which was unmistakably Obsidian. He was the one that had just punched my head, the pain of which was registering now.

I could not see Frank and had no time to worry about him as I tried to keep my feet underneath me and my centre of gravity low but off the floor. Go down now and I was in real trouble was the thought at the front of the queue. Obsidian was trying to get his hands around my throat from behind and I could not turn to deal with him as I was already engaged in

305

dealing with the vampire to my front who was already doing a stand-up job of throttling me. I wanted to launch a high elbow at Obsidian's head, even if I missed it should break his hold, but my arms were trapped.

From my right came the sound of a fist striking flesh followed by an unconscious looking vampire form landing at my feet. Big Ben was improving the odds. Then suddenly it was light in the room again as the door was opened once more and for the first time, and despite myself, I was pleased to see Vermont Wensdale and his two flunkies.

Cape flapping dramatically behind him, Vermont rushed down the stairs bearing a large crucifix of his own. He was yelling something I could not make out; it was Latin maybe. I saw him reach up to touch his throat and the cape released to land behind him. It was a cool move which revealed bare, muscular arms. He was wearing a white shirt with a ruffled neck opening and a leather doublet drawn tight with leather ties at the front.

His two flunkies had on combat gear much akin to my own, but with actual utility belts and far more red interwoven into the fabric than one usually associates with combat. It was reminiscent of Blade I realised later and wondered if they had ever tried doing all this with their sunglasses still on as Wesley Snipes would have.

Together, the three of them crossed the small chamber in a heartbeat. Vermont got to my position first and still moving at speed he struck the first of the two vampires in front of me across the back of his head with the metal crucifix. I half expected a comedy *boing* noise from the blow, but what I got was a sickening crunch from his skull and a flick of warm liquid on my forehead as blood came away from the wound.

Stefan and Arthur grabbed Obsidian and wrestled him away from me. The brief respite gave me a chance to find Frank who was now being

306

pulled to his feet by Big Ben. Big Ben looked over and offered me a thumbs-up as a question. I was hurt but it was superficial, so I returned the gesture. The door slammed open once again which drew our eyes to see two of the vampires running from the crypt. I guess they didn't like the odds and were feeling less invincibly powerful now.

'Do we chase?' asked Big Ben, clearly out of breath.

Before my brain could even consider the question and any options, I heard Obsidian behind me again.

'I'm not a vampire! I'm not a vampire!' he was yelling repeatedly.

Big Ben, Frank and I saw why he had changed his tune the second we turned in his direction. Arthur and Stefan had him pinned to the floor, one on each arm and Vermont was sitting astride his waist with a stake held to his heart and a bloody great mallet held over his head. The mallet was on the upstroke and nearing its apex!

'Let me go, I'm not a vampire!' cried Obsidian again.

His desperate cried mingled now with a combined, 'Nooooooo!' from Big Ben and Frank and me as we all dived to intercept the imminent murder. Seven of us crashed to the floor in a sprawling heap. I was spending far too much of my free time rolling around on the floor this week. I would not mind so much if there was a naked and happily willing lady involved but there never was.

Yet again we all scuffled, Vermont exclaiming his disbelief that we had dared to stop him dispatching the creature. Obsidian continuing to claim that he was not a vampire and everyone trying to hit someone else. I rolled off Stefan only to get kicked by Arthur as he struggled to get out of Big Ben's reach. I rolled again to find space.

307

'Alright. Everyone stop!' I bellowed. Incredibly they did, all of them turning to face me. Big Ben had hold of Frank's shirt and was about to hit him by mistake. Vermont still had the stake in his left hand.

And Obsidian was nowhere to be seen.

Staring at each other in the dim candlelight, I swore internally that our best chance to find Poison had just run out the door. I ran to the top step and outside yelling over my shoulder as I went, 'Don't let that moron stake anyone.'

Outside, there was no sign of Obsidian and numerous directions he might have gone. Did I guess and assume he leapt the wall to escape along the river path? It seemed more likely than him running further into the castle grounds. As I set off to cover the short distance to the wall though I heard a car start, a thrashed transmission and the spray of gravel as it took off. I turned and ducked to see out from under the trees. A small van was peeling out past what I took to be a swimming pool pump room. I could not see who was at the wheel, but I felt sufficiently convinced it was Obsidian.

I jogged back to the crypt and went inside once more. At the bottom of the steps, Big Ben and Frank were still engaged in a standoff with Vermont and his flunkies. On the stone floor, were two unconscious looking members of the Brotherhood of the Dead vampire-wannabe club and a third who was holding his head and sitting up.

Vermont had probably saved my life earlier just by turning up but the chaps on the floor needed first aid now. After that, I needed to get information from them and for that, I needed them unstaked.

'Vermont these are humans. Despite their appearance and behaviour, they are just plain, vanilla humans. Check their pulses please if you need to but no one is getting staked.'

'Mr. Michaels, they have been drinking the blood of a vampire's victims, they are no longer human even if they are not yet full vampire.'

309

How on earth could he know that?

'How on earth do you know that?'

'Um,' said Frank.

'Frank was filling in a few blanks while you were outside,' answered Big Ben.

Okay. 'Let's say that they are not full vampire then. Is it possible to turn them back at this stage?'

'Well, yes,' Vermont's admitted reluctantly.

'Then we have a duty to keep them safe and bring them back from their living-dead hell yes?' Ha! Get out of that Vermont.

'Technically vampires are not undead, Tempest,' supplied Frank unhelpfully.

I ignored him.

Vermont clicked the fingers of his left hand which caused Stefan to bend and check the pulse of the nearest unconscious vampire. As he did so, the vampire groaned a little and moved. Stefan stood up again and nodded at Vermont.

'Very well, Mr. Michaels. It would seem that these fellows are indeed not yet full vampires. You may proceed.'

'I am a vampire,' came the voice of the one that was still conscious, although he had made no move to get up yet.

'I bent down to him just as Vermont's stake hand twitched again. 'If you are a vampire, you are about to get staked.'

'Oh,' he said in a rather disappointed voice. 'In that case, I might not be after all.'

I asked his name while I was still kneeling next to him and asked Frank and Big Ben to check out the other two and make sure they were okay, administer first aid, that sort of thing. I checked to see if Vermont and his flunkies were going to help or hinder but they were happy to do nothing, it seemed.

'Thanatos Angelus.' He answered. I searched my memory but could not link the vampire name to the real name in my head.

'That's your vampire name, little man. I want your real name.' The tone I used was supposed to infer that compliance was a good idea.

He hesitated for a bit before giving it up, 'Louis Richmond.'

'Well, Louis, we have something of a problem to deal with. First, why don't you tell me the names of your two friends here?' I gestured to the two forms on the floor just across from us. I had a hand on his shoulder to ensure he stayed in place. Frank was helping one of them into a sitting position. Even in the dim light, I could see that he had a broken nose and two black eyes, although to be fair they were fairly black from makeup before he gained his new injury. He also appeared to have had an earring ripped out. His right ear lobe looked ragged and bloody.

Louis raised a shaky hand and pointed first to the vampire now sat up with Frank and then to the inert form that Big Ben was still checking over. 'That is Simon Holland and that is Sarah Gaine, although I know them as Draven Parris and Karayan Krystol.'

'Chaps are they badly injured?' I enquired. I sort of hoped they were, but not with life-threatening wounds as that would just complicate matters.

'I think this one is a woman,' Big Ben replied. 'But no, I don't think so. She just seems to have taken a blow to the head. There is a nasty lump by her temple.' Frank also gave me a thumbs-up.

'Mr. Michaels,' Vermont Wensdale raised his voice. 'You need to stand aside so that I can obtain from them the whereabouts of their master. The beast is still afoot!'

He actually used the word *afoot*. I looked up and locked eyes with him. He held my gaze unwaveringly. I dismissed him. I had bigger issues to deal with. I turned back the man on the floor in front of me. 'Louis, the police are on their way and they will have questions about the kidnap of a young woman. Where is she? You need to tell me so that I can find her before Obsidian or Ambrogio hurt her.' I was using a calm and soothing tone in a bid to get him to give up the information willingly. If he didn't, I was likely to grab his nuts and make them touch his nose.

'Mr. Michaels, I can get the information you want from him,' Vermont again. He was agitated and visibly impatient. His hands were twitching - a sure sign that he was going to do something very soon.

'Louis,' I started again, this time with markedly less patience in my voice. 'Mr. Wensdale here is quite happy to torture answers out of you. Tell me where Poison is being held.'

'Who is Poison?' he asked from the floor, sounding genuinely mystified.

'How many young women have you kidnapped that you don't know their names?' I shot back. My hand on his shoulder became a hand around his throat. My keenly balanced sense of how to act was shot to pieces by stress, threats and constant fighting over the last few days. I was tired and pissed off and I wanted to hurt someone. This idiot was guilty by association at the very least and he was going to tell me what I wanted to know.

'Ivy Wong ringing any bells?' I demanded. He shook his head again. 'Listen, dickbag. You think I won't hurt you? I am not the police and they are not here. Do you think the persons here will back your story if I break both your arms? Obsidian snatched a young woman yesterday and plans to kill her tonight so that you pricks can become whole vampires.' I had his head pushed back against the stone wall and I was right in his face. He was turning away from me, trying to be somewhere else.

'You mean the honour sacrifice?' he blurted with his eyes closed. 'Young, pretty, great tits, tiny waist?' Bang on description.

'Yes,' I hissed at him. 'That's Ivy. Where is she?'

'Obsidian has her stashed somewhere. I don't know where. Honest, he never told me. Only Obsidian, Ambrogio and Keith know.'

I slammed his head against the stone wall in frustration. I didn't believe him. I didn't want to believe him. I wanted someone to tell me where Poison was, so I could get her and have an end to this crazy vampire shit. I considered letting Vermont have a go at getting him to remember more detail, but that thought died on my frontal lobe as I heard voices approaching outside.

Reinforcements? The vampire dicks had been gone long enough to gather help, so I called a *heads up* to Big Ben and Frank and yes, I supposed to Vermont and his flunkies as well and I steeled myself for the next fight.

It was police that came through the door though, a tactical unit with all the weapons and gear. Their weapons were trained on me, several red dots showing up clearly on my vest as they spilled through the door shouting commands and issuing orders.

Hours later we had been handcuffed, questioned and released and were now just hanging around.

Once the police had turned up and taken over, the place got busy quickly. Within minutes of their arrival, more sirens had heralded the arrival of even more cops and then paramedics in ambulances. Then staff from the castle began to appear, undoubtedly drawn by the lights and noise. Most of the castle staff were kept at bay by crime scene tape that went up to make a perimeter, but there were a couple of persons in suits that I suspected were among the castle management team. Then the press arrived, and cameras were popping and flashing in the dying light.

Protesting our innocence made no difference at all. Big Ben, Frank and I were all cuffed within seconds and led from the mausoleum as were Vermont and his flunkies. Ironically it was the three idiots from the Brotherhood of the Dead that received the best treatment as their injuries were attended to. Our injuries could wait it had seemed.

Amanda had arrived, still in plain clothes and shortly after that, the cuffs were taken off. It was fortuitous that she was there as she was able to advise that we were the ones that had reported the kidnap and tracked the suspects. This meant that we could finally get some answers to the questions we had been asking since we had been arrested (again). There was no new news about Poison. Officially it was not a kidnap case and was not getting the attention Frank and I felt it deserved as there was no ransom note and the email I had from Ambrogio was insufficient proof to get anyone interested. It was a missing person case until they knew more.

Vermont had taken his henchmen and left the moment the cuffs came off, yelling various declarations of intended vengeance for his slights as he departed. I think several of his threats were aimed at me.

315

It had been castle staff that had called the police when they saw us coming in over the wall - so much for stealthy movement. Amanda said the report of two men, in what was reported as tactical gear, had triggered all kinds of alarms and it had been an anti-terrorist squad that had turned up to arrest us. Frank said nothing as this information was delivered. I made a mental note to listen to Frank more often.

Frank was fretting. It had been almost twenty-four hours since Poison had been taken and we had no idea where she was or if she was hurt. We may have interrupted the ceremony they had planned in the mausoleum for tonight, but there was no reason to believe they would not go through with it somewhere else or just kill her and dump the body.

I had run out of leads and ideas. I could not come up with a next step. I was tired and hungry and beaten and berating myself for being weak enough to acknowledge these things while Poison was out there still and probably in far worse shape than me. Once the cuffs had been taken off, I had tried calling Obsidian again and then called Angela but neither of the numbers was being answered. I also emailed Ambrogio and offered to meet wherever he wanted in exchange for Poison, but it felt like I was clutching at desperate straws when I wrote it.

No response came.

I got the impression that it was only through Amanda's direct involvement that anything had happened at all. Chief Inspector Quinn was on the scene but thus far had blithely, and I'm sure quite deliberately, ignored me, as if I was so insignificant that I was not worth speaking to.

Amanda reported that the three vampires of The Brotherhood of the Dead had been placed in custody after being treated for minor injuries and had since been taken away for questioning. They were denying any involvement with the murder of Brian Grazly or any of the other victims.

316

Additionally, they had never heard of anyone called Ambrogio and had definitely never drunk any human blood. They had been asked about Poison only because Frank, Big Ben and I were making so much noise about it. They had all denied any involvement and were now stating that they knew nothing about the alleged kidnap of a young woman. Thankfully, the castle manager was inclined to question why they were in the mausoleum or even on the property, so they were considered at least guilty of breaking and entering and someone in castle management intended to press charges. I was a little stunned that no one from the castle had known they were here until today, but the mausoleum was on the lee side of the castle, so I suppose it was out of sight from everyone unless they took a stroll out that way. Perhaps their movement via the door in the castle wall had kept their movement hidden and we had been spotted through pure bad luck.

The sun had set a while ago and it was getting cool. I checked my watch: 1958hrs. The dogs had been cooped up and asleep in the car for over three hours now. I was not overly worried about them, I expected to have to wake them up when I got back to the car as they were such lazy dogs, but they would be getting hungry now as it was after their usual dinner time.

I let Big Ben know I was going to shoot off to feed the dogs. He was busy chatting up a young woman in a police uniform, so barely even registered my presence.

Most of the police had already packed up and left. The tactical team was long gone, the castle staff had got bored or cold and had drifted away and the ambulance crews had departed which left only a scant handful of police cleaning up and taking down barrier tape. I was not convinced that Ambrogio would return, but equally, I had nowhere else on my list of places where I might find or intercept him with Poison.

317

As predicted, the dogs were both asleep when I got back to the car. Opening the door revealed the comforting smell of warm, furry creatures. I got into the car and petted them both as they poked their heads out from under the blanket on the passenger seat. Then I fetched their dinner from the boot and fed them on the grass beside the car. I knew they would not go anywhere or be distracted by anything while there was food on offer.

As they licked their bowls clean, I clicked their leads on, waited briefly for them to finish, then invited them to take an evening constitutional to walk off their dinner. They were happy to pull me towards the river path where I guess the more interesting smells could be found. Once there, it was clear to me that there was no one in the general area, so I unclipped them once more and let them snuffle freely. I didn't plan to take them far as I needed to put them back in the car before I returned to the mausoleum.

While the boys snuffled in the bushes behind me, I pulled out my phone in the vain hope that Obsidian might answer me this time.

I was facing the river, the cool air coming from it spooling around my feet to make my ankles cold. It was warm enough outside to not feel the chill too badly with my gear on, but the cold air always causes me to reminisce about my time in the army when I would be stuck outside trying to stay warm. It made me glad I now have the option to go inside for warmth when I choose to. Across the water, the sounds from the pub drifted out. It was muted by the doors and windows closed against the autumn temperature, what did escape dissipated on the surface of the river.

I felt the scream as much as I heard it. My adrenalin spiked immediately. I had heard people scream before and could tell the difference between a scream induced by pain, or by terror or just plain fake. This one was real, its creator gripped by absolute terror and it had been cut short. It was also female in origin and meant that someone was in trouble.

I was directly opposite the River Angel pub and therefore nowhere near anything else. No chance of back up, no idea what I would find ahead of me and my two tiny dogs were somewhere in the bushes snuffling for discarded food. The scream had come from further along the path, back towards the mausoleum. Maybe others had heard it and would react also, but I made my decision and started moving.

'Bull! Dozer! Get here now!' I bellowed as I took off toward the sound. Perhaps two seconds had elapsed, and I was accelerating into the dark. One of the dogs appeared by my feet, easily keeping pace with me. In the gloom, I could not tell which one it was, only that it was distinctly one of mine.

I got to the end of the paved area and hit the dirt path. The lights from moored riverboats on the far bank were behind me now, so I could see a bit better in the dark. However, with the next thought, I realised I was about to reach the denser trees and disappear under the canopy where even less light penetrated. There were lamp posts on the path, but they were not maintained, so either through vandalism or simple malfunction most of them were not working.

The darkness enveloped me completely, shards of light from the sky barely penetrated the foliage and I was forced to slow my pace lest I fall or trip or run into something. I was equally as concerned about kicking or tripping over one of the dogs as their ability to avoid people and feet had never been good.

I had covered fifty metres and my breath was starting to pull. Over a longer distance, my breathing would even out allowing me to maintain a good pace, but short sprints had never been my thing. I could already feel that I would tire soon and then the lack of fresh oxygen reaching my muscles would severely deplete my ability to deal with whatever I found ahead. Tempted to reduce my pace, I pushed it instead and saw movement on the path ahead of me, a brief shadow moving to obscure a faint light behind it.

Bull barked. It was a loud and sudden explosion of noise on the silent path. He was off to my left and a metre or so ahead of me. I heard his paws splash through a puddle although I could see neither it nor him. He barked again, and his brother joined in, a continuous statement of proposed violence. The dogs could see, or smell or perhaps sense whoever was ahead, their normal reaction to make noise quite welcome for once.

I still couldn't see much, it was just too dark, but now whatever it was I was running into was just a few yards ahead and the indistinct shadows were becoming shapes. What I could see was a human shape turning towards me. It was stood in the middle of the path and even in the poor light I could tell it was a man and I could tell he was big. Really big. Muscular. His shadowed outline was wide at the shoulder like a bodybuilder. I couldn't see anyone else. What was I running into? Was this just a guy out walking home from the pub? Or had he just clubbed a woman with nothing to stop him killing or raping her except me? There was no time for a decision, he was right in front of me. I was moving fast and if he had just attacked someone I needed to act now. If I stopped to make sure I was attacking the right person and not some innocent out walking his dog, then I would have handed the advantage over.

So, I slammed into the figure, using my weight and momentum to drive home a killer punch to his throat. Forget punching the skull: Jaws, cheekbones and anything else on the head are generally harder than your knuckles, so while you may land a stinging blow you stand a big chance of breaking your hand. The TV show knockout punch is rare to the point that I have never seen it. The best I have seen resulted in a dazed effect, but the throat, genitals and other soft bits have a devastating effect if struck correctly. I crashed into him and understood more fully just how big he was.

I could think of nothing now other than landing the next blow. I had committed to taking him down, all thought of whether he might be innocent dismissed. I grabbed his left wrist and pirouetted underneath it to force his elbow joint against itself then used my continuing motion to swing him around and onto the ground. His feet tangled, as I had intended them to, and he went down leaving me knelt on his back with his left arm in an armbar. It was a textbook move. I had never performed it that well in practice.

So, what now, dummy?

My breathing came in ragged lumps, my pulse through the roof from effort and adrenalin. If this guy had just attacked a girl then I needed to find her, I also needed to get help to deal with Mr. Enormous, because there was little chance of getting him up and back to where I would find people. I wanted to get my phone out, which meant dangerously juggling my hands and where the hell were the dogs?

All these thoughts fought for dominance as half a second ticked by. I looked up and around, wondering where the dogs were and hoping to spot the victim. My eyes were adjusting to the dark, but I could see nothing of value.

Mr enormous moved beneath me. He had only been down for perhaps three seconds, everything had happened so fast and he was trying to get up. 'Stay down.' I instructed. 'I can snap your arm in three places with almost no effort from here. Where is the girl?'

He said nothing. However, his head snapped up as we both heard movement a few feet away. The path was bordered on one side by the canal and on the other by a steep slope. The slope was mostly dirt and trees, not much foliage on the slope where local kids scrambled around on it. At the base though there were bushes, nettles, weeds and the obligatory litter. I heard one of the dogs sniff something, an odd but instantly recognisable noise of air being drawn into a canine nose for analysis. The next noise we heard sounded larger than a small dog, like a human limb moving.

'Is there someone there?' I asked. 'Miss? I have subdued the attacker, but I need to know if you are okay.' I got no response from her, assuming there was a her over there, but Mr. Enormous had decided he was getting up regardless of what I thought and was performing a one arm press-up with me on his back.

'Don't do it, man,' I warned as I increased the pressure on his left arm. What I was doing seemed to make no difference though - he was getting up anyway. I leaned my weight back and pushed against him, putting one leg back onto the ground for additional leverage. His arm was locked, and his resistance should have been ripping tendons in his elbow and shoulder. If it was, he showed no sign of pain. My foot slipped on the dusty path and I realised I was about to get a beating when he stood up. In one motion, he was on his feet. He turned around and grabbed me with his left hand.

Oh, my god. It was Ambrogio! His face swung into view for the first time as it moved through a light patch coming between the trees and here we were, finally face to face and grappling for a dominant grip.

My brain casually observed that his hand was massive as it closed around my left bicep and then the pain hit. There is a sweet spot where the two muscles that make up the bicep join. Push your thumb between them and the pain is instant. Whether he was doing this from knowledge or chance my left hand went slack and I was unable to keep my grip on him.

Focus. Move. Block and strike. I released his left arm. After all, my grip on it was having no effect. I pulled back from his grasp to create motion and switched to move towards him just as his balance shifted to follow me. He still had my right arm, but I drove forward ignoring his grip to crack my elbow into the side of his skull. The blow hit, jarring my arm and I landed another just the same followed by a knee to the groin and a kick to the inside of his left knee. His weight dropped again as his knee buckled, but he recovered immediately. The knee kick alone should have convinced him to let go, but as I considered what I might do next, he hit me. The blow caught under my rib cage as his left arm drove upwards to take me off my feet. Looking back with time to consider it, I still doubt I have ever been hit harder. It was like a sledgehammer smashing into my gut. My breath went from me before my feet came back to the earth. This is a terrible thing in a fight when you are already breathless. A next blow had to be coming, so with that singular thought, I settled my feet to provide a balanced base and spun my arms up and out. The move should have broken his grasp and allowed me to then kick away from him, but where his right arm held me my swinging arm just bounced off it and he yanked me into a headbutt.

The headbutt missed. Not completely of course, but rather it missed my nose and most of the impact was on my forehead. Headbutts are a close-range weapon, which when used effectively will end a fight instantly. The nose is the best target because it will smash completely, bringing tears to blind eyesight, instantaneous pain to stun and it will drastically affect the ability to breathe when the blood starts to flow. He missed my nose, but the strike had some serious force behind it. I was stunned anyway which gave him the chance to sweep my feet out from under me and follow me to the floor.

He landed on top of me and would have knocked the breath from me if I had been able to recover from the first pile-driver punch to my midriff. I reset myself mentally. I'm on the ground and on my back and that is a strong position if you know what you are doing. He was trying to force my head to one side and into the dirt of the path but using both hands to do this and basically sitting on my hips he had ignored all my limbs. I couldn't really see him still, couldn't make out the features of his face it was so dark. He had forced my right cheek flat against the path and I was pinned unless I could find some leverage. I threaded my right arm down between us and hooked it underneath his right armpit. He was leaning down like he planned to kiss me or something. I pivoted off the path with my hips, shoved hard with both arms and pushed him off me.

I spun away and got my legs back under me. We came to face each other as we both scrambled to our feet. My breathing was ragged, my pulse high but everything worked, and nothing was broken so I was still in the fight. Even though he was bigger, stronger and worryingly impervious to pain, I could still win.

A groan came from the scrub to my left. I had all but forgotten the girl I came running to help. She was moving now, coming around perhaps. My brain spinning fast now and I no time to weigh up my options. I had to get

325

Ambrogio under control or convince him to run and neither seemed entirely likely. Before I could move though she sat up, her face shining in the light coming through the trees. It was Poison! She was bleeding. That was my first thought, my second was that she was holding one of the dogs, both hands gripping its body while it tried to lick her face. Then her eyes focused on Ambrogio and she screamed.

The scream was incredible. She was staring at Ambrogio, eyes huge and mouth open, screaming from the very base of her soul. The scream ended when either shock took over or she ran out of breath, but neither I nor Ambrogio had moved in the seconds that passed. Then a whole load of things happened very quickly.

Bull barked. He was stood between Poison and Ambrogio. The little guy was defending her. Dozer wriggled out of her grip and joined his brother so that the two of them stood side by side. I started to move towards Ambrogio as he started to move towards Poison. In the dark, I didn't see his left arm swing up to swat me back and it stalled my progress. The blow threw me off balance and I stumbled and fell while he continued towards Poison. The boys barked once more, and I saw Bull launch himself forward snapping at Ambrogio's ankles. Ineffective, but ridiculously brave. Then Dozer joined in and I watched horrified as Ambrogio stopped, bent down and picked up the two dogs, one in each hand. Momentarily stunned into motionlessness, I saw him throw the two dogs away like they were toys. A yelp from one as it hit the bank behind Poison somewhere and a splash from the other as he threw it off the path and into the canal.

My brain exploded, all my emotions coming at once. The dogs! Dead? Injured? If I needed a boost to overcome this guy, then now I had it. Any coherent thought of what attack to lead with, how best to pin him or disable him were all gone. He was moving forward towards Poison again. I was insignificant it seemed, forgotten. Good.

I took two fast steps, leapt off the ground and slammed my right fist into the side of his head as I came down on top of him. He stalled, stumbling as I landed on him, but he didn't stop. I was so filled with rage. I wanted to find the dogs. One of them was in the water and Dachshunds don't swim well, their ridiculous bodies so poorly designed for it. I rained blows down on him, punches to the face, kicks to the legs. He went down to one knee and I grabbed his head and kneed him in the face with everything I had.

Poison had finally got enough sense back to get up and run. I noticed her scramble to her feet and head in the direction of the mausoleum. She was limping, but I had no time to focus on her. The knee to the head should have been the end of it, anyone else would have gone down with their nose spread across their face and either unconscious or concussed. As he fell back from the impact though, his face caught in a shard of light which revealed that he was bleeding, if the blow had hurt him, he showed little sign of it. His eyes locked on mine, his left hand went behind him to arrest his motion and he changed direction, coming up off the ground with an upper-cutting right fist.

The fist caught me under my chin and I knew I was done. Strangely, as I felt my feet leave the earth, I lost all my fight. I had never experienced this before, I was conscious still, but all my bells were ringing. Like an out of body experience, I could feel my senses shutting down. I could think, but not really feel anything. I crashed to the concrete path, wondering where the dogs were and if they would be okay. What about Poison? Was I losing consciousness now? Odd feelings, odd thoughts, odd sounds. I felt Ambrogio kneel next to me and felt him grab my head. He twisted it to the side again like he had earlier. I realised he was exposing my neck as he leaned down to bring his mouth to my skin.

I was dimly aware that I was going to die then. That I would be the sixth victim of the *Vampire*. Well done, Tempest. You solved the case, I silently chuckled inside my head.

His head snapped up, focusing on something else. I heard noise, then voices. They were getting louder and suddenly he was gone.

Footsteps now, footsteps coming toward me.

Someone was touching my arm and I could see shadows running past me. 'Tempest?' I knew the voice, but couldn't put a name to it. 'Tempest, are you okay? It's Amanda.'

There were voices further down the path now. I guess I was coming around because I could make out Big Ben's voice from the others. He was swearing which was not unusual, but his voice was carrying. Concern, was that what I could hear? Relief perhaps also?

'Tempest?' Amanda again and I realised that I had failed to answer her when she had spoken before. I turned my head to focus on her face. Lovely Amanda was kneeling on the path in the dirt looking utterly beautiful as always. Part of my brain was telling me that this was an opportunity to say something really cool, but I was not sure I could formulate the words. While I contemplated that, a thought occurred to me.

'Poison?' I asked.

'She's fine, Tempest. You did great. I have backup coming, but she is safe and not hurt.' Amanda was holding my hand and it felt great. I had to move though. Ambrogio had beaten me and had gotten away. It was clear to me now that he *was* the Maidstone Vampire.

'He is the killer, Amanda. I let him get away.'

I levered myself off the ground. 'Hold on, Tempest. You're in pretty bad shape.'

'I'm fine. It probably looks worse than it is. I don't think I have any broken bones, just a bruised face where I tried to break his fist with it.' I scraped my legs around through the dirt to get them back under me and let Amanda help me up. Her arm went around me, and I got a good whiff of her - expensive perfume mixed with woman. A flash of excitement zipped through my groin and I knew instantly that whatever damage I had suffered it was not life-threatening.

Then I remembered the dogs.

'Oh, God, my dogs! He picked them up and threw them. I have to find them.' I made a move forward and almost went back to the ground as my legs refused to cooperate. Amanda was keeping me upright thankfully though my sagging weight was a bit much to ask her to support for long.

'I have to find them.' I repeated and forced my legs to take my weight by pushing on my quads with my hands until they were back under me.

'What can I do?' she asked looking around for any sign of them and still holding my arm in case I fell.

'Just help me look please.' I said quietly. I had seen the force with which they were thrown, and my heart was so heavy I almost didn't want to find them, I was so convinced that it would be their tiny broken bodies I would discover.

'One was thrown somewhere up that bank I think.' I motioned in the general direction I thought was correct. It was a steep bank and littered with leaves, weeds and loose stones, so would be hard for a human to climb without slipping back down constantly. 'The other went into the water. I heard a yelp and a splash, but the current will have taken him downstream and they don't swim well.'

'You stay here, Tempest. I will look downstream.' Then she was gone, looking for my little dog and suddenly I was alone despite all the people around me on the path. I could hear sirens in the distance.

On my hands and knees, I started climbing the bank behind where Poison had been. I called for the dogs not knowing which one of them might have been thrown in this direction. There were nettles that stung my hands and then my face and neck in the dark, but I didn't care. I had too many other more convincing aches and pains to be concerned about a few minor stings.

The sound of someone coming back up the path towards me turned out to be Big Ben. He was jogging but moving slowly, probably because of the utter darkness cloaking the path. My eyes had adjusted to the gloom now; I had been away from the lights back at the mausoleum and elsewhere for long enough.

I cupped my chin and gave it a rub where the last punch had landed. It was going to bruise, and eating would be an unwelcome reminder for a few days to come.

'We need a light source down there. I think he is dead. I can't find a pulse anyway. I left Frank with him to guard the body. It looks like he ran into a piece of broken fence.'

My memory skipped to the piece of fence I had found just a couple of days earlier. I had tried to lever it back into place because I thought it was dangerous. He must not have seen it in the dark.

'Ben, I can't find the dogs, mate.' I said feeling the need to cry pulling at the back of my throat and causing my words to choke in my mouth. 'He got them and threw them. One went up here and one went into the river, Amanda is looking for that one now.' I was sitting on my butt, just miserable in the weeds and litter and probably dog crap a few metres up the bank.

'One of them is down by the body, mate, I think it is Bull. He seems fine. Come on, buddy, let's get you down there.' He took two confident steps up the bank and grabbed my arm. Getting to my feet and stumbling down the bank, I wanted to run to see which of them was there.

Big Ben said, 'I patted him, and he was dry, so whichever one it is, it did not go in the river.' My clever dog had probably seen the guy running off as Ben and the others closed in and decided to give chase. Absolutely something a dog would do.

Ben and I jogged very slowly along the path in the dark. My battered body was telling me to walk but I needed to find my dog and see if he was ok, so I forced myself to keep a steady pace. The path twisted around more than you might expect. We went into and out of light and dark patches as the tree canopy allowed light to pass in some places. We came around a bend and were met by a shaft of light coming through the trees. Momentarily blinded I stumbled into a bush and felt Ben grabbing my arm to stop me falling. The light was coming from a spotlight on a riverboat moored on the other side of the river.

'Sorry mate should have warned you about that. It got all of us first time.'

331

A step or so further and the light was obscured again by another branch and there in front of me was the man I had been fighting. It was quite a sight.

'Bull?' I called hopefully, a shadow moved through a patch of light on the ground near to the body.

'Come here, boy.' I bent down happily to scoop him up as he whizzed towards me seemingly propelled by his tail.

It was Bull and he seemed unaffected by his short flight and sudden stop. Perhaps he had landed on a bush or some leaf litter rather than the hard earth. I squeezed him into me and kissed the top of his head with relief. He was warm, and his heart was beating fast from all the excitement. I popped him back on the path and felt down his sides and limbs, squeezing hard enough that he would react if I touched a sore spot. There were none that I could find. Somewhat relieved but still very anxious about his brother, I stood up again to look at the body.

The fellow was neatly impaled through the chest by an old wooden fence post. The exact same one I had tried to put back into position earlier this week. He hung limply with the post sticking out through his back. It had not broken through the material of his shirt though, so was forming a tent with the cloth. The shirt he had on was soaked down the back with blood which shone darkly in the moonlight. The stake protruded perhaps twelve inches from his back, my guess was that it killed him instantly as he ran onto it in the dark.

A gap in the bushes allowed light from a lamp across the river to illuminate his back but all around was therefore even harder to see. He would have been blinded by the light as he rounded the bend, much like I had, and would not have been able to see the post sticking out in the dark.

Loathe to get too close and thus mess with the crime scene, I nevertheless went over to get a better look at the fence.

As we stood there not doing much I started to wonder again where Dozer was and if Amanda had had any luck in finding him. I wanted to look myself and was about to announce my intention to do so when the body started to move.

'Whaaaargh!' exclaimed Big Ben as he jumped back, taking me with him. My poor heart stopped briefly then hammered in my chest as a second later we saw that it was just the weight of Ambrogio's dead body pulling itself free of the post. His body slid backward off the post with a slight slurping, sucking noise and then toppled onto the ground to him lying flat on his back in the moonlight. The front of his shirt was equally doused with dark, sticky liquid. It was untucked and pulled roughly to one side, possibly by me during the short fight.

Distracted now by the body in front of me, I knelt to examine him. Bull wriggled to be let down, so I popped him on the floor, looping a finger through his collar so he couldn't get to the body which he was now desperately sniffing. The post had entered the chest a little to the left of his breastbone and perhaps an inch under the line of his nipples. To me, it looked like it must have gone straight through his heart. I could not manage to feel sympathy for him though, he had threatened me, had threatened my family and friends, had kidnapped Poison and possibly killed one of my dogs.

'You will note, Tempest,' said Frank, who had moved to bend down next to my ear 'That it was a stake through the heart that killed him.'

'You have got to be kidding me, Frank.'

'Tempest, how else does one slay a vampire? Had the wound been anywhere else he would have removed the post and escaped us. He would probably have turned himself into mist or a bat or something.'

Frank, of course, was dead serious.

'Frank my friend, the police will be here soon, and they will be able to provide Ambrogio's real name once they have his fingerprints. There is probably a set of car keys in his front pocket and a wallet in his back pocket with bank cards, driving license and a loyalty card for Domino's pizza.'

'Let's find out shall we,' said Amanda who had silently re-joined us. I stood up again and fished for Bull's lead in my back pocket.

'Any sign?' I asked, desperately hoping someone had found Dozer.

'Nothing, Tempest,' her voice soft and caring. 'There is a police boat coming down the river along with a SOCO team, so we can have a better look with the lights on the boat and there will be plenty of light on the bank soon and more people to help you look.' she paused for a moment and turned her gaze to the body.

'I should see if there is anything to identify him.'

She knelt and patted obvious places on his body where a wallet might be. There was nothing to find though. He had no keys, no wallet. Not even a watch or ring adorned his body.

I didn't need to turn around to know that Frank would be smiling to himself.

'There's the beast!' rang a fresh voice far louder and more excited than the situation called for.

Vermont Wensdale leapt dramatically into the small clearing we were gathered in and skidded to a halt by Ambrogio's head. Vermont was totally focused on the body. He was panting slightly as one might be after a short run and kneeling now to see the body more clearly. 'Already slain I see. A stake through the heart no less.' Flunky one and two appeared then just behind him. It was turning into a regular party there were so many of us now in the small space.

'Step away from the body please.' Amanda had produced her police ID. She had to lean over so that the card was in front of his eyes and could not be ignored.

Vermont stood up then. For a moment I thought he was going to comply, but he reached into his cape and produced a small sword instead. 'Quick men, there is not a moment to lose. Mr. Michaels, I must congratulate you on bringing the beast down, I must say that I underestimated you. Nevertheless, you have done well to survive thus far.'

Arthur and Stefan had doffed small backpacks and were now spilling equipment out onto the path. They both flicked on head torches, red light I noted, to better see what they were doing without ruining night vision.

'Your lack of experience in such matters shows I'm afraid, Mr. Michaels.'

'How so?' I was actually curious to hear what he had to say.

The beast is down, but with the stake removed he will soon recover. We must remove its head and burn the body.'

Big Ben had moved closer to Vermont, presumably to react if he did anything crazy; like actually try to cut the head from the body at his feet.

335

'Man, I want to spend some time in your head. You could sell tickets every Halloween and never run out of customers.'

Vermont looked squarely at Big Ben. He tilted his head slightly as if measuring him up then flourished his short sword which caused Big Ben to duck out of the way. Vermont swung it down towards the body.

Amanda though was stood less than a foot from him and seemed unwilling to watch a decapitation. As Vermont's arm went down towards the body, she stepped in behind him and kicked his feet out from under him while simultaneously gripping his sword arm. A second later Vermont was on the ground with Amanda on his back, the same move she had used on me a few days ago, albeit that I had not been carrying a sword. The fun was not going to stop there though, Stefan was moving already.

His foot crunched into the items he had spread out from his backpack and he went in low to drive Amanda off his boss. He was closest to them, so none of us could stop it. His shoulder slammed into Amanda, knocking her from Vermont and onto the path where the three became a sprawling mess.

Only seconds had passed since Big Ben had to duck the sword but that was more time than he needed to get back into it. I moved to intercept Arthur, who was also now heading towards Amanda. I discovered that I had no energy, no balance and no fuel left in my tank, so my first step resulted in a stumble, flail, and crash to the ground. I bounced my chin on the path but only lightly and was thankful for that as I was then able to watch Big Ben in all his glory.

Arthur, focused on dealing with Amanda and bent low to pull her off Stefan, seemed very surprised when his head simply stopped moving forward. Big Ben had his hand on it like he was selecting a bowling ball.

Beneath Arthur I could hear Amanda yelling that someone was under arrest, then a foot flicked out into the light with one of her boots on the end of it. From the position of the foot, I gauged that she was now on her back which meant that Stefan or Vermont, or perhaps both, were on top of her.

The light shining through the trees illuminated bits of the scene in front of me, much like a strobe light at a disco in the eighties, and what I saw next was this: Big Ben had one hand on Arthur's head and one hand on his trouser belt. Arthur had been running towards him, so Big Ben just continued the motion in a classic use of momentum. I watched with joy as he swivelled on his back foot and lifted Arthur up and then onwards towards the river.

Arthur let out a panicked, 'Aaaagh!' At a pitch far higher than he might have liked. It ended in a delightful splash a second or so later.

Without pausing Big Ben had reached for the next body on the floor, so that he had Stefan hoisted into the air and moving towards the river before his counterpart had made his splash.

'Swimming lesson!' he yelled with glee as he sent Stefan to join his friend. 'Any more for the pool?' he asked at volume. 'I'm sure there should be a third candidate for the synchronised swimming team.'

'Not this one,' insisted Amanda from the floor, causing Big Ben to pause.

'Are you sure?' he asked, clearly disappointed.

'Tempting though it is,' she said between laboured breaths. 'This one is in handcuffs.' We heard the metal on metal sound of the ratchet mechanism shutting.

'You fools! You must destroy the beast. You must, or he will rise to kill again.'

'Ah,' said Frank by my ear, 'he may be right about that, Tempest'

I let my head drop in resignation. 'Frank just when I think I have got you onside you have to remind me that you are bonkers.' I levered myself up off the concrete just as Amanda was pulling Vermont up and onto his knees. Big Ben was looking around for something to do, probably feeling unemployed now that there was no one left to hit.

'Listen to your friend, Mr. Michaels. This is not over,' yelled Vermont at full volume. I imagined spittle on his chin from his ranting.

'Where's Poison?' I asked Frank, completely ignoring Vermont

'I'm here,' she said from behind me. 'I can't believe you came for me.'

'We all came for you,' I answered.

'But you saved me, Tempest. He was about to kill me.' If Poison was badly hurt, she was not showing it but everyone could see the blood that had poured from the small wound to her throat and was now covering her neck and upper chest, her clothing and her arms. I had interrupted her murder.

'What are you doing here? You need medical treatment.'

'I'm fine, Tempest. I'm sure it looks worse than it is. It doesn't hurt. He was only just starting to bite when you showed up.'

I really did not know how to respond. On some level, she was probably right that I had saved her but then had I not pursued this case Poison would never have been in harm's way. Had I not been closest to her when she screamed it would have been any one of the others that had got to her and Ambrogio first. My actions had not been heroic, just necessary and without thought.

'Where were you held?' Amanda wanted to know.

'I woke up on a boat, they were all there leering at me, all except Obsidian. They drugged me with something, I was not conscious most of the time. Then I came around and I was over someone's shoulder being taken off the boat next to where Tempest found me. I started to fight which was when he bit me. He hit me when I screamed and the next thing I saw was you fighting him.'

'Well, I'm just glad you are alright, but let's get that wound looked at.' I turned to Amanda, intending to confirm that Paramedics were on their way. Before I could speak Poison crossed the short distance between us and grabbed my face with both hands to kiss me. What I expected to be a peck on the lips, given that we were surrounded by people, was instead a full-on, passionate tongue to the back of my throat kiss which she broke off only when I pressed my hand against her. Poison was staring right into my eyes when her face got far enough away for me to see it. She dropped her hands and snuggled into me, her head tucked under my chin. I held her mostly because I did not know what else to do.

Over the top of her head, Amanda was staring at me. I could not read her expression in the dark, though I silently cursed that she had seen me kissing Poison and I knew then that despite Poison's obvious charms I could not allow my hope for sex to land me in her arms.

Paramedics arrived then though with a procession of police and others with them. I kissed the top of Poison's head and handed her over to them for treatment. She would need to be checked over and was certainly heading for the hospital. As I let her go, the two paramedics were gently taking her to one side of the path out of everyone's way.

'Frank.' I called. Frank was a few feet away talking to Big Ben, both stood by the body.

At my call, he looked up and wandered over.

'Frank, do you want to go with Poison?'

'Of course, of course. Someone should be with her.'

'Do you have a number for her parents?'

'No, but I will get her phone and make sure they meet us at the hospital.'

'Thank you, Frank.' I left him then, so I could speak with Amanda. My priority now was finding Dozer. 'Amanda?'

'Mmm?' Amanda was talking to Chief Inspector Quinn who had appeared from the dark without me noticing. On the crowded path, there were now maybe twenty people and I could hear more coming.

'Mr. Michaels,' Chief Inspector Quinn addressed me. 'In the thick of it again, involved where you ought not to be.' He stepped forward now getting into my personal space. 'This time I have a dead body which was last seen alive by you. They tell me the death is accidental and you had better hope that we conclude that it is.'

'Chief Inspector,' Amanda began but was silenced once again by Quinn sticking his hand in front of her face to shut her up. He had done this several times now. Did he do it to everyone? Or was this a misogynistic thing? I wanted to punch him on the nose.

'I don't like you, Mr. Michaels. I don't like your methods and I don't like that you are interfering in police business. However, I recognise that you have assisted in solving this case and in bringing a dangerous man down.

340

We already have several members of The Brotherhood of the Dead in custody. Given the evidence to hand, I believe we have can announce *The Vampire* killings to be over and the perpetrators either dead or facing justice.'

I said, 'I need a favour.'

Chief Inspector Quinn made a snorting noise of derision. 'I am not in the favours business, Mr. Michaels.'

'One of my dogs was thrown into the river. They don't swim well, and I would like some help to look for him if you can spare me the boat for a while.'

He just nodded as if I was asking nothing. Perhaps I was. He turned slightly, spoke into his lapel microphone and told me that the boat would be along to pick me up in a few minutes.

I nodded my thanks, but he was already moving away.

'I'll come with you,' said Big Ben.

Between the trees, we could see the police boat approaching, its searchlight piercing the night. It could not get to where we were, so we left the body and moved back along the path to where it gets closer to the river. Behind us, SOCO was sealing off the area. I had lost sight of Amanda somewhere, but it didn't matter. I was dead tired, tussling between my desire for sleep and the absolute need to find my dog.

The boat had three different searchlights fitted, two fore and one aft. For the next hour, we scoured the river bank for over a mile downstream, searching up and down in the weeds and bushes for any sign of him. It was near midnight and it was cold out now. Bull had started to shiver after a while, so he was asleep now inside the cabin of the boat wrapped in someone's coat.

I had started calling loudly for Dozer when I got on board and had not stopped until my voice had started to crack. Big Ben and others had joined in but now we were all but silent as we headed back to where Big Ben and I said our cars were.

Dozer had been missing for over two hours. I knew he was gone but I was struggling to admit it to myself.

I thanked the guys on the boat as they put me ashore. The chap piloting the boat emerged from his cabin with the barely awake Bull in his arms. As always, the little dog had been an instant hit. He handed him over for me to tuck under my arm, I wanted to thank him, but my heart was so heavy I knew I would not be able to speak without my voice betraying my sorrow.

Bull wriggled to be put down and found a convenient bush on the way back to the car. My car keys were still zipped in my pocket where I had put them thankfully, after all the rolling around this evening I could easily have lost them. I waved Big Ben off and sat in my car. Bull climbed off the passenger seat and on to my lap. He looked up at me and made a sort of chopping noise with his mouth. To me, it seemed as if he was asking a question, so I answered.

'I don't know, little man. I don't know where Dozer is.' That was all I had left in me. I cried for a bit but eventually pulled myself together and drove slowly home. It was 0112hrs when I crawled into bed, still dressed and with Bull tucked in next to me.

Solving the Blue Bell Big Foot Case. Wednesday 29th September 0347hrs

The answer had woken me at 0347hrs, I could be accurate about the time as I had looked at the clock to see if it was worth going back to sleep. At some point in the last two and a half hours, I had shed my clothes although I had no memory of doing so. Bull was curled up under the duvet with me and stayed there as I threw on sports gear and went downstairs to the iMac. The exhaustion I had felt a few hours ago had faded to the background leaving behind a bone-deep ache from the recent exertions and injuries. My jaw was stiff from being punched, my hands were stiff from punching, it was all insignificant though and would be forgotten about within a week or so.

I searched Dr. Barry Bryson Ph.D. again and looked specifically for his research and the book he spoke about writing.

There was little reference to the book but what I found was its title: The Bluebell Beast. I swiped across to a new page and searched for the book to buy. I found it immediately.

First published in 2015 it was available for sale at £6.99 in paperback from Amazon. I read the inside cover blurb which revealed that the book was a supernatural crime novel with a hero and a *large fearsome bear-like creature*. The publishing house was not one I had heard of, so I clicked to a new page and googled them. Arthouse Publishing was a firm that would publish your work and distribute it for you if you paid for it all up front and they took most of the profit. Unfamiliar with the complexities of getting published, I suspected that this was a great way of getting your work out there but that most customers failed to recoup the initial outlay because their work was not worth publishing.

343

So, Barry was a failed author and had written about the very beast that now plagued the Kent countryside. I clicked on the file in which I had collated the information and notes I had on the Bluebell Big Foot. I scrolled around until I found the second newspaper article. It was the picture of the footprint, the best piece of evidence and the one that had got him into the limelight.

At a little after 0400hrs, I had a likely solution to the Bluebell Bigfoot mystery, I would follow up on it in the morning. I headed back upstairs to bed planning the next day in my head.

I woke up with the sun streaming through my bedroom window. I estimated the time at somewhere close to 0700hrs but didn't bother to lift my head to check the clock. The sun was lighting up the branches of the cherry tree in my garden, now almost devoid of leaves, there was a comforting autumnal look to it. From my angle in bed, I could see nothing else save for tree and sky.

Unusually for me, I just laid in bed not moving. A warm lump by my right hip moved slightly, reminding me of his presence. I reached down with my right hand to scratch his ears and pat his rump.

The loss of his brother had hit me harder than I was ready to admit to anyone else. Bull was more clingy than usual, sticking to my side where normally he would find his own space. It seemed likely that he felt the absence of his brother more keenly than I, they had been together since Bull was eighteen months old. I had gone back to the same breeder to get what I hoped would be an equally excellent dog.

A sad smile then as I lay there remembering just how dumb Dozer had been. Where Bull would use a paw to open a door, Dozer would just stare at it. Where Bull would climb onto something to get to what he wanted, Dozer would stand beneath it and bark. Dozer even looked dumb with oversized paws and jowls. A dumb dog was a happy dog, a vet had told me once, and he had certainly been that.

He had drowned and been washed downstream, I was certain of that now. Even if he had not drowned, he would have been swept downstream, so my search radius was enormous and had he managed to escape the river he would have fallen foul to traffic or a wild predator or something. Dachshunds were great pets but were not able to survive in the wild by themselves.

Struggling against tears once again, I threw off the covers and headed to the bathroom chiding myself for wallowing in grief.

Bull did a perfectly good task of scaring the birds out of the garden by himself and trotted back to the house for his breakfast kibble. I let him in and he shot through my legs to find his bowl. I had work to do today. It would provide a welcome distraction from the hole in my heart and it would be nice to wrap up another case and get Mrs. Sweeting-Brand off my back.

My own breakfast consisted of a spinach and mushroom omelette with sliced cold ham on the side and a glass of milk. The ingredients were store cupboard standards and I ate it several times a week in a bid to avoid carb and fat-loaded bacon or sausage toasted-sandwiches which is what I really wanted. Body fuelled up, I settled Bull in his favourite spot on the sofa, patted his head and with an instruction to be a good dog left him there. I glanced back as I exited the room, but he had already closed his eyes.

I parked the car back at Kent Predators and Prey Park at 0754hrs and climbed out into the cool September air. My right foot splashed into a puddle and I thanked myself for choosing the Caterpillar boots this morning and not the Italian-leather loafers.

The water dripped off my boot as I took my next step. There was only one other car in the car park which I felt safe to assume was Dr. Bryson's as it looked like crap and was still sporting a space-saver tyre from the puncture. The car was a mid-grey Vauxhall Astra that had seen much better days. It was tired and dirty, and most panels were either scratched or dented or both. The interior was likewise ruined, and the parcel shelf was missing so I could see the punctured wheel lying among typical boot detritus. I also noticed that the car was open as it was an old model that still had the pop-up knobs in the windows.

I checked the building and could see dim light from his office illuminating the foyer area but no other signs of life, so I moved around to stand between his car and mine, making my intentions less obvious. I slipped on a pair of contact gloves from my pocket and gently opened his door. I always kept some gloves in my pocket and had a box in the car just in case. They were great for making sure fingerprints were not left behind. It seemed that an alarm was highly unlikely although I reasoned that if it did go off, I could have claimed to have knocked it or tripped a motion sensor.

The interior smelled musty and vaguely of aftershave, it reminded me of the smell my grandfather's car use to have, old perhaps, yet somehow still manly. I was looking for the boot release which I spied on the driver's side footwell. I cautiously bent down to operate it, knowing that I could not easily explain accidentally opening a car and then its boot.

The boot popped audibly as if there was pressure pushing against it, or it was perhaps out of alignment and had to be forced closed each time. I checked the building for movement and satisfied there was none, I continued.

346

Quite what I expected to find I was unsure about, a nice big sign saying guilty would be nice, but before I could peer inside the now wide-open boot, Barry spoke.

From behind me a voice said, 'It's not in there, Mr. Michaels.' I spun around startled, to find Dr. Barry Bryson Ph.D. stood no more than five feet away holding a shotgun tightly in both hands. It was pointed down at an angle rather than at me, but he was clenching it tight from the white showing on his knuckles and he looked both stressed and upset.

Forcing myself to steady my breathing and heart rate, I opened my mouth to respond and hoped that my voice would come out sounding calm. 'What's not in there, Barry?' It had been a while since someone threatened me with a gun. However, it wasn't really something that one got used to with practice and I didn't like it.

'The Big Foot suit, of course. That is what you were looking for, isn't it?' he said it as a statement, both hands still on the gun. 'I don't keep it in the car, too much chance of someone finding it.'

It was an immediate admission of guilt that I had not had to prompt or trick out of him. A tiny bubble of jubilance over the forthcoming pay check died instantly in my chest as I remembered the shotgun. 'Why, Barry? Why the dressing up and scaring people?'

'Does it matter now? No one was supposed to get hurt, but they did, and it was my fault and now I can't eat or sleep or function.' He looked miserable, worse than the last time I saw him. Was he wracked by guilt? It seemed perfectly plausible, so then did that make him suicidal or homicidal? Dangerous either way with a shotgun in his hands.

'How did you know?'

347

'It was the footprint. The footprint was between the trees and it is autumn. There are fallen leaves everywhere. The only way you could have found that footprint was by clearing away the leaves and making it yourself.'

Looking at the floor, he nodded.

I shivered from the cool air I had not dressed for as I had expected to be inside. Barry was wearing a thick parka and heavy boots, so he was probably warm enough. If he had been outside for long though his hands might be getting cold and thus his reactions might be slow. If he elected to kill me to cover his tracks all he had to do was raise the barrel and shoot, a range of motion that might take half a second. It would be too little time for me to do anything to stop him. I took a half step forward and held my hands out to either side in a placating fashion. I focused on his eyes hoping I would see a decision there first.

Barry didn't move but the shotgun twitched upwards slightly. 'Don't move,' he ordered.

'Tell me what it was for, Barry,' I tried. 'If no one was supposed to get hurt then you won't be found guilty of murder. If it was an accident, then we can get this cleared up. No one else needs to get hurt here.'

Especially me.

I angled my feet so that I could better push off from my right foot and lunge forward to meet him should he elect to attack, but before I could consider another move, he slumped his whole body. His shoulders dropped, and his hands appeared to get a foot closer to the floor. His eyes were staring blankly at nothing. He sagged for half a second and then in a single move he reversed the shotgun and swung the double barrels up towards his own head.

348

I still don't remember consciously deciding to move but I crashed into him as the shotgun went off, my left hand instantly hot where I had grabbed the barrel. My left shoulder met with his chest and we pitched over into the mud as one.

I landed with my shoulder in his rib cage and heard the breath whoosh out of him. Left hand on the weapon, I whipped my right elbow around to connect with his head but missed and struck his throat instead. He went limp beneath me as any fight he may have had left him. I yanked the gun from his grip and rolled onto my knees next to him.

Wonderful adrenalin washed through my system, making me shake and feel sick. Barry was heaving and holding his throat, he posed no further danger, so I sat and watched while he slowly recovered. Gentle drizzle began to fall.

I wondered idly if anyone would react to the shot. It seemed unlikely in such a rural area where shotguns were common. I stood, broke the breach of the shotgun to eject the spent shells and moved to check what damage the shotgun had done. Barry had some carbon marks on the left side of his face where the shot had missed but got darned close to his skin. The blast would have taken his head clean off had he released the trigger under his chin.

'Barry?' I called to get his attention. My ears were ringing from the noise of the shotgun, so I was probably speaking louder than I needed to. 'Barry. Let's go inside and talk. I need a cup of tea and you need to get your head straight, so let's go and see if together we can make some sense of this.' Barry was looking at me from the floor. He was lying on his back still rubbing his throat, he didn't speak but he nodded, a brief dip of the head as if that was all he could manage. He didn't move though, and I let a minute pass.

349

I was about to reinforce the idea of moving when he rolled onto his side, then onto all fours and then onto his feet. I pointed with the shotgun and he trudged in front of me towards the park main entrance.

Pausing to fish in his coat pocket, Barry produced a large bunch of keys, selected one and opened the door. I followed him as he shuffled through the foyer and back towards his office. The kettle I had spied when I first visited must have been already full because he flicked it on without adding water and proceeded to organise two mugs and two teabags. He turned to face me with the sugar pot and a spoon. Wordlessly he enquired, and I declined, still leaning in the office doorway.

Tea made, the time to talk was upon us, but I did not have to prompt him this time, Barry started his story and kept going until it was told. I interrupted only to clarify bits and pieces and right at the start to advise him that I was going to record the conversation.

Dr. Barry Bryson Ph.D. had invested in the Park because he believed he could make it a flourishing attraction that would make him rich while allowing him to work for himself and interact daily with animals. For him, it was the greatest opportunity he could have been afforded. Against his wife's wishes, he remortgaged the house and plumbed everything into his dream. It failed miserably. He was a poor businessman and got further and further into debt. His wife had left him, and the subsequent divorce had applied even more financial pressure. The Park barely broke even and he needed capital for investment to make it more interesting. He had hit upon the idea that he could create a new area of the park devoted to British mythical creatures. There were not very many of them and most were very local to particular areas, it would be an informative area, rather than actually having mythical creatures in it, of course, he explained.

That idea had stalled though due to lack of funds but gave birth to the idea that he could write a novel that would generate cash, allow him to rejuvenate the park and prove all the doubters, especially his wife, that Barry Bryson was a winner. A novel costs you nothing but time, right? And since he had no life, and no money to go out and get one, he dedicated every spare hour to writing his first novel.

No one wanted to publish it though. He tried everyone he could find and then some, and finally, just as he was about to give in, he discovered that he could publish it himself. He felt convinced that the story was a masterpiece, a bestseller if he could only get it into people's hands. The publishers must be blind that they did not see its worth.

As luck would have it, a favoured aunt had died leaving him a small amount of cash, so he invested it in the book and bought ten thousand copies on the advice of a brother-in-law who had spoken very knowingly about the subject despite having no tangible link to the industry that Barry could perceive. Broke again, Barry pestered local bookshops, papers and radio stations until he was able to get some publicity and a couple of advertised book signings in the nearby towns. Start small and get the stone rolling was his philosophy. The book was slated by the critic in the local paper though, cited as being poorly written, confusing and boring. He sold twelve copies. That was two years ago, and he had taken some time to accept the shortfalls in his book and produce a new draft. This time though no one would speak to him at all and he had no cash to pay for a new run of books.

Unable to come up with anything else, he had hit upon the idea to create a real beast of Bluebell Hill one night while watching a documentary on the North American Sasquatch and the various faked pictures and footage. All he needed was a suit, he could make that himself, and to make sure that no one got a good look at it.

It had worked better than he expected although he went out in it five times before anyone reported what they had seen. He would set up in

351

places where he could park his car, spy over an area and then, when he saw people, put in a brief appearance before disappearing back into the bushes. He decided to make a report himself because he wanted to get some of the information correct and give his opinion as an expert. He could thus also plug his book and had a simple plan to make it onto daytime TV where he could show off his new book and get a publishing deal.

I let him ramble on for a while before I steered him towards the fatal incident.

Barry had been talking for half an hour by that point and getting more animated as he went. Now his mood shifted again. He said he had wanted to be seen a few more times but the accident happened, and he couldn't put the suit on again after that. On the morning of the accident, he had parked down a narrow lane and was just getting his headpiece on when he heard a car approaching. He was stood next to his car, unsure what to do as there was no time to go anywhere and getting in the car would give the game away. Instead, he chose to cross the road. It would ensure he was seen and with their attention on him, he hoped they would not see the car he had just left. Then the car passed him, jerked hard to the right, lost control and disappeared down the bank.

Barry had wanted to go to the rescue but terrified of being revealed he fled and hid the suit. He didn't know that the driver had been killed until the following evening when the details were read out on the local evening news. He burned the suit and tried to forget his involvement.

By the time he had stopped talking I could hear a car pulling across the gravel outside. Barry looked at me, something he had not really done at any point while telling his story. 'That will be Margaret arriving to open up and get ready for the day. Pointless really, but she has an easy job and no aspirations, so I think it suits her.'

'I need to call the police, Barry. They need to take your statement and decide what to do. I am just an investigator, I get paid to solve crimes or mysteries, what comes after is not within my power to decide.'

Barry looked at his desk and fidgeted a little. 'What will they do?'

I considered that for a moment before answering. 'I don't know.' It was the best I could offer him. 'You left the scene of an accident and it could be argued that you caused it. However, I believe it will be difficult to show intent to do harm. Other than that, I am not sure what they could charge you with.'

I left Barry to consider that, while I placed the call to PC Amanda Harper. I figured I might as well give her the collar. It would ingratiate me if nothing else.

She answered on the second ring. 'Hey Tempest, any luck finding Dozer?'

'No. No, I'm afraid not,' I replied glumly. I did not want to discuss the subject, so I told her about the Bluebell Hill Big Foot and got her moving in my direction.

I could hear Margaret approaching down the short corridor, so I leaned against the doorway a little harder and held the shotgun against my body so that it was less visible.

'Good morning, Dr. Bryson,' she chirped merrily. 'Can I get either of you a cup of tea?'

'Yes, please,' I answered. Barry nodded towards her expectant expression.

Margaret bustled off once again and I brought the shotgun back into both hands. 'Is this licenced?'

353

'Yes. I have a cabinet for it in the back.'

'Better put it away then. Clean the carbon off your face as well. The police take a dim view on discharging firearms near people.' I held the gun out for him to take and, trusting that he would not reload it and pop himself, I went back into reception to wait for Amanda.

The runtime from the Maidstone station to the park was only a few minutes and my tea was still too warm to drink when Amanda arrived. I was back outside where the sun had come out and the warmth from it had made the carpark pleasantly cool now rather than cold. I fiddled with my phone while I waited for the tea to cool but as the squad car swung into the carpark, I slipped it back into my left back trouser pocket and pushed away from the wall.

There was still a little mist hugging the trees as I looked up towards Bluebell Hill, it would burn off soon as the day took hold and warmed the earth. For now, it gave an eerie effect. I imagined then the Bluebell Big Foot emerging from the treeline and smiled wryly to myself that it would have been fun to see and questioned what I, as a total non-believer, would have made of it.

Amanda was in the driving seat of a silver, 2013 model, Ford Focus police car, beside her was PC Hardacre. I had learned his name last night when he had offered his assistance in looking for Dozer and I had gladly accepted it. She turned in a wide arc and pulled to a stop in an empty part of the car park opposite where Barry and I were parked. The front bumper nosed into the blackberry bushes that edged that side of the car park.

I could see them exchanging a few words and watched Brad pass Amanda her hat as they open their doors and got out.

'PCs Harper and Hardacre,' I acknowledged as they approached. 'Dr. Byson is inside. He has confessed to be the Bluebell Big Foot and I have it all on a recording on my phone. He seems genuinely very upset about the death of Simon Monroe.' I omitted to tell them about the attempted suicide this morning. 'My interest in this case is pretty much finished, I was only hired to solve the mystery.'

'Just like the Scooby gang,' smirked PC Hardacre.

'Yes. Just like the Scooby gang, but better paid,' I replied taking a slurp of tea and smiling.

'Will you show us to him?' asked Amanda taking the lead, her voice soft and friendly but professionally curt at the same time.

I nodded and led them into the Park reception, past a startled looking Margaret and through to Barry's office. He was sitting patiently at his desk with a half-drunk cup of tea by his mouse mat.

While they dealt with Barry, I made the call to Mrs Sweeting-Brand. It was not a call I was relishing, even though I could impart news of my success. Yet the call was less unpleasant than I had anticipated.

Mrs. Sweeting-Brand listened patiently while I explained how I had tracked down the culprit, as she liked to call him, then assured me that she would be following up the case with her own legal team. I immediately felt quite sorry for Dr. Bryson.

Mrs. Sweeting-Brand thanked me for my efforts, which surprised me, but then chided that I shouldn't have needed her pressure to get the job done, which I felt summed her up nicely.

Call completed, I tucked my phone away but remained leaning against the wall I had come to rest against. I was tired. The last few days had demanded I run on pure determination and it was taking its toll. Last night I had bagged a few scant hours of sleep, most of it broken by vivid dreams. I looked back in towards the reception area, made a decision and went home. Bull met me at the door, wagging his tail the same as any other day but sadly still very alone. I scooped him and the two of us went back to bed.

I had slept until just after noon. When I awoke, the time on the clock by my bed had said 1217hrs, so I had laid there for a bit and patted Bull before forcing myself up and into the shower.

I left the house because the absence of Dozer was so visible there and went to the office. Once there, I spent an hour phoning different vets, animal shelters, and the RSPCA offices to leave details of my missing dog just in case someone found him and made contact. I did not expect to hear that any of them already had him, so was not surprised when they did not.

I thought about making up flyers with his picture on but could not work out where I would stick them up given how far he might have gone downstream. I was getting hungry and had not organised myself at all. I had nothing to eat now and I needed groceries for dinner, so I locked the office again and headed down into Rochester High Street. I avoided the coffee shop and the chance of seeing Hayley because my face was a wreck. I had a vaguely black eye, just a little colour to the edge of the left orb really, a cut and swollen lip and a cut to my eyebrow plus numerous little scratches to both my hands and face where I had eaten dirt, scrambled around in thorny bushes and generally taken a beating.

I had consciously dressed smartly in a waistcoat and jacket to offset the drunken brawler look I was worried I might portray. Convinced that people were looking at my beaten face, even though they probably were not, I chastised myself for being so self-conscious and put up with it.

A few doors along from my office is a small supermarket chain outlet where I was able to pick up some fruit for lunch and fresh chicken to have for dinner. As I came out of the shop exit, the first thing I saw was Natasha

357

the barmaid walking towards me. I had never seen her outside of the pub before.

Natasha was wearing Ugg Boots and one of those knee-length woollen dress things with a suede bolero jacket over the top, all in shades of brown and cream. She looked great from the toes up. I tried very hard to focus on her eyes and not the wonderfully bouncy lumps in the front of her dress.

Natasha smiled a broad smile to match mine. 'Hiya, Tempest. Wow, what happened to you?' she said with a little wave.

'Good Afternoon, Natasha. I had a fight with a bear,' I said rather than explain in detail. 'What brings you to Rochester today?'

'I live here, Tempest.' Well done idiot, nice one. I bet she has told me that little snippet a dozen times and I have failed utterly to remember it. 'I heard about *The Vampire* case.' She was examining my face, which was suitably bruised. 'I didn't realise you got hurt.'

'It's all superficial thankfully, nothing broken.'

I was so brave.

'Looks pretty sore to me,' she said.

A thought occurred to me. 'I'm just off to get a little lunch, would you care to join me? My treat.' I figured I had a fifty: fifty chance, and she may well have something else she was heading out to do. I was just being nice though and lunch with a charming female companion seemed like a good idea.

'Well, since I am hungry, and you so generously offered, where would you like to take me?'

358

I let Natasha pick as she knew the area better than I and a few minutes later we were being shown to a table for two at a family run Italian place I had walked by for years but never once gone into.

'I love this place,' Natasha said with genuine warmth as we took our seats. I could see why. The building was a couple of centuries old I guessed. The inside was creaking floorboards that had heard the secrets of generations, wooden beams, and columns from the original structure were left exposed and there were little tables tucked into alcoves to create intimate spaces. In just one of those, I was now sat opposite the very lovely Natasha.

A young man in a waiter's outfit of all black brought us menus, wine, and olives and departed once more to let us chat.

We were talking about nothing much at all: Rochester and how lovely it is, The Vampire case, the weather recently and it was all very nice when Natasha stopped mid-sentence, took a sip of her wine and fixed me with a stare.

'You know, Tempest. I always wondered what it would be like to talk to you when you are not out drinking with the boys.

'Really? Why?'

'Because I only ever see you, and for that matter most of the men I know when you are getting drunk or already drunk.'

I felt a little defensive at this because I held the belief that I always stopped drinking while just a little merry and long before drunk arrived, but I guess that is just semantics, so I kept quiet and nodded acceptingly.

She continued, 'Everyone leers at me.' She saw my look of denial, 'Yes, Tempest. Even you at times. Most make comments. I have to expect most of it, I am a barmaid with big boobs after all, and no one ever tries to grab a handful, so I should be thankful for that, but I get terrible chat-up lines every week, so even when there is someone I might be interested in,' she paused to make eye contact, 'I never see them in the best light.'

I was not sure what my face was supposed to be doing. I was certain she had made lots of valid points. Was I just another leering, lecherous bloke at the pub? I had never given it much thought, had never placed myself in her shoes. I felt like I was being told off but suspected that was not her intention.

Perhaps sensing my struggle, she leaned forward to grab my hand. 'Don't go apologising, Tempest. You are the most gentlemanly among them.'

That made me feel a bit better at least. 'Natasha,' I began but she waved for me to stop.

'It's okay, Tempest,' she sighed. 'I'm not sure what point I was trying to make.' Natasha let go of my hand, leaned back in her chair and took a swig of wine while looking out the window. As she swallowed and placed the glass back on the table, she blew out a hard breath as if clearing her thoughts, grabbed her purse and stood. 'I'll be back in a minute.' As she took her first step she paused, leaned down and kissed me lightly on the lips.

By the time she returned to the table our food had arrived and I was still wondering whether it was *National hot girls kiss Tempest week*, or if my aftershave had taken on some kind of magical power.

We stared at each other for a moment when she sat, both of us waiting for the other to speak. She broke the silence before I had time to work out what to say. 'I'm not sure what I was trying to tell you, I feel a bit silly.'

'No need to,' I assured her.

She fell silent again and I felt a need to rescue us both. 'Why don't we eat these delicious pizzas before they get cold?' I smiled at her and picked up my knife and fork. 'We can just be two friends out having lunch.'

Natasha returned my smile but said nothing. As I dug into my pizza, she started in on hers as well. They were quite delicious, the only sound now from our table was the occasional scrape of a knife on a plate.

We finished our food at almost exactly the same time. This was deliberate on my part as I had slowed my pace to avoid finishing minutes before her. I had still not worked out what to say next, so did not wish to sit there doing nothing while she ate.

Natasha was impossible to not be attracted to. I was uncertain of her age, but my guess would be thirty-two ish. Her figure was womanly curves with a thin waist. Her hair, makeup, and nails were beauty shop perfect and she was both intelligent and engaging. If she were to grab my hand and instruct me to take her somewhere for an afternoon of sex, I would not be able to say no and could not possibly come up with a reason why I should. I felt that she had laid the ground for me to invite her out for an actual date, but I was holding back, and I was not entirely sure why.

My internal debate kept coming back to Amanda, but Amanda had shown no real interest. Poison was clearly interested, Hayley wanted simple no-strings sex. Natasha, I suspected was waiting for me to make a move, yet I could not get my head to stop thinking about Amanda.

The lunch was done. I paid the bill, took her phone number and promised to call her soon.

I was doing some number crunching for the business accounts when the sound of my phone ringing broke my concentration. I had left it in the kitchen to recharge, so pushed away from the desk, scooped Bull off my lap and went to get it.

It was not a mobile number, nor was it prefixed by 0800 or 0345 or any of the numbers that might suggest telesales or some other nonsense, so it was most likely going to be a client. 'Blue Moon investigations, Tempest Michaels speaking. How may I help you?'

'Hello?' came a wobbly little-old-lady's voice.

'Good morning,' I replied. 'This is Tempest Michaels. How may I be of assistance?'

'I think I have your dog.' My breath caught, and I swear my heart stopped briefly. They talk about hearts skipping a beat, well that is what mine did.

I calmed myself enough to speak. 'That is wonderful news,' I beamed. 'Can you please tell me where you are so that I can come to get him?'

'Oh, err, well I am not sure what the right thing to do is. Could you describe him to me, please? I don't want to give him to the wrong person.'

'Certainly, my dear lady. He is a slightly podgy, black and tan miniature Dachshund with a grey muzzle. He has large paws and a dopey looking face, and I have his brother at my feet right now.' I was desperately impatient to get her address and get him back, but I could only commend her caution. 'Furthermore, if he still has his collar on it is a brown and white canvass item with a red enamel tag.'

362

'Well, I suppose that is as good a description as I could ask for,' she replied. 'He is still wearing his collar, that's how I got your phone number.'

I got her address, thanked her several more times and agreed that I would arrive at her house in the next hour. Her address was number 42 Church Lane, East Barming. I checked the map for confirmation as it seemed incredible, but the little dog had travelled thirteen miles downstream. Whether he had been swept downstream and found a branch to cling to until he was washed to a point of the bank where he could get out or had exited the river almost immediately and had then just wandered until he lucked upon this lady I would never know, but he was alive and well and I would have him back in no time at all.

I whooped! I genuinely stood in my kitchen and whooped. I grabbed Bull and held him above my head like a prize and whooped again. 'We found your brother, little man.' I told him. 'We found your brother. Let's go get him.'

And so, we did. The lady had given her name as Mary Coalfell. I had her address and phone number and had given a brief description of myself and my car so that she knew who it was when I approached her house. I held the opinion that little old ladies living alone, which I guessed she did, were probably cautious about who they let in and were quite right to do so given some of the crimes I heard reported on the news each week.

The journey took longer than it otherwise might have as I stopped off at a florist and waited for them to turn a fresh fifty pounds note into an ornate bouquet for the lady.

Excitement and some trepidation that he might be hurt or starving, or something was making my right foot heavy. I narrowly avoided a speeding fine on the Tonbridge road heading for Barming. Soon enough, I was pulling up at the address she had given with Bull standing on my lap, craning to see out of the window. Usually, he would curl up and sleep on the passenger seat, though perhaps he sensed something in my excitement.

With the flowers in my right hand, I carried him down the path tucked under my left arm and towards the front door, from which barked a familiar voice before I could even knock. Bull's tail began to wag like mad as clearly, he also recognised the bark.

From the other side, I could hear Mary making gentle shooing noises and the door opened. Dozer swished out from between Mary's legs taking the hem of her skirt with him. It created an effect much like appearing from under a curtain but there he was, wagging his bum and leaping up at me.

I gave Mary a tearful smile, not trusting my voice to hold steady if I spoke. I handed her the bouquet soundlessly mouthing thank you and bent down to fuss him. I plopped Bull on the path with his brother and the two of them spun around each other in greeting, sniffing and nudging one another. Then after a few licks of my hand, I was forgotten again as he ran across the front lawn to look under a bush.

I turned to smile as the lovely little old lady. 'Would you like a cup of tea?' she asked me.

Inside Mary's house, she regaled me with her story of finding Dozer last night just before she went to bed. She had gone out to put some rubbish in the bin because tomorrow was bin day and the bin was already on the curb in anticipation. Her neighbour, Mark was a kind soul and took it in and out for her each week she told me.

Dozer had appeared, framed in the light from her doorway as she had turned around to go back in. The sight had startled her and at first she thought it was a badger and had tried to scare it off by making a noise and flapping her arms. He came towards her when she did that though and she saw it was small dog when light reflected off his tag.

She said she had never seen a Dachshund in any of the houses near her and her street was a cul-de-sac, so she felt it unlikely he had escaped from an owner out walking him. As it was so late, she took him in and offered him water and then when he started looking longingly at the fridge, she gave him some ham which he ate ravenously.

All the time she was talking, I had both dogs sat on her sofa with me, one on either leg sleeping peaceful doggy sleeps. I sipped my tea and encouraged her to talk as she seemed very happy to have company.

She apologised several times because it had not occurred to her to look for a phone number on the tag until this morning and should have called last night. She called herself a silly old woman, but I asked her to stop doing so as she was wonderful in my eyes.

This morning she had no dog food, so had cooked some sausages that she had in the fridge and had fed him those. 'Do you know, he scoffed the lot?' she exclaimed at that point. 'He just swallowed each of them and looked up again asking for another until they were all gone.'

He had probably not eaten much in the time he had been missing. It was no surprise to me that he had been hungry, but he would have eaten freshly cooked sausages even after a banquet if he had the chance.

I helped her get down a vase from a high shelf in her kitchen and assisted with arranging the flowers into it. I thanked her several more times, but eventually said my goodbye and took the dogs out to the car.

Driving home I was euphoric. I was having the best day and resolved to spend the next couple of days away from work walking the dogs and playing with them.

And that was what I did.

The sun had pretty much dipped below the horizon as I set out on my meandering route to the pub. Ambient light from the city below reflected off tonight's low cloud cover. Combined with the last rays of lingering light, I could easily see my footing and the dark shapes of the dogs as they snuffled around me. I walked past the last house at the edge of the village and through a gate designed to keep livestock one side or the other. By day the countryside near me was pleasant rows of vines bordered by bramble hedgerows, at night it was all still there but nothing more than indistinct shapes.

The paths were clear though and mostly free of potholes, so the only hazard I had to negotiate in giving the boys a walk was the mess left by less diligent dog owners.

Walking in silence, I reflected on the past week. It had been more eventful than most and I had the bruises to show for it. The successful conclusion of the Vampire murder case had become a National story headline. Chief Inspector Quinn had claimed all the glory when he held a press event in front of the mausoleum the morning after Ambrogio was killed. As he had outlined how his team had tracked the killer and cornered both him and his accomplices, someone sounding suspiciously like Amanda had shouted a question from the crowd.

'Is it not true that the police received a significant amount of help in this case from a local private investigator?' the voice asked.

Chief Inspector Quinn had mumbled something that the microphone had not picked up and then attempted to press on with his explanation. However, the reporters then began asking about the local PI and thankfully he had then named me as a special consultant that had been of some assistance.

367

Then the story of the Blue Bell Big Foot case broke later the same day and I was identified as the paranormal detective that had solved not only that case but had been involved in the Vampire case as well.

Interviews requests came by phone and email though I turned them all down bar one which went to Sharon Maycroft of The Weald Word. She had very been pleased to get the story first, which I had expressed seemed only fair given that she had got me onto the Vampire story in the first place. Interview done, she had kissed me on the mouth and whispered that I would be seeing her again soon.

Pleasing though that news was, I was now faced with a conundrum I had never really had to consider before. A few short days ago I had no women in my life and now I was being pursued by Poison, Sharon, Hayley, and Natasha yet found myself drawn most strongly to Amanda. Mr. Wriggly voiced that he was happy for me to tackle all of them, either one at a time or all together - he was *up* for anything. An enticing concept, but one that seemed doomed to deliver havoc rather than fantasy sex. Personally, I was conflicted about what to even hope for. Amanda was lovely, but apart from being continually nice to me, she had shown no real interest. She had kissed me, but only as a joke, she claimed. Poison was attracted to me, that much I knew, but I had not yet had the chance to speak to her and express my feelings on the matter. It was not something I felt could be handled by text. Was it a daddy thing with her? Was it now some kind of hero worship because she believed I had saved her? Hayley at least was clear about what she wanted, it wasn't really what I was looking for, but was I fool enough to dismiss harmless engagement with a willing lady? And then there was Natasha at the pub. That was a new development, but also one that I had been fantasising about for ages. I had no answers to my lengthy list of questions and it all felt too complicated to do anything about right now. Maybe doing nothing would yield a result and make the decision for me. A bit cowardly, but hey ho.

Several days had passed since Ambrogio had impaled himself. This had given reporters time to investigate him and the coroners time to conduct an autopsy. The autopsy of Ambrogio Silvano had revealed several things, chief among which was that he was human. Frank was still sulking over that one as he had bet money the coroner's office would be stumped and he was already claiming a cover-up. The fence post had punctured his right ventricle, killing him immediately. The crime scene people had determined somehow, angles and such I guess, that he had tripped on a raised edge in the path and fallen with his full body weight onto the fence post. The post had penetrated his chest between ribs five and six at a slight upwards angle. It had exited his back destroying his heart on its way through. His canine teeth were professionally fitted prosthetics fixed to the real teeth underneath. They were razor sharp, which had allowed him to inflict the deadly bite wounds.

The police, the press and everyone else were yet to work out who he really was. Perhaps his real name was Ambrogio Silvano, but I thought it unlikely. The money he had received from the Brotherhood of the Dead Vampire LARP club was out there somewhere. Amanda said they had forensic computer people employed for specifically this kind of task, so it would be found soon enough. I was unconcerned.

The papers were making various assumptions based on the limited information they had, but the prevailing theory was that he had discovered by accident that he resembled the Master vampire Ambrogio Silvano and had proceeded to exploit this by contacting the Brotherhood of the Dead and pretending to be their returned Master. So, why had he started killing? There was more writing on this subject, several *leading* criminal psychologists were giving their opinion on why he had gone on a murder spree. All conjecture at this point, but the theory I favoured was that having taken on the identity of the Master Vampire and revealed himself to the club he had then tried to fulfil their expectations and having killed once had liked it. Of course, it was such a dark and sexy subject that some papers were able to fill many pages with tales of sex parties - as reported by the people that were there! Also, recipes for fake blood-based cocktails and the obligatory pin-up girl dressed as a slutty vampire.

The Autopsy also revealed that he was pumped full of Human Growth Hormone Steroids and high on a cocktail of drugs at the time of his death. The HGH explained the enormous size and strength and perhaps the drugs explained why I had so little effect when I hit him. I would never know, and I was telling myself that it really didn't matter now.

Obsidian had yet to be found. Poison had, of course, identified him and Keith Teeth as the two that had grabbed her. It had happened seconds after I left her that night to rush home to my parents. They had pulled up in a transit van and bundled her in the back. She had been drugged with what turned out to be Rohypnol and stashed on a riverboat. The boat belonged to one Mr. Damian Fogerty, who had reported it stolen over a week ago. It seemed impossible that something that large could be stolen and not found immediately, but it had been painted a different colour and had new, but false markings applied to it. Poison, of course, fingered the other members of the senior circle as well. Her statement claiming that they were all complicit and that each of them had been witness to her being held captive. They had not made it out of custody.

Quite where Obsidian was hiding I didn't much care, although I admitted to myself that I had some concern that he might attempt to exact retribution and that he might not necessarily target me directly. Was he daft enough to come after me? Or my family and friends? Or was the better question: Is he bright enough to evade the police? I could choose to worry about it or I could move on and assume he was miles away. As a compromise, I elected to have a chat with my parents and friends about being vigilant for a while.

Dr. Barry Bryson had been arrested and taken into custody. The police had nothing much to hold him for though, so he had been released pending investigation. The News articles that followed had instantly made him into a quasi-celebrity and he was suddenly in demand. He had appeared on day-time TV only this morning, chatting to the hosts about why he had taken the step of dressing up and the most unfortunate accident for which he was gravely sorry. His book had leaped from obscurity to number one bestseller overnight. Half of all proceeds from the book were to go to a charity that supported disfigured models, (I was amazed such a thing could even exist) although I suspected that the other half would soon be won by Mrs. Sweeting-Brand as she seemed likely to sue for damages and perhaps she was justified to do so. Michelle Sweeting-Brand's testimony was that the accident was exactly that. The Big Foot costume has scared her, but she did not believe that Barry should be blamed for the car crash and her boyfriend's death.

I reached the end of a long hedge and turned the corner to face back towards the lights of the village. Dozer was by my feet. Bull would be somewhere not far away, but he was generally more independent and likely to wander off on his own. I stopped and called for him until he appeared a few seconds later. Reassured that I would not have to search for him, I started back along the path and shortly left the scrubland and emerged back onto the pavement of the village.

I clipped the two boys back onto their leads, just in case any cars were about and just in case they saw a cat. The village was pleasantly lit, both from the street lighting and from the houses where lounges, kitchens, and bedrooms had lights on but the curtains still open. I imagined the dynamic of the families in some of those houses - dad home from work, kids in

371

from school, dinner in the oven and the weekend ahead of them. Pleasing concepts that I had yet to realise for myself.

Crossing the car park at the pub, the door opened, and a smoker came out with her unlit cigarette in hand. A burst of noise from the conversation inside mingled with some laughter to make it feel like a great place to be heading.

I gave the smoker a quick good evening as I passed since she was smiling at the dogs, then let them drag me inside.

'Hey, here he is!' Big Ben knelt and scooped Dozer before I could even get into the pub.

'Hey, brother,' I replied, grasping his offered hand for a firm shake. The other chaps offered similar greetings and I headed to the bar to get a round in as usual. Natasha was missing which struck me as unusual. I tried to remember when she was last not serving on a Friday night. Behind the bar was the landlord instead - an equally pleasant chap but not quite the same visual effect.

'No Natasha?' I enquired after I placed my drinks order.

'Asked for the night off. Said she had something she had been meaning to do for ages and it was time to get on with it. Didn't say what it was though.' The Landlord was pouring drinks while talking and setting them on the bar. He had the face and skin pallor of an undertaker with very thin and dead looking brown hair covering his balding scalp. Perhaps he recognised his genetic shortcomings, and this was why he employed a young attractive person to work the bar rather than do it himself. On his thin white shirt were numerous damp marks. In some places, the shirt was sticking to the flesh beneath and I could see thick black hair on his belly showing through. Occupational hazard I surmised. As he handed the last pint over, he flicked the spilled foam from his fingers and got yet more on himself. He didn't seem to notice or perhaps just didn't care.

I took the first three drinks to the table and returned to collect my change and the other drinks before settling into my seat.

Jagjit and Hillary were discussing a new TV program they had both watched the night before, Big Ben was texting quietly, probably to some girl he met earlier today and would be done with before the weekend was out and Basic was humming to himself. I struck up a conversation with Basic about rugby because I knew he followed it and it was a subject we could debate. Big Ben joined in after a while, giving his thoughts on the Saracens season so far and why he thought Harlequins needed to replace their hooker.

Then his phone beeped from an incoming text and we lost him briefly while he dealt with his sex life again. The evening was like so many others before it. Full of laughter, stupidity, and conversations about nothing much at all.

Not very much later I was four pints in and getting to my limit. It was 2134hrs and now full dark outside. I took the dogs outside just in case either of them felt inclined to find a bush. To the right of the door were two chaps I did not know, they were smoking but were good enough to make sure the smoke was blown away from me as I exited the building.

The dogs tugged at their leads, taking me to the grass verge at the edge of the carpark. I had guessed right, as both took the chance to lift a back leg. They went back to snuffling in the bushes soon enough and while they did, I pulled my phone from a back pocket.

No new messages.

Back inside, Big Ben was talking about women again when I re-joined the table with a final pint and a bag of pork scratchings for the dogs and me, as a rare Friday night treat.

'So, what happened with Poison?' Jagjit asked. 'Ben says she kissed you. Are you planning to follow that up?'

I put my drink down and sucked on my teeth for a moment. Now that I was forced to consider how I was going to answer the question I found that I knew the answer - she was simply not right for me. 'I don't think so,' I replied.

'Mate are you crazy?' Big Ben wanted to know. 'She is a totally hot, little, oriental chick.'

'She is. She is. But I am actually old enough to be her father.'

'So?' Jagjit asked. 'She is actually old enough to be your girlfriend.'

'I don't know mate. It just doesn't feel right.'

'Well, she would feel right to me,' said Big Ben. 'Tiny little thing like that. The damage I could do...' he tailed off wistfully.

'She is a free agent mate. Feel free to pursue her.'

'I'm not so sure about that, Tempest,' he replied. 'I saw her look at you down by the river. It was a look that said she wants to cover you in toffee sauce and eat you with a spoon. She doesn't look at me like that.'

'Then I will have to let her down gently I guess.' Was Big Ben right? Was Poison really into me? The flirting had gone from innocent but fun, to kisses that felt like foreplay. Was I throwing away a chance for great sex? This was too complex to consider with several pints in my system.

'What about the Policewoman?' Hilary wanted to know.

374

'What about her?'

'Jagjit said that she already kissed you and that you are totally in love with her.'

'Oh, did he?' I fixed Jagjit with a look.

'Hold on, when did she kiss you and why do I not know about this?' asked Big Ben.

'A few days ago, and there was nothing to tell.'

'Well, you should feel a need to tell me these things. Otherwise the girls you want to chase will fall into the gravitational pull of Big Ben and you will have nothing to pursue but my cast offs. The only way to protect yourself is to put a dibs marker on them so I switch the charm off when they are around.'

'You are such a dick,' said Hilary. 'How many girls have you actually shagged?'

'I don't know mate, I lost count somewhere after three hundred.'

'Three hundred women? In your life, you have shagged over three hundred women?'

'God no, Hilary, I thought you meant this year.'

We all laughed at him and to me the mirth felt like a cathartic release after the last few days of terror, righting and drama.

My phone rang, breaking the conversation. Checking the screen, I saw it was not a number I recognised. I switched it to silent and put it back in my pocket. The lapse in conversation gave me the opportunity to down my drink and bid my friends a good evening. It was close to last orders, I was tired, and I had already drunk my fill.

The stroll home took a little over a minute as usual. I let myself in, let me dogs out into the back garden, waited for them to return and instructed them to hold it now until morning.

As I walked back through the house to the stairs the pair of them began barking and ran to the front door. I chastised them for making so much noise when children nearby would be in bed, but they kept going and then I heard it too - a knock on my door.

I shooed the dogs into the kitchen and shut them in there.

The outside light was illuminating a person who I could see through the frosted glass of my front door. It looked to be just one person, but a second or third could easily be standing further back in the shadows.

I wondered then if this was going to be members of The Brotherhood of the Dead come to seek revenge for bringing down their master and leaders, but I refused to be cowed into asking, 'Who's there?'

I opened the door with forced confidence, but it was not vampires. It was not anyone I was not pleased to see.

She had on a pair of tall heels, expensive looking to my untrained eye and a long, but elegant coat undone to reveal a cocktail dress inside. She was wearing her hair up which exposed the skin of her delicate neck wonderfully.

'Are you going to invite me in?' she asked smiling.

The End

But don't miss the cool stuff on the next few pages!

376

What's Next for the Blue Moon Crew?

The Phantom of Barker Mill

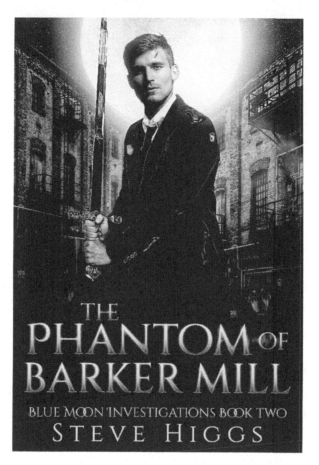

Why can't I turn down a woman in distress?

I just took a case from the tearful, but very rich, widow Barker, whose husband supposedly died at the hands of a century-old phantom. He was the owner of the Barker Steel Mill and it doesn't take me long to realise that something very weird is going on there.

That's not all though, a spectral dog has eaten a bloke at a junkyard and I'm supposed to work out how to get him back.

Everyone is lying to me about everything, but my toughest test is dealing with the aftermath of my stupid decision to hire Amanda Harper. Not that she isn't talented, intelligent, and capable, because she is. She is also drop-dead gorgeous and massively distracting.

She'll prove to be an asset no doubt, assuming we live through the week that is.

Click the link embedded in the cover picture to get your copy and find out who was at his door!

Note from the Author:

Hi there, I first published this book in June 2017, and it was less than perfect. I will admit that I had no idea what I was doing. Had no concept about how to edit or find help with proofreading, and the book got slammed in early reviews.

It took me five years to write and then sat on my desk as a big lump of A4 sheets for another eighteen months because I couldn't work out how to get it published. In the end, found my way to Amazon and Kindle and haven't looked back since. Of course, I had to learn a lot in the first year, during which time I wrote five more books in this series, found people to help me proofread and learned how to market and advertise. I also retaught myself grammar, though I except that my early books could still do with a serious fine-toothed comb through.

At the time of writing this note it is June 2020 and I have just finished writing my thirty-seventh full-length novel. I am a full-time novelist now with a career that rewards and excites me, and I get fan mail every day. I consider this book to be flawed as it picks at people unnecessarily. Debbie, the overweight but hopeful blind date, and other besides get a roasting by me, even though Tempest wishes to be fair and even to all people. I thought long and hard about editing the book to remove those passages but elected to leave them be as the book continues to please more than ninety percent of those who pick it up. Perhaps that view will change in the future.

If this is the only book of mine that you ever read, then I thank you for doing so, and wish you many hours of reading pleasure with other authors. However, if you are willing to give me one more try, you will find a growing library of books at your disposal. My boxed sets are especially good value.

On the pages below, you can read an extract from the next book in this series. The Phantom of Barker Mill picks up where this one leaves off and you can discover who was at his door.

Perhaps though you would like something for FREE. And who could blame you? Scroll down a few pages, read the extract, and after it you will find links to my other books and to an offer of FREE books. I have 3 to give you and all you need do is give me an email address to send them to.

Take care

Steve Higgs

June 2020

There are secrets buried in the Earth's past. Anastasia might be one of them.

The world knows nothing of the supernaturals among them ...

... but that's all about to change.

When Anastasia Aaronson stumbles across two hellish creatures, her body reacts by channelling magic to defend itself and unleashes power the Earth has forgotten.

But as she flexes her new-found magical muscle, it draws the attention of a demon who has a very particular use for her. Now she must learn to control the power she can wield as a world of magical beings take an interest.

She may be damaged, but caught in a struggle she knew nothing about, she will rise, and the demons may learn they are not the real monsters.

The demons know she is special, but if they knew the truth, they would run.

Every second generation of the Hale line dies at the hands of an unnameable monster on his 80th birthday. The current Lord Hale turns 80 this Saturday.

To protect himself, Lord Hale has invited paranormal investigation experts Tempest Michaels and Amanda Harper plus their friends and a whole host of other guests from different fields of supernatural exploration for a birthday dinner at his mansion.

As they sit down for dinner, the lights start to dim and a moaning noise disturbs the polite conversation. Has Lord Hale placed his faith in the right people, or just led them to share his doom?

Finding themselves trapped, Tempest and Amanda, with friends Big Ben and Patience must join forces with a wizard, some scientists, and occult experts, ghost chasers, witches, and other assorted idiots as they fight to make it through the night in one piece.

Could this be their final adventure? Will Tempest finally be proven wrong about the paranormal?

More Books by Steve Higgs

Blue Moon Investigations

Paranormal Nonsense

The Phantom of Barker Mill

Amanda Harper Paranormal Detective

The Klowns of Kent

Dead Pirates of Cawsand

In the Doodoo With Voodoo

The Witches of East Malling

Crop Circles, Cows and Crazy Aliens

Whispers in the Rigging

Bloodlust Blonde – a short story

Paws of the Yeti

Under a Blue Moon – A Paranormal Detective Origin Story

Night Work

Lord Hale's Monster

The Herne Bay Howlers

Undead Incorporated

The Ghoul of Christmas Past

The Sandman

Jailhouse Golem

Shadow in the Mine

Patricia Fisher Cruise Mysteries

The Missing Sapphire of Zangrabar

The Kidnapped Bride

The Director's Cut

The Couple in Cabin 2124

Doctor Death

Murder on the Dancefloor

Mission for the Maharaja

384

A Sleuth and her Dachshund in Athens

The Maltese Parrot

No Place Like Home

Patricia Fisher Mystery Adventures

What Sam Knew

Solstice Goat

Recipe for Murder

A Banshee and a Bookshop

Diamonds, Dinner Jackets, and Death

Frozen Vengeance

Mug Shot

The Godmother

Murder is an Artform

Wonderful Weddings and Deadly Divorces

Dangerous Creatures

Patricia Fisher: Ship's Detective

Patricia Fisher: Ship's Detective

Albert Smith Culinary Capers

Pork Pie Pandemonium

Bakewell Tart Bludgeoning

Stilton Slaughter

Bedfordshire Clanger Calamity

Death of a Yorkshire Pudding

Cumberland Sausage Shocker

Arbroath Smokie Slaying

Dundee Cake Dispatch

Lancashire Hotpot Peril

Blackpool Rock Bloodshed

Felicity Philips Investigates

Real of False Gods

Get sneak peaks, exclusive giveaways, behind the scenes content, and more. Plus, you'll be notified of Fan Pricing events when they occur and get exclusive offers from other authors because all UF writers are automatically friends.

Not only that, but you'll receive an exclusive FREE story staring Otto and Zachary and two free stories from the author's Blue Moon Investigations series.

Yes, please! Sign me up for lots of FREE stuff and bargains!

Want to follow me and keep up with what I am doing?

Facebook

Made in the USA
Monee, IL
17 December 2022

22265484R00229